Prologue

Callie Jamieson was eight years old when her mother was taken from their home in a straitjacket. From the window of her bedroom, she watched in silent horror as her mother kicked and squirmed in a vain attempt to wrench herself free from the two burly, white-uniformed men who had come to get her. She heard her mother's screams, her entreaties to her husband, to Callie, to God, to anyone who would listen. She saw neighbors gather on their lawns and crane their necks to get a better view of the proceedings, holding back just in case whatever Mara Jamieson had was contagious. Callie cringed as the doors to the ambulance slammed shut with stunning finality, yet her eyes remained riveted to the scene. It was only when the ambulance pulled away from the curb that she turned from the window, pressing her hands against her ears, refusing to listen to the screech of the siren announcing to the world that her mother was so crazy she needed to be whisked away as quickly as possible.

Within minutes, it was as if nothing had happened. The sun continued its ascent. Quiet was restored. The crowd of onlookers retreated behind closed doors to discuss what they'd just witnessed. Whatever cars drove by did so at a respectable thirty miles per hour and without accompanying fanfare. Birds chirped. Next door, the Goldsteins' dog, Dudley, ran through the sprinkler spray, barking excitedly. Life on Meadow Drive was back to normal.

Inside the Jamieson house, however, there was a sharpened silence that felt like a knife poised over a thread. Also, there was a profound stillness, as if everything within—animal, vegetable, and mineral—was holding its breath. Other than the soft whir of the air-conditioning units outside, nothing stirred.

For a long time, Callie remained by the window staring out at the empty street. Half of her prayed that whatever power controlled the universe would rewind the tape, erase the scene that had just been played, and return her mother to the house. The other half acknowledged that bringing her mother back physically without bringing her back mentally would mean that the exact same scenario would be played out a week, a month, or a year later.

When Callie couldn't stand her solitary confinement any longer, she ventured out of her bedroom into the hall. The last time she saw her father he was outside, his back turned away from the street so he didn't have to see his wife being strapped onto a gurney and sedated with a needle. Callie hadn't heard the door close, but it must have. She hadn't heard him climb the stairs, but he might have.

Cautiously, Callie tiptoed down the hall toward her parents' bedroom. The door was open and her father, Bill, was standing in the midst of the debris caused by Mara's latest outburst, his face drawn, his cheeks damp with tears. Callie's eyes widened at the sight of her parents' drapes lying in a heap on the floor, curtain rods dangling precariously from hardware that was supposed to anchor them to the wall. The mirror over her mother's vanity table was smashed. A chair lay on its side, its back broken. Elegant crystal perfume flacons that Mara used to collect and proudly display had been flung up against the wall, their colorful shards shattered on the carpet, the heavy scents contained within mingling into a sickening blend. Clothes that had been ripped off hangers had been slashed and cut into ragged slivers. And there was blood.

Her heart pounded inside her chest as she followed the track of the stains from the carpet to the bedsheets to her father's clothing, up to a huge gash above his left eye that had swelled into an angry purple bulge. His right arm also bore ugly red scars. Unmindful of the glass on the floor, Callie ran to him, threw her arms around his waist, and burst into tears. Without saying a word, Bill lifted his daughter into his arms, cradled her against him so she wouldn't gaze upon the destruction wrought by her mother, and carried her out of the room, away from the shambles.

Callie and her father spent the rest of that Saturday in June trying to come to grips with the impact of Mara's madness on their lives. Her father tried to explain it all to Callie, but it was clear that even he didn't fully understand what had happened.

"What started it, Daddy?" she asked, unable to reconcile what she'd seen in that bedroom and the woman who last night, before the hysteria began, had read her a story and tucked her into bed.

Bill Jamieson shrugged. Years of trying to fathom what had initiated his wife's mental descent weighed on his shoulders. He said he supposed her mother's mind had snapped, which was why he sent her away.

"I was afraid she might hurt herself, or you," he said, holding Callie close, as if even now she needed protection.

While Callie wanted to protest that her mother would never hurt her, the wounds on her father's arm and face attested to the very real potential of violence. Mara had gone after him with a scissors.

When Callie apologized on her mother's behalf and whimpered that surely, Mara wouldn't do anything like this again, Bill reminded Callie of the times Mara had rampaged through the house breaking lamps and furniture with a fireplace poker, shrieking about invisible intruders; of the many nights Mara would carry on heated conversations with the darkness, claiming that the empty space before her was filled with people intent on doing her harm. He recounted the times they found Mara muttering incoherently or sitting alone in the backyard, mourning the loss of someone neither Bill nor Callie had ever heard of.

"I'm not blaming your mother, sweetheart. She's ill. She can't help herself." He rubbed his tired, bloodshot eyes, wincing at the pain. "And much as we'd like to, we can't help her either. She needs medical attention. You do understand that, don't you?"

"Will Mommy ever be okay?" Callie asked, her lower lip pursed and trembling.

"I hope so," Bill responded honestly.

While he couldn't promise a cure anytime soon, he went to great lengths to reassure Callie that Mara would be well cared for.

"Dr. Freedberg is the one who recommended Stonehaven. He wouldn't send Mom anyplace that wouldn't be kind to her."

Callie nodded. Dr. Freedberg was the family internist. He always made her feel better. Surely, he would do the same for her mother.

As her father spoke about the tragedy of it all, how difficult mental illness was to treat and to live with, Callie couldn't help but notice the strain in his voice. These past few years had been hard on him. When Mara was really bad, Bill stayed home from work and tended to his wife, relying on Ruby, their housekeeper, to help out with Callie. There were nights when Callie was certain he didn't sleep a wink, days when he was exhausted from maintaining a prolonged vigil, months when he acted as if everything was fine, yet remained constantly on guard, alert for even the slightest hint of manic behavior.

Even now, Bill didn't hesitate to reaffirm his love for Mara. He promised Callie he would stand by her mother and do everything in his power to make her well and bring her home so they could be a family again.

Callie tried to mimic his optimism and be brave, but inside, she was a whirlpool of confusion. She didn't know how to define mental illness, so she couldn't imagine what kind of treatment it might require. She had no explanation for her mother's bizarre behavior, so she had no other solution, but there was much she didn't understand.

Like when exactly had her mother gotten sick? One min-ute they were a happy little trio, living an ordinary, happy little life. Then, suddenly, about two years ago, it started. At first, it was simply a case of sleeplessness. Mara claimed something awakened her in the middle of the night—a strange noise, a feeling that someone was in the room, a scary dream—something inexplicable, but frightening enough to keep her from falling back to sleep. After several nights of this, she'd grown moody and agitated, often turning harsh and snippy.

Then came the phobias. And the odd shifts in person-ality.

At what exact moment in time, Callie wanted to know, had her mother's brain gone on the fritz? And what, or who, had caused it?

While her father constantly assured her that schizophre-nia wasn't caused by something anyone said or did, that it was a mysterious illness that simply took over the rational side of one's nature, Callie often wondered if she had been a contributor to her mother's mental demise.

She also wondered why, when her parents were so ob-viously devoted to each other, her mother wanted a divorce. Several times over the past few months, Callie had over-heard Mara and Bill arguing about that. Her mother would demand a divorce. Her father would refuse. He'd say Mara was acting irrationally, that she still loved him, he still loved her, and they both loved Callie. Mara would admit that what Bill had said was true, that, of course, she loved him and Callie. But then, Mara would say it was because she loved them that she wanted a divorce. Something about her being sick, about wanting to spare them and free them.

For months, Callie agonized about what Mara meant by that. Ultimately, she concluded that since Mara couldn't possibly want to free Bill and Callie from her, it had to be the gray people.

Mara rarely explained where she went and what hap-pened when she got lost inside the dark caverns of her mind, but several months before, Callie caught her in an unguarded, desperate moment. It was after she'd returned home from an appointment with her psychiatrist. Usually, after a session with her doctor, Mara was so drained she retired to her bedroom for a long, restorative nap. That day, she was alert and eager to talk. She seemed particularly eager to explain her behavior to her daughter, which was why she told Callie about the gray people, evil specters that came to her, unexpected and uninvited, at odd times during the day and night. It was their fault she was like this, Mara confided.

There were several other windows of lucidity during which Mara spoke of the gray people, but as her condition deteriorated, those clear windows were boarded over and nailed shut. Callie tried raising the subject with her mother again, but Mara acted as if she didn't know what Callie was talking about.

Callie had always been an obedient child, one who trusted her parents to make the right decisions on her behalf. But that had been before the strangeness had invaded her home and changed everything. Before her mother began to get lost in a place known only to her. And her father began to withdraw to a place only large enough for him.

In the months following Mara's commitment, though Bill continued to dote on Callie, he began erecting a wall around himself. Like Callie, he'd wished for a speedy recovery. He'd expected that a heavy assault of therapy and medication would result in a quick reversal of Mara's illness and a hasty return. Like Callie, he was sorely disappointed when none of that happened.

He coped by fencing in his feelings, refusing to share his heartbreak or discuss the devastation that had become his daily companion. Instead, he focused on his work and his child, to the exclusion of everything else. Slowly, painfully, he faced his new reality: his wife had been institutionalized, was not showing any signs of improvement, and, according to her doctors, would probably remain where she was for the rest of her life.

He also became fiercely protective of Callie. He screened her activities, sifted out playmates who might tease her about her mother, chaperoned many of her play dates, and kept her as busy as he could so that she wouldn't have time to brood. Their only bone of contention was that he refused to allow Callie to visit Mara at Stonehaven.

Bill couldn't see the benefit in exposing Callie to the hideous sights and sounds that accompanied his visits to the sanitarium. He didn't want her to witness the hellish cobweb of personal torment that mental illness wrapped around its victims. He didn't want her to leave feeling frightened for her own mental health or to be plagued with the guilt that clung to him for days after each journey. The problem was, he was so enmeshed in his own net of woe, he couldn't see that rather than protecting his daughter, he was increasing her anxiety, as well as her determination to find out what he was keeping from her.

After more than nine months went by without a visit—or any promise of one—Callie went on a hunger strike. Her father might not notice—he'd been trying to rebuild his business and often came home past Callie's dinner hour—but Ruby would. After two days of pushing her plate away and ingesting nothing more substantial than a glass or two of milk, Ruby relented. She would hire a car and take Callie to Stonehaven.

Stonehaven sat on the horizon like a monarch, a gracious stone structure that reigned over acres of magnificently manicured grounds in the Connecticut countryside. A huge mansion modeled after Blenheim Castle in England, it appeared to be a place where fox hunts were held on Sunday mornings after guests recovered from elegant dinner parties held the evening before. But there were no fox hunts, no elegant dinner parties, no guests. And, according to the managing director, no way that an eight-year-old, unaccompanied by a parent or guardian, was going to visit one of his patients. After brusquely ushering Callie and Ruby into his office, he excused himself and called Bill Jamieson immediately.

Ruby was sent home in the hired car. Callie rode home with her father.

"Why would you do something like this?" Bill asked, his hands gripping the steering wheel so tightly his knuckles were white.

"I wanted to see Mommy."

"I told you the doctors didn't think that was a good idea."

"I don't care. I wanted to see Mommy."

Bill glanced over at her. Callie sat face forward, her eyes staring straight ahead, her hands clasped in front of her. Her posture was so rigid, her manner so completely unrepentant and insistent, it unnerved him.

When had Callie become so independent, so willing to challenge his authority?

"Mommy's sick, Callie," he said.

"I know."

"If you know, then why don't you help me and the doctors so we can make her well?"

"You don't want her to get well."

"What!" Bill almost lost control of the car. "Why would you say such a thing?"

"Because it's true. You want Mommy to stay sick so she can't divorce you!"

Bill Jamieson found an opening in the traffic and pulled onto the shoulder. He put the car in park and turned to face his daughter.

"That's a terrible thing to say!" He stared at her, his face ashen. "What would make you think such a thing?"

She didn't move.

"Callie, I'm speaking to you."

She still didn't move.

"Look at me, please."

Callie obliged, and slowly turned her head.

"What makes you think Mommy and I would ever even consider getting a divorce?"

"I heard you fighting about it. A bunch of times."

"We did discuss it, that's true, but it was only because she was afraid of what the future might bring, that she might do something that would cause you and me to be even more unhappy. Mommy thought she'd become a burden and she didn't want that."

"She could never be a burden," Callie whimpered.

"Of course not." He stroked Callie's hair. "If you were listening carefully, then you must have heard me say just that. And that I would never divorce her."

Callie nodded. Small tears tiptoed down her cheeks.

Bill gently pulled her to him and hugged her, trying desperately to make her feel safe.

"I told your mother and I've told you, we're in this together. We're a team and we're going to win this battle, Callie. You'll see."

Again, Callie nodded, but the hitch in his voice and the gruffness of his embrace told her that her father didn't believe a word he was saying.

"I called Auntie Pennie from that man's office," Callie confessed, as she pulled away from her father. "She said she'll take me to visit my mother."

Bill started to object, but Callie stopped him.

"If we're a team," she said with quiet firmness, "it's time you let me into the game. Okay?"

Bill swallowed all his concerns for her safety and all his objections. What he couldn't swallow was the lump of paternal pride that had lodged in his throat, so he smiled, winked at his eight-year-old daughter and gave her a shaky thumbs up.

When Bill and Callie pulled up to their house, the driveway was blocked by a long black limousine. Bill honked his horn. A crisply uniformed chauffeur appeared, opened the door for his client, then stepped aside. Penelope James, Bill Jamieson's younger sister—a successful actress and complete godamnit—got out of the car and purposefully strode over to Bill's window, peering inside so she could get a good look, particularly at Callie. Pennie was Callie's god-mother, a title she took seriously.

"Well, fancy meeting you here," she said with exaggerated brightness. "Did we have a nice trip to the country?"

Bill turned off the engine and quickly got out of the car. He and Pennie moved several paces away and faced each other.

"I gave Ruby the night off," Pennie said as if she were the mistress of the house. "I repaid her for the cost of the car service and threw in a little extra, just in case you decided to inflict a bit of pain and suffering for her wanton disobedience."

Pennie smiled to show her brother she was teasing, but his face remained sallow and somber.

"She shouldn't have taken Callie to that place," he said wearily.

"Ruby took Callie there because the child was desperate to see Mara. Personally, I think Ruby did the right thing."

Bill shrugged. "You know what, Pennie, I don't think I know what's right and what's wrong anymore."

"I don't either, but Callie's already witnessed more than her share of psychotic outbursts. You've said they keep Mara medicated and relatively calm. It might be good for Callie to see that."

"You may be right," Bill said. "But there are a few complications."

"Like what?"

"Mara's contacted a lawyer and filed for divorce."

Bill had told her that Mara mentioned that possibility several times but, like Bill, Pennie hadn't taken it seriously.

"One of the reasons I haven't taken Callie to Stonehaven is, I was afraid if Callie had a negative reaction to seeing her there, it would reinforce Mara's resolve."

"Why is she doing this?"

"She wants me to be free to move on, to find someone to be a wife to me and a mother to Callie."

"Maybe she's right," Pennie said softly.

"At this point in time, I don't agree. A divorce would make her feel alone and unloved!" His voice choked on emotion. "I won't let her do that to herself. I can't."

Pennie had never seen her brother so worn-out, so confused, so defeated. She smoothed her hands over his arms, which were as tense as girders.

"Mara and I have always been close," she said. "I've been wanting to see her. Let me take Callie. You never know. It might help."

"I appreciate what you're trying to do, but this is tough stuff, Pennie."

"I'm tough stuff," she said, taking his hand and leading him back to the car. "And don't you forget it!"

Pennie walked around to the passenger side. Callie was still sitting with her hands folded neatly in her lap. Pennie's heart grew heavy. Her niece was clearly miserable: sad about her mother, concerned about what trouble she might have caused for Ruby, nervous about whether or not her father was going to punish her.

"Bill, my dear, you can do whatever you please about dinner. My niece and I are going out!"

She opened Callie's door and reached inside for the young girl's hand. "Come, sweetheart. Come with Auntie Pennie," she said softly.

Some fairy godmothers waved sparkly wands. Others had big black limousines, but as much as Callie needed a little magic just then, she was torn.

"Go," Bill said, leaning into the driver's side window and blowing her a kiss. "Have fun."

"You sure?" she asked, scanning his face for any signs of disapproval.

"Absolutely!"

With that, Callie took the hand that was offered and gladly followed her aunt.

Bill waited until they had pulled out of the driveway and driven off. Then, he walked into the dark, empty house, closed the door behind him, and cried.

• • •

Pennie spent most of the ride to Connecticut trying to prepare Callie for what she might see. She told her not to expect her mother to look exactly the way she had when she lived at home; Bill had warned Pennie that Mara had lost quite a bit of weight. She explained that many of the patients talked to imaginary friends, that sometimes they yelled and threw things and that Callie shouldn't take anything personally.

Callie listened without comment, but Pennie was certain she heard most of what was said. Her back was straight and Pennie could tell she was trying to be very much the grown-up, but every now and then, her hands clenched and unclenched, as if she were girding herself for a bad time.

On the floor sat a basket of goodies Callie had brought for Mara: Hostess cream-filled cupcakes, a new bottle of Shalimar, Mara's round roll neck pillow, its white eyelet cover freshly washed and ironed, a lipstick in Mara's favorite shade of red and a pound cake which Ruby had baked especially for her. Callie had wanted to pack several of Mara's nightgowns, but Pennie convinced her they probably would be taken away.

"Save them for when she comes home," she'd told Callie, wondering when that might happen, if ever.

When they arrived at Stonehaven, the director greeted Callie more respectfully than he had the last time. Even so, she clasped her aunt's hand, refusing to separate from her for fear that if she did, he would put her in that room again and only allow Pennie to see Mara. Since Mara was just finishing her lunch, they were asked to wait. It was only fifteen minutes, but to Callie it felt like an eternity.

A nurse escorted them down a long hallway to the solarium where patients were permitted to visit with their guests. It was a large, glass-domed room that overlooked luxuriously planted gardens. It was June; so many of the shrubs were in full effulgence: azaleas, rhododendrons and peonies created beautiful splurges of pinks and purples amidst a backdrop of unremitting green. Artfully staggered bunches of yellow irises and white hydrangeas edged many of the carefully sculpted beds, interrupted here and there by low clumps of lilac ageratum and pink and white phlox.

The couches and chairs within the room were upholstered in bright, floral-patterned fabrics that mimicked the garden scene outside. Pennie didn't think Callie noticed, but the furniture was bolted to the floor, nothing in the room had sharp edges, and the upholstery was coated in a thick, hard plastic that resisted cuts and stains. High above them, ceiling fans whirled about at moderate speed, trying to circulate the air and whatever unpleasant smells might accompany the patients into this room.

When Pennie and Callie walked in, many of the seating groups were already occupied. Callie spotted an empty loveseat in the far corner and made a beeline for it.

It wasn't long before an attendant brought Mara in. Pennie heard Callie gasp as she spied her mother in the doorway. Bill hadn't been exaggerating: Mara was beyond thin. Her blond hair was pulled back into a ponytail, exaggerating the sunken, craggy look of her face. She was wearing a shapeless smock dress that hung on her like a sack and soft, slipper socks on her feet. She was thirty years old, but looked twice that. As she approached, however, there was a sparkle in her eyes that was definitely the Mara both Callie and Pennie knew and loved.

As Callie ran to embrace her mother, Pennie choked back tears. She was Bill's sister, but from the minute he brought Mara home, Pennie had loved her as if she, too, were blood.

Mara grinned as Callie led her to the loveseat she'd commandeered. Pennie hung back, allowing mother and daughter to chat for a bit without being interrupted. It disturbed Pennie that the attendant hovered nearby, watching as Callie opened her basket and presented her mother with all her little gifts. Pennie could see the matron making mental notes about what Mara could keep and what would be taken away. Equally disturbing were the other patients, some of whom were clutching themselves and bobbing back and forth to the horror of their families. One man, who had been shouting obscenities nonstop, was being led away.

"Do you really have to be here, Mommy?" Callie whispered as Pennie quietly joined the reunion. "Couldn't you get your treatments at home?"

It was a question Pennie had also wanted to ask. Mara seemed so normal.

"I don't know," Mara answered, as if she had wondered the same thing many times. "They tell me I'm a danger to myself."

"Are you?"

Mara kissed her daughter's cheek and stroked her hair. "I don't think so, but I do have those dreams. And they are scary."

"Can't the doctors make them go away?"

Mara shrugged. "They haven't been able to so far."

"Are they worse?"

"A little." The sparkle left Mara's eyes.

Callie shook her head, clearly exasperated. "Then these doctors aren't very good! I'm going to tell Daddy to find some new ones."

Mara laughed, but Pennie saw tears beginning to gather in the corners of her eyes.

Quickly changing the subject, Mara asked Callie if she'd get her a glass of water.

"Those cupcakes made me thirsty," she explained.

Callie, eager to do anything to help, immediately went off on her errand.

"What's up?" Pennie asked, recognizing a ruse when she saw one.

"I want you to convince Bill to sign the divorce papers." She was blunt, concise, and extremely lucid.

"Why?"

"Because that child deserves a mother."

"She has one."

Mara shook her head. "No. She has the memory of a mother and a fantasy of a mother, but she doesn't have a mother to·take her shopping for school clothes or help her with her homework or make sure she's getting enough sleep. I want Bill to move on and he won't as long as he feels responsible for me."

"He loves you, Mara."

"And I love him. That's why I'm doing this." Again, she looked around, as if demanding that Pennie absorb the reality of Stonehaven. "They're never going to let me out of here," she said.

"You don't know that."

"Yes, I do." Her hands were shaking. She was getting agitated. "Bill doesn't deserve to be shackled to someone like this," she said, looking down at herself, drawing her shoulders in as if repelled by the thought of who she'd become. "And neither does she." Mara's lips quivered as she watched Callie walk across the floor holding a small paper cup obviously filled to the brim with water.

"Here you go!" Callie said, proud to be of assistance.

Mara drank the water and then turned her attention to Callie's gift basket. She rummaged around, retrieved the bottle of perfume and handed it to Pennie.

"They're not going to let me take this up to my room," she said, handing it to her sister-in-law. "See if Cerberus can find a plastic bottle for us to put the perfume in."

"You bet." Pennie took the bottle and went to sweet-talk the matron.

When they were alone, Mara asked Callie how she was doing in school, about Ruby, her friends, and finally, about Bill. Callie answered all her questions, elaborating with funny stories where she thought it would amuse Mara. She was careful not to mention that her father was spending a lot of time in the office and rarely smiled anymore; her mother didn't need to know those things.

"How are you doing?" Mara asked Callie, staring deep into her daughter's eyes. "Are you all right without me at home?"

Callie sniffled. "I miss you," she said.

Mara pulled the child to her chest and hugged her so tightly Callie could barely breathe. "I miss you, too."

Suddenly, abruptly, she pushed Callie away and looked

around, as if she feared she'd done something wrong.

"What's the matter, Mommy?"

Mara's eyes grew wide and a little wild. Her voice was low and hoarse, as if she were sneaking it out of her throat. "If they think I'm too emotional, they'll stick me with a needle and I'll go all numb and I hate that." Again, she looked around, nervously. "I don't belong here, Callie. They know it, but they give me those needles so they can keep me here."

Callie's heart began to pound inside her chest. Her mother was behaving strangely, the way she used to at home sometimes.

"Can't you say no to the needles?"

Mara shook her head. Her fingers tapped a silent staccato on her thighs. "I try, but they don't like me so they don't listen." Her eyes sought out the matron who'd accompanied her into the solarium and glared in her direction. The tapping stopped. Her fingers clutched the fabric of her dress. Then, she turned back to Callie, leaning toward her so she couldn't be overheard.

"They don't want me talking to my friends." Her voice got even lower. "You know. The ones I brought with me from home."

Callie nodded, but she was getting scared. She wished Auntie Pennie would hurry back.

"They're the only friends I have. Maybe if I had other friends, they'd go away."

Mara tilted her head to the side, as if she hadn't thought about that before, but needed to consider it now. When she righted her head and looked at Callie, her eyes seemed normal again.

Callie wanted to cry. Her mother wasn't getting better.

"Do they still visit you?" Mara whispered.

Once, when Mara described her dreams to Callie, Callie had confessed she had some of the same dreams. Mara had been so upset they'd never discussed it again. Until now.

When Callie didn't respond, Mara asked her again. "Do they still visit you?"

"Sometimes."

Mara shook her head from side to side, almost violently. "You have to get rid of them!" she ordered. "Make them go away!"

"I've tried," Callie confessed. "But they come back."

Mara took a deep breath and wiped her eyes with the sleeve of her dress. Tears flowed anyway.

"You have to make them go away, Callie," she said, gripping her daughter's shoulders with her hands, her entire body quaking. "Promise me you'll try harder. It's important."

"I promise, Mommy." Now, Callie was crying. "But what if I can't make them go away?"

Mara pulled Callie close and whispered in her ear. "Then you keep them a secret and you don't tell anyone. *Ever!*"

That night, after Callie went to bed, Pennie told Bill all about their visit, including the private discussion she'd had with Mara.

"A divorce might help ease her sense of burden," she said. "Maybe if she doesn't feel responsible for anyone but herself, it might hasten her recovery."

The next day, Bill called Mara's doctor to discuss the matter. He dismissed it, preferring instead to harshly admonish Bill for allowing Callie to come to Stonehaven.

"The visit with her daughter and sister-in-law left your wife in a highly agitated state. She was so out of control we had no choice but to sedate and restrain her."

Bill called again the following day and the day after that. Each time, the doctor repeated his gloomy prognosis: Mara was deeply psychotic, haunted by a collection of malevolent strangers who so terrified her she was afraid to leave her room, let alone the sanitarium. She was going to need years of treatment and confinement.

It was several months before the doctor agreed to let Bill come to Stonehaven.

Mara was emaciated. He could find only a few vestiges of her former beauty: Her eyes, while still a beautiful blue, were dulled by drugs. Her cheeks, once high and proud, were hollowed and gaunt. Her lips, which once had brightened his day with a smile or pleasured his nights with their touch, were dry and pinched. But worst of all, the spirit of Mara, the ebullient, clever, sassy essence that had defined his wife, was all but gone.

At first, he spoke about innocuous things: the change in the weather, her health, what Pennie was up to. There was no response. He presented her with a card hand-drawn by Callie. She put it on her lap and never looked at it. He told her how much Callie missed her, how he missed her. Her eyes remained vacant. He asked about her treatment, how the attendants and doctors were treating her. Was she eating well? Sleeping well? Nothing. Mara was a shell, a void, emptied of all curiosity. He told her how much he loved her and how he looked forward to her recovery and homecoming.

That's when she spoke and when she did, she broke his heart.

"I want a divorce," she said. "Give it to me. Please."

Bill heard the words, but refused to believe they were sincere.

"I took a solemn vow, Mara, to stick by you in sickness and in health," he told her, still believing the strength of his love was more important to her well-being than a legal document granting him freedom. "I intend to keep that vow and love you 'til death do us part."

Without uttering another word, she got up from her chair, turned her back on her husband, and walked out of the solarium.

Two days later, Mara Jamieson hanged herself.

---------------- 1 ----------------

The Grill Room of The Four Seasons restaurant buzzed with the excited exchange of gossip that accompanied every lunch at the prestigious watering hole. Since most of the diners were regulars, the chatter followed a prescribed order: Those on the upper tier whispered about those on the lower tier. Those on the lower tier snickered about those at the bar. And those at the bar prayed that when their reservations were called, they would be put anywhere other than the Pool Room. That was for tourists.

From his privileged perch—lower level, corner table—Wilty Hale commanded an unfettered view of most of the room as well as of the entrance. The prestige of that prime placement—and the reason for it—was not lost on him. His was a boldfaced name; this was a place that thrived on the loyalty of the see-and-be-seen crowd.

While others of his ilk could be observed reaffirming their own importance by assessing who was at neighboring tables—and with whom—Wilty couldn't have cared less. When he wasn't becoming one with his martini, his eyes remained fixed on the stairway leading up to the Grill.

He didn't know why he expected her to be on time. She would never even consider being anything less than twenty minutes late.

An investment banker who handled several of Wilty's accounts stopped to pay obeisance before moving on to his table. Several other money men ambled by, also pausing to engage in a moment or two of social banter. Each of them took a moment to give Wilty a companionable slap on the back and say they really should get together for a round of golf, or a spot of lunch, or a late-day drink. Wilty managed to be charming but, inside, he roiled at the hypocrisy. They'd always been happy to chat him up and brag about what a great job they were doing managing his wealth, but until this year, none of them had ever called him for lunch or golf or a drink at any time of the day. Suddenly, he was a hot commodity. Why? Because while he'd always had money and a name, soon he would have power.

He looked around and wondered how many people in that room envied him his name. Probably most. They thought it was a ticket to easy street. In some ways, they were correct: being a Hale meant he'd never have to worry about money. It also meant that no matter what he did, he'd never measure up.

When you're the scion of a dynasty, you're the heir to someone else's genius. Wilty could start a business from scratch and build it into a financial behemoth and he'd still never get the respect he coveted. *They* would say he never really started from scratch because his seed money had come from the family trust, that his name had opened all the right doors, that success bred success. To *them,* he'd always be the cluck with the inheritance.

Wilty winced as he swirled his vodka around in its glass.

He and that glass had a lot in common, he thought wryly. They were both vessels. The difference was, no one expected the glass to do anything more than sit quietly and hold its liquor. He was expected to do that *and* to sow the seed for the next generation of Hales, to keep the family flame burning bright, and not to do anything that could tarnish the luster of the Hale name.

That name would be the death of him, he thought, a lifelong bitterness rising in his throat like a bilious belch.

Then again, if what he found out was true . . .

He swallowed hard, forcing the bitterness down, back into the place where he kept most of his emotions hidden from public view. It wasn't as easy to digest the possibility that he wasn't who he always believed he was.

How ironic! Up until six months ago, Wilty had spent a great deal of time bitching about his dynastic obligations—sitting on the board of Hale Holdings, as well as on the boards of several of New York's finest cultural institutions, making an honest, concerted effort to contribute ideas and energy to all of them. And bemoaning the fact that no matter what he did, no one took him seriously; that to his fellow board members he had no distinction, no track record of personal success.

How often had he fantasized about how wonderful it would be to be free of the Hale yoke, to be respected for what he'd done, not for what the late, great E.W. Hale had accomplished.

"Be careful what you wish for," he muttered under his breath.

He checked the stairway, then his watch. Five minutes more, ten at the outside. He signaled the waiter, who was already on his way with another martini.

Despite his rising vodka buzz, he felt several sets of eyes on him. They weren't from those who disapproved of his drinking or pitied him because he was alone. He had a built-in radar system for those stares. No, these gazes were from women on the prowl.

It wasn't exactly a new experience. Wilty was as handsome as he was rich. Tall, with broad shoulders and a slim waist, he wore his expensive suits and bespoke furnishings well. He had deep set, engaging blue eyes that peered out from beneath a wide brow and a carefully tousled head of sandy hair. His face, angular with sharply planed cheeks and an aquiline nose, seemed to emphasize his patrician lineage, describing him as someone who conducted his public life according to rules established by society's peerage. To some extent that was true. Wilty had all the manners and grace and poise that one accrued attending the finest boarding schools and universities and having all the advantages great wealth could afford.

But Wilty's dimpled chin and a full lower lip that always looked as if it had just been kissed, attested to the puckish, rebellious side of his nature, the side that was ready, willing and more than able to cast aside his nobility whenever the spirit moved him.

Unfortunately of late, there were too many spirits in Wilty's life and too few rules.

His latest admirers were at a table on the upper tier; two young fashionista types who smiled fetchingly the minute he looked their way. He raised his glass and tipped it toward them, knowing they wanted him to ask for their numbers or buy them a drink or do something equally gallant. Instead, he looked away. He'd learned a long time ago the worst thing that could happen to any woman would be to become Mrs. Hale. All he had to do was look at his mother.

Speaking of the devil, and she was that, Carolyne Hale had arrived. He watched with amusement, and a bit of perverse pride, as she greeted the maître d' and allowed him to escort her to the table. Just as she'd intended, for a moment all eyes were directed toward her, and rightfully so. Say what he would about her—and he said plenty—Carolyne was a stunning woman.

Blond and slim, with the long neck and classic bone structure coveted by sculptors, she walked with a regal bearing that befitted her station. Her face was pale and artfully done; this wasn't a woman who championed the natural look. Her mouth, wide and full, but not overly generous, was rouged in a ladylike pink and set in an expression best described as inscrutable. Her hair, coifed in a loose twist, drew attention to large cornflower blue eyes that took in the room and separated social chaff from wheat with a single sweep.

She air-kissed Wilty on both cheeks, slid onto the banquette and immediately dispatched the waiter for a glass of white wine. Wilty tacked on an order for a refill of his libation.

"Hello, Mother," he said. "Nice of you to join me."

"It's good to see you, too, dear."

Carolyne checked her place setting, then aligned the flat-ware so that the various forks and knives and spoons were all the exact distance from the edge of the table.

"So sloppy," she sniffed. "You'd think that with their clientele they would take greater care."

Wilty slapped the palm of his hand against his forehead. "Drat! I completely forgot! Tuesday is bridge and tunnel day." He looked around with comic exaggeration, leaned up against her ear and whispered, "They let things slide when it's not exclusively the A crowd."

Carolyne pushed him away and made a show of disciplining a stray strand of hair. "Don't be snide, darling. It's unbecoming."

The waiter replaced Wilty's empty glass with a fresh martini and set Carolyne's wine down. She lifted it up and with practiced grace, took a small sip. Her collection of gold bracelets jangled at her wrist.

"How was your stay in the country? Was it productive?"

"If you're asking whether I went out to the Hamptons to dry out, no, I didn't."

Carolyne heaved a sigh. She leaned close to her son so that no one would overhear. "Why must you be so difficult?"

"I can't help it. It's in the genes."

He laughed. Carolyne shook her head.

"How many of those lethal weapons have you consumed?" she asked, pointing to his martini glass.

"As many as it took to fill the time between when you were supposed to be here and when you actually showed up."

The captain appeared, anxious to tell them the specials of the day. When he'd completed his recitation, Carolyne ordered her usual salad, Wilty the filet of sole. After the captain departed, Carolyne turned her attention to her son, looking him over as if he were a piece of fruit she was checking for signs of rot.

"Your color is poor," she announced, as if he could—

and should—immediately change the tone of his complexion to one which she found more pleasing.

"Don't worry, Mother, one more drink and I'll be nice and pink again."

"I wish you would stop," she said.

"Drinking? Or flushing?"

"It's not funny, Wilty. You're becoming an alcoholic."

The honest concern in her voice startled him. He wasn't used to it.

"That'll show you how long it's been since we've seen each other. I already *am* an alcoholic." To drive his point home, he speared an olive and licked it dry before popping it into his mouth.

Embarrassed and at a loss, Carolyne examined the basket of bread as if its contents had been smuggled into the country from Afghanistan.

Their lunch arrived. Carolyne picked at hers. Wilty didn't even bother pretending to eat his. Instead, he emptied his glass. He was about to order another, but Carolyne stopped him.

"Please! I need to talk to you. I'd like you to remain sober enough to listen."

A slow, sardonic smile passed over Wilty's mouth. She needed money. He should have known. Why else would she be having lunch with him?

"How much?" he asked, bluntly.

Quickly, Carolyne looked around, nervous that someone might have heard him.

"You make me sound so mercenary," she complained.

"If the Manolo Blahnik fits . . ."

Carolyne's blue eyes went cold. "In case you've been too *indisposed* to read the papers, the market isn't exactly roaring these days. I loathe having to come to you with hat in hand, but thanks to the collective insanity of your father's family, *you* control the money."

"It's a pisser, isn't it?" Wilty signaled the waiter for another drink.

"You may find this situation amusing, Wilty, but I do

not. It's unseemly that I should have to ask my *son* for money every time I want to make an investment."

He agreed with her, but they both knew there was nothing he could do about it. E.W. Hale had been dead since 1938, yet thanks to an ironclad will, he still held sway over all of them.

"If I wasn't the one holding the purse strings, Mother, would I ever see you?" It was an obvious question, one he'd asked many times before. Why he bothered, he didn't know. He was never going to get the answer he craved. Yet he couldn't stop himself. "Do you even care whether I live or die?"

Wilty's voice was low. He sounded the way he used to when he was a little boy and wondered whether she was lonely without her husband and whether it was hard being a mommy when there was no daddy.

"Of course, I'd see you," she said, truly moved. "And while you may not believe it, I do love you, Wilty." He harrumphed. She shifted in her seat, clearly uncomfortable. Carolyne didn't like public discussions of private disputes. She liked questions about her personal sentiments even less. "I didn't love your father. You know that. He was a brutish, horrible man. And I loathed your grandmother. But my feelings about them have nothing to do with my feelings toward you."

Wilty felt the vodka slide down his throat. It was smooth and sedative, but not strong enough to numb him to the hurt he felt whenever he and Carolyne were together.

"Did you want me?" he asked.

It was an odd question coming from a thirty-four-year-old man, but, Carolyne ruefully admitted, Wilty was odd.

"How could you even ask such a thing?"

He wanted to say the same thing to her, but they both knew this conversation had gone as far as it was going to go. The mother would never be able to convince the son that she loved and wanted him, because the son had never felt loved and wanted.

He tilted his head and stared at her through eyes growing rheumy with drink.

"What would you do if the money was taken away? And I mean every last *centavo* of it."

A chill raced up Carolyne's spine. "That's never going to happen, Wilty, and you know it. Your great-great-grandfather may have been a colossal prick, but he was smart, especially when it came to money."

Carolyne noticed a smirk flit across Wilty's lips. It was fleeting, but unsettling. Smirks usually meant someone knew something you didn't. For some time now, he'd been alluding to a nugget of information he'd uncovered that had the power to change their lives. When he refused to elaborate, she dismissed it as another of his attempts to torment her for past maternal offenses. But he continued to bring it up.

"I didn't say we'd lose our fortune because he was stupid. I just said it was possible for us to lose it."

Carolyne leaned in very close. Her jaw clenched and her voice trembled with annoyance. "I don't appreciate being toyed with. Either tell me what you're talking about, or drop it!"

Wilty poked a plastic toothpick into an olive and stirred his drink, an incipient flush of power pinking his cheeks. He could feel the strength of his mother's anger just as acutely as if she'd wrapped her fingers around his neck.

"The last time I was up at Long House," the Hale family's Adirondack retreat, "I spent my evenings rummaging through E.W. Hale's memorabilia. Sometimes I think I lose sight of what an incredible man he was." His eyes widened with honest reverence. "The diaries were particularly fascinating. They are, after all, a first-person history of America at the turn of the century."

"Get on with it." Carolyne had little patience for anyone waxing poetic about the Hales. She hated everything about them, except their money.

Normally, Wilty sloughed off his mother's loathing of the Hales. It was as much a part of her everyday routine as having her hair blown out. Today, however, her disrespect of his ancestry rankled. In response, he debated whether to cut this conversation short and leave her hanging, or tell her what he'd discovered. Since the latter would definitely devastate her, that was the course he chose.

"It was serendipitous, really. I was returning a journal to its respective shelf when I noticed a tiny piece of paper sticking out from the back of a pilaster. When I looked more closely, I realized I'd come upon one of those secret compartments the Victorians were so fond of. The door to this little hideaway must have come loose over the years and the paper must have shifted enough for a corner to peek out." He paused, relishing the nervous flutter of her eyes. "You'll never guess what it was," he teased.

"Nor am I going to try."

"It was Charles Hale's suicide note."

Carolyne looked bored.

"I realize you're not a Hale history buff, so I'll enlighten you. In 1900, Charles Hale was thirty years old, happily married, and firmly ensconced as the undisputed heir to the Hale fortune. Suddenly, for no apparent reason, he blew his head off. A month later, E.W. Hale ripped up his will and created the Hale Trust to replace it.

"It's been over a hundred years, yet not one historian or biographer has been able to explain why Charles would have taken his life, and why that singular event would have prompted E.W. Hale to wrest control of his fortune away from his wife and his remaining children."

"Well, thankfully, you've found the answer. The universe can breathe a sigh of relief."

He ignored her sarcasm. "His farewell wasn't as specific as I would've liked. I'm still at a loss as to why he put a gun to his head, but he does say a few things that explain why E.W. would've wanted this note buried."

"Please don't keep me in suspense. What was so unnerving?"

"Charles said he was a fraud and his entire family was living a terrible lie. He blamed his father for getting them into this 'hideous predicament,' as he called it, but admitted that his actions were the ones that would bring shame upon the Hale name. He said, 'he'd opened Pandora's box and let the secret out.' "

"What secret? How was he a fraud?"

Wilty shrugged. "I don't know. He said he tried to make things right, but instead, things went terribly wrong." Wilty crinkled his forehead as, again, he tried to make sense of Charles's words. "He said that thanks to him, they would be coming to take what was theirs: the Hale name, the Hale fortune. And their revenge."

"Who are *they?*"

"I don't know that either, but his fears must have had some merit. The guy blew his brains out rather than see it happen."

Carolyne was growing impatient, and more than a little nervous. "What does any of this have to do with us?"

"If these are the ramblings of a lunatic, nothing. But if his not-so-subtle inference about E.W. Hale doing something that might have compromised the integrity of the family is true, the entire line of descent could be called into question." His blue eyes fixed on hers. "I'm the last of that line, but if I'm not a Hale, the money isn't mine."

"Is there corroboration for any of this?"

"None that I could find. And believe me, I've looked."

That worried Carolyne because as dissolute as Wilty seemed to be, he was compulsive by nature. If he said he hadn't been able to unearth anything to back up this note, either there was nothing to be found, or someone was making certain it couldn't be found.

"Then file it under miscellaneous historical garbage and forget it," she said with a wave of her hand, as if she could wish this unfortunate discovery away.

"I can't."

"Why not?"

"In case you've forgotten, my thirty-fifth birthday is less than two months away."

Carolyne would never forget about June first. That was

when Wilty was due to inherit hundreds of millions of dollars. On that date, the principal of the Hale Trust, and the power that came with it, would be turned over to him if, "in the judgment of the trustees, he had proven himself competent and qualified to take care of same." Several years before, the Trust was terminated, allowing the interest from the estate to be bequeathed to Wilty. He had from then until his thirty-fifth birthday to prove himself worthy of the Hale mantle on three counts: philanthropy, profit and prestige, which E.W. Hale defined as being of moral character. Wilty had achieved two out of the three.

"According to E.W. Hale's will, after the trustees decide whether or not I've passed the old man's test, they're free to consider any information developed by them or others as to whether or not I'm up to the challenge of being the head of Hale Holdings."

Carolyne shook her head in disgust. "Stupidest thing I ever heard of."

"Maybe so, but it's not your call," Wilty reminded her. "I've done enough charity work and made enough good investments to clear the first two hurdles, but as we both know, I lose points on character." Almost as a reflex, Wilty pushed his drink away. "That's the bad news. The good news is that since no one on the Hale board craves lurid publicity, I can't see them rejecting me and risking a media field day just because I have one too many martinis at lunch."

Carolyne's look warned him not to bank on that.

"They're too self-serving. Instead, they'll figure out a way to fulfill the mandate of the Trust and marginalize me at the same time."

Carolyne had to agree. As long as the men on the board could maintain their control on the *Courier* and the rest of Hale Holdings—and therefore justify their bloated incomes—without having to suffer any interference from Wilty or her or anyone else outside their tightly drawn circle, they wouldn't deny Wilty his inheritance.

"What does make me nervous, however," Wilty continued, "is the surprise, the person out there who knows about Charles's claim that he, his siblings and their descendants don't have a rightful claim to the Hale Trust."

He furrowed his brow and rubbed his temples to soothe an incipient migraine. He'd had a lot of those lately. "I know you don't care about this, but aside from the obvious financial ramifications, that claim goes to the heart of who I am."

Carolyne groaned. "It does not. Stop being so paranoid and insecure. It was a claim made by a man who moments later put a gun to his head. And, in case you've overlooked this fact, despite his whiny confession of some unmentioned wrongdoing, the Hale fortune was passed down through the original family line. No one took him seriously then. No one's going to give credence to his rantings now."

Wilty said he wasn't so sure.

Carolyne was right. Wilty was obsessed with this note. From what she could surmise, he'd been stewing about this for six months already. What worried her was what he intended to do with this information.

"Okay, you've discovered that the great E.W. Hale wasn't infallible. That his son might have tried to clean up some mess his father created and made the mess worse. So what? This note is literally ancient history. It has no bearing on the Trust and your right to receive it, especially if you're smart and keep this foolishness to yourself."

"It may not be completely up to me," he said.

"What do you mean?"

"There were dozens and dozens of diaries at Long House, all of them arranged chronologically according to year. Four diaries were missing. I've tracked down three of them, but the most conspicuous one, the one from 1900, the one that could back this letter up or refute it, is gone."

"So?"

"So, something happened. Something big enough to motivate Charles to kill himself. For Winifred Hale and her other children to be punished as a result. And for E.W. Hale to do his damnedest to cover up the reason why. Whoever has the missing diary knows what that something is and is waiting for just the right moment to spring it on the public. June first might be that moment."

A heavy silence parked itself between them as both Wilty and Carolyne considered the consequences of such a revelation. Carolyne spoke first.

"I take it you're assuming that E.W. Hale laid out the details of whatever put his family into that so-called predicament in his diary."

Wilty nodded. "He was a detail man."

"Without the diary, the letter is damning, but vague. Without the letter, the diary could be dismissed as merely E.W.'s private thoughts or flights of fancy. It would be difficult to portray anything written in a personal journal as proof of any specific action."

"Granted. But together, they could bring down an empire. My empire, to be more precise."

"Are you still looking for the diary?"

"Of course."

"Where's the letter?"

"In a safe place."

Carolyne glared at her son as if he were an idiot, but instead of chastising him, she withdrew, studying the bread crumbs on the tablecloth, finishing her wine, taking the time to consider a myriad of possibilities. When she finally looked up, her mouth was set.

"No place is safe," she said to Wilty. "Get rid of that damned note."

2

Peter Merrick's office was designed to be soothing. The walls were paneled in an ash-toned wood which prevented the room from turning dark and threatening even when the lighting was lowered. The fabrics that upholstered the chairs and made up the elegantly swagged drapes had been carefully chosen to please and disarm. The analytic couch was leather, a beige that looked like coffee with an extra splash of milk. Sheer, accordion-pleated blinds filtered whatever outside light found its way inside. Plush carpeting absorbed sound.

There was no desk, nor were there any personal effects in the room. It looked like a library in a home except there were no family photographs or snapshots of favorite vacation sites. No art other than two "decorator oils" selected simply because they matched the color scheme. Even Merrick's diplomas were relegated to another, smaller space adjacent to the consultation room, where patients waited for and were received by the therapist.

Early in his training, one of Peter's supervisors cautioned him about putting anything in his office that might reveal personality traits or biographical data. According to the trainer, it was essential that a patient not have access to knowledge about the therapist's personal interests or family life. The therapist was supposed to be a blank slate onto which the patient could transfer attitudes and feelings that might offer clues about unconscious biases.

Peter didn't believe one needed to be completely enig-
matic to be effective, but since he was reticent by nature,
a certain amount of anonymity was fine with him.

Peter enjoyed his work because it was a challenge and
the effort was worthwhile. Also, thanks to his own psycho-
logical pathology, he could relate to many of his patients.
He was one of four children in a family of extraordinary
achievers: his father helped pioneer organ transplants, one
of his brothers was a Nobel nominee in nuclear physics,
his sister was on track to become governor of Connecticut,
his other brother was a world-renowned surgeon, his
mother a pediatrician/author whose books on child care
were de rigueur for any new parent. In the Merrick clan,
anything less than greatness was failure.

Like most analysts, Merrick believed in dreams as a
shortcut to the unconscious. He also shared the view that
dreams connected the past to the present and therefore
needed to be thoroughly explored. In many cases that was
easier said than done. Some dreams could be satisfactorily
analyzed and explained: they expressed anxiety or frustra-
tions or tensions brought about by everyday problems. Others remained stubbornly resistant to interpretation. They
couldn't be explained, wished away, talked away, or
drugged out of existence. They were night terrors: horrific
nightmares that appeared to have no relevance to the
dreamer's external life, provided no clues to the dreamer's
inner life, yet recurred again and again and again—in exactly the same form each time. They were the ones that
intrigued Merrick the most.

Merrick's fellow analysts believed night terrors resulted
from overwhelming stress. Peter believed invariable, frequently recurring dreams weren't dreams at all. They were
memories passed on to us from someone else.

While Peter wasn't the first to put forward the notion of
genetic memory or the only one to pursue evidence of the
theory, he was one of the few who vigorously promoted it.
He'd written a book, *Before and Again*, which had done

quite well, and frequently lectured on the subject. Still, he was considered a maverick.

To the general public, the idea of being able to tap into a secret part of the brain and relive the pasts of distant relations seemed remote, implausible and, perhaps, a bit spooky. Most laypeople preferred the notion of past lives and reincarnation, even though it was far less likely.

To many of Peter's colleagues, genetic memory was simply instinct by another name: Like birds flying south in the winter. Squirrels storing nuts. Bears hibernating in caves. To them, elevating genetic memory to something more than repetitive, animalistic behavior felt like too great a leap.

Peter remained undeterred. To him, the concept was simple: If we passed on genetically transmitted disorders like sickle cell anemia, Tay-Sachs disease and cystic fibrosis, why not memories? If experiences were imprinted on brain cells as memories, why wouldn't they be imprinted on DNA as well? If we agreed that some individuals were capable of extrasensory perception, why weren't other individuals capable of ferreting around in the recesses of their brains to retrieve hidden memories?

Just because something couldn't be readily explained didn't mean it should be dismissed.

Once it was announced that several highly respected biotechnology institutions were engaged in a colossal project to map a human genome that would identify all the genetic material in the chromosomes of a single human being, everything changed. The press jumped on the Human Genome Project with an enthusiasm usually reserved for major sporting events or juicy scandals. The general public, who usually considered science something only smart kids took in school, and genetics the thing that gave you blond hair and good skin, was actually excited about the Human Genome Project. Because this was about them. Who they were. What their bodies were made of. What diseases would probably attack them. And what the odds were of them surviving.

There was also an irresistible sense of mystery surrounding the Project. What secrets might be hidden inside the human body and the human mind? What could we do or know that had never been imagined before? Among other revelations, Peter was certain that once the researchers had deciphered the genetic codebook, they would find that one of the three billion bits of information within that book not only controlled memory, but contained a door to the past.

And when they did, he would not only be rich, but hailed as a visionary.

Even by his family.

Peter was first introduced to the concept of genetic memory twenty years before. He had just begun a fellowship at a private sanitarium when a young man was admitted with a diagnosis of schizophrenia. He heard voices, which was indeed typical of the illness; he saw people who weren't there, another standard symptom. But the voices weren't urging him to commit violent acts to others or himself, as would be typical. They were exhorting him to save himself. And the people he described were not of this time. The women wore long woolen skirts and big, fabric bonnets. The men wore blousing shirts and full pants tucked into high leather boots.

One of the more puzzling aspects of this particular case was an abject fear of water. This young man quaked at the sight of a bathtub or a swimming pool or a pond. Even a rain puddle could unhinge him.

After months of following standard protocols—including heavy doses of Thorazine—with no visible improvement, Merrick began to question the accuracy of the diagnosis. In his search for another explanation for this patient's distress, he remembered hearing one of the psychiatrists senior to him discuss genetic memory. Peter had been intrigued. He read the research, spent hours talking with his colleague about how to distinguish between symptoms of schizophrenia and genetic memory and even observed the other man's attempts at regression therapy. The more he learned, the more convinced Peter was that his patient wasn't suffering from schizophrenia. Strange, inexplicable memories were overwhelming him to the point of madness.

Without telling anyone at the institution—other than his mentor—Merrick substituted a placebo for the Thorazine, hypnotized the patient and began to regress him.

At first, Abel, as Merrick dubbed him, took to the hypnosis with tremendous ease. He recalled details easily, spewing tales about a family that was part of a larger community. Everyone he mentioned was very tall, which prompted Merrick to conclude these were the memories of a child. He described a journey in a vehicle with large wheels, but no engine. He spoke of dust and heat and freezing nights and blowing snow.

For six months, Merrick pushed Abel to remember more and more, encouraging him to confront the images that appeared before his mind's eye, to work harder to explain them. Sometimes their sessions were satisfactory. Sometimes, they were utter failures.

One afternoon when Abel seemed particularly relaxed, Merrick asked him to paint a landscape. He spoke of endless, flat expanses of golden yellow that suddenly erupted into caverns of blue-green, sharply peaked mountains. He described a journey not unlike a cross-country migration.

Merrick accompanied Abel on his trek, listening carefully as the young man's voice became more shrill with each mile logged, his breathing more erratic. They crossed a range of mountains. Abel continued to be unsettled, yet remained in the trance and clearly focused. Merrick had a difficult time keeping his own emotions in check.

Then, Abel stopped speaking. His hands shook. Huge tears flooded his cheeks, his eyes stayed closed. His head snapped back and forth, his mouth opening and closing like a fish out of water gasping for air. Merrick asked where he was. Abel described a riverbank. Merrick asked how wide the river was. Abel's eyes popped open. They were agog. He tried to take Abel across the river, but the child in the man refused to go. Merrick urged him on, using phrases from Abel's dreams. Abel resisted, begging Merrick to stop, to not make him go into the water. Merrick, who believed this was the only way to free Abel from his nightmares, insisted.

Abel called out to people Merrick assumed were the boy's relatives. He cried. He screamed. He gagged, as if his throat had suddenly filled with water. Merrick continued to push the dream child forward, telling him to complete his journey, to fight the restraints of the present so that he could conquer the past. He was merciless.

That night, they found Abel dead in a bathtub. He'd tied a plastic bag around his head and drowned.

No one blamed Merrick for Abel's death; suicide was the number one cause of death for schizophrenics. Nonetheless, Peter conscientiously reviewed his behavior. He acknowledged that perhaps he had pushed too hard, that youthful impatience might have overshadowed professional caution. But he didn't alter his diagnosis, especially after research turned up a snippet of history that changed his life: a small paragraph within a larger piece about the migration of the Mormons from Nauvoo, Illinois, to Utah in 1847.

Along the way, a small colony of mostly women and children strayed off course. Eager to rejoin the caravan, they decided to ford the Colorado River. Unaware of how wide the river was and how fierce the undercurrent could be, they ventured into the water. The few men who'd accompanied the group saved as many as they could. Most of the women drowned. Only a few of the children survived. Peter believed Abel had been one of them.

He also remained convinced that Abel's illness was caused by traumatic ancestral memories forcefully manifesting themselves. The problem was that when Abel arrived at the crux of the memory, he couldn't separate the past from the present. Peter vowed to do better the next time.

Over the next twenty years, there were two next times.

Both patients were diagnosed as schizophrenics. Both evinced clear signs of genetic memory. Both eventually committed suicide.

Everything's gray. Kind of vague and murky. The air looks thick.

It feels uncomfortable, crowded almost, like the gray has turned into a huge glob that's spreading quickly and will soon overwhelm the area. The closeness makes me gag.

A man and a woman are silhouetted in the shadows. They're facing each other. Their postures are stiff with barely restrained anger.

The gray man is tall. His body is lean, his face sharply planed. He's dressed like a fancy man, with a colorful vest and neatly pressed pants.

The woman is smaller and softer, yet her posture speaks of internal structure girded with steel. She's not a fancy woman. Her hair is loose and undone. Her hands appear roughened by work. Her clothes are homespun and plain, but she's not. Her features are refined, her carriage rather elegant.

The gray man bends over, deliberately cramping her space. She resists the temptation to step back and stands firm, her eyes locked on his. His voice rises. The veins in his neck protrude. His lips seem pinched, as if his words are being forced through gritted teeth.

I'm afraid for her. I stand, ready to rush to her defense when I'm stopped by a huge burst of blinding, white light. It paralyzes me.

I'm frightened for her. And for me.

"When I clap my hands, you'll awaken. You'll remember everything, but instead of being agitated, you'll feel calm and relieved."

He clapped his hands three times. The woman's eyelids fluttered. The tightness that had described her body only moments before disappeared.

"That was excellent, Callie," the doctor said.

Callie Jamieson looked around the room, momentarily disoriented. She felt a dampness on her cheeks and automatically ran the back of her hand across her face, swabbing the tears she'd shed while under hypnosis.

Peter Merrick studied her carefully as she emerged from her trance.

Callie Jamieson had been his patient for nearly six months. She'd come seeking help because she felt she'd arrived at a crossroads in her life. She believed she'd made an unwise decision, one that had more to do with the baggage she'd carried with her from her childhood than anything related to the current situation and wanted to prevent that from happening again.

Over the course of their sessions, she confessed that one of the reasons she'd chosen Merrick as her therapist was because of his expertise in the field of dreams. She'd suffered horrible nightmares as a child. They'd visit, ravage her, then disappear, often for years at a time. She said that what made them particularly terrifying was the fact that her mother had experienced the very same dreams.

For Peter, that moment was a miracle. He had begun to think he'd never find another candidate for genetic memory regression, that his chance at meaningful success had passed him by and that he was forever relegated to couch-counseling neurotics. When Callie confided in him about Mara, it took every ounce of restraint he possessed to hold himself in check and wait for her night terrors to return. Sooner or later, he knew they would.

The other night they had. She said they were nebulous and less defined than they'd been in the past, but she feared the reappearance of this chimera was simply a foreshadowing of what was to come. Rather than subject herself to the hell she believed awaited her, she agreed to be hypnotized.

"This was a wonderful beginning," Merrick said, his basso voice soft and soothing.

"I couldn't protect her," Callie said, agitated despite his instruction to the contrary. "He hurt her. I know he did."

"Who are they, Callie?" He was intrigued that the dream was more powerful than his command.

The young woman's large turquoise eyes pooled with frustration and despair.

"That's why I'm here," she said, tremulously. "I don't know."

Her fear was so strong, Merrick could feel it.

"Did your mother know who they were?"

"If she did, she didn't tell me."

Callie sighed, her breath fluttering over a sudden rush of feeling.

"Why do you think the dreams have returned?" Merrick asked, changing the subject so she wouldn't become overwhelmed by emotion.

"I wish I knew. They've been dormant for years." Her eyes misted and her voice stumbled over a lump in her throat. "I thought I was rid of them."

Merrick was grateful that she wasn't.

"Are you feeling any extraordinary stress at work?"

Callie was an investigative reporter for a major newspaper, the *City Courier,* a job that frequently required her to be in precarious situations, but she shook off the suggestion that her nightmares were work related. "I am working on a major story involving some unsavory characters, but I'm careful. I've done this often enough to know what precautions to take."

"Any social pressure? A new man in your life, perhaps?"

Callie offered him a small smile. "Sadly, no."

"Are you open to a new relationship?" Since she'd come to him after a failed romance, this detour wasn't without therapeutic purpose.

She said yes, but her body language screamed uncertainty.

"Are you afraid that if you enter a relationship it'll end badly?"

"They all do."

"Because of the men or because of you?"

"Mostly me. When you get right down to it, I'm afraid

history will repeat itself. I'll wind up like my mother and whoever I'm with will end up like my father, lonely and withdrawn and permanently scarred." Her lower lip wobbled as painful memories were revived.

"Do you believe the dreams brought on your mother's insanity?"

Callie thought about that for a moment. "Since I have the same dreams, my response is probably self-defensive, but yes, I think that's entirely possible."

The dread she expressed told him how depleting and ruinous these nightmare sieges could be.

"Besides," she said with a self-conscious smile, "it's easier for me to believe that than to believe that insanity created the dreams."

Merrick nodded. Point well made.

"Did your grandmother have these dreams as well?"

Callie sat up, turned around and looked at him. "Why would you ask me that?"

"Because it's possible that these nocturnal visitations aren't dreams, but are in fact memories of an event that occurred several lifetimes ago." He said it quietly, knowing that insinuating genetic memory was provocative and often disturbing. Then again, Callie had come to him because of his book on past lives. On some level, he assumed she suspected that something like that might be true.

He waited while she pondered the question. From experience, he knew she was trying to provide an honest answer while at the same time, trying to decide what she wanted the answer to be.

"My grandmother was an extremely closed-mouthed woman with a highly exaggerated sense of privacy," she said finally. "She never would have shared her dreams with me. Good or bad."

Callie lay back down on the couch and rubbed her eyes. Merrick could see she was exhausted.

"Is she still alive?"

"She died six months after my mother."

"How did she die?"

Callie screwed her face into a grimace and dropped her face into her hands. Merrick rose from his chair and walked to her side. He bent down and gently laid his hand on her back.

"What's wrong, Callie?"

She lifted her head and turned toward him. Grief and fear streaked her face.

"She died in a mysterious car accident. It was a bright, sunny day. She was driving down a wide street that wasn't heavily trafficked and for some reason, her car ran over a divider and plowed into a wall. There was nothing wrong with her car. The police had it checked out. They thought something might have spooked her."

Callie stared at Merrick. Her eyes were moist.

"What if my grandmother had the same dreams I have? The same ones my mother had?" Her body was trembling. "The gray people could have spooked her. They could have been what killed her." Her breathing was rapid and erratic.

"These gray people are visions, Callie," he said. "They're frightening, but they're not real. They can't hurt you."

Callie's eyes hardened and her lips pulled into a tight line.

"You're wrong," she snapped. "Dreams. Memories. Visions. Whatever you call them, they killed my mother. Possibly my grandmother. And if I don't figure out who the gray people are and what they want with me, they're going to kill me, too."

3

Wilty Hale had a stable of attorneys, most of them pedigreed partners at high profile, white-shoe law firms. For this particular matter, however, confidentiality and trustworthiness were key, which eliminated most of Wilty's legal minions. This would hit too close to home for any of them to be effective.

Instead, Wilty called Dan Kalikow, a college chum who'd left Sullivan & Cromwell to open an office with several other lawyers who'd also tired of big-firm bureaucracy. Wilty had tossed Dan a few things in the past and found him immensely capable. He was also unsparingly loyal, hungry enough to want the job, but too proud to prostitute himself.

Dan had agreed to meet Wilty in the Tap Room at the Yale Club. Though he, too, was a member, it wouldn't have been his first choice; the fact that it was Wilty's struck him as out of character, but that only served to pique his interest.

The maître d' led them down the steps into the long, faux-medieval room, seating them at a small table set into a windowed niche. With its stone walls and glazed brick floor, the room was noisy, which, Dan assumed, was what Wilty had wanted; upstairs, there was another dining room, one that was far more elegant and subdued. After their lunch had been ordered, Wilty handed Dan a sealed envelope, along with a single sheet of paper: a Xerox of a section from E.W. Hale's will.

"I need you to read these paragraphs first."

"Okay."

Dan noted that Wilty hadn't ordered anything alcoholic. Also, his manner was focused and matter of fact, words not usually employed to describe this particular gentleman.

"Take your time."

Dan read the highlighted paragraphs several times.

E.W. established the Hale Trust in 1900 to govern his estate. Included in the trust was fifty-one percent of the *City Courier-Journal*'s common stock, making the trust, rather than a single individual, the controlling owner of the *Courier*. Family members were to receive monthly allowances from the trust as well as compensation for serving on the *Courier* board.

In the year 2000, the trust was to be terminated in two stages. In stage one, the interest was to be divided among E.W. Hale's living, legitimate issue, described as those of his bloodline born in wedlock or legally adopted. Five years later, or on the eldest heir's thirty-fifth birthday, whichever came first, the trust was to be completely terminated, the principal to be divided among those living issue who met previously described criteria, the eldest receiving the lion's share of the money as well as chairmanship of the board.

If there were no living issue, or if there were questions about the recipient's competence, the money was to be distributed evenly to a variety of cultural institutions and medical facilities. According to newspaper estimates, in the year 2000, the Hale Trust was worth nearly five hundred million dollars.

"According to this," Dan said with a slight whistle, "while you've always been a rich son of a bitch, you're about to become stratospherically wealthy."

"That's true, but I didn't invite you here to celebrate my enormous good fortune."

He drew a breath and held it, as if oxygen contained courage. Then, he handed Dan several sheets of paper, copies of stored originals. Dan only needed one reading for him to understand the source of Wilty's edginess.

"Where'd you get this?"

"That doesn't matter," Wilty said quickly.

Dan leaned in close. "Wilty, if I read this correctly, this implies that you and your antecedents might not be legitimate issue."

Wilty nodded glumly. "What happens if it's true?"

The answer was stunningly simple: he wasn't entitled to inherit E.W. Hale's fortune. Worse, whatever money he'd already received from the Trust would have to be refunded.

"Of course," Dan counseled, "there might be other documents out there that would refute this, provisions of a subsequent will that if implemented could short circuit the main inheritance clause, challenges to the trust over the years that weakened it in some way."

Dan said he'd investigate each and every possibility.

"But honestly, I don't believe this would hold up in court without proper corroboration."

"What kind of corroboration?"

Dan shrugged. "I don't know. An invalid marriage certificate. Falsified birth certificates."

Wilty looked quizzical. Dan explained.

"A wealthy man and his wife discover one of them is sterile. They buy a child, falsify the birth records and claim it as their own. Often, aristocrats bought the children of their servants."

Wilty panicked at the thought of some unknown family passing that kind of secret down through the generations. What if there was a "bill of sale" signed by E.W. Hale floating around somewhere; that would be even more devastating than the diary.

Again, he felt the beginnings of a migraine.

He asked Dan what would happen if something like a bill of sale for a child came to light, or if a diary penned by E.W. Hale surfaced that seemed to corroborate the claims in Charles's note.

"It depends. The burden of proof is on them. They'd

have to show that whatever they're presenting is accurate beyond a reasonable doubt before the line of descent could be invalidated."

The waiter came with their lunch. Wilty used the time to mull over what Dan had said. It was nothing he hadn't suspected. He'd simply needed his suppositions verified. He also wanted to know what his options were, if any.

"What if I destroy this note?" he asked after the waiter had gone.

Dan suddenly realized that the envelope Wilty had handed him at the beginning of this meeting contained a check; by paying for Dan's services, Wilty insured Dan's silence—attorney-client privilege and all that.

"It wouldn't solve anything, Wilty. If those other things you mentioned came out, there'd still be a scandal. On top of having to weather that, you might have to explain why you destroyed something as historically important as Charles Hale's suicide note." He shook his head. "It's a lose-lose situation."

Wilty nodded, but remained deep in thought.

"This letter is simply a record of the last words of a man who was not of sound mind," Dan reminded Wilty, trying to reassure his friend and client. "If you'd like, I know a couple of private investigators with a scholarly bent who might be able to help verify or debunk it."

"Thanks, but no. Poking around in Hale family business tends to be hazardous to one's health."

Dan held up the unopened envelope. "That may be, but since I'm officially on the case, at the very least, I'm obliged to give you my best advice. So here goes. Don't dive into shark-infested waters unprotected and alone."

Again, Wilty nodded, but his expression was mixed. Dan could see that curiosity was tangled with fear, and with good reason: The unknown was as intriguing as it was alarming.

"What if I'm not the official prince of Hales?"

Wilty stared at Dan, but his eyes were focused else-where. Dan couldn't tell whether it was at what Wilty thought might be coming up in his future. Or what he feared was about to come out of the past.

The music seemed louder than usual. Then again, Wilty was more sober than usual. Seeking to rectify that, he snaked his way through the throng and headed directly for the back end of the bar. By the time he got there, a very cold martini was waiting. He took a hefty swallow and licked his lips appreciatively. Of all the downtown havens he frequented, Onyx was his favorite. Gus, the bartender, was one of the reasons why.

"How're you doing tonight, Wilty?" Gus asked as he poured scotch on some rocks and handed it to a woman whose leather outfit was so tight it looked as if she'd been shrink-wrapped.

"Hangin' in."

"Can't ask for more than that."

Wilty laughed. "You can ask for anything, Gus. You just can't count on getting it."

"True enough."

Wilty liked the atmosphere at Onyx. It was dark without being morbid or, heaven forbid, chic. As the name implied, everything was black, from the highly glossed walls to the leather banquettes, to the granite bar, to the velvet curtains that hung in front of the privacy booths along the back wall. Even the umbrellas Gus put into the occasional Mai Tai were black. The crowd consisted mainly of downtown denizens who believed they needed a life-and-death reason to venture above Fourteenth Street.

The reason Wilty liked doing this scene was because in Alphabet City no one cared about pedigree. If people liked him, it wasn't because of who his relatives were. If he and a couple of guys went on a bender together, no one expected him to pick up the entire tab. If he shared a bed with a woman, it was about having sex, not about shagging some corporate prince. And if someone didn't like him, it wasn't because of his name, his contacts, or how much money he had. It was because they flat-out didn't like him. Wilty was fine with that. It was honest.

Occasionally, the curious did ask questions about his family and those who had projects that needed funding did approach him for help. Wilty answered the former and did what he could for the latter.

This night, however, he wasn't in the mood for questions, especially those which involved money.

"I thought I might find you here."

As if on cue, Dan Kalikow sauntered over and took possession of the bar stool next to Wilty. Since Dan was also a regular, Gus didn't have to ask what his pleasure might be. It was a glass of single malt scotch, two rocks and a twist.

"Thanks for lunch," he said after a long swig. "And for the check. It was extremely generous."

Wilty grinned. "Take advantage of it while you can!"

Dan laughed. He'd always enjoyed Wilty's wry sense of humor. "Yeah, okay," he said, "but you didn't have to buy my silence."

Wilty's mien turned serious. "I was insuring your safety. If this turns out to be accurate, it's going to piss off a lot of people. That check gives you cover."

Dan worried more about cover for Wilty. There was another side to this tarnished golden coin: the rightful heirs to this vast fortune had been denied the money, the prestige and the power that came from being a Hale. Talk about being pissed off!

Dan slid his barstool closer to Wilty's. "This afternoon, you hinted that you might want to get rid of that letter. Are you still considering that?"

"No. That's one of the reasons I wanted to speak to you. I needed someone with a level head to tell me I was right to just put it away for safekeeping." He laughed. "There are those who vehemently disagree with that decision."

Carolyne had called him at least three times a day every day since their lunch demanding that he get rid of Charles's last words.

"Resist whatever arguments they're putting forward," Dan counseled.

"I'm trying." Dan had no idea how insistent Carolyne Faessler Hale could be when she thought her income was threatened.

"My offer to help still stands."

"I appreciate that," Wilty said. "Right now, I'm gathering information, stuff that may or may not prove to be relevant. Down the line, if there's a question about authenticity or admissibility, you'll be sure to hear from me."

"Good," Dan said. "In the meantime, I'd like permission to look into the legalities. There have been dozens of changes to inheritance laws since that will was drafted. You could be agonizing over nothing."

Somehow, Wilty doubted that.

The two remained huddled until Dan finished his drink. When he checked his watch, he slapped a couple of bills on the bar and slid off the stool.

"You leaving so soon?" Wilty sounded distressed.

"Got to." Dan could see that Wilty was in need of his company, but Dan was in a new relationship, one he sensed might actually go somewhere. "I'm meeting someone for dinner. I'd ask you to join us, but . . ."

". . . two's company, three's a ménage." Wilty smiled, hoping he didn't sound as jealous as he felt. "Have fun."

"I'll call you next week," Dan said.

Wilty watched Dan race for the door and a wave of loneliness sluiced over him. Needing a moment of privacy, he lowered his head, shaded his eyes with his hands and stared down into his drink, conjuring the image of the woman he used to run to see. As her face floated in the clear liquid, Wilty grieved for what might have been. She was singularly beautiful and disarmingly bright, but more than that, she was the only woman who'd ever taken the time to get to know the man behind the name.

As he stirred his martini and began to feel sorry for himself, he could almost hear her chanting, "Stop crying and start trying!"

She used to recite that motivational mantra whenever he rued the golden prison he believed held him captive. She dismissed that as rubbish. Life was about choices and if he was stuck, it was because he chose to be stuck. All he needed to do to climb out of the rut he was in, was to take advantage of the vast opportunities available to him.

"Use who you are to be what you want to be," she used to say.

What he wanted to be was welcomed as the head of the Hale Board, yet the closer the day came when that title would be bestowed upon him, the more frightened he became of failing, of letting his great-great-grandfather down, of sullying the noble Hale name. So instead of readying himself for his ascension, he began his descent into dissolution. She tried to stop him, tried to reassure him about his ability to lead and the depth of his intellectual resources, but he allowed his insecurities and his fears to overwhelm his better instincts and her Herculean efforts. He became a drunk. She left him.

"Hey, Hale!"

A thin man with bloodshot eyes and a sweater flecked with crumbs from bar nuts, elbowed his way toward Wilty. A second man, this one shorter, thicker and sloppier, followed close behind.

"We have to talk!" Judging by the bullhorn tenor of his voice and his defiant, my-feet-are-planted-in-concrete stance, the man had an agenda that required an audience. "Now!"

As intended, several heads turned in their direction.

"Do you have an appointment?" Wilty asked with patrician cool.

Those at the bar buried their faces behind drinks or napkins and tittered. The guys in the cheap seats laughed out loud.

"Fuck you!"

"Well, then, step into my office."

The man actually moved a step closer. His muscle remained where he was.

"You were supposed to get back to me three weeks ago. I'm still waiting."

Wilty finished his drink. Gus brought him another. As he put it down, his eyes asked if Wilty needed help. He didn't.

"I'm terribly sorry," he said. "If you would be so kind as to refresh my memory. What was I supposed to get back to you about?"

Gus turned away and chuckled.

The man's complexion alternated between livid pink and stunned white. His eyes narrowed and darted about in the hopes of dismissing the very spectators he'd been so eager to assemble. As with all good theater audiences, however, no one was leaving until the denouement.

"You were going to invest in . . . well, something I told you about."

"Which was?"

"I'd rather not go into the details now . . . here."

"I thought that's exactly what you wanted," Wilty said, his lips tight and even. "Otherwise, why would you have stormed over here, with a bodyguard in tow, and invaded my space?"

The man's jaw was so tightly clenched, it looked as if his teeth were pushing through his skin.

"If you simply wanted to chat, I'm not in the mood." Wilty picked up his drink. "Now, if you don't mind . . ."

The two men slinked away. When he was certain they'd left the club, he fluffed off the obvious shakedown and, because he hated being the center of attention, grandiosely bought a round of drinks for his fans.

Inside, however, the incident unsettled him. He only vaguely remembered this man; he recalled even less about whatever project he was supposed to be looking into. And while he'd managed to convince everyone that the man's claim was bogus, something in his manner rang true. He and Wilty probably did have a discussion that resulted in Wilty magnanimously offering to help out. Whether he meant it or not was another story; he was always generous

when he was drunk. Either way, Wilty was at a loss and
that scared him. This kind of thing was happening a lot
lately. Forgetting names and faces. Losing small stretches
of time. Suddenly, the number of brain cells wiped out by
a single martini became important.

"Hey!"

Wilty turned toward the familiar voice and smiled at
Savannah Larkin, another Park Avenue émigré. After his
breakup, he and Vanna had gone out a couple of times, but
she was too much of a wild child, even for Wilty.

"What're you doing here?" he asked. "I thought you
swore off this scene." She'd been arrested in a drug sweep
at one of the nearby clubs; her father bailed her out, calling
in every chit he was owed to keep her name out of the
papers.

"Daddy did threaten to cut off my allowance if I didn't
change my lifestyle, but really! I can take just so much
uptight, uptown bullshit before I feel the need to kick
back."

"Just don't kick too high," Wilty admonished as he
watched her slide behind the velvet curtains into one of the
private booths.

A young man wearing a black tee shirt and skin-tight
jeans meant to show off his incredibly buffed body slid in
behind her. Wilty exchanged worried glances with Gus, but
there was nothing either of them could, or would, do. She
was a grown woman. Her companion was above the age of
consent. And those booths were private.

Two drinks later, Wilty thought he heard scuffling. He
had to listen hard. It was late, his head was fuzzy, and the
noise level had risen to near deafening. Again, he heard
what sounded like a struggle, accompanied by a muffled
groan.

In an instant, he was off the barstool. Though a bit un-
steady, he pushed aside the heavy curtain, assessed the situation and attempted to pull the bodybuilder off his
intended prey. Gus and Onyx's bouncer, both of whom
could have been poster boys for the World Wrestling Fed-

eration, helped Wilty extract the mauler from the booth, then showed him the door.

Wilty moved into the booth and closed the curtain behind him.

"What happened?"

Vanna's makeup was smeared, her blouse was ripped and her nose was bleeding.

"He got a little carried away," she said, as she tried to fasten her bra.

Wilty wiped her nose with his handkerchief.

"Let's clean you up and then I'll take you home. Okay?"

Her eyes filled with tears. Wilty took her in his arms and let her cry. He knew how she felt. He was no stranger to self-inflicted public humiliation.

When Gus appeared with two cups of coffee, Wilty went to make room on the table. As he pushed Vanna's belongings aside, he noticed a couple of pills lying next to a small pile of white dust.

"What're these?" he asked Gus, as he stirred Vanna's coffee to cool it.

"Don't know. Don't wanna know." Gus shrugged and nodded toward the semiconscious woman in the booth. "She's been into some heavy shit lately."

"Call for a car, will you?"

Gus went back to the bar. Wilty pocketed the pills and raised the cup to Vanna's lips. She slurped a little, then pulled back and pressed her hand against her cheek. The inside of her mouth was cut.

"I can't," she whimpered. She was barely conscious.

He gulped his coffee and waited for his head to clear. When he was able, he gently extracted her from the booth and steered them through the bar to the door.

The minute they hit the air, Vanna staggered toward the curb and vomited.

Wilty was rocked by the sight of this elegant young woman on her hands and knees, heaving her guts into the street. It was positively Dickensian. In a moment of terrifying clarity, he knew he was staring at what his future could be if he didn't get off the debauched road he was traveling.

Looking at Vanna, thinking about how he'd screwed things up, he, too, felt sick to his stomach.

Maybe if he turned himself around, she'd take him back.

His head began to throb, pulsing with spasms of regret and recrimination.

When Vanna had completely voided her stomach, he cleaned her up and poured her into the waiting car. The door closed and Vanna passed out, for which Wilty was grateful. He had nothing to say to her and he wasn't interested in anything she had to say to him.

After he finished taking care of his charge, he walked back to his apartment, all the while trying to figure out how to take care of himself. Tonight had rattled him. Vanna's drunken degradation had served as an epiphany.

He had to get his life back on course. He wasn't sure he could do it, nor was he certain what direction his life was going to take. The only thing he did know was that the first step to recovery was to swallow his pride. The second, was to ask for help.

4

The blinding white light fades. A second man storms in through a large doorway. He moves quickly, purposefully, his footsteps riling the dust with each thud of his boot.

The new arrival looks slightly older than the first. He positions himself in front of the woman, clearly protective. He makes a declaration of some sort. The gray stranger with the fancy clothes snorts. He takes a step forward. The other man shoves him away. They glower at each other and yell some more. They square off and take each other's measure. The woman tries to arbitrate, but they're deaf to her entreaties.

The woman moves to separate them, but fails. They're stronger than she is. And angrier. The two men start flailing at each other. They hurl nasty words and vicious accusations. They seem fueled by a fury that frightens me.

The gray stranger looks in my direction. His eyes narrow with irritation and hostile curiosity. He makes a move toward me, but as he does, the other man's fist lands squarely on his ear. He continues to glare at me, but he's stunned by the blow. Both the woman and the other man shout at me, demanding that I leave. I don't want to, but I obey.

The fighting resumes. The two men tumble to the floor, rolling over and over on the ground as they beat each other's faces. The woman jumps on the back of the stranger, pounding at him. He rallies all his strength and *throws her off him. She falls up against a partition. Something hard hits the ground. As the stranger defends himself, he gropes around until his fingers find something solid. Feinting and parrying until he senses an opening, he swings a two-by-four over his shoulder and smashes it into the head of his opponent.*

That man's body goes limp. His head lolls to the side. Blood stains his brown hair and his pale flesh.

I start to run, but I'm stopped by a monstrous burst of orange thunder! It's like I opened the door to a furnace. My skin is blistering. My eyes sting and tear. I can't see. I can't raise my hands. I'm having trouble breathing.

I need to get help, but I'm trapped.

Finally, the orange is fading. I can see again.

The fire's devoured nearly everything. All that's left is a heap of smoking cinders.

The stranger's gone. The man whose head was so badly crushed lies in a new spot, just outside the smoldering ruins. The woman's lying near him. A scarf that wasn't part of her ensemble before is tightly wound around her neck. Her eyes are open and bulging. Her body is still.

Callie quaked in the darkness. Her eyelids snapped open. Anxious, slightly bewildered, she searched the room, scanning the fading black of night for malevolent shadows, grateful to see only familiar forms. Her hair felt damp and sticky and her head throbbed as if every vein was about to burst. On her cheeks, she felt the wetness of tears freshly shed. Clammy from fear, she tucked her blankets up under her neck, clutching them close in an attempt to quell the shivering.

A pained, pitiful sob burst from her mouth, replacing the fraught stillness of the room. The gray people were back— with a vengeance. She should have known. Their punishing visits were never one-night stands. They came in waves, torturing her night after night until she was completely whipped. Then, they'd disappear, staying away just long enough for her to believe she was free of them.

What depressed her most was that it was always the same. Same dream, same response, same sense of defeat. Nothing varied. Nothing changed. Each time she was bedeviled by these unwelcome visitors, she awakened feeling like a failure. It was as if she were supposed to extract from these visions some significant truth, some kernel of knowledge powerful enough to change the world. Whether it was the world at large, or her own little universe, she didn't know, but it didn't matter, because it was always the same.

Callie sighed. One of these days she was either going to stop caring about what happened to those three people in the grayness or she was going to purge herself of these nocturnal torments.

Unfortunately, this was not that day. Callie still worried about that man with the side of his head smashed in and that woman who had fought so valiantly. She still wondered about the third player in the drama, why he'd come to that place, what he'd said and why he'd committed those despicable acts. She wiped a tear from her eye. She also worried about herself.

This wasn't normal. Yes, people had recurring dreams. She'd scoured enough psychology books on the subject to know that. Yes, there were common dreams: incidents and objects that appeared in the same form in different people's dreams, like falling or being chased, or snakes and clouds. But rarely did the *exact* incidents and the *exact* objects appear in the same person's dream again and again and again for over twenty years.

Callie glanced at the clock radio on the nightstand next to her bed. The green digital numbers told her it was a little past five in the morning. She groaned and cursed the thieving spirit that continually hijacked her sleep. It felt way too early to start her day, but she was too worked up to ever get back to sleep. Annoyed, she grabbed two Tylenol from a bottle she kept by her bed for occasions such as this, gulped them down and prayed for relief to be swift.

Minutes later, stymied and restless, Callie rousted herself out of bed, went to the kitchen, where she put up a pot of coffee, and headed for the shower. If she couldn't sleep and she couldn't make sense of this crazy dream, she might as well do something productive and finish polishing the first installment of her series on pill mills, which was due on her editor's desk that morning.

With her hair turbaned in a terry cloth towel, she brought a steaming mug of coffee into the bathroom, placed it on the vanity and got her hair blower out of the cabinet below the sink. After squeezing the water from her hair, she put the towel on the bar behind her and turned on the blower. She was nearly finished when the towel fell onto the floor. Without stopping what she was doing, she turned around, bent down, replaced the towel on its bar and turned around again. As she raised the blower to dry the top of her hair, she looked in the mirror. The cord from the hair blower was wrapped around her neck like a noose.

Like a holograph, the image of the gray woman lying on the ground strangled with a silken scarf superimposed itself over Callie's reflection. The visual stunned her. With her heart thumping wildly in her chest, she shut off the blower, uncoiled the cord with shaking hands and put the appliance down. Trembling, she grasped the edges of the sink, gripping the porcelain with a wretched distress that paled her skin to an appalling white. Her eyes filled with hot, frightened tears, blurring the double-exposure in the mirror. She tried to escape the taunting portrait by shutting her eyes, but her eyelids refused to close. She pleaded with the spectral artist to erase what he had drawn. But the picture refused to fade.

The insistent *brrrrring* of the telephone jolted Callie back to the present. She ran into her bedroom and grabbed the phone, suddenly panicked. At six o'clock in the morning, whoever was calling wasn't the bearer of good news.

"Callie? It's Luke." Luke Crocker was the editor on the metropolitan desk at the *Courier*. "A guy took a flyer near where you live. I need you to cover it for us."

Callie started at the *Courier* as a beat reporter on general assignment, the lowest rung on the journalistic ladder. Diligence and talent had boosted her up to being one of the paper's investigative reporters. She didn't do on-scene coverage anymore, but if Luke was asking, he needed her.

"I can be out the door in fifteen minutes," she said.

"Make it ten."

"Okay." She grabbed a pad and a pen to write down the particulars. "Just tell me where to go."

"Right around the corner."

Callie's apartment was on Eighty-fourth between Park and Lexington Avenues. As she turned onto Park, she saw that a group of people were already gathered outside a building between Eighty-fourth and Eighty-fifth. A police car, an ambulance and several TV vans had clogged the space in front of the elegant co-op and forced the uptown traffic into a single lane, prompting a barrage of indignant horn blowing and creative name calling.

She raced up the block and elbowed her way into the pack. Mike O'Connell, a reporter from a daily tabloid known more for its headlines and its gossip column than its journalistic prowess, was in his usual spot—right in the thick of things.

"What's up?" she asked.

She had to crane her neck to see what was happening. The body had been discovered in the narrow alleyway that separated the two buildings on the block. The high wrought-iron gate that separated the alley from the street was being guarded by police.

"Jumper. Nineteen stories." Mike was nothing if not concise.

"Move aside!"

A man and a woman in blue coveralls and baseball caps that identified them as detectives from the NYPD Crime Scene Unit made their way through the crowd and into the alley. Callie knew from her days on the beat that suicides were treated as homicides until proven otherwise. Immediately, the area was cordoned off with yellow tape; another set of uniforms was upstairs doing the same in the victim's apartment.

While the CSU duo examined the victim and documented the scene of his demise, two detectives conducted a preliminary canvass. Callie began her own canvass, interviewing anyone willing to talk to her. At the same time, she eavesdropped as the detective nearest her, an intense Hispanic man named Alvarez, questioned several of the building's residents. Their curiosity had been aroused by the ruckus and they'd come downstairs in their robes and slippers. He was trying to ascertain whether anyone actually witnessed this tragedy. No one saw or heard anything.

Alvarez's partner finished up with the building superintendent and was headed toward the alley when O'Connell stopped him.

"Any ID on the vic?"

The detective turned toward Mike and Callie. His eyes scanned them quickly, but so thoroughly Callie felt as if she'd just been through a radar screen.

"According to the super, the deceased is Wilton Hale."

Callie gasped. Both men looked at her. She was obviously stunned.

"Are you all right?" the detective said.

Mike's upper lip lifted into an expression that fell midway between a smirk and a sneer. "She works for the *Courier,* which is owned by the Hale family. In a sense, that guy was her boss," he said, nodding in the direction of the corpse.

And my lover, Callie thought.

Callie and Wilty's meeting was as trite as it gets: they met at the *Courier* Christmas party, two years before. She was standing at the buffet, debating about whether there could ever be such a thing as too many shrimp, when he sauntered over and struck up a conversation with her. They flirted for a while, then he left. She assumed that was that; Wilty had a reputation as a ladies' man. But the next day, he called and invited her to have dinner with him at Le Cirque.

Callie was as nervous as a six-year-old at a ballet recital, and just as clumsy. She tripped walking up the stairs leading into the restaurant, almost fell over a chair on her way into the smaller, red dining room and when she slid onto the banquette, she caught the edge of the tablecloth and dragged it with her, dislodging pieces of the place settings. It took an alert, swift-handed waiter to prevent glasses and dishes from crashing into each other and creating a disaster.

She smiled now, remembering that when the waiter went to pour red wine into her glass, she hesitated. Wilty quickly tucked a napkin into his collar, spread it across his chest for protection, and instructed the waiter to pour away. She fell in love with him then and there.

Their romance advanced quickly because according to Wilty, "he was an instant gratification guy and she gratified him instantly."

Callie couldn't believe how lucky she was. Aside from being great-looking, bright and more involved in the world around him than people gave him credit for being, Wilty was fun. He had a quick wit and an easy laugh and was up for just about anything.

What was wonderful was that they seemed to energize each other. He wined and dined her in the expensive, three- and four-star restaurants that made up his culinary universe. She introduced him to the other New York, the one with hundreds of fabulous places to eat that didn't require frou-frou clothes, major jewelry and a trust fund. He went with her to lectures at the 92nd Street Y, most of them political roundtables or speeches by famous journalists. She went with him to Yankee games, U.S. Open tennis tournaments, Knick games, and, once or twice, Ranger hockey. In each venue, they sat in the Hale luxury box and dined on catered food, yet Wilty behaved like a bleacher creature. He stood and cheered every home run or three-pointer scored. He could have owned the team, but he was the ultimate fan and Callie found that endearing.

She also found him incredibly exciting. He was a man who loved his sports as much as he adored the cultural arts, was as addicted to the theater as he was to fine wine and was as passionate about loving her as he was about loving life.

He claimed she was Valium in a size four dress. "You have the power to keep me calm," he used to say. And she did, up until the previous summer.

Once June first passed and he was officially into the year of his inheritance, he began to change. He drank more and slept less. The fuse on his temper became shorter, the intervals between him being relaxed and easy to be with and those times when he was snappish and difficult to be around, became longer. Instead of running on the beach or playing four hours of tennis, he'd lock himself in a room and submerge himself in material he thought would round out his breadth of knowledge about all things financial. When he emerged, he'd be depressed, convinced he'd waited too long to educate himself in the finer points of managing an empire and was destined to fail.

Callie tried to be supportive. She pointed out numerous things he'd already accomplished, assuring him that those victories were harbingers of greatness to come. She dismissed the condescension of Hale board members as old fogyism and entrenched arrogance and reminded him that he wouldn't be running Hale Holdings alone. There were advisors aplenty and surely, no one expected him to do anything earth-shattering within the first month of his reign.

Unfortunately, Wilty's fears were a lot stronger than her love.

By August of that year, Callie had had enough. They rarely slept together; as Shakespeare once pointed out, alcohol increased the desire, but lessened the performance. They were fighting more often about less important things. Callie found his precipitous dissipation upsetting and his mood swings way too chaotic. To her, he seemed on the verge of something similar to madness.

Reluctantly, she told him she didn't think they should see each other until he stopped drinking and got his act together. He told her she could either accept him as he was, or she could get out. They hadn't spoken since.

"Can you tell me when this happened?" she said to the detective, snapping out of her mournful reverie and trying to regain her professional footing.

"Sometime between three and five this morning when his body was discovered by the janitor. Of course, that can't be confirmed until the autopsy's complete."

It unnerved Callie to think that just as she was being dragged from the peace of sleep by her ghosts, Wilty leaped to his death.

Why would he do something like this?

"Did you know Mr. Hale, Ms. . . ."

Too consumed by her thoughts to speak, Callie showed him her press badge.

". . . Jamieson."

He waited for her to respond. When she didn't, he repeated his question.

O'Connell hovered so close she could feel his breath on her face. Since he worked for one of the city's largest tabloids, O'Connell must have known all about her affair with Wilty. Yet he'd kept his mouth shut. Callie found that uncommonly decent. "Yes, I did," she said, finally.

"How well?"

Thankfully, the van from the Medical Examiner's office arrived, sparing her. Two men in navy blue jackets with bright yellow lettering reached into the back bay. They removed a gurney and a body bag. Both detectives left their respective interviews for a brief confab with the ME team, while the policeman guarding the gate opened it just long enough for them to enter the alley.

O'Connell, eager to have a visual advantage, squeezed past Callie to the front of the crowd. Callie also managed to wriggle close enough to the gate to watch two of the men unzip the body bag and lay it out alongside the victim. When one moved aside, she caught sight of a head of bloodied blond hair, a swatch of shiny fabric and an oddly positioned body crumpled on top of a pile of garbage.

Callie visibly recoiled when she glimpsed Wilty's mangled body. She choked back a sob, but a flood of tears could not be stemmed. As the man she once wanted to marry was put into a navy blue bag, she cried openly, so riveted by the sound of the zipper closing, she didn't notice the detective watching her.

Another TV crew arrived and set up camp. The cameraman focused his lens on the ME crew as they lifted Wilty's remains onto the gurney. All around, people were buzzing like flies on carrion.

Callie wiped her eyes and swallowed her grief. She had a job to do. Valiantly, she continued her interviews, trying hard to tune in to what they were saying, to her, and each other.

It upset her that no one seemed shocked by the news that Wilty appeared to have killed himself. His neighbors viewed him as an eccentric with a knack for getting into well-publicized scrapes. Several eagerly pointed out his reputation for recklessness, citing helicopter skiing, cliff diving and mountain climbing as proof of his willingness to take big risks in search of big thrills.

Callie had always found his sense of adventure exhilarating. If not for him, she never would have gone hot-air ballooning or white-water rafting.

One man described Wilty as pathologically indulgent. He was particularly appalled by the fact that Wilty's obsession with golf had prompted him to create a makeshift driving range in his apartment.

Callie remembered him being passionate about the game, but she had to admit, laying down AstroTurf and attaching mattresses to the walls to absorb a fusillade of golf balls made him sound positively bizarre.

She asked when Wilty had moved into the building. When they were together, he lived in a six-room penthouse on Sutton Place which she thought was fabulous; he told her he'd bought a place on Park Avenue, but it was under construction and he didn't want her to see it until it was finished. He promised it would wow her. According to his neighbors, he'd been living there for nearly seven months.

Several residents called him a drunk. Callie hated hearing that, but the ME guys did tell the detectives the deceased reeked of alcohol.

When asked about his everyday demeanor, some said his most common facial expression was brooding. Others claimed they only knew him as manic.

Callie knew him to be both. As well as funny, kind, and very loving. It upset her that no one seemed to have anything positive to say about Wilty.

Had he changed that much?

A man standing behind her tsked. "How old was he?" he said, not directing his question to anyone in particular, yet fully expecting an answer.

The superintendent provided it. "Mid-thirties, I think."

Callie's stomach lurched. Wilty used to say he'd never have to worry about old age: other than E.W. Hale, no Hale male had ever reached his forty-first birthday.

"Ms. Jamieson." It was that detective again. "If you don't mind, I'd like to continue our discussion about Mr. Hale."

Callie shoved her notebook into her backpack and made a show of being very busy. "I'm sorry, Detective, but I have a deadline. I'm sure you understand."

She started to leave. He caught her by the arm.

"You know what, Ms. Jamieson, we've all got jobs to do. Mine concerns the guy whose body was carted away in that van, so I believe it takes precedence."

Callie shifted her weight uncomfortably. There was no arguing that point.

"You said you knew the deceased. I noticed you seemed uncomfortable in front of your colleague, so I backed off, but he's gone now. Let's talk."

"I don't see what I could possibly contribute to your investigation, Detective. I did know Mr. Hale, but I haven't seen or heard from him in months."

He wasn't swayed. Instead, he handed her a card: EZRA

CHAPIN, NYPD DETECTIVE, FIRST GRADE, 19TH PRECINCT. "I'll tell you what. I'll let you go do your thing on the condition that you come by the station."

She started to offer another excuse, but he cut her off. "Today."

Indignant, Callie slid his card into her pocket, turned and walked away.

"If you don't come to me," he called after her, "I'll come to you."

The *City Courier-Journal*'s offices were in the Hale Building on Fifty-second Street and Sixth Avenue. The newspaper, the only New York daily that truly rivaled the *New York Times*, occupied twenty floors of an architecturally splendid glass and steel tower. The remaining floors were divided between the corporate headquarters of Hale Holdings, bureau offices for the other newspapers in the *Courier-Tribune* chain, Hale Books, one of the better publishing houses in the city, and Hale Paper, the seed for the Hale empire. The top floor was reserved for WHAL, an FM radio station devoted to classical music.

Callie's office was on the twelfth floor. She wasn't important enough to have a corner office, but thanks to a promotion three years before, she had shimmied high enough on the success ladder to merit moving out of the bullpen and into a closet with a window.

It was barely eight o'clock when Callie clocked in. Fortunately, Amy, an assistant Callie shared with two other writers, was already there. She greeted Callie with fresh coffee and the morning edition of the *Courier*; it was considered politically incorrect to read the *Times* on the job, although everyone did. They had to keep abreast of what the competition was up to, after all.

"Did you hear the news?" Amy asked, closing the door behind her.

Callie extracted her notebook from her backpack, eased into her chair and booted up her computer, her mind already forming a lead.

"International? National? Corporate? Or personal?" she said, distracted.

"Wilty Hale committed suicide. He jumped out a window." Amy scrunched her face in horror at the thought of it. "Ugh! Can you imagine?"

"I don't have to imagine. I saw it. Crocker called me at six and assigned me to the story," Callie explained.

Amy fell into the chair on the other side of Callie's desk, her mouth agape. Thankfully, Amy had only been at the *Courier* for five months, so if she knew about Callie's relationship with Wilty it was from whispered gossip and not open for discussion.

"Was it awful?"

Callie recalled the image of Wilty sprawled on top of a pile of garbage, his body twisted into a position that would have been impossible if all his bones hadn't been broken.

"It wasn't pretty," she said.

"They mentioned his name on the news," Amy reported. "That means the Widow must have been notified."

Both women groaned. Carolyne Hale, known as the Widow Hale to fans and detractors alike, was a woman who seemed to compel people to take sides. There were those— mostly society matrons—who found nobility in her enduring widowhood and her unwavering insistence that she would always be married to Huntington Hale. After all, she would say, she knew how important it was to her beloved Hunt that their son, Wilty, be raised as a Hale. To her, that meant mother and son had to bear the same name.

Another, more cynical, school of thought decried all of that as pure bunk. This faction assumed the Widow had lovers hidden in every closet, but hadn't remarried because her income was tied to a clause in her late husband's will that said if she gave up the name, she forfeited the money. Also, they found it difficult to award her the *Good Housekeeping* Seal of Approval for motherhood. Carolyne Hale had always been very much the merry widow, partying constantly and traveling often. She was absent for such long periods of time, many wondered if she could even pick Wilty out of a crowd.

Since Wilty was not among Carolyne Hale's admirers, Callie had never met the much-talked-about Widow. He always said being around his mother was like getting a flu shot: you only did it when necessary, because it was never a pleasant experience.

"I'm not a member of the Widow's fan club," Amy said, "but Wilty was her only child. And he committed suicide. You've got to feel for her. It must be awful to have to wonder whether you could have done anything to prevent it or, worse, if in some way you were partly to blame."

Callie's face paled and her eyes dimmed. "It is awful," she said quietly.

Amy suddenly felt as if she was intruding on a private moment and she didn't know why.

"Did you eat anything before you left your apartment?" Amy asked, hoping Callie's lack of color was due to a lack of nutrition.

Callie shook her head. "No time."

"How about if I call downstairs for herbal tea, a couple of slices of seven grain bread and a container of all-fruit jelly?"

"Better yet," Callie said, needing a heavy dose of comfort food, "how about a gooey cherry Danish and a frappachino from the coffee shop around the corner?"

"All that sugar isn't healthy, you know."

Callie appraised her thin body, then looked at Amy. "You're always telling me I should put on a few pounds. Let's start now."

"It's not about weight," Amy protested, knowing she sounded like an ad for the latest diet tome. "It's about insulin and glycogen and metabolism and . . ."

Callie raised her arms in a gesture of surrender. "Okay, okay. Call Alfalfa's and order me something healthy. While you're at it, would you get me whatever bio there is on Wilty Hale? I need background."

Callie hoped his file could tell her what he'd been up to since their breakup.

"I'm on it."

"Thanks." Callie motioned for Amy to close the door on her way out.

It felt strange to be writing a piece about the death of someone she knew so intimately, but Callie soldiered through it, relying on her reportorial skills to relate the facts while at the same time struggling to keep her emotions at bay. When she read her first draft, she was disgusted. The column was perfunctory, nothing more than a simple recitation of who, what, where, and when. As for the why, she didn't have a clue.

A rush of grief sluiced over her, washing her in a thundering wave of sadness. Wilty had been out of her life for months. She didn't love him anymore, at least not the way she had, yet in some corner of her heart, she supposed she kept hoping he would shape up and come back. Knowing that now that was impossible, she put her head down on her desk and wept.

When Amy returned with breakfast and the material Callie had requested, she also had a message.

"Brad Herring has requested your presence in his office."

"Really." Brad Herring was the executive editor of the *Courier.* "Did he say why?"

"Nope." Amy shook her head as she poured the frappachino from a paper cup into Callie's Big Apple mug. "But there was no detectable growl in his voice, so I presume you can leave the suit of armor here."

"Good to know. Did he say what time?"

"Ten-thirty."

"Give me a ten minute heads-up?"

Sometimes Callie got so involved in her work, she forgot to check the time.

"Will do."

Amy left and Callie opened the file marked *Wilty Hale.*

It depressed Callie to think that a person's life could be reduced to a thin, colorless folder.

On the first page, she found a brief summation of his life: Wilton Colfax Hale was thirty-four years old, the only child of Huntington Albert Hale and Carolyne Faessler Hale. Born in Memphis, Tennessee, he had prepped at Exeter, graduated from Yale and was the sole heir to the Hale newspaper fortune.

She knew all that.

Amy had fleshed out that skeletal report with a compilation of interviews conducted over the years with neighbors and friends. The older pieces painted a portrait of a bright, creative, well-meaning fellow doomed by his enormous wealth and social prominence to life as "the son of" and "the heir to," with little chance of establishing his own resumé. He was also portrayed as a man of enormous generosity. He contributed to charities, volunteered at a soup kitchen, and every now and then, when he found someone who inspired him, served as a benefactor to young actors and artists.

She knew that, too.

The more recent commentaries were all negative, beginning with a string of drunk and disorderly complaints to the police department. Then, there were interviews with obvious detractors who listed Wilty's main talent as partying to the extreme. They claimed he was loud and improper and threw bacchanals that were more appropriate to a downtown loft than his fancy spread on Park Avenue.

That was the Wilty Hale his neighbors seemed to know. The Wilty she hadn't wanted to be with.

She'd hoped to find more, particularly gossipy pieces that might have provided names of recently acquired friends—he'd stopped seeing most of those she'd met during their courtship—and in particular, whether he'd had a special lady in his life. But there was nothing. Apparently, even the yenta press had given up on him. Then again, there weren't any pieces about her romance with Wilty; he'd made a deal with the gossip columnists that in exchange for exclusives on really important news about him, they would leave his private life private.

She opened her notebook again and went over the interviews she'd conducted that morning at the scene. While most people were honest enough to admit they weren't intimately acquainted with the newly departed, there appeared to be a recurring theme: while Wilty's early death was tragic, it was inevitable. There was his dissolute lifestyle. And there was history: many believed the family was cursed.

Callie knew that history and it did demand some acknowledgment. Not only had no male Hale other than the founder of the dynasty lived past forty-one, but aside from two who died in infancy, none of E.W. Hale's male progeny died of natural causes. There had been a shooting and a fall off a cliff in Martha's Vineyard. Wilty's uncle, Cole Hale, electrocuted himself while rewiring the stable that housed his thoroughbreds. His father, Huntington Hale, died piloting his high-speed motorboat around Lake George; he fell into the water and had his head sliced off by the motor's propeller. Both of those deaths were listed as accidental, but were considered highly suspicious. With the addition of Wilty's leap, there were three suicides.

A chill wrapped around Callie's shoulders like a shawl. She closed her notebook and gripped her mug, eager to feel its warmth.

Was there a curse hanging over the Hale family? Was Wilty a victim of his heritage?

It was a thought that terrified Callie. She shook her head, physically rejecting the notion that one's fate was sealed at birth. She refused to believe that a person didn't have control over her life, that she couldn't make informed choices and direct her path accordingly, that nature was more powerful than will.

Amy buzzed. "This is your wake-up call," she said, reminding Callie about her meeting with Brad Herring.

Callie thanked her, opened a drawer, took out a small mirror and checked her appearance.

Her hair was the pale yellow of Caribbean sand, straight and cut in a silky, freewheeling bob. Today, she wore it parted in the middle and tucked behind her ears, simple and neat. She never wore a great deal of makeup and this morning was no exception, just a light touch of liner and mascara and a pale pink gloss on her lips. Her skin was creamy, her cheeks high and round. Her nose was small and narrow, speckled with a profusion of freckles she didn't attempt to conceal.

She was thin, Amy was right about that, but it wasn't the result of dieting and it wasn't something Callie thought others should envy. She viewed herself as skinny, hardly an ideal. True, she rarely had to worry about squeezing into a skirt or a pair of pants or covering up an undisciplined bulge, but she did have to guard against the potato sack effect and the poor-thing-hasn't-eaten-in-months look. When she did go to the gym, she understood the stares and barbs tossed at her by women battling to sweat off a couple of pounds. But she wondered if they understood her desire to add muscle and tone to a body she feared would otherwise look like a stick. Or that she'd been studying martial arts since she was a kid—and was now a brown belt in karate— because she feared being a weakling. Probably not.

As she replaced the mirror, her hand sought the small, silver-framed photograph she kept tucked away in the drawer. Lifting it so she could see it clearly, her lower lip wobbled as she gazed upon a woman who looked almost exactly like her. Same round apple cheeks, same big, turquoise blue eyes, same straight, slightly upturned nose. As always, Callie touched a finger to her lips, then to the photograph and returned the picture frame to its place with the reverence she felt her mother deserved.

It had been twenty-two years and Callie ached for her mother as deeply now as she had when she was eight and her mother left their home. Another twenty-two years could pass and Callie was certain nothing would change. She would still have a hole in her heart and she would still find it impossible to reconcile the notion that her bright, curious, cultivated, fun-loving, perpetually gentle mother was insane.

Callie exited on the twenty-fifth floor and told the receptionist she was there to see Brad Herring. As she waited to be buzzed inside, she indulged in the elegant silence that characterized the executive floor. Elsewhere, noise was part and parcel of the environment: computers, faxes, telephones, footsteps echoing off uncarpeted floors, voices raised to carry over partition walls. Status, such as it was, was marked by a small office walled by glass panels that looked out into the bullpen, a door and maybe a window. Sometimes, there was room for a plant.

Here, the front desk was a half moon of polished teakwood. The walls were upholstered in thick, gray flannel material. Museum-quality black-and-white photographs of various New York City landmarks hung behind the desk and above facing black leather couches. Charcoal-colored carpeting absorbed traffic noise. Authentic Tiffany table lamps provided color. And the receptionist's voice never rose above a whisper.

As she did whenever she visited the famous twenty-fifth floor, Callie felt proud and slightly awed. Proud to be part of a quality publication like the *Courier,* awed by the power and influence that dwelt behind the hand-carved wooden doors. That vaunted assembly of personnel could not only change public opinion but, sometimes, the course of history. They affected the outcome of elections with their endorsements of particular candidates. They influenced public policy via their critiques on the way the economy was being managed and the way the government was conducting the business of state. They didn't shy away from expressing outrage or demanding sympathy. They weren't cowed by world leaders nor mass demonstrations. They viewed the situation, arrived at a conclusion and, then, put it out there for all to see and comment upon.

But their success came not from their collective intelligence and talent, which was prodigious, but rather from the way the managing editors adhered so strictly to the philosophy of their founder, E.W. Hale: The task of a good newspaper was to inform. To do that, it had to assure the public that while they might not read every word printed, every word they read was the truth.

A loud click signaled that the security lock had deactivated. Callie pushed open the door and strode down the thickly carpeted hall to Brad's office; someday, she'd like to make this walk without a nervous flutter in her stomach. At least this morning, the reason she'd been summoned to the executive editor's office appeared obvious. Judging by the high pitched buzz around the newsroom, the demise of Wilty Hale was definitely the topic du jour.

Brad Herring, a tall, reedy man in an impeccably tailored suit, rose to greet her. He had an engaging smile and bright blue eyes, both of which he used to his advantage. He always struck Callie as someone who'd taken a course on how to be elegant; his aspect and demeanor were that studied. Still, Callie liked and respected him.

"Welcome," he said, as he shook her hand and escorted her inside.

Luke Crocker from the metropolitan desk and Harold Josephs, the deputy managing editor, were also in attendance. Callie said her hellos and took a seat. Mercifully, Brad didn't insist on a lot of small talk. He came right to the point.

"We called you up here, Callie, because we'd like to run a feature-length piece on Wilty Hale. We felt your talent as an investigative reporter, and your ability to write longer articles, more than qualified you for this assignment."

Callie hadn't expected this. Often, it was difficult to know if the higher-ups even knew who you were, let alone what kind of job you were capable of doing, so she was flattered by their faith in her. She was also nervous and conflicted. This was a major assignment, one which could boost her reputation and catapult her into prominence within the journalistic community. But it was about Wilty.

"We're thinking of running it in *Courier Weekend*, or

possibly in *EVENTS*," the Hale weekly news magazine, "as a series."

Callie's head raced with ideas about how to present Wilty to the world without crucifying him or compromising her professional integrity by covering for him.

"Wilty was the last of the Hales," Harold Josephs, the *éminence grise* of the *Courier,* said in a quiet, respectful way. "If for no other reason, the end of such a prominent American dynasty demands more than a news column and an obituary."

"Speaking of columns, I read yours before coming up here," Luke told Callie. "I especially liked your inclusion of bystander commentary. It painted Wilty with some much-needed humanity."

Callie smiled her thanks. She considered praise from Luke an accomplishment.

"It's sad to say, but most common folk aren't exactly sympathetic toward people like the Hales."

"It's not just common folk who lack sympathy," Callie said, an idea beginning to percolate. "A couple of his so-called peers were of the opinion that Wilty's death was as untidy as his life."

"It was," Luke said, matter-of-factly.

Luke was probably aware of every visit Wilty Hale made to the local police precinct. It would have been his decision to report those stories or squelch them. Most had been squelched. Callie wondered if that was because Wilty was a Hale, or because Luke, a recovering alcoholic, had a certain empathy for the guy.

"I think I should tell you that I received a call from Carolyne Hale this morning," Brad said. He noted the silence and the arched eyebrows that accompanied it. The Widow's reputation as a meddler preceded her. Also, he guessed they were as surprised as he was that only moments after hearing of her son's violent passing, one of her first thoughts was to protect his reputation *and,* of course, hers. "She's concerned about how her son's death is going to be reported."

"Factually," Luke said, with undisguised disdain. "Callie's piece is unbiased and uncolored. As it should be." Luke didn't like anyone questioning his reporters' objectivity.

"I'm sure this initial column is in perfect order," Brad soothed. "That's not why I brought up Mrs. Hale's call." His gaze settled on Callie. "I have two concerns. First, I need to ask about your relationship with Mr. Hale. My understanding is that, for a time, you and he dated. Is that correct?"

Callie flushed red. She was embarrassed, but not insulted. Brad wasn't a gossip. He was trying to discern whether or not her being assigned such a major piece about a former beau presented a conflict.

"It is true that Wilty and I shared an intimate relationship, but it ended almost a year ago."

"Did it end amicably?"

Callie thought about that. They were both hurt and angry at the time, but she didn't hate him. And she didn't believe he thought ill of her.

"Few romantic relationships end on a truly amicable note," she said carefully. "But, over time, I'd say we both got there." She looked around the room, then at Brad. "If anything, it's because of my past relationship with Mr. Hale that I'd like to do this piece. I think I can bring to it an honesty and a clarity that someone else might not."

Brad nodded appreciatively. Obviously, her answer allayed some, if not all, of his concerns.

"My second consideration is the seemingly obvious linkage of Mr. Hale's recent decadence to his impending assumption of the chairmanship of Hale Holdings. Even if it's true, it doesn't serve us or him well to insinuate that he preferred to drink himself into oblivion rather than take the reins of his family enterprise."

Even if it's true . . .

Callie was grateful to hear that perhaps someone other than her wasn't completely convinced that Wilty dove out a window because he feared he wasn't up to the task ahead of him.

Callie's job was to look at life through a what's-wrong-with-this-picture lens. When she spotted something that didn't feel right, or look right, or seem right, she was supposed to find out what was wrong and expose it so it could be fixed. Well, something was very wrong here.

When she and Wilty split, he wasn't in great shape, but he wasn't suicidal. In between then and now, it was certainly possible that the pressure of inheriting the mantle of the august E.W. Hale had mounted to a point where Wilty believed it was truly beyond him. But he could have abdicated the chairmanship. He could have hired a thousand advisors. He could have done a lot of things other than what he did.

Callie was beginning to wonder if something else had been thrown into the mix.

"The last thing any of us wants is to advertise the dark side of our founder's progeny," Harold Josephs was saying, "but let's face it. It's a pretty safe bet that in one way or another, Wilty's rather wild lifestyle contributed to his death."

Reluctantly, Luke Crocker agreed.

"With all due respect, gentlemen," Callie said, "I don't want to use Mr. Hale's unconventional lifestyle as the hook for this piece. I'd rather concentrate on his family's unconventional death-style."

The three men looked at her.

"The Hale curse." She tossed it into the center of the room as if it were the proverbial hot potato. Clearly, no one wanted to touch it. "Wilty's death invites an investigation of that long-propagated myth. Is there a curse on the Hales? If so, who invoked it and why? If not, why do people whisper about it as if it's true? Even this morning, people at the scene were muttering about how this curse finally destroyed the Hales. To me, *that's* the story."

It was also a way of deflecting blame and detouring public attention.

Brad Herring pursed his lips and tapped a finger lightly on his desk. Callie guessed he was running through a mental checklist of pros and cons—including how many more phone calls he'd get from the Widow. Callie found his silence encouraging. If he out-and-out hated it, he would have said so immediately.

Harold Josephs leaned back in his chair and folded his arms behind his head as he contemplated the ramifications of Callie's suggestion.

"I've always found it fascinating that of all the nineteenth-century titans the only family that bears the burden of a curse is the Hales. There's no Rockefeller curse, no calamitous invocation on the house of Morgan, no scent of unavoidable doom surrounding the Warburgs or the Schiffs. Each of those families had its share of deaths and failures and scandals. And certainly, the founders of those dynasties were just as ruthless as E.W. Hale and created equally powerful enemies. Yet only the Hales had a whammy placed on them. It does make you wonder."

Precisely, Callie thought.

Josephs plunked his chair back onto the carpet and looked Callie squarely in the eye.

"Frankly, Ms. Jamieson, I agree with you. It's about time someone confronted that blasted curse head on. Brava!"

Callie couldn't restrain a smile from forming. "Thank you, Mr. Josephs."

Luke, delighted to hear his protégée praised by the likes of Harold Josephs, turned from Harold to Callie. "It is eerie to realize that this story is bookended with two suicides. The first son blew his brains out. The last son splattered himself all over an alley."

"Let's not forget the many unexplained deaths in between," Harold said, warming to the subject.

Brad, who had refrained from speaking until his comrades had their say, finally expressed his opinion.

"It's good, Callie." He nodded his head approvingly. "It's gutsy and I like that. But I have one word of caution.

Make sure your facts are solid. First and foremost, this is a news story."

"I understand." For Callie, it was also a way of assuaging her guilt.

"Since public interest is notoriously fickle, I'd like this ASAP."

A look of panic skated across Callie's face.

"You have a month. Six weeks, if need be. Do you think you can do it in that time?"

Callie gulped. "I'll do my best, sir."

And she would. She owed it to Wilty.

5

Carolyne Hale's morning ritual was sacred. She was awakened at seven by her housekeeper, Lourdes, who brought in a wooden tray with a small pot of steaming mocha java coffee, a slice of unbuttered, lightly toasted whole grain bread, and the morning edition of the *City Courier*. After helping prop her mistress up against a tuft of pillows and setting the tray down on the bed, Lourdes pressed a button that mechanically drew the draperies back and allowed daylight to enter the peach-toned chamber. If there were no other requests, she exited.

Carolyne sipped her coffee and skimmed the headlines. When she was more awake, she'd go back to read the articles that interested her in full. She took no calls until eight-thirty. Anything earlier was simply uncivilized, which was why, when someone dared to ring her doorbell before the appointed hour, she glared at the space beyond her bedroom, appalled at the obvious breach of etiquette.

Lourdes appeared at the door and identified the visitors as Lieutenant Caleb Green and Detective Ezra Chapin of the 19th precinct.

Carolyne's eyes narrowed to a peevish squint. "What could he possibly want at this ungodly hour?"

"He wishes to speak to you, Madam. I told him you were not prepared to receive him, but he insisted." Lourdes was wringing her hands and staring at the floor. She didn't like to bring Mrs. Hale unpleasant news.

A sense of unease and premonition gripped Carolyne. The police were not common visitors to her apartment at any time of the day. For a lieutenant to come to her door at eight o'clock in the morning did not bode well.

"Tell him I'll be out shortly."

Lourdes, grateful to have a task, quickly retreated, closing the door behind her.

Several minutes later, Carolyne appeared swathed in an ecru silk robe and matching mules. Her face looked freshly scrubbed, her hair hastily brushed. Her expression was a mix of worry over the reason for their visit and pique that she hadn't been given enough time to prepare her appearance.

Two men presented their badges and identification for her appraisal.

"Mrs. Hale, I'm Lieutenant Caleb Green. This is Detective Ezra Chapin. I'm sorry to intrude on your morning, but we have some disturbing news."

Carolyne said nothing. Her silence gave the lieutenant permission to deliver his distasteful tidings.

"Sometime between three and five-thirty this morning, your son apparently leaped to his death."

"What?" Carolyne was genuinely stunned. Her complexion blanched and for a moment, she staggered. The younger policeman, Detective Chapin, reached out and took hold of her arm. When she'd regained her balance, and her composure, she shook him off and turned to his superior.

"Are you certain it's Wilty?"

"Our preliminary identification is considered highly reliable, ma'am, but we will need you to come downtown."

Carolyne nodded, but the rest of their conversation was a blur. The lieutenant offered his condolences and whatever other facts were available. As he was about to leave, he informed her that Detective Chapin would escort her to the morgue—at her convenience, of course. They agreed he would return at noon.

After they left, Carolyne returned to her bed. She was exhausted and emotionally spent. Lourdes had left a fresh cup of coffee on her nightstand. She drank it slowly, Lieutenant Green's voice playing over and over in her head, telling her that her son, Wilton Colfax Hale, had jumped out a window in order to end his life.

Carolyne set her coffee cup down and for a long while simply stared at her lap, as if her Porthault bed linens had been sewn with oracular threads that would explain how this could have happened. It seemed inconceivable that Wilty was actually dead. She'd spoken to him just the other day. Fought with him would be more accurate, but since when would that raise a red flag? Bickering was normal behavior for them. When they'd parted Wilty was keyed up, but he didn't seem dangerously overwrought. She certainly wouldn't have described him as suicidal. Then again, she never would have thought Wilty had the courage to jump out a nineteenth story window. Sadly, he'd surprised her.

Her stomach knotted at the thought of Wilty crashing onto the cold, hard pavement of that alley, but maternal warmth was not a quality Carolyne had in abundance. Once she'd absorbed the fact of his death, rued the circumstances surrounding it, and admitted to herself that she was genuinely upset to learn of it, she put her emotions into a "to be dealt with later" file and turned to more practical matters.

Wilty was a Hale, which meant his funeral service had to be steeped in ceremony. That required detailed planning.

Wilty's death created a number of serious financial complications. Those required careful manipulation.

Carolyne finished her coffee, left her bed and headed for her dressing room. She had a lot to do.

The rest of the morning was a flurry of activity. Carolyne called Brad Herring, the executive editor of the *Courier,* to discuss how Wilty's death was to be reported and to get him to agree to fax over an obituary for her approval.

She called her lawyer, Harlan Whiteside, to counsel her on what she needed to do and when. She also charged Harlan with tending to the other unpleasant tasks occasioned

by Wilty's death. He would call the funeral home and arrange to have Wilty picked up from the morgue and prepared for a proper wake and burial. He would reserve the
church. After he and Carolyne discussed the details of the
service, he would call the rectory and pass along whatever
information was pertinent.

She called her houseman out in Southampton. She'd assigned him several errands the day before, but he'd never
checked in to tell her whether they'd been completed. Also,
she wanted to talk to him about Wilty.

Then, she called Arthur, Wilty's valet and asked him to
gather clothing to send over to the mortuary. As always,
Carolyne's instructions were explicit: a dark blue Zegna
suit, a white Turnbull & Asser dress shirt, a royal blue silk
Charvet tie, Wilty's favorite Lobb shoes, and the gold in-
taglio cuff links with the initials E.W. carved into a re-
cessed oval that had been passed down from Hale to Hale
to Hale. Since Wilty was the last of the dynasty's sons, it
seemed only fitting that he should be buried wearing something belonging to the founding father.

That would play well with the press.

At noon, Detective Chapin arrived. Carolyne announced
immediately that there were to be no questions. She also
refused to ride in a police-issue vehicle. Instead, she insisted they use her limousine. Chapin sat up front with her
chauffeur. She sat in the back. The window between them
remained closed.

When they reached the morgue, she was led through a
dark, narrow basement hallway to a large curtained window. Detective Chapin explained what was about to happen, gave her a moment to compose herself, then rapped
his knuckles on the glass.

In a jarring flash of déjà vu, Carolyne felt as if she were
standing before the window in the nursery area of the hospital where Wilty was born. Then, she was accompanied
by her husband and mother-in-law, a small coterie of Hale
hangers-on, as well as a photographer and reporter from the
Memphis Courier-Journal who'd been summoned to record

the moment. She recalled being giddy with relief that she'd borne a boy and heir, at the same time proud and exhilarated, as if the act of giving birth was such an exceptional triumph, it deserved media attention. Surviving a pregnancy and a birth attended to by the likes of Huntington and Eppie Hale was actually the more notable accomplishment, but only Carolyne knew that.

Now, she was standing next to a stranger in a dark, quiet hallway, alone and anxious. There were no flashbulbs or microphones, yet she was certain that more than one reporter and photographer lurked nearby. As the curtain was drawn she girded herself. She wasn't being asked to view a tiny, blue-blanketed baby lying in a plastic bassinet. Rather, it was the body of a grown man on a steel table, his mangled remains sheathed in an expanse of stiff white paper.

A tall, thin man garbed in medical whites stood alongside the table waiting for her to signal that she was ready. She nodded. He retracted the covering just far enough to reveal the dead man's face.

Carolyne averted her eyes. She felt the detective's hand on her elbow. He asked if she was all right. She mumbled that she was. He asked if the person on the table was her son. She braced herself with a deep breath, then slowly turned her head toward the window.

His blond hair was matted, his complexion a dun white. There was an unnatural puffiness to his features as well as a hideous array of purple shadows alluding to the trauma that had caused his death. His nose appeared flattened and askew. His eyes were shut, his mouth turned down in a permanent pout.

He looked so dispirited, she thought, so dejected.

Weeping, she turned away. The sadness that masked his face was more upsetting than the lifelessness that distinguished his body.

When she turned back again, the curtain was closed. Behind the glass, she heard the muffled slam of a door and flinched. That was her son being pushed into a refrigerated, metal drawer. That was a Hale, being stored like a piece of meat.

When Callie walked into the stationhouse and asked for Detective Chapin, she was directed up a flight of stairs. Chapin was on the landing waiting to greet her.

"Ms. Jamieson," he said, extending his hand. "Thank you for coming."

Callie thought about reminding him that this was a command performance and not something she'd done voluntarily, but she restrained herself.

"This is my partner, Detective Alvarez," he said, acknowledging the man standing next to him. "Jorge, Callie Jamieson from the *Courier*."

Alvarez, slightly shorter than his partner and as wired as a small dog, offered a barely perceptible nod of his head and muttered something along the lines of "nice to meet you."

Amenities concluded, Callie was led into one of the interview rooms, a spare, grim space that made no attempt to make its occupants feel comfortable. She took the seat offered, shifted her backpack onto her lap, folded her hands in front of her and placed them on the metal table, wondering when, and if, it had last been washed.

Chapin offered her a beverage.

While he retrieved a bottle of water and Alvarez scrutinized her with his piercing obsidian eyes, she studied the two of them. Chapin was about six-foot-two, broad-shouldered and ruggedly handsome, with a strong physique and casual manner that seemed better suited to an outdoorsman than a New York City detective.

Alvarez, whose skin tone looked like rich cream flavored with a drop of espresso, was totally city. His entire being emitted an alertness that told Callie very little got past him. She also got the sense that he viewed the world through a much darker prism than she did. While her work had exposed her to a great deal of unpleasantness and created a cynicism she tried to keep in check, his work dealt with human beings at their most violent and most corrupt.

Chapin, who obviously dealt with the same nefarious element, came across as a man better able to prioritize the various elements of his life. While Callie had no doubt he took his job seriously, his manner wasn't as edgy as his partner's, nor were his looks.

His face was long and oval, with a hint of a five o'clock shadow shading his jawline. He had thick, reddish brown hair, that looked like it had been chopped rather than cut, and hooded, deep-set eyes that were a mesmerizing mix of gold and brown. She recalled from their previous encounter, however, that their amber color was deceiving. Rather than exuding the warmth normally associated with such burnished tones, his gaze was hard and steely. She also noticed that while his lips were full and his mouth was generous, his chin was square and determined.

"How well did you know Wilty Hale?" Alvarez had grown impatient with the foreplay and decided to get right down to it.

"Very well. We dated for nearly a year." As much as she loathed revealing personal things to strangers, in this case, honesty was the only policy.

"Sounds like it was a big-time romance."

"We were rather heavily involved."

Chapin wasn't surprised. Not after what he'd witnessed at the scene.

"When did you stop seeing each other?"

"About nine months ago."

"Did you dump him or did he dump you?"

"We dumped each other," she said, refusing to rise to Alvarez's bait.

"What was he like?" Chapin asked. "Nice guy? Spoiled brat? Angry drunk? All of the above? None of the above?"

"Despite what you might have read in the press, Wilty was a really terrific man," Callie said with obvious affection. "Being a Hale, he couldn't help but be spoiled, yet he was always very considerate, very nice. As for what kind of drunk he was, I'm hardly an expert. During the period of time we were together, he was sober more often than not."

"Funny. According to our sources, the guy was sloshed more often than not."

That blanket, one-dimensional kind of characterization of Wilty as a hopeless boozer bothered Callie beyond measure.

"Wilty changed a great deal over the past year," she admitted.

"How so?" Chapin noted that she was reluctant to bad-mouth her ex. He wondered whether she was concerned about his reputation, or hers. She wouldn't be the first woman who didn't want to own up to a relationship with a drunk or a deadbeat.

"He was drinking more," Callie said. "He'd stopped seeing many of his longtime friends and frequenting his favorite haunts. Instead, he was becoming a regular at an assortment of downtown bars and clubs. Also, he'd let a number of his philanthropic obligations slide."

"What kind of philanthropic obligations?"

"Wilty spent a lot of time and money helping sick and disadvantaged children. He loved baseball and had organized a peewee league down on the Lower East Side. He got local merchants to sponsor the individual teams, but he paid for all the uniforms and equipment. He even paid for the ball field."

It pleased her to note that both detectives appeared surprised by Wilty's generosity and a bit chagrined at their preconceived prejudices against him.

"I made some calls today," she continued. "He didn't go to one game this past season. He also stopped going to the soup kitchen on Fifteenth Street. He used to do that most Sundays. Lately, he's been a no-show."

Alvarez tipped his chair back onto its rear legs and studied her. "Did you do that to him? Was he so ripped up after you two split that he became a drunken recluse?"

Callie glared at him with obvious dislike, yet beneath the coarse verbiage was a fair question, something that had been eating at her all day. From the moment Chapin identified Wilty as the jumper, Callie had wondered about her role in his death. If she'd stuck by him a little longer, if she hadn't abandoned him to the bottle, if she had helped him find his footing in the new world he was about to enter, would he have found his way into that alley?

"The circumstances that were ripping him up preceded our breakup," she said, swallowing hard.

Chapin eyed her curiously. "Can you be more specific?"

Callie hated revealing Wilty's secrets, but they wanted to know what might have propelled him out that window. So did she.

"On June first, Wilty was slated to inherit the Hale fortune. He was also supposed to take his place as the chairman of the board of Hale Holdings."

Alvarez whistled.

"It was an awesome prospect, one that filled him with enormous pride and, at the same time, overwhelming fear. There was a lot of history for him to live up to. He wasn't sure he could do it."

"I can dig it," Alvarez said, with an unexpected show of understanding.

"So rather than run toward it," Chapin said, "he ran away from it. As hard and as fast as he could." Callie nodded. "Which is why you walked away from him."

That stunned her. First, that he could intuit her feelings and second, the horrible way he made it sound.

"I tried to remind him of who he was and how much good he'd already done, but in light of what his great-great-grandfather, E.W. Hale, managed to contribute over the course of his lifetime, Wilty felt inadequate."

Her eyebrows drew together as she remembered how many times she'd held him in her arms and tried to soothe away his pain of feeling less than.

"Once he was in the year of his thirty-fifth birthday, he changed. He drank more. He worked less. And he began to have reactions to things that never bothered him before," she said in a low voice.

"Like what?" Chapin wanted to know.

"A maître d' seating him before others who'd been waiting. Someone soliciting a donation for their favorite charity. People asking him for box seat tickets to Yankee games or tennis matches. He used to give those away without a second thought. Then, all of a sudden, he started complaining about everyone hitting him up for something. About people taking advantage of him because he was a Hale."

"Was that a big thing with him? Being a Hale?" Alvarez asked.

"When we first started dating, he seemed to view it as a golden albatross, a weight he had to carry around, albeit one which afforded him the chance to go, do, see, and buy anything he wanted."

"And later?"

"It became something he was both defending and avoiding."

"Was it important to you?" Chapin said. "Being a Hale?"

Callie didn't like the implications inherent in his question. "Do you mean was it important that *he* was a Hale? Or was it important that ultimately *I* became a Hale?"

He shrugged and smiled, as if to say it didn't matter how she answered, he'd already come to his own conclusions.

"Since you've obviously missed the point, Detective Chapin, let me reiterate: being a Hale might seem like a really great thing to someone like you, but at the end of the day, it was more trouble than it was worth."

"Why'd he call you the night before he died?"

"What are you talking about? Wilty never called me."

"Yes, he did. Twice. We have the phone logs."

Again, Callie didn't like his tone. This time, it was barbed and accusatory.

"I did have two hang-ups on my answering machine," Callie said, reining in her temper by reminding herself this so-called interview had been initiated by a death.

"Does your machine give the time the call was made?"

Callie said it did. She told them she'd gone to dinner

and a movie with a friend and gotten home around midnight. The two calls came in between eleven-thirty and a quarter to twelve. The detectives exchanged glances. Obviously, those times corresponded with their log.

"Any idea why he'd call out of the blue like that?" Alvarez said.

"None whatsoever."

"Did Mr. Hale wear glasses?"

Callie turned toward Chapin, surprised by the question and the sharp change of direction. She was also suddenly aware of a strange undercurrent in the room.

"He wore contact lenses. He only wore his glasses when his eyes were tired. Or, when he'd had too much to drink. Why?"

"A pair of glasses belonging to Mr. Hale were found next to the body. Most suicides don't wear their glasses on the way down."

Callie shivered, visualizing Wilty watching the ground coming up to meet him. She shivered again when she realized what might have prompted the question.

"Are you insinuating Wilty's death might not be a suicide?"

Chapin shrugged again, but there was nothing casual about it.

"I don't insinuate, Ms. Jamieson," he said, his gaze fixed on her. "I simply ask questions, listen to the answers and see where it all takes me. Not too different from what you do, right?"

Callie had had enough of his arrogant attitude and his hairpin subject shifts and his nosy intrusions. Also, she was unnerved by his suggestion that something untoward might have happened to Wilty.

"Speaking of what I do," she said, pushing back her chair and rising to her feet. "I'm done here. If you think of anything I might be able to add that would prove *truly* germane to whatever it is you're doing, give me a call. Otherwise, see you around."

She marched out of the room, closing the door hard behind her.

Ezra Chapin stared at the door for a moment, then turned to his partner. "That went well, don't you think?"

6

Peter Merrick prowled the perimeter of his office, listening to a tape recording of his session with Callie. He'd done little else since she'd left the other day. While his step was firm, the carpeting absorbed his footfalls, maintaining the undiluted silence he required for contemplation.

He's dressed like a fancy man, with a colorful vest and neatly pressed pants.

Merrick listened hard to the soft voice of Callie Jamieson as she recounted the vision that had plagued her for most of her life.

Fancy man.

What an interesting term for a modern young woman to use. Merrick stopped the tape and considered her phraseology. It felt old-fashioned, sort of bucolic. Yet according to Callie, who was just thirty, she was born and bred in the metropolitan area.

Colorful vest. Neatly pressed pants.

Today, in this era of casual Fridays and dressed down Wednesdays, few men wore vests and those who did rarely selected one that was colorful, the exception being a groomsman in a wedding party or an overly enthusiastic New Year's Eve celebrant. But even twenty-some-odd years ago when she claimed these visions first appeared, vests were rarely rainbowed. They were the third piece of a suit, usually cut from the same cloth. Western attire included a vest, but for those, leather and suede were the most popular fabrics.

And why would she notice whether or not a man's pants were pressed? While he considered those in the media boorish and today's youth downright slovenly, he doubted that wrinkled slacks had become de rigueur.

He clicked the tape back on.

She's not a fancy woman.

There was that term again.

Her hair is loose and undone.

Callie's blond hair was loose, unrestrained by gels or clips or bobby pins; her hairstyle might be called undone. So why would the dream woman's unfettered mane be unusual enough to be committed to memory? His own observations told him that most women had forsaken the tight French twists and neatly coiled rolls of days gone by. True, formal occasions often called for more elaborate, more structured coiffures, but there was sunlight in Callie's dream, marking it as something occurring during daylight hours. Also, nothing that she recounted even vaguely resembled a formal get-together.

Her hands appear roughened by work and her clothes are homespun and plain.

He rewound that segment and replayed it. Why use the term *roughened by work* when the more commonplace phrase would be *dishpan hands*? And since when was anything other than a crocheted afghan *homespun*?

A powerful fizz started in the pit of his stomach. It rose rapidly, tickling his lips into a smile. He replayed the tape one last time, increasing the volume so he didn't miss a word or a tonal nuance. He picked the dream apart, then put it together with things she'd told him during their talk sessions to determine if the conscious had influenced the unconscious. He warned himself to be objective and not to make the puzzle fit the piece, but his excitement continued to build.

She didn't know it, nor did she need to know it, but

Callie Jamieson's predicament was Peter Merrick's providence: Her past was going to insure his future.

Carolyne had left word with her doorman that the only visitor she'd see that evening was her attorney, Harlan Whiteside. They were to turn away *everyone* else.

She combed her hair before admitting Harlan, but did nothing else to improve her appearance. It was rare that Carolyne was minus the armament of makeup and couture, but after the day she'd had, she had neither the physical nor the emotional energy to don her usual camouflage. She bathed, towel-dried her hair and slipped into lightweight, cashmere drawstring pants and a matching sweater.

Harlan Whiteside was a New York powerhouse. Well-connected, well-heeled, and highly regarded by his peers, he was known for his keen intellect, his elegant manners, and his take-no-prisoners style. He inspired fear in those on the lower rungs of the Whiteside, Bannister, Howell and Revere ladder who in some way demonstrated a poor work ethic or a lack of loyalty, as well as those who sat across the negotiating table from him and attempted to deny him something he wanted for himself or for his clients. His obsession with winning was absolute, whether it was in a board room, a court room, on a golf course, or at a bridge table.

Harlan was a man who wore his age well, boasting a full head of silver hair and a body that so far had avoided the paunch that seemed inevitable in men who'd passed the sixty-year mark. He worked at looking fit and younger than his years, because in a society preoccupied with youth, age had suddenly become synonymous with disability: the older you were, the less you knew. Which, of course, was the complete reverse of the way it used to be and the way Harlan believed it should be. Once upon a time, age equaled wisdom, youth connoted inexperience. Then, for some absurd reason, the world turned on its axis and decided youth was cutting edge and everyone on the far side of forty could be cut out. He didn't understand it, nor would he ever accept it, but he was doing his damnedest to keep up.

Carolyne and Harlan went way back. She'd been acquainted with his second wife—he recently divorced number four—a congenital social climber who'd affixed herself to Carolyne believing that befriending the Widow Hale provided instant access into the upper echelon of New York society. Not only did she fail to gain entrée, but her marriage failed as well. In the months after her exit and before Harlan located the third love of his life, Carolyne and he indulged in a passionate intermezzo. The romance was short-lived, but the friendship had endured.

Carolyne led him into the den, fixed him a drink and refreshed her own. They talked about the day, what he'd accomplished, what she'd done. He asked how she was doing.

Unwilling as ever to let anyone get too close to her, she responded with the pat: "As well as can be expected."

"You made our meeting tonight sound urgent."

"It is. I had some questions that required immediate answers."

"About?"

"My . . . situation. I know you're not Wilty's lawyer, but you once said you were familiar with the Hale Trust. Is that true?"

"Slightly familiar is more like it, but ask away." He leaned closer. Her voice had grown so soft, for a minute he thought his hearing had gone bad.

"As you know, I have very little of my own. I have a modest stock portfolio, several money market accounts and an income from a trust Huntington left me. I'm not poor, but I am not, by any stretch of the imagination, wealthy. I was able to live my oh so glamorous life without any real resources because most of my expenses were taken care of by Wilty. With him gone, I'm worried about my very survival."

As well she should be, Harlan thought. As dependent as Carolyne had been before the dissolution of the Hale Trust,

after, she became completely beholden to her son's benef-
icence. And having witnessed the strangled machinations
of their relationship over the years, he suspected Carolyne
wasn't Wilty's sole heir, perhaps not even his primary beneficiary.

More the pity, he thought, since as her attorney he, too,
would greatly profit by her inheritance.

"Did Wilty ever discuss the terms of his will with you?"

"No."

That surprised him. Knowing Carolyne's need for
money, he would have expected that after Wilty came into
the first part of his inheritance, she would have hounded
him about settling some of his millions on her. Then again,
maybe she had and had been denied.

"Do you know who drew it up?"

"No. He had a number of attorneys on retainer, as you
know."

Harlan had handled several matters for Wilty over the
years, but he was neither his personal lawyer, nor did he
represent Hale Holdings. He'd lobbied for a greater percentage of Wilty's business at one time, but Wilty made it
clear he knew of Harlan's relationship with Carolyne.

"She needs your friendship more than I need your legal
expertise," he'd said, explaining his desire to avoid any
possible conflict or confusion.

"He probably assigned his personal matters to an estate
and trust guy at the firm that oversees Hale Holdings," Harlan said.

"Or to a storefront lawyer in Harlem!" She was exasperated and on edge.

"Wilty was a generous man, Carolyne. I can't believe
he didn't provide for you."

The lines around Carolyne's mouth tightened. "He was
thirty-four years old, Harlan. Since I don't think he expected to die so young, I have no reason to believe that he
took the notion of a last will and testament seriously."

Her entire body was tense and she was trembling. Low

blood sugar, Harlan concluded. Too little food, too much drink.

"There are two things to remember, Carolyne. One, Wilty wasn't an ordinary thirty-four-year-old. He was a Hale. Several years ago, he came into an enormous amount of money. Had he lived, in a few weeks he would have inherited a veritable fortune. You can be sure that his attorneys, as well as those representing the board of Hale Holdings, made certain that Wilty's will was up to date.

"The second thing, though it makes me uncomfortable to discuss it at this moment, is that Wilty committed suicide. It's quite possible that he was considering this for some time. If so, it's also possible that he put his affairs in order before . . . well, before."

"No!" Carolyne snapped, the lioness side of her personality emerging. "He wasn't considering suicide. Whatever order things were in last week, is the way they are today."

"How could you know that?" Harlan asked.

"I don't *know* that, but suicide is an impulsive act."

"Not always."

"Wilty was an impulsive man. Who else do you know that went on canyoning expeditions, or bungee jumping?"

Harlan found it odd, and a bit chilling, that she would trivialize her son's death that way, as if a plunge from a nineteenth story window was a puckish impulse.

"I know that Wilty enjoyed sports with a bit of danger attached," he said, "but I never interpreted that as a suicidal bent. Frankly, I saw it as his attempt to defy death."

She frowned, her mouth twisting with an odd resentment. "He had a nasty streak. Did you know that?" Her lips pinched together in a distasteful sneer. "That was the Hale side of him, that hateful, self-aggrandizing, self-impressed Hale side that taunted and tormented those who didn't accord him the proper respect. Me, especially."

She gulped the last of the scotch.

"You're not implying that he leapt from that window to torment you, are you?"

"No!" She must have realized how ghoulishly absurd

that sounded, because her denial was immediate and insistent. "Absolutely not, but . . ."

She hesitated, seeming to debate revealing something else. Whatever it was, Harlan guessed it was the real reason he'd been summoned.

"But what?" he prodded, gently.

Carolyne cast her eyes downward. She began to fidget with the strings of her pants, rolling them around in her fingers as if they were rosary beads.

"Wilty found something," she suddenly confided, her voice barely audible. "Something positively ruinous."

"To whom?"

"All of us. Him. Me. Hale Holdings. All of us."

Harlan had known Carolyne long enough to recognize when she was exaggerating and when she was telling the truth. This was not one of her drama queen attempts to do an end run around whoever or whatever she thought was standing in the way of something she desired, be it a designer purse or the chairmanship of a charity ball. Whatever Wilty discovered was obviously invested with the potential to devastate.

"What did he find, Carolyne?" He didn't have to remind her that anything she told him would be held in the strictest confidence.

"Something that denied his birthright." She could barely bring herself to allow the words to cross her lips. "Something that said he might not be a true Hale."

Which meant, Harlan finished the paragraph in his mind, there was no fortune, no power, and no money to leave her.

She told him about the suicide note. "It was written in 1900."

Interesting, Harlan thought. That was the year E.W. Hale established the Hale Trust.

"Was any of the information in this document verified?"

Carolyne shrugged. "He said no."

The last time she'd asked him if he destroyed the

damned note he told her he hadn't, but he thought he might have figured out how to get his hands on the missing diary. They fought over what to do, but she didn't tell Harlan that. Not only was airing one's dirty laundry completely unseemly, but she didn't want her contretemps with Wilty to be misinterpreted.

"Where is this note now?" Harlan asked.

Again, she shrugged. "He showed me a copy. He wouldn't tell me what he did with the original."

She'd begged him to tell her where it was. If he wasn't going to get rid of it, the least he could do was let her help him authenticate it. He refused, mocking her interest as being completely self-motivated which, of course, it was.

"Okay, let's forget that for the moment and get back to Wilty's will," Harlan said. "It's possible any endowments he might have wanted to make were restricted by the original stipulations of the trust."

"You mean he didn't have the right to leave anything to me? I'm his mother, for God's sake!"

An ancient anger rouged her face. Once, in a rare moment of confession, Carolyne had told Harlan about the denigrating way she'd been treated by the Hales, so he knew the root of her rage.

"I didn't say that," he cautioned. "What I'm saying is that there might have been provisions for what would happen to portions of the estate in the event of Wilty's death, particularly the shares of Hale stock. As for those components of the estate that would have been considered personal, my guess would be that Wilty was free to designate bequests."

"Like?"

"He could have bequeathed you ownership of this apartment as well as the houses in Palm Beach and Southampton. He also could have assigned you a portion of his stock in Hale Holdings, enough to secure you a place on the board. And, if he was feeling particularly generous, he might have left you a big, fat chunk of cash."

The look of panic that had insinuated itself onto Carolyne's face, eased slightly.

"However," Harlan said, bursting Carolyne's balloon, "if what you just told me is true, it's possible that the entire estate could be voided and the terms of his will invalidated."

"In other words, there'd be nothing to bequeath."

What little color had tinged Carolyne's face, disappeared.

"Correct."

"What happens now?" she asked. "I mean under normal circumstances."

"Wilty's will has to be probated. That could take up to sixty days. Once that's completed, it will be read and its stipulations fulfilled."

"And if this document comes to light?"

"The court would hold off any and all distribution until the conflict is addressed and satisfied, and a thorough search for the so-called legitimate heirs is conducted and concluded."

Carolyne braced her elbows on her knees and dropped her head into her hands. For several minutes, she sat quiet and still.

"I can't let that happen," she said, lifting her head and staring at Harlan with such fierce determination it took him aback. "Do you understand that? We cannot let that happen!"

"What is it you want me to do?" he asked.

Her voice was strong, but tremulous with insistence. "What do you think I want you to do? I want you to squelch any and all hints about Wilty not being a Hale. I want that damned piece of paper ripped up, thrown out, burned to a crisp, buried on the bottom of the ocean or otherwise permanently suppressed. That's what I want!"

No surprise there, Harlan thought. Also no surprise that Harlan had already decided in his own mind to do just that, if she asked. Half a billion dollars was a lot of money for a woman to handle on her own. She'd need a strong, intelligent, trustworthy man by her side to give advice and counsel, as well as love and support.

"I'd be more than happy to grant your request, Carolyne, but first, you have to find the original."

"Trust me, Harlan," she said. "I intend to do just that."

7

The Round Bar at the Royalton was so crowded Callie could barely get inside, let alone find her friend, Paula Stein. Standing on tiptoes, her head snaking from side to side like a periscope, she scanned the area, trying to see beyond the clamorous mass. Since it was three deep around the dimly lit bar, four in some spots, and loud, this was not an easy task, although Callie's height helped.

She shifted slightly to the left, saw an opening and wriggled past a cluster of men speculating about what the volatility in the stock market meant to their individual portfolios and how long the Yankees could dominate New York baseball. One or two smiled at her, but she disregarded them. She already had a date, of sorts.

As she maneuvered closer to the epicenter of the action, she eyed the faces of the first ring of the humanity hugging the bar. They were young, well-dressed, mostly single and bunched in groups. Three young women, four young men. One woman, one man. Two of this, three of that. Rarely, if ever, did anyone venture into this high pressured mating ritual alone.

Suddenly, above the sea of heads, a hand waved. Callie grinned at the woman directly across from her. Tall, raven-haired, boasting a deep red lipstick that was her signature shade, Paula was perched on a bar stool, oozing confidence as she fended off potential seat poachers, in her usual take-no-prisoners mode.

As Callie made her way around the room, she laughed at how little had changed since the first time she saw Paula. They were ten years old. Bill had remarried and the newly configured Jamieson family was moving onto Pennington Road. When the family arrived, Paula watched the moving men unload the truck and welcomed the Jamiesons to her neighborhood, especially the quiet blonde who was as tall and gawky as she was. Sensing a kindred spirit, Paula asked if Callie wanted to ride bikes. They'd been best friends ever since.

Their relationship worked because in so many areas what one was missing, the other supplied, right down to their family situations. Paula's parents were happily married, she had a younger brother, a dog, and two sets of grandparents alive and well and wintering in Florida. Callie's family was more like a badly patched quilt. When Bill remarried, Callie gained a stepmother and two step siblings, none of whom she particularly liked. She tolerated Serena and her children because she loved her father and desperately wanted him to be happy. Also, she thought if he could be happy again, so could she. Unfortunately, it didn't work out that way.

Before they could even exchange how-are-yous, Paula was signaling one of the bartenders to bring Callie a drink. Within seconds, a bubblegum pink libation in a martini glass was placed before Callie by a young man answering to the name Harry. A loud gasp from Paula stopped Harry dead in his tracks. He looked at Paula, then down at the drink. Apologizing profusely, he eased a tiny wedge of lime into Callie's drink and mopped the overflow with a white cloth.

"Much better," Paula sniffed.

"A thousand pardons," he said, lightly, offering Paula a salaam before moving on to his next customer.

"Harry makes the best Cosmopolitan around," Paula declared, whispering to prevent Harry from overhearing the compliment—as if he could with all the noise. "I can't believe he left off the lime, though."

"He should be beheaded," Callie harrumphed, trying to raise the glass to her lips without spilling half of it onto her blouse. "Better yet," she said, replacing the glass on the bar and smacking her lips, "the man should be knighted. Oooh! Is that good!"

Paula's smile was triumphant and pleased, as if Callie's enjoyment was yet another validation of Paula's uncanny ability to discriminate between the good and the great.

"He makes it with lemon vodka."

"Whatever," Callie said, blithely taking another sip.

Paula laughed and wondered aloud why she bothered. They both knew Callie couldn't care less how something was made. It was different for Paula. As associate food editor for the *Courier,* it was her job to know where to find the best food and drink in New York. Callie saw no need for both of them to do Paula's job, particularly when Paula did it so well.

As she set down her drink, Callie noticed that Harry's special concoction was extremely popular, particularly with women. She wondered if it was because they were pink and pretty. Then, typical of Callie, who often ruminated about minor observances until she'd elevated them into major social commentaries, she tried to connect individual women to their drinks. She wanted to see whether the Cosmopolitan was the drink of choice for the attractive or the unattractive, whether less than beautiful women ordered them to feel pretty, or attractive women ordered them because they seemed a fitting accessory.

Paula poked her. The woman next to Paula was leaving and had generously bequeathed her bar stool to Callie, who had exactly one second to take possession of it before the herd stampeded.

"What was all that woolgathering about?" Paula asked, as Callie fought off an overly aggressive barfly.

"Women. The kind of drinks they order. What it says about them."

"And society at large. Yada. Yada. Yada." Paula's eyes rolled around in her head. "Callie! Give it a rest, will you?"

"Okay," Callie promised. "Philosophy class is over."

"Good. Now we can get onto serious business," she said, tipping her head in the direction of someone across from them. "Like what was that woman thinking when she bought that sweater!"

Reserving anything even remotely substantive for later, they catted mercilessly about the people surrounding them, dishing about clothes and hairstyles, who had on too much makeup, too little clothing, as well as the *Gentlemen's Quarterly* type whose stares were so lecherous Callie was sure he had visions of threesomes dancing in his head.

After downing a second of Harry's fabulous drinks, Callie declared herself ready for dinner.

"I'm getting blitzed," she announced. "I need sustenance!"

"I don't understand how you can be so buzzed," Paula grumbled, clearly not ready to leave. "You ate all the nuts."

"Sue me. I didn't get a whole lot of sleep last night and . . . let's just say this was a long day."

Paula took a last swig of her pink drink, paid the tab and the two of them elbowed their way to the coat check.

"I heard about Wilty," Paula said quietly as they waited for their coats. "That must have been tough for you. So personally painful."

Again, Callie recalled the sight of Wilty's battered body lying atop a heap of garbage.

"That it was," she said, feeling an unexpected chill arpeggio up her spine.

Quickly, Callie went to slip into her coat, eager for whatever warmth it might provide. Someone bumped her from behind. Her vision blurred and she was momentarily disoriented. She blinked, trying to clear her eyes and get her bearings, but when she looked up, the person she faced was someone who didn't belong there—the gray stranger. He wasn't clearly defined, his features looked as if they'd been drawn with chalk then smudged, but it was him. She staggered slightly in disbelief.

Paula grabbed hold of Callie and held her. "Are you okay?"

Callie nodded, but it was a lie. She didn't feel okay at all. In truth, she was terrified. Her heart was thumping and she was finding it hard to breathe.

The gray people only visited at night.

Callie stared at the space which just seconds before had been occupied by that vague, ashen specter she'd come to associate with midnight and death.

Why had he followed her here? Where had he come from?

"You need to get out of here, girlfriend," Paula said, taking charge.

She put her arm around Callie's waist and piloted her outside. She hailed a cab and gave the driver Callie's address.

"What are you doing?" Callie sounded frightened.

"What does it look like I'm doing? I'm taking you home."

"No!" Callie's voice was shrill. "I don't want to go home!" He might be waiting.

"But . . ."

"You told me you had to check out some new restaurant. That was the plan and that's where I want to go."

"Okay, I just thought . . ."

"Look. I had too much to drink. As soon as I eat something, I'll be fine."

Rather than argue, Paula gave the cabby the address of a restaurant in the thirties.

The ride was silent. Callie stared out her window. Paula stared at Callie. She had had too much to drink. And food would make her feel better. But knowing Callie as well as she did, Paula suspected that drinks were not the problem and food was not the solution. Something had spooked the hell out of Callie Jamieson.

The bread came in a small loaf on a wooden board, warm and crusty and smelling of butter and dill. After two thick slices, Callie's Cosmopolitan buzz had disappeared and her stomach had calmed, but not enough to join Paula in a glass of Chardonnay.

"Feel better?" Paula gratefully noted that some color had returned to Callie's face.

"A little."

"Good." Paula was relieved when their starters were set down. Maybe after she ate, Callie would reveal what had unnerved her back at the bar. "I stopped by your office this afternoon to find out how you were."

"I was at the police station."

"That's a place to be," Paula said, surprised. "And you were there because?"

"Detective First Grade Ezra Chapin of the nineteenth precinct invited me to stop by." Callie fluttered her eyelashes sarcastically. "He and his equally charming partner, Detective Second Grade Jorge Alvarez, wanted to know all about my relationship with Wilty."

Paula could see how annoyed Callie was at having been called in and questioned about her love life, but under the circumstances, Paula thought interviewing friends of a suicide was appropriate and said so.

Callie agreed, then thought about what Chapin had said about Wilty's glasses. She'd been mulling that over ever since she left the stationhouse, but for now, she decided to keep it to herself.

Instead, Callie told Paula about being called to Brad Herring's office and being assigned a major feature. When she explained her plan to key the series around the Hale Curse, Paula wanted to know why she chose something steeped in such murderous mythology.

"Because too many men have died before their time of unnatural causes. Because I used to care a great deal about one of those men. And," she added with sudden realization, "I suppose because deep down, I've often wondered if my family's cursed."

"Ah," Paula said. "The nightmares."

Callie nodded. "I have them. My mother had them. Yesterday, someone asked me if my grandmother had them."

"Did she?"

"I don't know, but if she did, what would you call this generation to generation haunting? A blessing?"

"Not exactly." Paula remembered several times when Callie slept over and woke up screaming in the middle of the night. Her body was always drenched with sweat, shaking uncontrollably, and her eyes were always wide and vacant, as if something or someone had sucked the life out of her. Paula had never witnessed terror like that. "Are they back?"

"They returned the other night."

"Are they worse?" Paula was unable to imagine anything worse than being continuously tortured by a nightmare.

Callie choked out a frustrated laugh as bitter tears pooled in her eyes. "They were a little fuzzier than usual, but yes, they're the same," she said, as if she, too, were amazed at the persistence of these phantoms. "They're always the same."

The waiter cleared their plates and served their entrees. Callie didn't object when he poured wine into her glass. It was false courage, she knew, but just then, she was fresh out of the real kind.

"Do you remember when we were in the coatroom?" Paula nodded. "He was there," Callie said.

"Who was there?"

"The stranger. The gray stranger. He was standing right there in front of me." Callie's eyes darted about the room, as if she feared the stranger had a ghostly posse that had followed her to the restaurant and would punish her for revealing their leader's location. "He was there," she said, her voice as hushed and hollow as the wind. "I saw him."

"I believe you, honey."

Callie heard it in her voice. Paula hadn't seen anyone, nor did she understand how Callie could believe she saw anyone.

"Maybe I just had one too many of Harry's happy hour specials," Callie said, with a dismissive shrug.

Paula shook her head. "That's too easy, babe."

"Trust me," Callie said, a pall clouding her turquoise eyes. "There's nothing easy about this."

Paula realized she was about to enter a mine field, but the question begged to be asked. "Maybe it's time to see someone about this. You know, professionally."

Paula expected Callie to have one of her usual outbursts about shrinks being an unctuous bunch of know-nothing quacks who made things up to make others look crazy and themselves look good.

Callie surprised her by saying, "Believe it or not, I've been in therapy for about six months."

"Really? Who are you seeing?"

"Peter Merrick. A couple of months after Wilty and I broke up, I began to beat up on myself for cutting out on him when he turned weird. Instead of sticking by him, like my father did for my mother, I ran away as fast as I could." She grimaced. "That bothered me. A lot. I decided it might be time to pry open my psyche and do the shrink thing. So, I researched the subject."

Paula laughed. There was nothing Callie didn't research. Paula knew never to ask where a phrase came from or who the best bunion doctor in the city was.

"And you chose him because?"

"I read his book, *Before and Again*. It's a series of vignettes about patients suffering from recurring nightmares." Callie gulped her wine, then made a feeble attempt at humor. "And I thought I was so unique. Who knew there were thousands of people out there being awakened in the middle of the night by strange, gray people?"

"I don't care what put your butt on the couch," Paula said, ignoring the sarcasm. "I'm proud of you. I know how hard it was for you to start therapy."

"It was harder to do nothing."

She explained that even before Wilty, the minute she felt herself growing close to someone, the fear of becoming her mother would insinuate itself on her consciousness. She'd see herself exhibiting bizarre behavior, saying inexplicable things. She'd envision fights and misunderstandings, emotional shutdowns followed by hysterical flare-ups. She'd see the man she loved slipping away from her, seeking solace with another. She'd see herself taunted by demons instead of surrounded by a husband and children.

"Imagine my surprise when suddenly it was Wilty who was exhibiting all kinds of strange behavior." She smiled, but her eyes welled. "His life was going to ruin and instead of being steadfast like my dad was with my mom, I turned my back on him. And now look . . ."

Miserable, she shook her head, not even bothering to wipe the tears that flowed down her cheeks.

"You couldn't have saved him," Paula said. Callie began to repeat what she'd said about her father's loyalty. "Your father stuck by your mother, but he couldn't save her either."

Callie blinked.

"He stood by her, that's true, but in the end, her madness was stronger than he was." Paula took Callie's hands in hers and held them tight. "Wilty's problems were bigger and stronger than you are. Grieve for him. Miss him. Regret the time you didn't have with him. But don't think that you could have saved him."

Callie nodded and grew silent, mulling over what Paula said.

"Will I be strong enough to save myself?" she wondered aloud.

"From what?"

"From going nuts and ending up like my mother."

"That is not going to happen," Paula said, with calm, firm assurance.

"You don't think tonight's coatroom episode is enough to categorize me as psychotic?"

"No, I don't!" Paula dismissed Callie's self-diagnosis with a wave of her hand. "But don't ask me, ask your shrink."

"Next time I see him," Callie said, wondering whether there would be a next time.

"Speaking of Dr. Merrick. What's the significance of the title, *Before and Again*?"

"He claims to have done a lot of work with people who believe they've lived before."

Callie and Paula had discussed the notion of past lives many times. Paula found it comforting, and maybe even a little racy, to think that when a person died her soul hovered about until it found an enticing receptacle for its next incarnation. Logically, that didn't work for Callie. She simply couldn't buy into the notion of an atmospheric holding cell for souls. If pressed, she might accept the concept of the soul leaving the body after death and traveling to heaven or hell, but once it arrived at its destination, that was it. When you died, you died.

"I've always said you were an old soul," Paula reminded Callie.

"And getting older by the minute."

They both laughed, but it was brief and tentative.

"Did he regress you?" Paula's curiosity was peaked.

"We tried it the other day for the first time." As Callie began to recount the session, the color drained from her face. "Maybe that's why the stranger ventured out of the dream," she said, more to herself than Paula. "Maybe the hypnosis triggered something."

"Like what?"

Callie's eyes were wide, but vacant, as if she were looking beyond Paula into a gray void populated with predatory specters.

"Something that would've been better left untouched," she said.

It was late when Callie got home. She dropped her keys, heard a faint beeping noise and headed straight for her answering machine. She couldn't explain it, but she was actually hoping to hear from Detective Chapin. She supposed what she wanted was for him to say his speculation about Wilty's death was just that—speculation. It was tragic, but not criminal.

There was one message. Callie pressed the PLAY button.

Callie, this is Dr. Merrick. I don't see your name in my book. I wondered if you forgot to make an appointment or there was a scheduling problem. If you're ill or if you have a conflict related to your job, please let me know. I'll make every effort to accommodate you.

When her answering machine clicked off, Callie turned her back on it. On the way home in the cab, she debated continuing therapy. Tonight's coatroom incident rattled her. While she admitted that this had been a particularly difficult day and that it was entirely possible that fatigue and grief and guilt and a myriad of other nagging emotions might have precipitated her hallucination, it had frightened her.

She busied herself emptying her backpack and sorting through her mail, employing an energy level completely inconsistent with such mundane chores.

Dr. Merrick sounded anxious to see her again.

Why not? Someone like her must look like an annuity to a shrink. A history of inexplicable night terrors. Irreconcilable differences with key family members. Problems maintaining relationships.

Ka-ching.

He was right about one thing: she did have a major conflict. Only it had nothing to do with scheduling. Callie didn't want to be hypnotized again. She wasn't even sure she wanted to be analyzed. What she wanted was for her life to be normal.

Callie shook her head, banishing all morbid thoughts about ghostly encounters and recriminations about failed relationships. She and Wilty had fun, but they weren't right for each other. They never would have made it as lifetime partners. He had issues about who he was and what his family history insisted he become. Callie had issues with whom she feared she might become. Both had pasts that got in the way.

Which was why she'd sought therapy in the first place. If she couldn't erase the past, perhaps Dr. Merrick could help her find a way of marginalizing its influence so that she could actually think about a future. He told her it would take a lot of time and work, with absolutely no guarantee of success. He also said it would demand a willingness on her part to venture into a very dark place.

Callie had seen firsthand what visiting that place could do to a person's life.

She spun around, pressed a button and erased Dr. Merrick's message. The whir of the rewinding tape sounded like a reprimand.

"I'll find another way," she declared as she took a deep breath and shooed away the shadows she felt gathering in the kitchen. "I can't go there."

Because once you go in, you don't come out.

8

The leather guest book was from Cartier, the silver sign-in pen from Tiffany. The lightly scented candles that bathed the room with a flattering golden glow were from Slatkin, the elegantly arranged flowers from Rémy. Her dress was Chanel, as were her shoes. The handkerchief she used to dab her cheek was from Frette, her hair by Fekkai. Her pearls were South Sea, her diamonds Harry Winston. The only thing faux about Carolyne Hale was her grief.

Seated in a high-backed chair with imperial allusions, she received the many mourners who came to offer their condolences with stoic grace. She bobbed her head sadly and knowingly when people spoke of Wilty's many gifts, about how handsome he was, how charming, how generous. She sniffled delicately when they rued a life of such promise cut so short. And then, she watched those same people walk over to the casket, look down at Wilty and chat among themselves about what a drunk he'd become and what a wasted, non-productive life he'd led.

Beneath her sangfroid, Carolyne seethed. No matter the quality of their relationship, Wilty was her son. He had died a violent, premature death and this was a place of mourning. Visitors were supposed to offer their respects, get in and out quickly, and keep their big mouths shut. The ones with class did. The others were placed on a list for immediate banishment to Carolyne's societal gulag. They didn't know it, but they had attended their last Hale function.

After an hour, the room was filled to near capacity. It was like a dry cocktail party, with people standing about in small clusters talking about . . . whatever. Mostly, Carolyne assumed, it was the fact that Wilty had chosen to die and in such a messy, public way.

When she could not bear the tedious burden of bereavement another second, she rose from her seat of state and made her way over to a twosome in the far corner. Peter Merrick and Guy Hoffman were probably the only ones in the room not trashing Wilty, and by inference, her.

Carolyne sat on the board of Hoffman's company, GenTec Sciences, a biotechnology concern that was involved in mapping the human genome. She had invested in GenTec several years before, just as she had invested in several other start-ups her financial advisors had brought to her attention. Not all of those companies made it past the first stage. One or two had; they'd repaid her investment, with interest. GenTec was on the brink.

Peter Merrick was a frequent escort and a sometime lover.

Several months before, she'd hosted a dinner party at which she'd introduced the two men. She knew about Merrick's interest in genetic memory; Hoffman believed he had isolated the gene that controlled memory. Carolyne thought they were a good fit. It appeared as if her instincts had been correct.

"I wanted to thank you again for coming," she said, with just the right amount of somber gratitude. "Your presence means a great deal to me."

The two men reiterated their condolences, making certain to commend her on her emotional strength and physical fortitude. Carolyne's constant need for homage was well known.

Merrick was sincerely saddened by Wilty's death. He'd known Wilty and liked him, a fact Carolyne found curious. She was fully aware of her son's ability to charm, but she never viewed him as someone with the keenness of mind to appeal to a cognoscente like Peter Merrick.

"I enjoy his wry way of looking at the world," Peter said once, when she wondered aloud what Wilty's attraction was. "He's creative, curious, and amusing."

At the time, Carolyne thought one might say the same thing about a cocker spaniel, but she kept those kinds of comments to herself. They weren't good for her image.

"I can't imagine why he would do this," Carolyne said, shaking her head and snuffling. She was being honest. She couldn't imagine what had pushed Wilty out that window. She was hoping Merrick would give her a quickie analysis.

"He must have been in terrible pain, Carolyne. Most suicides are hurting so badly, death is a relief."

As he began to explain how psychic agony overwhelmed reality in potential suicides, she spotted Harlan on the other side of the room. She wanted to know if he'd had any luck tracking down Wilty's estate lawyer.

"Would you excuse me?" she whispered, looking as pathetic as she could. Then, she turned and homed in on her attorney. She'd heard all she wanted to about Wilty's pain. She had other, more pressing, priorities.

Once she'd gone, Merrick and Hoffman returned to their original conversation. Merrick had asked Hoffman how his Mnemonic Project was coming along.

Hoffman was a rangy man with slightly stooped posture, white hair and wire-rimmed glasses magnifying tired green eyes. As he responded to Merrick's question, it appeared as if an extra wave of fatigue washed over him.

"Science moves slowly. I wish it proceeded at the rapid pace preferred by business, but it doesn't." Hoffman's benefactors were growing impatient and he was in danger of losing his funding.

"How much time do you have remaining on your patent?"

"More time than my investors have patience," he said with obvious frustration. "I'm in the midst of several research trials on p-316. If my hypothesis is correct, proper application of this protein will unleash the mnemonic gene and allow it to retrieve ancestral memories."

Hoffman's eyes glowed with the possibility of his work being validated and ultimately hailed by his peers. Peter understood. He, too, had experienced the "eureka moment."

"How about you?" Hoffman asked. His trials with rats hadn't proved conclusive yet, but he was close enough to hope that Merrick might provide a candidate for the human trials, someone who'd already indicated an acquaintance with another time.

Peter revealed he'd recently performed a successful regression. Hoffman's eyes widened.

"It was only one session, Guy. It was positive and highly encouraging, but it'll take many more of the same caliber before I can honestly declare her a reliquary of the past."

"My protein is designed to hasten the process."

"I know, but we both need to do more work before we inject this woman with a volatile chemical."

Reluctantly, Hoffman agreed. "Speaking of work," he said. "I'm going to take my leave and head on home. Lab rats are early risers."

Merrick was about to follow Hoffman out, when Callie Jamieson walked in.

Callie approached the casket slowly. She'd expected to find colleagues from the *Courier,* but it was late. They may have come and gone. Since there was no one else who knew her, she was afforded the privacy to visit Wilty alone. She snaked her way toward the niche where the casket rested on a velvet-draped bier. Just before she reached it, she paused. She was never comfortable viewing the dead. She preferred remembering them as they were in life, not lying in a box, pumped full of formaldehyde, dressed up and painted by a mortician. In this case, however, she needed all of that. She needed to see Wilty fully "prepared." That was why she had come tonight. She couldn't allow the image of him in that alley to be the way she remembered him.

When she finally summoned the courage to look at his face, she smiled. He was handsome, even in death. Obviously his eyes were closed. To Callie, that was a shame.

They were such a beautiful blue and so wonderfully expressive. So often, he'd say something and his eyes would contradict his words. Someone would engage him in a battle of words and walk away feeling as if Wilty had coldly cut him down. He had been too engrossed in the debate to catch the glint in Wilty's eye and the crinkle of a smile stifled by a man thoroughly enjoying the joust.

Despite the subtly applied blush, Callie thought his skin tone was too sallow, too flat. Wilty was so athletic, it was rare to see his cheeks without a ruddy cast. His hair was also a bit too done. The one feature that looked just as it did in life was Wilty's mouth. To Callie, that was his sexiest feature: full and lush, with a cleft in his lower lip that felt so good when they kissed. She flushed, remembering how passionate Wilty was. He loved making love. He once told her it was a relief to be alone and naked, doing something that was born of everyone's basic yearnings. Sex wasn't something one bought or learned or got a degree in or deserved more than anyone else. It was, according to him, the most common of denominators.

"I loved you," she whispered to the man in the casket. She brought her fingers to her lips, then touched his, recoiling at the cold stillness of his flesh.

What happened to you? she wanted to scream.

Tears dribbled onto her cheeks. An elderly couple approached the casket. Quickly, Callie wiped her eyes, and turned to go.

She'd intended to express her sympathies to the Widow, but Carolyne Hale was on the other side of the room, engaged in conversation with the chairman of the board of Hale Holdings.

Callie worried that it was rude to just leave, but since no one noticed her come in, and no one seemed to notice she was there, it followed that no one would notice she was gone.

She couldn't have been more wrong. Two people had watched every minute of her emotional farewell to Wilty: Peter Merrick. And Carolyne Hale.

9

The morning of Wilty's funeral, Callie was at her office by eight so she could check her phone messages and e-mails for early responses to the opening installment of her series on pill mills—"Dr. Drug: Provider or Pusher?"—which was appearing in the morning's edition.

She'd been working on this for months: a major exposé of doctors and pharmacists who doled out unnecessary prescriptions for feel-good pills. Not only did Callie explain how this scam worked, but she named names—in particular, Martin Orlando, the doctor credited with setting up the pill mill network operating within the five boroughs.

The process was simple: People went to a physician, paid for the office visit, plus a fee for the scrip. Then, the patient went to the doctor's partner in crime—in Orlando's case, the Sunshine Pharmacy run by Hakim Raju—and filled their prescriptions at a hugely inflated price.

Orlando wasn't the first doctor to abuse his privileges, but he was one of the few to work in tandem with pharmacists to help create an illicit drug-dispensing organization. It began when one patient's bad back wasn't feeling quite right and he wanted to continue with his Vicodin or, worse, OxyContin. Another patient decided life was simply better on Xanax. Since they were willing to pay whatever Orlando wanted for relief, he happily doled out scrip for refills. Those two patients told two friends who told four friends who told eight friends. And before anyone could say, "pharmacological fortune", a mini-industry was formed.

On the street, grateful addicts had even named a drug cocktail after him, "Orlando Magic," a deadly combination of OxyContin, the painkiller Lortab, Xanax and the muscle relaxant Soma.

The narcotics squad, off information provided by Callie, had rounded up most of the pharmacists and bogus doctors involved in the scheme. The only one who'd avoided capture was Martin Orlando who, for all intents and purposes, had vanished.

Future installments would deal with HMOs and how their bottom-line approach to medicine was changing the administration of health care, investigate the role of pharmaceutical companies in the escalation of painkiller addiction and, finally, would confront the public and its role as stock-buying, pill-buying enablers.

A finger-pointing series like this was expected to generate threats. Already, there were several on her voice mail from irate—albeit anonymous—doctors, all of whom loudly decried her tarnishing of their profession. None sounded particularly venal, but Callie would alert Security anyway.

After returning some other calls and accepting the congratulations of her colleagues, Callie left for the church.

Anticipating a traffic jam, she had the taxicab drop her off several blocks away on the corner of Twenty-fifth and Park. She was about to cross Park and head down when she heard someone call her name.

"Dr. Merrick," she said, surprised to run into him.

"Are you attending the service for Wilty Hale?"

She'd never mentioned the name of the man with whom she'd been having an affair, but having witnessed her emotional good-bye the previous evening and noting her presence here today, it seemed safe to assume that her ex-lover was none other than the recently departed, a fact that intrigued him.

"Sad, isn't it?" he said. "Someone so young."

She nodded as she fell into step beside him.

"By the way, did you get my message?" When an answer wasn't immediately forthcoming, he continued. "I was concerned. My receptionist told me you didn't reschedule. Is there a problem?"

Callie hastily debated her response. Should she put him off by saying, yes, she'd been in a rush, but she'd call to make another appointment? Or should she tell him the truth?

"Sort of," she replied, opting for truth.

He tilted his head to the side and furrowed his brows quizzically, as if he was looking through a microscope at an unidentified organism.

"I'm not sure I want to continue therapy." She said it quickly, as if even a second's hesitation would erase her resolve.

"The hypnosis upset you, didn't it?"

She stopped and faced him. "Yes, it did." So did my recent encounters with a ghost.

She expected him to grill her about what the aftereffects had been and to make every attempt to reassure her that the next time would be better. Instead, he resumed his stroll down Park Avenue.

From the corner of her eye, she studied his profile, trying to read his thoughts.

He was a tall, gym-trim man of fifty or so with a thick, well-groomed mustache and closely cropped hair that implied an insistence on neatness. His forehead, wide and subtly lined, described a man who navigated his life along strict, carefully plotted paths. There were no wrinkles, no laugh lines, nothing that even hinted at a playful, impetuous side. Even his eyes, a vibrant blue that bore the color of delphiniums, conveyed no more warmth than a girder of steel. Peter Merrick's cover was attractive, but impenetrable.

"I'm sorry," she said suddenly, feeling like a six-year-old fearful of displeasing her father.

He turned and offered her a smile that teetered between patronizing and sincere.

"So am I, Callie, because I think the reason the hypnosis upset you is that it worked. It helped open your mind and you found that disturbing."

His voice was quiet and even. Callie found it intimidating nonetheless. Especially when the thought crossed her mind that he might be able to hypnotize her right there on the street. She blinked her eyes hard and shook her head, willing away whatever spell he might have tried to cast.

"I didn't like the way it made me feel," she said bluntly.

She decided that with someone capable of telepathic manipulation, a show of strength was essential. She didn't want him to know how vulnerable she felt. Nor did she intend to tell him about the gray stranger accosting her in a public place.

"It's your decision, of course, but I don't think you should stop treatment."

They were nearly at the church. Callie saw Brad Herring and Harold Josephs standing on the side of the entrance, about to go in. If she hurried, she could catch up to them and hide in the familiarity of their company, but she didn't. She couldn't let this matter hang in the air.

"Why not?" she said, sounding more peevish than she intended.

Merrick looked at her, full of sympathy. She wondered if it was for the nightmares and emotional anguish she suffered in the past or the terrors he knew she would experience in the future without his help.

"First of all, you came to me with other problems that still need to be dealt with. Also, because the dreams will continue." He spoke with quiet conviction. "And they will get worse."

"Even so," Callie muttered, utterly unsettled.

"May I make a suggestion?"

"Yes."

"Why don't we continue talk therapy and leave off the hypnosis until you've grown more comfortable with the idea of it? There is much that can be accomplished simply by talking, you know."

Callie didn't wish to be rude, but after six months of chatter she didn't feel appreciably better—about herself or her breakup with Wilty. And after her last session, she didn't believe hypnosis would do anything except exacerbate her fears and accelerate her nightmares.

"I'll think about it," she said, in a way she hoped didn't sound like a brush off.

"Please do." His smile was quick. His "good afternoon" was quicker.

Callie suddenly found herself stranded on a busy corner.

"Was that guy bothering you?"

The voice was vaguely familiar. Standing alongside her was Detective Ezra Chapin. She almost didn't recognize him. He was wearing a suit, a tie and a genuine look of concern.

"No. Not really."

He stared at her, waiting for some sort of explanation.

"We were talking about a possible project," she said, finally. "He'd like to go forward with it. I'm not interested."

A slow, knowing smile ambled across his mouth. "Some guys just don't take rejection well."

Callie was willing to bet he was one of those guys. "To what do I owe the unexpected pleasure of your company?"

"Wilty Hale." The light changed and they both crossed the street. "I thought it might be a good idea to scope out the crowd at his funeral. See who's there, who isn't, who cries, who doesn't. That kind of thing."

Callie was about to ask him why a homicide detective was being so compulsive in his follow-up for a suicide when he said, "I read your piece in this morning's paper. It was damn good."

"You sound surprised."

"Hey, I'm a longtime fan."

"Yeah, right."

"Okay, so I did a quick search on Yahoo and downloaded some of your stuff. The series you did on hotel thefts was actually another gutsy piece of detective work."

A ring of thieves had conscripted an army of hotel service staff to rob unwitting tourists. Over a period of several months, Callie checked into various New York hotels pretending to be a Midwestern innocent in town on business. She'd act flustered when trying to extricate money from her wallet, allowing the bellman or room service waiter to see a large stash of bills. She'd leave credit cards out on a dresser, alongside a computer and perhaps some jewelry. Then, she'd drop her key off and go out, leaving her room vacant and vulnerable. She was robbed in two of the hotels. In a third, someone attempted to break into her room while she was in it. Callie pressed the panic button given to her by the police. The man was arrested, named names, and the ring was broken.

"This story isn't going to get you the pats on the back that one did, you know."

Callie looked at him quizzically.

"I'm sure the Chamber of Commerce and the entire hotel industry hailed you as some kind of savior. Not to mention the thousands of tourists whose hard-earned vacation money you saved."

Callie couldn't tell whether he was mocking her or warning her. "People were grateful that gang was caught."

"No one's going to be grateful to you for exposing this scam. The doctors and pharmacists are going to hate you for taking away their profits. The addicts are going to hate you for stopping the flow of their happy pills. And Orlando, who could be facing up to thirty years in prison, is going to want your head on a platter."

"That's just too damn bad!" Callie said, her dander up and flying. "I hate knowing that people who are supposed to be caregivers only care about lining their pockets."

He held up his hands. "Whoa! I'm on your side."

Callie took a breath and emotionally regrouped. "I believe in the power of the press," she said simply. "If it can shine a light on activities that thrive in the darkness of indifference, it should."

"I wholeheartedly agree." He nodded and tipped his head respectfully. "What gave you the idea for this series?"

"There were too many deaths being reported that involved prescription painkillers, especially OxyContin."

"That's one dangerous pill."

"Handed out like candy by dangerous men like Martin Orlando."

"How'd you get onto him?"

"I kept hearing his name, so I went to see him. I told him I had neck spasms. He gave me a prescription for Percocet. I went back three times for refill scrips. He wrote them out without ever even examining me."

"You should have your head examined for putting yourself in harm's way like that."

Callie bristled. That sounded a lot like "don't worry your pretty little head about it."

"How do you think investigative reporters get their stories? Do you think we make it up or phone it in? We work it. Same as you."

He tilted his head and studied her. She was passionate about her work. He liked that. "You're a regular Crusader Rabbit, aren't you?"

"Since when is that a bad thing?"

"It's not," he said, backing off. "I'm sorry. I didn't mean to sound like I was putting you down."

He actually sounded sincere. It was a nice change.

"Apology accepted."

"Good. Then you won't mind if I tag along with you," Chapin said as they approached the church. "Makes me look less conspicuous. Know what I mean?"

"Why do I suddenly feel used and abused?"

Chapin smiled. "Used maybe. Abused? Not my style!"

It was a magnificent day, with the sun gloriously yellow against an azure sky, a day far more suited to a Van Gogh palette than the steady stream of black that poured into the old Calvary Episcopal Church. There were police barricades set up at both ends of Twentieth Street to allow the family privacy upon their arrival. Out front, half a dozen mounted police guarded the sidewalk along Park Avenue South. More barricades were set up across the street to keep the crowds corralled and separated from the hundreds of mourners who were expected to pay their last respects to Wilton Colfax Hale.

Callie and Ezra made their way inside slowly, both of them slightly intimidated by the size and the celebrity of the crowd. There were politicians from both sides of the aisle: Senators from New York, Ohio, Pennsylvania, California, New Jersey and Tennessee, as well as prominent Representatives from half a dozen states. Callie identified several state legislators, a number of well-known writers—including one or two who owed their careers to Wilty's early sponsorship—stars from television and the movies, a large contingent from the theater, and an impressive percentage of the *Forbes* 400.

"I've never seen so many boldfaced names in one place," Callie whispered as they entered the sanctuary.

"It's the end of an era," Ezra supposed as he and Callie paused in silent respect.

At the foot of the altar, a mahogany casket stood blanketed in a black velvet pall laden with a spray of lilies that was gently bound with a purple ribbon. Tall, brass torchères flanked the coffin, their ivory candles illustrious guardians of Wilty Hale's remains. Behind the bier, a dozen large bouquets of white gladioli stood like a prince's regiment, stiff and at attention. Two young boys in white robes smartly collared in black, went about the task of readying the altar and the podium for the service. They checked and double-checked their work. This was a funeral for a Hale; the bishop of the diocese would conduct the mass.

Callie and Ezra found seats in a pew midway down the aisle.

Somber-faced ushers handed out programs.

"There must be five hundred people here."

"It's the power of the Hale name." Ezra's eyes roved the hall slowly and deliberately, taking careful note of who was there. "How many do you think are here for Wilty? Personally, that is."

Callie's eyes were riveted on the casket, her mood sober. "Not a lot," she said with obvious sadness.

She scanned the mourners, then nodded to a section in front of them on their left where a large, hybrid group of thirty-somethings had congregated, downtowners, easily identified by their edgy, avant garde attire. A few uptown compatriots Callie recognized had chosen to honor their late friend by seating themselves in that section rather than across the aisle where the rest of their social set was encamped. They hugged each other and spoke in soft, measured tones about the man who was their common denominator, all of them truly grief stricken.

"Those are Wilty's friends. They're the only ones here who really feel a loss from his death."

"Other than you," Ezra said.

Callie agreed. "Other than me."

There were plenty of glum expressions and sad eyes spread throughout the church, but Callie guessed that while most of the attendees regretted Wilty's passing and, over the past several days had commented many times about what a tragedy this was, to them, Wilty was a cliché—the proverbial "young man who had everything to live for." Wilty's friends knew the man, what he was living with, what he'd be giving up if he exited this life, and what he'd be leaving behind.

Callie used to know all those things. But Wilty had made new friends and a new life for himself.

"Why do you think he did it?" Ezra asked, watching her carefully.

She shook her head. "I wish I knew. What do you think?"

"Are you reporting on the funeral or are you here in a nonprofessional capacity?"

"You didn't answer my question."

He didn't even bother to look at her.

"I don't have an answer. When I do, I'll let you know."

"Fine." Callie wondered whether he worked at being this disagreeable or if it came naturally. She was sorry she let him piggyback on her invitation.

Behind them, the large wooden doors closed and the rich, full tones of the organ overwhelmed the stately hall with a sound so powerful it was almost palpable. As the music swelled, Callie felt as if she could reach out and grab each note as it passed by her. Her eyes closed and she let the rumbling vibrato of the bass sweep over her. Something deep inside of her trembled. She swayed.

Ezra felt her body fall onto his. Quickly, he slid his arm around her waist to steady her. It looked as if she was in a faint. He fanned her with his program. Her eyelids fluttered, then snapped open.

"Are you all right?"

She was still slightly out of it. She was looking at him, but she was looking beyond him as well.

"I feel odd." Her voice sounded cottony, as if she were in a stupor. "Misplaced, kind of."

"Take a deep breath. It'll pass."

Callie breathed deeply, but again, seemed to wander off. Her eyes were glazed and her head listed to the side, as if she were straining to hear every note, every nuance of the music being piped into the large sanctuary.

"They played this at E.W. Hale's funeral service," she said quietly. "It's Beethoven's *March on the Death of a Hero,* adapted from one of his piano sonatas."

Ezra stared at her. Her voice sounded like a recording. "How'd you know that?"

Callie turned to face him, blinking as if still trying to regain focus. "I don't know." She seemed bewildered.

Ezra, a history buff, had read a couple of biographies on E.W. Hale, but he couldn't recall seeing anything about the music played at his funeral. Even if he had, something that obscure would never stick in his mind. He opened his program to see if perhaps that was where she'd picked up this little informational gem. The first musical interlude was indeed credited to Beethoven, but there was no title given and no mention of the piece having been played for Wilty's great-great-grandfather.

"No wonder you're such a good reporter. With research trivia like that stored in your memory bank, you should go on *Jeopardy!* You'd make a fortune."

His tone was light, but he felt as if he were tiptoeing through a mine field. Worse, Callie looked like she was right there with him, confused and afraid.

Peter Merrick had waited for Callie to enter the church before taking his seat. Rather than appear conspicuous, he'd taken cover within a small group of mourners at the front who chatted quietly in the aisle adjacent to the family pew. He'd positioned himself so he could keep his eyes fixed on the door. He didn't want to miss her. When she finally made her entrance, he watched carefully while she located a vacancy and settled into a pew. He wondered who her companion was.

The large crowd took its time filling the sanctuary, giving Merrick ample opportunity to observe Callie and her friend. They studied the program, gawked at the various celebrities present and spoke amiably, but not intimately.

He could be a colleague from the *Courier,* Merrick thought.

When the time came to be seated, Merrick encouraged the others to slide into the pew ahead of him, saving the aisle seat for himself. While the inevitable stragglers scurried to find a place to sit, Merrick stole a quick glance in Callie's direction to reassure himself that she hadn't moved. He needed to know where she was, because he needed to know whether what he'd said to her on the street had had an effect. If his prediction of escalating night terrors had upset her, she'd be fidgety, impatient, disconnected from what was going on around her. That would be good. If, however, she appeared calm, that would mean she'd discounted his dark auguries and was resolute in her decision not to continue therapy. That would not be good.

A door behind the altar opened. Carolyne Hale, her face

hidden behind a black chiffon veil, supported by a priest
and her lawyer, Harlan Whiteside, was ushered to her seat.
Once she'd been settled and the bishop had mounted the
altar, the throaty tones of the organ and the resonant knell
of chimes signaled the beginning of the service.

Merrick tried to keep his eyes front and to maintain a
facade of solemn concentration, but it proved impossible.
When he couldn't stand the suspense any longer, he succumbed to temptation and turned around. Just as he did,
Callie looked as if she grew faint. Merrick was desperate
to know why.

The young man next to her cradled Callie and fanned
her with a program. She appeared somewhat disoriented
when she opened her eyes, yet *he* seemed able to comfort
her.

The other day, Callie had told him she didn't have a
boyfriend. Was she lying or was this relationship too new
for her to label him as such? Either way, Merrick wasn't
happy. One of the keys to the success of this kind of therapy was dependency on the therapist. The more complete
the dependency, the better. A boyfriend became the third
wheel, someone else for the patient to talk to and confide
in. Which made a boyfriend a threat.

The service was short and strictly orchestrated, devoid of
any warmth or personality. The bishop led the congregation
through the various rites that attended this solemn passage,
as well as offering the only eulogy, which was flattering,
but perfunctory. The choir performed a selection of musical
tributes. The assembled mass joined in the singing of whatever hymns were so designated in the program. The names
of the honorary pallbearers were read—the Hale Holdings
board, Harlan Whiteside, and Wilty's valet—and precisely
forty-five minutes after the organ intoned the onset of the
service, it chimed the beginning of the recessional.

Ever since her swoon, Ezra had been keeping an eye on
Callie. While she insisted she was all right, the stoop of her
shoulders and the ashen cast of her complexion said oth-

erwise. She seemed to be lost in the middle distance, wandering around a faraway place that was somehow related to the day's events.

As Wilty's coffin made its way up the aisle, he could feel her body stiffen. Out of the corner of his eye, he saw tears dampening her cheeks. Both reactions were consistent with the stark realization that someone you loved was gone. Nonetheless, Ezra couldn't shake the feeling that something else, something outside of this death and this funeral, had been tossed into Callie's emotional mix.

Slowly, the cortege made its way toward the church doors.

First, the casket. As it passed, some of Wilty's friends added their own floral tributes by tossing roses on top of the elegantly tied spray of lilies.

As it moved toward Callie, she wept and gripped the pew in front of her. Ezra took the liberty of sliding his arm around her waist, just in case. She must have been afraid of fainting because she didn't object to the gesture.

Following the casket, and marching two by two, came the stone-faced pallbearers; only Arthur, Wilty's valet, showed signs of honest mourning.

Then the bishop, four priests and various other church officiants, led by the two altar boys who struggled to hold gargantuan golden crosses aloft.

And finally, there was Carolyne Hale. She walked several paces behind and alone, emphasizing her status as the sole surviving Hale. Her steps were slow and measured, her posture regal, her head bravely held high. In her gloved hands, she carried a single calla lily and an old family Bible. Her face was heavily veiled, leaving people to guess at the state of her emotions. The consensus was that she was grief stricken and utterly heartbroken. How could she not be, after all?

On a scale of one to ten, Ezra, who'd seen her shed a tear or two—and no more than that—when she viewed her son's body at the morgue, placed her desolation at about a four.

As she approached their row, a brief burst of sunlight from the front door sneaked past her veil and illuminated her face. In that instant, Ezra caught her looking at him and Callie. Her eyes turned away quickly, but he had seen it: annoyance bordering on anger. Ezra couldn't help but wonder why.

Callie and Ezra waited for their pew to empty, then filed out of the church. As they stepped into the light and Ezra took a good hard look at the tall blonde next to him, he suggested they go for a cup of coffee.

"Frankly, you don't look so swell," he said.

"Thanks for sharing."

"I didn't mean it that way. I just thought you might like to grab a bite before heading back to the paper." Her face was still frozen in a look of distaste. "Come on, let me buy you a sandwich or a bowl of soup or a corn muffin. Something. It's my way of thanking you for letting me slide in on your coattails."

Callie, who was still a little embarrassed by her odd reaction to the service, threw her hands up in a gesture of surrender. Delighted by her capitulation, Ezra smiled, grabbed her arm and steered her through the crush of people.

From the church steps, Peter Merrick watched them go.

"Peter. Have you had lunch?" Guy Hoffman had come up alongside Merrick, who couldn't take his eyes off Callie. "Peter?"

"Good idea," Merrick said, his jaw set. "It'll give me a chance to learn more about your experiments."

Carolyne Hale spotted them as her limousine turned the corner and followed the hearse uptown on its way to the cemetery. As soon as she was far enough away so that no one could observe her actions, she reached into her purse, took out her cell phone and speed-dialed a number. It was answered on the first ring.

"What?"

"The blonde who was at the wake last night just left the church with one of the detectives assigned to Wilty's case. Find out who she is."

10

Six blocks north was The Globe, a large restaurant that catered to office workers in the neighborhood. The noon rush was waning, so instead of having to sit at a small table in the middle of the room, Callie and Ezra were ushered to a spacious booth toward the back. He ordered a hamburger and a side of fries. Callie opted for a salad.

When the waitress left, Ezra shed his jacket, undid his tie and opened the top button of his shirt with such exaggerated relief, one would have thought his clothing was made of ten-gauge steel. He rested his arms on the table, leaned toward Callie, smiled charmingly and said, "By the way, you never answered my question. Was your presence at the funeral solely personal, or are you covering the story for the *Courier*?"

"Both." Callie, imitating his pose, but leaving off the charm, rested her arms on the table and leaned toward him. "You never answered my question about why you think Wilty killed himself."

Ezra sat back. His smile was gone. "Wilty Hale was murdered," he said, plain out.

Callie felt the breath go out of her. "No!"

"I spoke to the Crime Scene Unit this morning. The preliminary tox screens came back from the lab. Not only did Wilty have enough vodka in him to float a barge, but his blood was loaded with chemicals, including barbiturates like Seconal."

"Was Wilty dead before the fall?"

Callie hoped he was. Then, his landing would have been painless. And he wouldn't have had any second guesses on the way down, or moments of unqualified, unimaginable terror.

"That'll be determined by the autopsy. What the toxicity levels tell us is that there's no way this guy walked from his library to the kitchen, climbed out onto the fire escape and played Greg Louganis. Someone had to help him."

Callie's stomach did its own dive.

"Drag him, actually," Ezra continued. "Vodka and Seconal isn't exactly an energy drink."

They both fell silent as the image of a semiconscious young man being dragged to a window and pushed over a fire escape railing to a horrible, bone-crushing death settled over them like a pall. Callie closed her eyes and rubbed her forehead as if a fingertip massage could erase the grisly scene.

Ezra leaned in again and lowered his voice. "Look, I didn't mean to spring this on you, but you were going to find out sooner or later. I thought, considering your relationship with him and all, I'd give you a heads up."

"I'm okay," she lied. Her heart felt weighted down by sadness and an inexplicable sense of guilt. "I just can't imagine someone drugging someone, then throwing him out the window like a scrap of garbage."

Ezra didn't want to tell her this wasn't the first time he'd covered a case like this, nor did he have any illusion that it might be the last.

"Do you have any leads?"

"Not yet, but Alvarez is back at the house working on it even as we speak."

Their lunch came. Ezra dug into his burger. Callie picked at her salad.

"Come on," he urged. "Eat up. If the city was paying, I wouldn't care what you ate, but this meal's on me."

She forced herself to find something appealing in the large vegetable collage.

"What else did CSU come up with?"

Ezra should have shut this conversation down, but he didn't. Callie Jamieson was a sharp woman with a nose for news. In a sense, they were both working the same case. Feeding her a tidbit now just might bring him a chunky lead later on.

"Whoever did Wilty in was looking for something."

"Like what?"

"We don't know, but according to the CSU lead investigator, someone rummaged through Wilty's drawers."

"Then why couldn't robbery be the motive?"

"There was no forced entry, which means Wilty probably knew his killer. His valet said nothing of any significant value was missing. Plus, this was premeditated. It's not exactly usual to visit a friend with a stash of Seconal in your pocket."

"Was the apartment ransacked?"

"Nope. The uniforms said it was beyond neat."

Callie nodded and smiled. "That's so Wilty."

"In what way?"

"He was compulsive about appearances." She riffled through images of Wilty at some of the parties they'd attended. "No matter how drunk he got, he never loosened his tie or had a hair out of place."

"We'd heard that," Ezra confessed. "That's why the tech on the case drew the conclusion she did. According to her, while the contents of his closets and dressers weren't tossed, his desk and bureau drawers were disturbed, as if someone had been on a hunt.

"Also, she said that in the library, there were a dozen or so books that were upside down or somehow out of order. Anal compulsives don't have messy drawers and they don't allow their bookshelves to become disorganized. Take it from someone who knows."

Callie pushed some lettuce around on her plate and considered that.

"Yet, instead of leaving the books on the floor, the killer put them back on the shelves. Which means whoever it was knew Wilty well enough to know how fussy he was. And that if there was a mess, it wouldn't look like suicide."

Ezra was impressed. "Excellent, my dear Watson."

The killer had also placed Wilty's slippers neatly on the floor in front of the window from which he presumably leaped, but Ezra kept that to himself. While he was secretly astounded by the attempted thoroughness of whoever it was that pushed Wilty Hale out that window, it was that kind of small, yet overreaching mistake that often provided the one piece of evidence that insured capture and conviction.

"So," Ezra said, leaning back and smiling slyly, "I've shown you mine, now you have to show me yours."

"What?" This guy changed subjects the way skiers avoided each other on the steeps, sharply zigging wherever someone wasn't.

"Are you going to be the pen on this case?"

"Yes. And . . . I'm not sure."

"That's clear."

"I've been assigned a series on the Hales," she said, patiently trying to disavow him of his obvious conclusion that she was an airhead. "I'm not certain whether or not I'll be covering the day to day details of Wilty's death. The assignments come off two separate desks."

"Hell! They can't break this team up," he said, appearing crestfallen. "Not after we've built up such a wonderful rapport."

Team. Rapport. Was he on the same planet? "You felt it too?"

He chuckled at her sarcasm, but his amber eyes remained fixed. "So, what's your angle on your Hale story?"

"They're cursed." That wiped the supercilious grin off his face.

"I beg your pardon."

She explained about the truncated lives of E.W. Hale's male descendants. "Wilty's uncle was in his thirties when he died. So was his father."

"I think I read about him. Didn't he have his head sliced off by a propeller?"

Callie pushed her salad plate away. Her appetite was gone for good.

"What about the uncle? How'd he die?"

"He was electrocuted."

"Nice. Anyone charged with either of those two crimes?"

Callie shook her head. "After extensive investigations, both were ultimately listed as accidents."

"Bullshit! They're just cases that haven't been solved yet." His entire face had hardened.

"Why couldn't they simply be bizarre accidents?"

"Most cases that remain unsolved are those that were abandoned because of lack of funds or lack of commitment."

"And not because of insufficient evidence?"

Ezra leaned forward, his expression intense. "Insufficient evidence just means the proof hasn't been found yet."

Callie was dying to know why he'd gotten so hot under the collar, but before she could pursue it, he zigged. Again.

"Who do you think put the hex on the Hales?"

She decided to stop trying to figure him out and just go with it.

"A lot of wild rumors swirled around E.W. Hale during his lifetime and are still whispered about today. I guess the first step is to either verify or debunk those rumors."

Callie enumerated the various rumors. Some were so outlandish as to seem totally ridiculous: E.W. Hale was gay and someone else had fathered his children; he was black or Jewish and had successfully managed to pass in WASP society; he had a harem of mistresses and each of his four children was mothered by a different woman.

Other rumors were more serious: he manipulated bankruptcies to buy up companies and cheated everyone who ever partnered with him—including his brothers—in order to gain sole control of the business. The most serious was that he killed his first wife.

Callie believed that hidden somewhere amidst those rumors were the seeds of a curse that just might have killed Wilty.

"And the second step?"

"To determine whether any of it can be tracked from one death to another."

"Want a piece of advice?"

"No."

"Because I'm such a nice guy, I'm going to give it to you anyway." His voice was light, but he wasn't smiling. "Don't waste your time sifting through esoteric, pseudo-psychological, will-sound-good-in-a-sound-bite type crap."

"I had no intention of doing any such thing," she snapped.

"I'm just trying to give you the benefit of my vast experience."

"Bless you." She gave him a sarcastic salaam, then glared at him. "This may be hard for you to comprehend, Detective Chapin, but I'm good at what I do. I don't need you telling me how to write a story or research a story. So thanks, but no thanks."

Unfazed, he met the heat of her anger with the cool confidence that what he was saying was the unassailable truth: "Most great fortunes begin with a crime."

Callie spent the rest of the afternoon at the library, reading up on Emmet Wilton Hale. And thinking about Wilty.

She still couldn't wrap her brain around the fact that he was murdered. Neither could she comprehend the mind-set of the person who would have committed such a crime. Why not kill him in his apartment and be done with it? Perhaps part of the thrill of the crime was humiliating Wilty. What other reason could there have been for insisting that his body be on public display?

And what was the murderer looking for? Wilty never kept large amounts of cash at home. Since it appeared that his murderer was acquainted with at least some of Wilty's habits, he or she would have known that. Also, while Callie was certain he had a small safe, she was just as certain it was well hidden and held nothing more valuable than a few cuff links and his collection of watches. The only other items worth robbing would be Wilty's art or antiques, and there was no way a thief was climbing down nineteen stories of fire escape with a sack of priceless antiques on his back and oil paintings under his arm.

As for enemies, Wilty wasn't without them—it was hard to be as rich as he was and not ruffle a few feathers—but Callie couldn't believe any of their grievances had risen to a murderous pitch.

Then again, who knew what trouble he'd gotten himself into since she last saw him?

A little before five, Callie admitted she was too distracted by the present to effectively research the past. She selected several biographies and checked them out. She figured when she got home, had a cup of tea and got into comfortable clothes, she'd find it easier to delve into the life of the infamous E.W. Hale.

She thought wrong.

When she walked into her building, her doorman handed her a package. The name of the sender was Wilty Hale.

She closed her door, raced to the kitchen, cut through the packing tape and ripped into the box.

There was a note written on Wilty's personal stationery and three claret leather journals. Callie opened one and was confronted by page after page of penmanship distinguished by old-fashioned flourishes and letters emboldened by the pressure of the hand against the page. The paper had yellowed slightly, but the ink remained black, so the words were clear, if a bit difficult to read.

Callie looked at the dates of the diaries: 1888, 1896, 1902. The name engraved on the fronts of all three was Emmet Wilton Hale.

Confused, she reached for Wilty's note. As she lifted it out of the box, she could feel the tears gathering in her eyes. The postmark on the package said it had been sent the morning of the day he died. Her hand shook as she removed the note from the envelope.

Dear Callie,

About six months ago, in the midst of what was obviously a premature mid-life crisis, I discovered something that drew me into a project of personal discovery. Basically, it has to do with who E.W. Hale was and what that makes me.

I tried to work this out on my own, but I'm afraid I might have wandered too deep into the forest. In a flash of modesty, I decided it might be a good thing to have an objective eye make certain there are actually trees in that forest. You always had a greater sense of clarity than I had. You wouldn't be affected by the outcome. And at the end of the day, I don't think you'd care whether I am who we thought I was, or not. The fact that you're a big time investigative reporter doesn't hurt either.

These journals were among E.W. Hale's personal papers. At some point they were separated from the others up at Long House. I don't know why, but my gut says that's important. There was another diary, one that probably explains everything, but naturally, it's still MIA.

I know none of this makes sense, but when I see you, I'll spell it all out for you. So, take time to read and absorb. (And to dismiss all the really good reasons you have to tell me to take my diaries and my dilemma and get lost.) I need your help, Callie. And I miss you terribly. Speak to you soon.

Love, Wilty.

Callie stared at the note.

It has to do with who E.W. Hale was and what that makes me.

She rebelled against the thought that invaded her brain. Chapin had warned her. Was he right? Did the curse on the Hales begin with a crime?

If so, what the hell did E.W. Hale do?

11

"I have something that might interest you," Callie said, approaching Ezra's desk.

"I'll just bet you do," Alvarez mumbled.

Callie ignored him.

Ezra noticed how tired she looked, also that she was wound pretty tight. He rose to greet her and offered her a seat. She declined.

"Not here."

"Okay. Follow me." He stood and escorted her to one of the interview rooms, knowing Alvarez would follow and watch through the one-way mirror.

When they were settled, Callie opened her backpack, lifted out several leather bound journals, a torn piece of brown wrapping paper and an envelope. She placed them on the table in front of Ezra.

"These were delivered yesterday," she said, handing him the piece of wrapping paper with the postmark on it. "The package was mailed the day Wilty was murdered."

Ezra was appropriately stunned. He examined the postmark and the return address, then looked at the claret leather diaries.

"What are these?"

"Some of E.W. Hale's diaries."

Ezra was a dedicated detective. Every case he worked was important because each one started with an unnecessary death. He'd started out thinking Wilty's was no different, but these diaries underlined the fact that it was. This corpse's great-great-grandfather was E.W. Hale, one of America's titans.

"Why did Wilty send them to you?"

She handed him the note. He read it slowly. Then he read it again.

"CSU said the killer was looking for something. Maybe it's the fourth diary. The one Wilty said was missing."

That sounded plausible, but Ezra's experience said there was more to this case than finding a diary. Assuming that Callie's initial premise was correct and E.W. Hale had a secret, the likelihood was that Wilty knew the secret; diary or no diary, the killer felt the need to eliminate him. Whatever the secret was, it was powerful.

"What did he mean, 'It has to do with who E.W. Hale was and what that makes me'?"

"I'm not sure. I read all three journals, twice, and still can't figure it out. But," Callie said, with almost palpable reluctance, "I'm beginning to buy into your theory about fortunes beginning with crimes."

Ezra flashed her an aha! smile. "The old man offed his wife, right?"

"That is certainly a crime, but I don't think it's *the* crime. First of all, Hale's fortune was well established by the time she died. And second, while there was a great deal of speculation about Winifred Hale's medical treatment, it was all out in the public. Nothing was hidden."

Callie explained that one theory had been that E.W. instructed Winifred's doctors to withhold certain treatments. Others believed he out-and-out poisoned her. He insisted she died of severe asthma complicated by alcoholism. Since both Winifred's asthma and excessive drinking were well known, Hale's accounting was accepted.

"He could have exacerbated the situation, though," Ezra said, thinking out loud. "An inappropriate mix of medication. An overdose of something. Negligence."

"The only ones who'd know for certain would have been

Winifred's doctors, who hid behind doctor-patient confidentiality."

"And E.W. Hale."

"True, but this is the 1902 diary," she said, pointing to one of the journals, "and there's no confession in it. If anything, his writings substantiate the stories about her breathing problems."

"Okay, if he didn't kill the missus, what do you think he did that would have put a hundred-year hex on him and his?"

Callie pointed to the diary marked 1888. "I don't know what the crime was or where it was committed, but I think I've narrowed down the when."

Ezra's amber eyes glinted with admiration and amusement. "Crusader Rabbit. Nancy Drew. There's no end to your talent, is there?"

Callie rolled her eyes, but since there had been an undertone of actual respect in that last gibe, she let it go.

"The reason most of those rumors surrounding E.W. Hale survived was because from day one, anyone who'd ever investigated E.W. Hale ultimately came away feeling that old E.W. wasn't who he seemed to be.

"The man would disappear for months at a time. No one knew where he went, what he did, or whom he was with. The conclusion was unanimous and obvious: E.W. Hale had a secret life."

"Any theories about what kind of secret life he led?"

"Not really, but there is one period of time, from 1859 to 1864, when for all intents and purposes, Emmet Hale went missing."

"The Civil War was on. Maybe he was a soldier for the South and wanted to hide that treasonous fact from his Northern family. He was nineteen. He could've gotten caught up in the passion that always surrounds a war."

"E.W. Hale never struck me as the altruistic type."

Ezra had read enough about the man to agree. E.W. Hale's main concern was to make as much money as he could and to wield as much power as his wealth afforded him.

"Was that the only time he disappeared?"

"He'd take off for a couple of months here, a couple of weeks there."

"He started out as a peddler. They made their money traveling from town to town. Long absences weren't unusual."

Callie found it interesting that he knew anything about E.W. Hale.

"That would account for the years before 1859. After 1864, there were also times when he left home on business, but those trips were well documented. It's those five years in between that are a mystery."

"What's your best guess?"

"I don't have one. All I know is that when he returned to Stroudsburg, Pennsylvania, in 1864, he was no longer a peddler. And he was no longer poor."

Ezra was fascinated. Questions without answers always got under his skin. He looked at Wilty's note, then opened the diary and leafed through it.

"What did you find in here that makes you think he committed some kind of crime during his absence?"

"I marked several key passages. Do you have time to go over them?"

"I was supposed to meet Prince Charles for breakfast, but he'll understand."

She swallowed a smile as she sought the page she wanted.

I found my way back to the place with minimum difficulty, but returning to a former time will prove impossible, I fear. So much has changed. Skeletons remain where once there was flesh, silent screams where once there was laughter.

I journeyed here alone, as I had so many times before. This time I carry a burden far weightier than my pack had ever been, yet I dare not com-

*plain for I deserve this Punishment. And so much
more.*

"He wrote this in March of 1888."

"The year of the Great Blizzard."

"Yes. Evidently, he was marooned in some rickety cabin during the worst of it. If you read his account, he's lucky to have survived at all."

She showed Ezra several other passages, intrigued by the intensity of his interest.

*I cannot get warm. My teeth will not cease their
chattering and my vision seems bleached. I wandered blindly, my compass stymied by the volu-
minous heaps of snow that fell unabated from the
Sky.*

*It began shortly after I arrived and strength-
ened quickly. I tried to make it back to town before
I too became another morsel in its beastly jaw, but
I had lingered too long in the past to effect my
own rescue.*

"He and his horse took refuge, but the horse bolted soon after. Fortunately, Hale had a pack stocked with a candle, matches, and a knife. Since he thought he'd only be gone for the afternoon, he only had enough food for a snack. He was snowed in for three whole days."

Ezra had heard about the Blizzard of 1888, but he'd never read a personal account of it. He tried to imagine being confined to a cabin for days, drinking melted ice, nibbling birdlike portions of bread and cheese, all the while reliving his sins and paying penance for his mistakes. It sounded like a situation more suited to a monk than a mogul.

"You have to tip your hat to the guy for his fortitude."

"He referred to his ordeal as his 'Exile in the Wilderness.' "

"What was he doing wherever he was?"

Callie allowed E.W. Hale to answer Ezra's question.

I came to this place in search of the Blessings and despite what has happened to me here, despite the cold shoulders of those I once considered warm hearted, I shall continue to seek them out, because I believe it was God's Will that I come to this place at this time. I needed to be brought near to death so that I might appreciate life. I needed to confront my wrong doings so that I might come out on the other side a better man.

I'm thankful for the experience and hereby dedicate myself to finding the Blessings, no matter what it takes. For it is through them that I hope to find Faith, as well as the Truth.

"Faith?" Ezra groaned, dismissing this last entry as an I-was-tested-and-found-religion exultation.

"He's talking about a woman." Callie told him Faith was mentioned in another diary, then continued. "I figure E.W. Hale lived wherever this was. He worked there, made friends there, established a life there and met a woman there, a woman he'd loved and left. His abandonment of one of their daughters didn't sit well with the townsfolk."

Ezra reread the pages of this particular entry. Something terrible had happened in this place. Hale referred to an Apocalypse. He spoke of deserving Punishment and the need to search for Blessings and find Faith. But what could he have done that would have caused enough devastation to warrant an entire town's hostility?

"What does any of this have to do with Wilty's death?"

"The most obvious answer is money. Wilty said he wanted my help because I wouldn't be affected by the outcome. Anyone close to Wilty would be, which is why he went to an outsider for help."

"What did he want you to do?"

"He never got the chance to tell me, but since he mentioned my being a reporter, my guess is he wanted me to employ my investigative skills to help him dig around in E.W. Hale's life."

"To find what?"

Callie shrugged. "For all I know, he also wanted to figure out why the Hales have had a hundred-year run of bad luck. I don't know, but I'm going to treat it like I would any other story and see where it takes me."

Ezra tapped his finger on the table as he considered the various routes an investigation like that might take.

"You think these diaries and Wilty's note indicate some kind of curse."

"If it looks like a curse and sounds like a curse and feels like a curse, it's not a duck," she said, reaching across the table to retrieve the diaries and the note.

"What're you doing?" Ezra slapped his hand down on the journals, preventing Callie from picking them up.

"What does it look like I'm doing?"

"These are now part of a police investigation. They stay here."

Gritting her teeth, Callie reached into her backpack and handed Ezra a copy of Wilty's note. "This can stay. The rest comes with me. You have a problem with that, call a judge."

With that, she grabbed the journals and the original note and left.

After she'd gone, Alvarez sauntered in, a huge grin on his face. "Man, you just can't help pissing her off, can you?"

Ezra listened to Callie's receding footsteps. "It's a gift."

It had been a positively dreadful day. First, Carolyne's manicurist hadn't shown up. Apparently, the girl had an immobilizing cold. Then Carolyne had gone downtown for meetings with her banker and her broker, neither of whom had good news for her. When she returned to her apartment, Lourdes added to her doldrums. The police had called. They had some questions for her.

As she waited for them in her living room, she stared out the window, busying herself with the scene below. Across the street, Central Park was beginning to hint at the coming of spring. On a bench just outside the entrance, an elderly man sipped from a paper cup and read his newspaper. A stooped-over old woman, assisted by an aide in a white uniform and a pink sweater, leaned on her cane and hobbled past him. Inside, streams of joggers ran along the designated paths, keeping their own pace as traffic sped through the park. Men in business suits with cell phones glued to their ears stood beneath trees or in the middle of sidewalks and conducted outdoor meetings while young mothers steered prams and strollers amidst the green lawns and budding gardens.

Carolyne's gaze fixed on these city mommies blithely ambling about New York's living landscape, so carefree and confident about their place in this world. When she was their age, she had none of their assuredness. It was difficult to feel confident when everyone around you said—in so many words—that you didn't fit in. It was impossible to feel carefree when everything you did was second-guessed and criticized by a know-it-all mother-in-law and an abusive husband.

She watched one young woman lean over and chuck her little boy under the chin. The mommy shook her head back and forth, gently tickling his face with her hair. The baby giggled and kicked his feet with delirious abandon. Carolyne tried to remember how it felt to nuzzle a child, but the memory was vague.

Behind her, the door to her apartment closed. Lourdes approached and announced that two detectives were in the foyer asking to see her. Carolyne responded with an almost imperceptible nod. Lourdes interpreted the gesture as the okay to usher the detectives in, which she did. The two men entered the lavishly decorated room and politely waited for the mistress of the manor to acknowledge them. Carolyne lingered at the window, unwilling to tear herself away from the mother and child below.

Ezra was not a patient man. As far as he was concerned, he had a murder to solve. She could soak up the view after he left. "Mrs. Hale."

Carolyne turned. She was not pleased to see Ezra Chapin, but she covered it well. "I'm sorry, gentlemen," she said. "Please. Take a seat."

As the three settled themselves—Carolyne in a gilded bergère, the two men on a tufted silk sofa—Ezra ran his eyes over the Widow Hale. She was striking, he'd give her that. Blond hair, black suit, great legs and tons of jewelry. A flower brooch of rubies and diamonds rested on the collar of the jacket; its companion pieces glittered on her ears. A diamond the size of an egg weighed down one hand, a collection of gold and diamond bracelets the other. Everything about her was tidy, expensive, neatly tailored and perfectly coordinated; there seemed little question as to where her son, Wilty, got his compulsion for order.

"Again, we're terribly sorry for your loss, Mrs. Hale," Ezra said, offering the requisite condolences. Jorge solemnly nodded in accordance. Carolyne Hale didn't respond. She barely even blinked. She simply stared at Ezra—impatiently, he thought. "I'm also sorry to have to be the one to tell you that we don't believe your son committed suicide. We believe he was murdered."

That got a response. Carolyne's delft blue eyes widened and her left hand slapped against her chest as if her heart had given off a sharp pain.

"No!"

"Forensics confirm a large quantity of alcohol and barbiturates in his system," Alvarez told her.

Her silence was long and difficult to watch. It was as if the batteries of her brain were low and it was taking an inordinate amount of time to absorb this news. Alvarez also sensed an enormous effort being expended to maintain her dignity. When, finally, she spoke, her voice was small and shaky.

"My son was a borderline alcoholic. It wasn't unusual for Wilty to drink more than he should."

"We're aware of that, Mrs. Hale." Ezra thought she looked embarrassed. "Was he also in the habit of taking sleeping pills?"

Her eyes blinked as if she didn't understand the question.

"According to the lab, the alcohol was combined with a large quantity of Seconal. The level of toxicity in his blood was such that it would be virtually impossible for him to have walked from the library to the kitchen, let alone climb out the window onto his fire escape. We think someone helped him to his death."

Carolyne rose slowly from her chair and returned to the window that overlooked Fifth Avenue. Her shoulders stooped slightly from the weight of what she'd just been told. Ezra thought he saw something glisten on her cheek. Then again, maybe not.

"Did your son have any known enemies?" he asked. She shrugged and shook her head. "Anyone who might've held a grudge?"

Alvarez, who'd been looking around the living room in search of some family photographs, wondered if people like Carolyne Hale had a special room where they displayed things like that. In his house, there wasn't a surface that wasn't covered with pictures of his kids, his nieces and nephews, and other assorted family members. Then again, his house didn't have expensive fabrics on the furniture and fine art on the walls.

"Were you close with your son?" he asked, instinctively knowing the answer before it was given.

"No. It's one of my deepest regrets."

"Would you know the names of any of Mr. Hale's friends or associates? We're going to need to question them as well as other members of the family."

Carolyne sighed. "There are no other members of the family. I'm the last of the Hales. As for Wilty's friends, I'm afraid I can't help you. He didn't bring anyone around to meet me, nor did he invite me to his infamous soirées."

Ezra was certain he detected an edge in her voice. Was

it impatience with the interrogation or regret over the distance that existed between her and her son?

Alvarez must have heard something as well, because he followed up immediately. "How often did you and your son see each other?"

Carolyne turned away from the window and looked squarely at the young detective with the pitch-black hair and the obsidian eyes that narrowed when he spoke.

"I already told you. We weren't close."

"Did you see him once a week? Once a month? Once a year? Ever?"

"I resent that!" she snapped.

"Forgive me." Alvarez bowed his head obsequiously. Ezra recognized it as a taunt; it was Jorge's turn to play bad cop. "I'm simply trying to establish the parameters of the relationship between you and your son."

Carolyne glared at him. Ezra rushed to change the subject before she reared up and tossed them out.

"Was Mr. Hale employed at the time of his death?"

Carolyne moved her eyes off Alvarez onto Ezra.

"My son was never *employed*. He lived off his trust fund. Occasionally, he dabbled."

"In what kind of things did he dabble?"

She stepped away from the window and began to walk around her ivory aerie. As she strolled about the room, her hand grazed the backs of chairs, the tops of several bronze sculptures, the petals of her orchids. It was as if she needed reassurance from her possessions that she was someone who knew how to care for and cherish those things that gave her pleasure.

Ezra wondered if she was trying to tell them, in a far out way, that if Wilty had given her as much joy as these things had, she would have been a better mother.

"He adored physical activity and indulged himself in every sport imaginable," she said, slipping back into her gilded bergère. "He was rather astute when it came to the stock market. I never understood why he didn't make a career of it.

"Also, he considered himself something of a thespian and often financed off-Broadway plays and one-man shows."

She appeared to drift off for a brief reverie. When she returned, an amused smile had insinuated itself on her lips.

"I once saw him perform in an absolutely hideous play. He was quite good, despite the paucity of material."

Ezra wondered if she'd told Wilty that while he was still alive. And if it might have made a difference to him.

"Did he ever work at a real job?" Alvarez asked.

"He held a seat on the Hale board." She sounded defensive.

"And that means he did . . . what?"

Her brow furrowed as some unbidden memories asserted themselves.

"Wilty tried to contribute to the conduct of the business, but no one would listen."

Ezra's ears perked. That was the first honest note of sympathy he'd heard since they began this interview.

"Hale Holdings is a major conglomerate," he said. "Did Mr. Hale favor one business over another?"

"Not really. He preferred to view the corporation as a whole, rather than a series of parts." She reflected further. "Wilty was quite proud of Hale Holdings and its long history of success."

Hard to knock a global behemoth, Ezra thought. "So what suggestions did Mr. Hale bring to the table?"

Again, Carolyne seemed defensive. "Wilty felt that the present-day company was adrift, that they were investing in companies completely unrelated to the core industries."

"What's wrong with that?" Alvarez asked. "Big companies buy little companies all the time. It's all about padding the bottom line."

"He believed that, ultimately, that kind of scattershot buying would prove disastrous," she replied with an undertone that implied Alvarez knew less about the business world than he did about fine French furniture. "My son wanted Hale Holdings to return to its base, to rededicate itself to the underlying philosophy and singular sense of purpose set down by its founder, E.W. Hale."

"Times change. Maybe the board had adopted a different philosophy and had set different goals," Ezra offered.

"The one and only goal of the board of Hale Holdings is to make everyone on that board as rich as possible."

"Including you and Mr. Hale."

Alvarez had caught the Widow off guard. She shifted in her chair, embarrassed by the truth.

"Money isn't everything, detective."

Alvarez snorted. "Why is it that only rich people say that?"

Ezra shot his partner a warning. Alvarez ignored it.

"So if it wasn't money, what was it that Mr. Hale wanted? Power, maybe? A better position at the table? A bigger cut of the pie? What?"

Carolyne was bristling. "He didn't have to want power and a bigger cut of the pie, Detective. In little more than a month, he was due to inherit the bakery. What my son wanted, was for the men who ran his great-great-grandfather's company to remember that he, not they, carried the Hale bloodline." Her voice trilled with a surprising burst of passion. "For that reason alone, he deserved respect."

"I gather they didn't give it to him."

Ezra, the good cop, was delighted that Alvarez had pushed that button. Maybe now they'd be able to find the chinks in Carolyne Hale's designer label armor.

"No," she said with sincere sorrow. "They didn't."

"Did they give you any respect?" Ezra asked.

She looked as if she wanted to laugh, but her expression wasn't at all mirthful.

"If they didn't hold the last male descendent of E.W. Hale in high regard, how do you think they dealt with a woman who simply married the name?"

Alvarez and Ezra exchanged glances. That was a chink if ever they heard one.

"When was the last time you saw Mr. Hale?" Alvarez

asked, watching the Widow bury a long-held anger beneath a cultivated aristocratic facade.

"We had lunch about a week before his death," she said, her hauteur restored.

"Where?"

"At the Four Seasons."

"Just the two of you?"

"Yes."

"You said you and your son didn't get together often. Was this a special occasion?"

"No. Just lunch."

"What did you talk about?"

"I don't really recall."

Alvarez could spot a lie a mile away. That was a whopper.

"Was he upset about anything?" he prodded, noting her discomfort and playing off it. "Was he edgy? Angry?"

"I didn't notice," she answered sharply. "And frankly, Detective, I don't enjoy being badgered."

"And I don't enjoy investigating murders of thirty-four-year-old men with everything to live for, so I'll ask you again, Mrs. Hale. At lunch, only days before your son's death, was there anything unusual about his behavior or his conversation? Did he say or do anything that might have alerted you to a problem?"

"No."

"In hindsight, was there something you realize now that might have been a clue as to what was to come?"

"No."

"Did you see him on the day of his death?"

"No."

Both men stood. That startled Carolyne.

"Is that all?"

Alvarez looked down at her for a very long moment, his eyes very dark and very narrow. "For now."

"If you have the guest registry from your son's memorial service," Ezra said, "we'd like to see it so we can go over the names of everyone who attended. You never know. The person, or persons, who murdered your son might have been there."

Carolyne stood, her face pale and drawn.

"My son was a wealthy young man who often made the mistake of flaunting his wealth in front of strangers. Perhaps his death was a robbery that went horribly, horribly wrong."

Ezra and Alvarez didn't respond. They headed out of the living room toward the door. Carolyne followed closely behind.

"Have you considered that possibility?" she asked with barely restrained insistence.

"We did, but nothing was taken." Ezra met her disapproving gaze head on. "We believe your son's death was a cold-blooded murder, Mrs. Hale, but since we haven't been able to come up with a compelling reason for anyone wanting him dead, we're open to suggestion."

He extracted a card from his pocket and handed it to her.

"If you happen to think of something Wilty had, or knew, that might be a motive for murder, give us a call."

12

Paula lived in a Chelsea loft that had taken two years and every cent of her savings to renovate. Even during the worst of it, she didn't regret her decision or the expense. While many accepted the saying that only two things in life were certain—death and taxes—in Paula's life there was a third certainty: She couldn't live in a standard apartment; standard kitchens weren't big enough to house her cookbooks, let alone her culinary tools. So instead of a two bedroom apartment with a kitchen, she created a kitchen with one big bedroom and an open space where guests could sit and talk to the chef while she cooked.

When Callie reached the sixth floor, the huge elevator door opened and let her into the loft. Immediately, she knew dinner would be of the Italian persuasion; there was no mistaking the aroma of fresh tomatoes, garlic and basil. Paula was holding court at her usual place in front of the stove. An open bottle of Chianti and a glass awaited Callie.

Callie poured herself some wine and leaned against a counter.

"Good news," Paula announced. "We can have the Hampton house six weeks early if we want. No extra charge."

Callie smiled. That was good news. Every summer for the past four years, she and Paula and several others from the *Courier* rented a small house in Bridgehampton. There were eight of them; they alternated weekends, four to a shift.

"How'd you work that out?"

"The Smythes," the owners of the house, "have to go out of the country. Fred's setting something up in Indonesia. Whatever, they need housesitters. I volunteered us!" Paula was so pleased with herself, she was as puffed up as a beignet. "You and I have the house to ourselves for the months of May, September, October and the rest of April. The rest of the crew joins us for June, July, August."

"Sweet!" Callie toasted Paula's genius.

She bowed her head with imperial grace. "Thank you. All accolades gratefully accepted." Her brown eyes suddenly opened wide and she bit her lower lip sheepishly. "This is a rotten segue, but I haven't spoken to you since the funeral. How was it?"

Callie gave her a rundown of the who's who, as well as the basics of the slam-bam-thank-you-ma'am ceremony.

"And who was sitting next to the Widow? A Senator? A Hale board member? One of her many lovers, perhaps?"

"I didn't get an up-close look," Callie confessed. "The family pew was pretty empty. There are no more Hales. As for the Widow's family, my sources say she distanced herself from them years ago."

"Distanced?" Paula guffawed. "From what I heard, she couldn't run away from that trailer park fast enough!"

They laughed and exchanged gossip about Carolyne Hale's journey from filth to Fifth, as Paula liked to say, enjoying every juicy little tidbit.

She didn't know why, but then Callie told Paula about running into Detective Chapin and sitting with him during the service. That raised an eyebrow. Callie hastily explained why he needed her to accompany him inside.

"What's he look like?"

Callie described him.

Paula made a yummy sound.

Callie rushed to correct that impression. "The fact that he's good-looking is offset by the even bigger fact that he's arrogant, chauvinistic and very, very full of himself."

Paula shrugged. "Still sounds appealing to me."

"If you're interested, I'd be happy to give him your number."

"Why not? You never know when Mr. Right's going to come along."

"This guy is not Mr. Right," Callie insisted. "He's not even Mr. Right Now."

Paula turned around and pointed a spoon at her friend. "Maybe not for you, but my criteria isn't quite as exacting as yours. My fantasy is a hunk who's great in bed, wants two kids and a dog and has a sizable trust fund. Since that's probably out of the realm of possibility, I'll take someone who makes me happy and makes me feel good about myself."

"Where is that so different from what I want?"

"You're looking for a guy who comes complete with a written guarantee for a happily-ever-after." Paula's voice softened. "And who's not afraid of ghosts."

Callie's eyes darkened.

"Uh-oh." Paula put the spoon down. "Did the gray stranger come back?"

"It wasn't quite as spooky as that." Callie returned to the church the previous afternoon. In her head, she heard the music filling the sanctuary. She tried to recall how she felt then, but the sensation remained on the edge of her consciousness. "It was a déjà vu kind of thing."

Paula visibly relaxed. "I have those moments all the time. You're sure you've been somewhere before or done the same thing before. Right?"

Callie nodded. Paula, accepting Callie's experience as unnerving but not critical, returned to her cooking.

"But I knew something I had no business knowing."

Paula didn't like the sound of Callie's voice. It was haunted, sort of. Low and echoing, almost as if it were coming from a deep hollow inside her soul.

"Like what?" she asked, keeping her gaze fixed on Callie's face as she mixed the shellfish in with the tomato sauce.

"The music. I'm certain that same piece was played at E.W. Hale's funeral. How would I know that?"

"You probably read it somewhere. You know how retentive you are." Paula gripped Callie's arms and gave her a little shake. "Don't make more out of this than it is."

Callie forced a smile. "You're probably right. I do have a brilliant mind. I don't know why I question that."

Paula groaned playfully. They each returned to their chores, Callie finishing up the salad, Paula reducing the remaining sauce while the pasta cooked. The silence between them was companionable, but fraught. Again, like the night the gray stranger came to Callie outside of her dreams, neither of them had a satisfying explanation for what had happened. They had excuses. Then, it was too much to drink and not enough sleep. Now, it was a good memory and an overheated church.

Callie had another thought: perhaps this déjà vu moment was the result of some post-hypnotic suggestion planted by Peter Merrick.

But how could he have known what was going to be played? And why would he want her to know that arcane bit of information?

She dismissed the thought as a burp of paranoia.

"I ran into Dr. Merrick on my way to the church."

Paula knew she wasn't going to like this. And she didn't.

"What's up with this guy pleading his case with you on the street? On the way to a funeral, no less! No wonder you had this . . . moment!"

"You think?"

"Damn right, that's what I think!"

Paula instructed Callie to bring the salad plates inside. She grabbed the wine and put her seafood concoction on simmer.

"Now," she declared, taking her seat and rapping her knife on the table like a scepter. "There is to be no more depressing talk. It riles the stomach juices."

She sipped her wine, munched on her salad and smiled with delight. There was a delicious aroma coming from the kitchen, the tang of a perfect salad dressing on her tongue, an outstanding Tuscan wine breathing in her glass and her best friend across the table. All was right with the world.

Until Callie said, "So let me tell you about the package I got from Wilty."

Their shift was over. Alvarez started packing up his things. Ezra was scribbling on a note pad. He'd been writing and ruminating for over an hour.

"What's up?" Jorge looked over his partner's shoulder at a primitive family tree with names of various Hales sitting on the branches. "She really got to you, didn't she?"

"What're you talking about?"

"You're buying into this curse thing."

"I'm just checking it out. The woman brought in some important journals. She made a couple of good points. It would be irresponsible to discount her entire theory."

"Irresponsible." Jorge pursed his lips together, narrowed his eyes and nodded. "Yeah. I'd hate for us to be irresponsible. So, what've you come up with?"

Ezra flashed Jorge a look that said, hear me out. Jorge folded his arms across his chest as if to say, lay it on me.

"Logic says this is simply a matter of statistics. If you have a large family, and you stretch it out over several generations, you're going to have a bit of everything: divorces, infant deaths, suicides, homosexuality, infidelity, sterility, tragic accidents. The Hales had them all, but no more or less than any other family of their size. The difference is that their statistics were made public. And that many of the deaths in that family smelled like murder."

"Fascinating," Jorge said, clearly finding Ezra's recitation anything but. "What does this have to do with our vic?"

"The deaths of Wilty's father and uncle were highly suspicious accidents, yet no one could ever find any hard evidence of foul play."

"That doesn't mean there wasn't any."

"Precisely." Ezra knew the minute the discussion turned to unsolved crimes, Jorge would be in. "Someone could've planned those accidental deaths knowing that if they were bizarre enough and spectacular enough, they'd be credited to the curse, which would remove pressure from the police to spend time and money attempting to solve a sticky crime the public had already dismissed."

"And you're thinking that same thing might have been at work here. That's sick, man," Jorge said, his face a map of disgust. "But possible."

"And clever. By making certain Wilty's death would be splashed all over the newspapers and picked at by media vultures hungry for another bloody story about a celebrity and a curse, the killers assure themselves that everything else about the case, including motive, becomes obfuscated."

Ezra watched Jorge process his hypothesis. He could practically see the gears of Alvarez's brain dissecting Ezra's theory, trying to link that suggestion to facts already known, then tracking it through to a conclusion. Ezra could tell by the look on Jorge's face, he was moving into Ezra's corner.

"Was Carolyne Hale ever a suspect in either man's death?" Jorge was convinced the Widow's hands were dirty.

"No one ever brought any charges against her."

"It might be interesting to see what they asked her, why they dropped it, and who was around her then that may still be around her today."

"My thoughts exactly."

"So where are you going with all this?"

"I'm going to make a couple of calls, poke a stick in a couple of bushes and see who or what runs out. Where are you going?"

"Home."

Ezra covered his ears. He knew what was coming.

"It's a place where there's a wife and kids who are actually happy to see you. Dinner that's served on a plate and not in cardboard cartons. And people who kiss you good night who'll still be there in the morning. It's nice. You really ought to try it."

"Yeah, yeah."

After Alvarez left, Ezra tracked down the Sheriff of Warren County, New York, to find out more about the bizarre 1970 death of Huntington Hale.

Hunt had been speedboating around Lake George, offshore from the Hale family's Adirondack retreat, Long House. Apparently, Hunt was sitting on the edge of the boat, fell off and into the water. The swell of the waves jerked him back in the wake and swirled him about in such a way that his head was sliced off by the motor's propeller. It was definitely gruesome. Ezra wanted to know if it was murder.

A secretary came on the phone to tell Ezra that Sheriff Carlson was out of the office and wouldn't be back for several weeks. She asked if anyone else could help him. Ezra said no, thanked her, left a message for the sheriff to call him as soon as he returned, and hung up. Better not to let too many people know what he was up to. It gave people time to prepare answers. Or lose evidence.

His next call was to the Memphis branch of the Tennessee Bureau of Investigation; they provided assistance to local law enforcement agencies, particularly in the area of criminal investigations. As luck would have it, Gideon Bryson, the TBI Special Agent in Charge, was the son of Noah Bryson, the Sheriff of Shelby County at the time of Cole Hale's death in 1969.

"I remember my father saying the man was fried like a catfish!" Gideon told Ezra.

"According to the reports I have, he was doing electrical work on a horse barn."

Gideon confirmed the report, but corrected Ezra by explaining this was no ordinary barn. "Cole Hale bred fine racehorses. Some of the finest in the state. This so-called barn was more like a horse hotel, stabling something like fifty bluebloods."

Ezra remained puzzled. "So why didn't he hire an electrician?"

"I asked the same thing. So'd my father. The answer was that Hale doted on his animals, almost to the point of obsession. He controlled everything even remotely related to their care. Also, he wasn't completely ignorant about electronics. Apparently, he'd gotten some training in the field when he was in the army." Gideon paused. "In fact, I think he worked alongside the crew that installed the electricity when the barn was constructed."

That confused Ezra even more. "Then what went wrong?"

"I don't know, exactly. According to the Memphis PD, he was replacing a broken fixture, one of the huge, high voltage lights that ran down the center of the barn, parallel to the sprinkler system. He was disconnecting the fixture, must have spliced a couple of wires together and boom! The man was toast!"

Ezra knew nothing about electricity except that it worked when you turned a switch on and off, you didn't stick your finger in a socket unless you wanted your hair to stand on end, and you never played with anything electrical while standing in a puddle.

"You said he was up near the sprinkler system. Were the pipes wet?"

"Nope. Neither was the ladder he was standing on. And, he was wearing insulated shoes."

Ezra had no idea what that meant so he jotted it down, but if Gideon's father checked it out, it must have been relevant.

"Was he the careless type?"

"Not usually. Especially not around his horses. That's why this accident was so damned freakish."

"Was the power on when he started?"

"First thing they checked. The switch was in the off position."

"Could someone have turned it on while he was working?"

"That's the sixty-four-thousand-dollar question, isn't it? Everyone on the farm at the time had an alibi and a corroborating witness."

That didn't mean they were all telling the truth, Ezra thought.

"Did Mr. Hale have any known enemies?"

"Breeding thoroughbreds is a fierce business. To be honest, I wouldn't rule out any of those guys as having the potential for committing murder if they felt they'd been crossed or cheated, but Cole Hale was considered a fair trader and a good horse man."

"Was he a good boss? Did his staff like him?"

"Yes and no," Gideon said.

"What does that mean?"

"He paid a fair wage, but the Hales were racists. They weren't exactly evenhanded when it came to overtime or days off or other kinds of favors."

"Was he married?"

"Nope. Man swung the other way, if you know what I mean."

"Was his homosexuality common knowledge?" Considering the times and his elevated station, Ezra doubted it, but he felt he had to ask.

"Everyone knew he was gay, but no one talked about it. It was like some public secret."

"Is it possible an ex-lover was trying to shake him down, got ticked off when Hale wouldn't pay hush money and waited for an opportunity to whack him?"

"Hey! Anything's possible," Gideon admitted. "By the way, my father did go down that road. The problem was no one knew the names of any of Cole's lovers. Or, if they did, they didn't want to say."

"Were there any gay bars in Memphis back then?"

"Oh, sure. Plenty. They were underground, but they existed. The detectives on the case interviewed every bartender on that circuit. Every now and then, Hale would show up at one of their establishments, but he never used the same name twice, so none of them knew his real identity. Those that did figured live and let live."

"How about Carolyne Hale? Any thoughts about her?"

Gideon laughed. "None that I'd say in polite society or that I'd want printed in the newspaper."

"Not a member of her fan club?"

"Hardly!"

"Why not?"

Gideon paused, as if he wanted to phrase his opinion just so. "She had an attitude she had no right having."

"A bit uppity?" Ezra said, hoping to draw him out.

"You might say. Carolyne Faessler grew up on the river with a no-account father who gambled away every cent he ever earned and a mother who some folks believe worked the prowl for a time. Now don't get me wrong," Gideon continued, softening his tone as if he realized he might come off sounding petty, "youngins can overcome their parents' shortcomings and she did. She worked hard, got herself some schooling, cleaned up nice and married real well, but *we* all knew where she came from."

"I take it her memory wasn't as sharp as yours."

There was a momentary silence. "You know, Detective Chapin, I'm a plain sort of fella. I work hard. I'm honest. I'm good to my family, loyal to my friends, and I generally try to do the right thing. A bunch of us have known Carolyne since she's a girl. We used to play together as kids. My mamma often watched over her when her mamma was . . . well, when her mother wasn't around. Then, she became a Hale. No one begrudged her good luck. But it was like she woke up one day, realized her bank account was fatter than everybody else's, and suddenly began treating us as if we were dirt under her feet. I don't take real well to behavior like that."

"I don't blame you."

He wondered how Carolyne's haughty attitude toward the locals had influenced the way she was treated by the police. Did they cast aside her slights and treat her with kid

gloves because of her husband's family's exalted position?
Or did they investigate her within an inch of her life and
come up empty?

"Why would anyone even suspect Carolyne?" Ezra continued. "What would she have to gain from her brother-in-
law's death?"

"For one thing, Cole Hale couldn't stand her. He thought
she was gold-digging trash and wasn't quiet about it. He
was almost as outspoken in his dislike of her as his mother,
and believe me, that's goin' some." Gideon chuckled, but
in that better-her-than-me kind of way that displayed a certain sympathy for Carolyne. "For another thing, she
might've thought that with Cole out of the picture, she'd
be the sole beneficiary of Hunt's estate."

"But she wasn't. From what I understand, the money
passed from one generation of blood to another. The best
she'd ever get would be an allowance, of sorts, from her
son."

"Yeah, but I'm not sure she knew that then."

"Interesting." Ezra scribbled the names Cole, Hunt,
Wilty and Carolyne on his notepad. He drew thick lines
through all three men. Carolyne was the only one standing.
"Do you think she had a hand in his death?"

"I think she's a greedy woman and a major-league
climber, so I wouldn't put it past her. I just don't have any
hard facts to back it up."

"Do you think she killed her husband?"

"Again, I wouldn't fall over in a faint if you said she
did it or hired someone to do it for her, but I don't think
our counterparts in New York came up with anything to
link her to Hunt's death either."

"I've got a call in to them," Ezra said, discouraged, "but
somehow I think when I speak to the Sheriff up there, he'll
verify what you just said."

"This is all about Wilty's death, isn't it?"

Ezra assumed the Memphis newspapers reported Wilty's
demise.

"As a matter of fact, it is."

"It wasn't a suicide, was it?"

"No. We don't think it was."

"Crazy, isn't it?" Gideon said with an ironic chuckle. "All these rich Hales dying these weird deaths? It sure makes you wonder whether there really is something like a curse hanging over their heads."

"It's been mentioned as a possibility," Ezra said, thinking how pleased Callie Jamieson would be to hear that. "But it's a little difficult to arrest and prosecute a curse."

"I hear ya!"

The two men spoke several minutes longer. Despite the fact that the case appeared to have been properly worked, Ezra asked Gideon to look into it again. Specifically, he was interested in the names of everyone who worked the farm with Cole, people who associated with the brothers Hale during that time, and any close friends of Carolyne Hale who made the transition from her old life to her new life. Gideon promised he'd forward whatever he could find.

Ezra hoped it would be sooner rather than later.

The taxi dropped Callie off on the corner of Eighty-fourth and Park. As she walked the few doors down toward her building, her eye was drawn to a man standing in the corner of the entrance to the parking garage diagonally across the street. She probably never would have noticed him except the gate to the garage was down. Usually, that meant the attendant was inside watching television, eating or taking a snooze. Also, he didn't look like any of the men who worked there. Most of them were Hispanic and on the small side. This guy was big and burly and wasn't wearing the uniform of the chain that owned the garage. His head was shaved. His skin was the color of cappuccino.

He was leaning against the gate, smoking a cigarette and watching her.

Callie quickened her pace, then chided herself for overreacting.

It must be the threatening phone calls, she thought. Having someone tell you it's going to be hard to type your next article with all your fingers broken is enough to make you jumpy. Even the *Courier*'s security chief thought that one needed further investigation.

She tried not to, but instinct forced her to look over her shoulder as the door to her building opened. The hulk smiled at her. He didn't make a move toward her. He didn't do anything that in any way could be perceived as threatening. He simply stood in the entrance to the garage and smiled. Yet something about him creeped her out.

"Hey, Tommy," she said, greeting her doorman.

"How're you doing, Callie?"

A portly man, in a gold-braided uniform he claimed made him looked like a tuba player in a marching band, he closed the door behind her and waved as she headed to the mail room.

"Great. How about you?"

A broad mouth smiled beneath a fluffy, black mustache. "Hangin' in."

They went through the same routine every night. In its own way, it was comforting, like coming home to a puppy who wagged his tail for the joy of seeing her.

She went into the back room where the mailboxes were. Hers was on the top tier; for Callie, that was eye level, so she didn't mind. She noticed a flyer announcing that the building would be undergoing some renovation within the next several weeks. As she read the dates and times when residents could expect the water and the electricity to be turned off, she rummaged around her backpack, grabbed her keys and opened the small brass door. She went back to reading the flyer and reached in for her mail.

She smelled it almost before she touched it. Her hand felt it for only a moment before she looked inside, withdrew her hand and yelled for Tommy. Her heart was pounding.

Tommy rounded the corner, huffing nervously. Callie was pressed against the wall across from the open mailbox, her skin dead white, her eyes bulging.

"Get that out of there!" Callie cried, pointing to a dead rat with a hypodermic needle sticking out of its belly.

Attached to the needle was a note made out of words clipped from a newspaper: **You'll be sorry.**

Tommy took Callie's arm and gently led her out to the lobby. "Let me get something to put it in," he said.

As they approached Tommy's desk, something clicked. Callie raced to the door and looked across the street. The big, burly man was gone.

13

Callie showed her credentials to the policeman guarding the door. He inspected them carefully and checked her name off the list of those permitted to visit the premises before removing the yellow crime scene tape that blocked the entrance to Wilty Hale's apartment.

"Please don't touch anything without these," he said, handing her a pair of latex gloves as he opened the door.

She took a deep breath as she walked into the entrance gallery. While this had been Wilty's, she had never been here, making everything seem strange yet familiar at the same time. She recognized some of the art and many of the antiques, but they were in new settings, surrounded by different rugs and moldings and wall coverings.

"You have to hand it to him. The guy had great taste."

This time, Callie recognized the voice.

"Were you waiting for me?"

"I'm on a case."

"Where's your other half?" Callie looked around as if she expected Alvarez to pop out from behind a plant.

"Jorge was here, but our shift was just about over. He went back to the house to do some paperwork. I took some lost time. He'll be happy to know you missed him."

"Why didn't you go with him?"

"I heard you were coming. I wanted to find out how you were." She eyed him suspiciously. "I heard about the rat in the mailbox."

Callie shrugged, as if death threats were part of the territory.

"I told you this pill pusher series wasn't going to win you any popularity contests."

"Congratulations. You were right. Now, is it all right if I do what I came to do?"

"How about if I tag along beside you? Who knows, I might learn a thing or two." He gave her his most enchanting smile.

She wasn't enchanted. "This tagging along thing is getting to be habit."

"I don't smoke. I drink in moderation. I call my mother at least once a week. I'm kind to stray dogs and cats. And despite the needs of my enormous ego, I'm willing to give credit where credit is due."

"Meaning?"

"I know you don't think I take you seriously, but after our last conversation, I made a couple of calls about Wilty's father and uncle."

Callie's eyes widened in surprise.

"In my line of work three unexplained, yet possibly connected, deaths isn't a curse. It's the work of a serial killer. But tomato, tom-ah-to, no matter how you say it, we're both after the same thing: who killed Wilty Hale. There! Are we buds now?"

"May I ask what prompted this unprecedented act of cooperation?"

"I have a thing about cold cases."

Callie gathered that the other day.

"The idea that there are at least two unsolved crimes in the same family as my current case intrigues me, as does the fact that initially all three presented as accidental deaths."

"And the fact that the family in question is the Hales?"

"All the more intriguing," he said. She smiled knowingly. "Now that we're on the same page, how about beginning the tour?" Callie nodded her assent. "I already did a walk-through with Alvarez. There are ten rooms. One is more impressive than the next. Other than the driving range, of course. That's just plain weird."

When Callie first heard about Wilty's so-called range, it had sounded bizarre. Envisioning it as part of this incredibly glamorous surround made it more so.

"I have to admit, I'm overwhelmed," Ezra said, as they walked from one room to another.

His knowledge of American antiques was limited, but even to his inexperienced eye, Wilty's furnishings were exquisite examples of nineteenth-century decoration. The highboy in the living room, the enormous mahogany table and Chippendale chairs in the dining room, the gilded mirrors, the framed samplers and needlework in the entrance gallery, the Chinese-patterned vases, the satinwood inlaid tea tables—all were collector's items.

A stand in the dining room holding a highly polished box aroused Callie's curiosity. She slipped on the latex gloves she'd been instructed to wear and paused to examine it.

"What's that?" Ezra asked.

"A wedding gift." She directed his attention to a small brass plaque glued onto the lid.

ON THE OCCASION OF THE MARRIAGE OF WINIFRED HUNTINGTON COLFAX TO EMMET WILTON HALE. 6 NOVEMBER 1869.

Carefully, she raised the lid. Inside were several crystal decanters, each one filled with a different liqueur. "This must be what people used before they had built-in bars."

Ezra noted the sterling silver pendants hanging around the necks of the decanters. Each was engraved with the name of a different libation. "How many of the antiques in this apartment originally belonged to E.W. Hale, do you think?"

"I'd say more than half." She closed the lid of the decanter case and took a second look at the table and chairs, as well as the breakfront and the set of five Chinese vases that sat in a row on top of it. "They were probably part of his father's estate."

Ezra glanced at the brass plaque announcing the marriage of E.W. Hale to Winifred Colfax. "You'd think the Widow would've inherited her husband's furniture."

"In an ordinary family, she would have, but the Hale Trust owns everything. Huntington Hale had no choice but to pass it on to Wilty."

"E.W. Hale sounds like a major-league control freak."

"Spread the wealth was not one of the old man's mottoes," Callie said, as they exited the dining room and headed down the hall.

Near the back of the apartment, Ezra opened a door and stood aside, inviting Callie to enter what she presumed was the infamous "driving range."

"In your life!" she exclaimed with an astounded laugh.

The floor was carpeted with the same artificial turf one might find at a domed ballpark. Red lines and netting divided the area into two cages. Near the lines, rubber tees of various heights sprouted up out of the carpet like headless flower stems. Next to those tees were metal boxes, each with a small screen that Callie assumed displayed something when the boxes were turned on. Along the wall adjacent to the door were four large buckets, two filled with regular golf balls, two with wiffle balls. In addition to the protective netting, the far wall and the ceiling were *papered*, so to speak, with thin mattresses designed to absorb sound and prevent damage. Two windows that overlooked the alley had shutters that closed from the inside—also covered with mattresses.

In the corner nearest the door was a large closet that had been refitted to store Wilty's golf equipment. Four long leather containers leaned out from the wall like quivers: one held an assortment of woods; the second, irons; the third, a conglomeration of wedges. The fourth held a set of antique golf clubs.

Callie lifted one out of its bag. Carved from hickory wood, it had a gleaming shaft and a bulbous head, also made of wood. Callie found it quite beautiful, the warm, bourbon-like color of the wood making it appear so much softer than the sleek, functional metal clubs in the other bags. There was a thin band attached to the handle. It was made of paper, covered by a protective piece of plastic. In a flourishing hand, the band identified the club as a "bulger." She smiled. Looking at the head of the club, there was little question about the derivation of the name.

She pulled out several other clubs, each identified with the same kind of handwritten band. There was a "baffy," a "brassie," an iron club called a "cleek," a hickory-shafted iron called a "mashie," a very old-looking club called a "longnose" and something that had to be the precursor of the modern putter. The band around that club said, "Liberty."

"I figured out what these metal boxes are," Ezra said, calling to her. "Grab a club and come on out here."

Callie heard him, but she extracted the Liberty and was stroking it against the carpet. She liked the feel of the club in her hands, the look of it as it swept the green turf at her feet.

Ezra stood at the door and watched as she continued stroking the turf. "You play golf?"

Callie turned to him, an embarrassed flush rouging her cheeks. "No."

"You could've fooled me."

"Well, don't be fool enough to enter me in any golf tournaments," she said as she slid the Liberty back into its container. "That was sweeping, not putting, and in case you didn't notice, there was no ball and no cup. Now what's this about those metal boxes?"

Uncomfortable for reasons she couldn't fathom, she quickly walked out of the closet, into the room. Ezra followed, carrying a metal driver.

"Watch this."

He placed a golf ball on the rubber tee and took a wicked swing. There was a ping as the club hit the ball, a thump as the ball hit the mattress. On an LCD screen atop the metal box, a number appeared: 270.

"That's how many yards that drive would've been."

Ezra's face was aglow, like a kid at a carnival who just knocked down enough pins to win a stuffed animal. "Life must be fun when you can afford toys like these." He spoke without thinking. "I'm sorry. That was so inappropriate."

Callie turned off the machine. "We were caught up in the moment."

Ezra returned the driver to its bag, steered her out of the room and closed the door behind them.

Down another hallway was the master suite, a series of rooms consisting of a bedroom, a bathroom, a dressing room and a sitting room/office. The sitting room was like a mini-library, with two comfortable armchairs, an ottoman, shelves filled with novels and magazines like *National Geographic, Art & Antiques, The Connoisseur,* and a host of catalogues from the New York Antiques Show held every year at the 67th Street Armory.

Beyond a gently curving arch and separated from the main sitting area was a modest alcove outfitted to hold Wilty's collection of travel folios and maps. There were three walls of cabinets and shelves, plus a peninsula large enough to accommodate a completely unfolded map. Neatly arranged and catalogued on the shelves were black cardboard boxes that contained the maps. Alongside those boxes were guide books relative to the country or city listed on the box's label. Aside from the usual what-to-see, where-to-go, where-to-shop, there were books ranging from the wildflowers of the Himalayas to the different kinds of coral that could be found in the Great Barrier Reef. Callie also noted books pertaining to whatever activity might have lured Wilty to that locale: fly fishing, skiing, golf, scuba diving, hiking, biking, wind surfing, etcetera. There were also restaurant guides and Berlitz language dictionaries.

"He was so anal," she said, noting the strict organization of this small, specialized room.

"That reminds me." Ezra started flipping pages in his ubiquitous black notebook. "I have to ask CSU if there was anything out of order in this room, or if it was only in the large library where things were a little screwed up."

Callie scanned the shelves in the alcove. Everything appeared to be in its proper place.

On the peninsula, she noted a photograph on an easel. On the table in front of the easel was a book opened to a full page spread of a house that matched the one in the photograph. It was the famous Long House, the Hale Adirondack retreat. Wilty had taken her there one weekend during the winter. They'd gone snowshoeing and sledding during the day, and ate dinner in front of an enormous hearth in what Wilty called "the great room" at night. It was incredible.

Callie turned several pages of the book. It was a pictorial tour of the lakeside mansion and its grounds.

"Look at this," she said, drawing Ezra's attention to a photograph of a golf hole. "Old E.W. was also a bit of a golf nut. I didn't see it because there was snow on the ground, but he built a three-hole golf course on his property: a par five, a par four and a par three."

Ezra studied the photograph, admiring the par-three green. Set amongst a background of sturdy pines and surrounded by deeply carved sand bunkers, its red flag was slightly furled, as if the camera caught it in the midst of a tussle with a gust of wind.

"This may explain Wilty's fascination with the game," he said.

"And the antique golf clubs." Callie thought about that. Her eyes turned wistful. "How wonderful to have something that belonged to one of your ancestors."

"Don't you have anything from your grandmother? Like a cameo pin or an old handkerchief?"

Only her nightmares.

"Nope." She wondered if her mother had jewelry from her mother or grandmother and, if so, what her father had done with it. "Besides, those golf clubs weren't from his grandfather. They were from his *great-great*-grandfather!" She was awed and it showed. "What did your relatives pass on to you, other than your extraordinary wit?"

"I'm adopted," Ezra said matter-of-factly. "So, I don't

have any handkerchiefs or golf clubs either."

Callie was humbled by his blunt admission. She was still trying to figure out how to respond when she realized he'd already moved on. The subject was closed.

As she followed him down the hall to the main library, the first line of Callie's favorite novel, *Anna Karenina* by Leo Tolstoy popped into her head: "Happy families are all alike; every unhappy family is unhappy in its own way."

Childhoods were like that, she supposed. She grew up without a mother and had always felt robbed of something precious. Her father loved her, Auntie Pennie doted on her, and she had the added blessing of Paula's friendship. But none of that made up for the gnawing pain of Mara's absence.

Wilty grew up without a father and, for all intents and purposes, without a mother. He had unimaginable wealth, prestige, and a remarkable history to inform and comfort him, yet, as he told Callie on more than one occasion, he always felt alone.

Ezra grew up with parents who didn't create him, but chose him. He'd offered no clue as to whether or not he'd been happy as a Chapin, but since he appeared balanced and at ease with himself, she assumed his childhood had indeed been happy. Of course, that didn't mean he didn't have an enormous blank that constantly begged to be filled in.

Since she had spent so much of her life wondering how different things would have been if her mother had lived—and hadn't been crazy—she couldn't help but wonder what he thought about, whether he fantasized about his birth parents and how his life might have been with them.

Her heart wrenched when she realized that for Wilty, all that was left were might-have-beens.

On one of the tables in the library, she noticed two pictures of Hunt and Wilty she'd never seen before. In one, they were fishing off a pier, the small boy nestled between his father's legs. In the other, Wilty and his father were dressed alike in white suits with pale blue shirts and white ties. While those standing alongside them had been cut out of the photo, Callie could see black dresses and black shoes. She guessed they were at a funeral.

Callie recalled seeing similar pictures in the sitting room. She thought about the pictures of herself and Mara that she'd distributed throughout her apartment, the small one she kept in her desk, the one behind her driver's license in her wallet.

She wondered if she and Wilty had been drawn to each other because he'd lost his father as a child just as Callie had lost her mother. And because life with the remaining parent had been less than ideal.

She knew what it was to feel like a stranger in her father's house, to wonder why suddenly you were a burden rather than a treasure. Her father hadn't totally abandoned her and, certainly, he hadn't stopped loving her; he had withdrawn. She'd had Auntie Pennie to cry to and, in later years, Paula to lean on.

Did Wilty's grandmother, whose fierce enmity toward Carolyne was well known, pick up the emotional slack and nurture her grandson? Was there a nanny? A high school chum? He never mentioned anyone in particular.

Maybe that's why Wilty partied until he was senseless. Maybe that was how he cried. But what happened in those frightening moments when he was sober and forced to confront his reality? Whom did he lean on then?

A sharp pain stabbed her heart. He'd tried to lean on her, but she rejected him.

"Find anything?" she asked Ezra, hastily trying to shoo her demons.

"A picture of you and Mr. Hale."

He handed Callie a silver frame with a photograph of them on top of a mountain. They both had on khaki shorts, tee shirts, fleece vests, tough-looking boots and baseball caps. They were arm in arm and grinning.

"We were in Vail," Callie said, smiling back at the two happy hikers. "May I take this?"

"I'm afraid not. It's . . ."

Callie nodded and returned the picture to him. "I know. Part of a crime scene."

Quickly, she turned her attention to the bookshelves. For a while, they worked in silence, Callie trying to concentrate on anything other than her memories, Ezra trying to concentrate on his job rather than Callie.

"I found a couple of books on suicide," she said, riffling through one with dog-eared pages. "This one has a number of highlighted passages."

"Faded or fresh?"

"They look relatively new."

"What are the highlighted passages about?"

"Why people kill themselves."

Ezra slid the book he was looking at back into its slot. "Okay," he said, serious and focused. "Why do people kill themselves?"

"Shame. Debt. Guilt. Despair. Madness." Callie's lip trembled at the last, but Ezra had begun to pace so he didn't notice.

"Interesting," he said, as he perambulated around the room. "The killer banked on the police buying into the notion that Wilty committed suicide. Which item on that list do you think the aforementioned murderer thought the police would most likely believe was the reason for Wilty's dive out the window?"

"Shame." Callie answered quickly, but she sounded quite certain. "Wilty knew everyone gossiped about how he wasn't living up to the Hale name, about what a total embarrassment he was to the family. My guess is that whoever did him in felt protected by Wilty's reputation as a degenerate."

"I'm sure you're right," Ezra said. "I felt the same way, until I saw this apartment."

"And now?"

"There's a lot of pride displayed throughout these ten rooms. And intelligence. Wilty Hale took great pains to showcase his heritage and to take care of its artifacts. The guy was an admitted drunk, but I think the label of family waste product was way too harsh."

"It was. I'm glad you see that."

"Me, too." Ezra saw how much this walkabout was affecting her. Again, he had to give her credit. The woman was a gamer. "What else have you got?" he asked.

Callie turned the book around so Ezra could see what she'd been looking at.

"We're assuming Wilty highlighted these passages, right?" Ezra nodded. "Wilty may have felt tremendous shame about his lack of notable accomplishment, but the word that's circled in red, is guilt. I can't imagine what Wilty would feel guilty about."

Callie flipped through the next few pages, seeking additional clues.

"If shame is the most common cause of suicide," Ezra said, thinking aloud, "revenge has always been a major motivation for murder. After passion, it's the first thing a prosecutor looks for. It's an obvious incentive and easy to explain to a jury." He paused, measuring his words. "I know you don't want to believe this, but Wilty might have done something really awful to someone and felt guilty about it. That someone might have decided to seek revenge."

"Revenge may be the motive," she said, closing the book and looking at Ezra. "But you know what, Detective? I have a feeling that nothing about this murder is obvious. Or easy to explain."

Callie left Wilty's apartment at around five and headed back to the office. When she arrived, Amy was waiting.

"Boy! Am I glad you showed up," she said.

Callie dropped her backpack on a chair, grabbed her messages and began to walk behind her desk.

"Do not sit down," Amy commanded. "Brad Herring wants to see you."

"About?"

"When it comes to the upper strata," she said as she

exited, "I maintain a strict, don't ask, don't tell policy."

Amy's credo of deliberate ignorance made as much sense to Callie as the government's.

She gave her hair a quick brush, checked her appearance in a mirror and raced to the elevator banks.

When Brad's secretary escorted Callie into his office, she was more than a little surprised to see Carolyne Hale seated on one of the couches.

"Good afternoon, Callie," Brad said as he shook her hand and brought her inside, positioning her directly in front of the eminent Mrs. Hale. Callie felt as if she were having an audience with the Queen, which, in a way, she supposed she was. "Carolyne, this is Callie Jamieson. Callie, Mrs. Hale."

Callie extended her hand, accompanying it with a quick, respectful smile.

"May I express my sympathy on the recent passing of your son?" She thought about mentioning that she and Wilty had been friends, but she was intimidated and uncertain about whether or not such a personal revelation was appropriate in a business setting.

Carolyne brushed her hand against Callie's rather than shaking it. She made no attempt to even acknowledge Callie's expression of condolence.

Brad invited Callie to take a seat on the couch opposite from Carolyne's. He sat next to Mrs. Hale. Callie thought he looked tense. His jaw was tight and his brow was furrowed.

Callie had seen the Widow at a number of office gatherings and in dozens of newspaper photos, but never up close. Aside from her high ticket ensemble and surgically-assisted appearance, the eminent Mrs. Hale exuded extreme presence. Callie found it daunting.

No wonder Wilty always said he couldn't have been a mamma's boy even if he'd wanted to be.

"I was telling Carolyne that the *Courier* is planning a major feature on the Hales," Brad was saying. "She's expressed some concerns about the project. I thought you might be able to put her at her ease."

"I'll do my best," Callie said, wishing she were anywhere but here. "What we're working on is a series that will be published in the *Courier Weekend* and excerpted in *EVENTS*. It focuses on E.W. Hale and his descendants, the greatness of their lives and the odd preponderance of their premature deaths. Our hope is that history will provide context to Wilty's passing."

Carolyne Hale turned to Brad Herring. "I want this project canceled and this woman fired."

Callie felt as if she'd just been told she had a fatal illness.

Brad Herring's face flushed. "What? Why?"

"First, the *theme* of this project is not history, it's hoodoo. There is no such thing as a curse on the Hales and I will not have my son's legacy tied to such rot." Without moving her head, she pointed a perfectly manicured finger at Callie. "As for her, she and Wilty had a brief affair. He told me he ended the relationship because all she was interested in was his money and his status. I believe she volunteered for this project so she could extract her revenge for his rejection."

"That's not true!" Callie was stunned.

Brad, whose jaw was tight enough to break, stood, his anger too fulsome to contain.

"Ms. Jamieson didn't volunteer for this project, Carolyne. I chose her based on her talent and her experience."

The Widow continued to afford Callie nothing but her profile. "You made the wrong choice," she said to Herring. "I'm giving you the opportunity to rectify it by assigning someone with greater credibility to produce something for the *Courier* that will honor my son, rather than savage him."

"I would never do that." Callie couldn't believe the things the Widow was saying.

Also, she felt betrayed by Wilty. He told her he never

discussed their romance with his mother; he claimed he never even mentioned her name.

"Three dates with me and Carolyne sends the dogs out after you," he'd said.

Callie had believed he was protecting her. Yet here she was, accused of being a social-climbing money-grubber, not only by Carolyne Hale but, posthumously, by Wilty as well. She felt as if she were being stabbed.

Finally, Carolyne faced Callie. Her blue eyes had turned black. "Didn't you ever wonder why he never introduced us? It was a fling, my dear. No more, no less."

That's not the way it was, Callie wanted to scream.

She didn't know why Carolyne Hale had such a hate going for her, or where she'd gotten her information, but Callie was the one being savaged and she didn't like it.

"Mrs. Hale, I object to your insinuations, both personal and professional. I take great pride in my journalistic integrity. It's true that your son and I were romantically involved and yes, I was disappointed when that came to an end, but I am not, nor have I ever been bitter. Also, I am not now, nor ever was after your son's money. I find the fact that you would even suggest such a thing highly offensive."

Not one of Carolyne Hale's feathers appeared even slightly ruffled.

"I was assigned a feature on the death of Wilton Hale. The consensus of the editorial board was that his death should be put into context with previous Hales who died earlier than their biblical allotment. And that is what I intended to do."

Callie would have liked nothing more than to tell this deluded harridan that Wilty had been digging into the Hale history when he died, but the less Carolyne Hale knew about those diaries, the better.

"If I wanted the world to know E.W. Hale's dirty little secrets, I could publish his private papers and be done with it," the Widow said with great hauteur. "Since I don't, those secrets will remain secret."

"Actually," Brad said calmly, but in a way that made

both Carolyne Hale and Callie sit up and take notice. "According to E.W.'s will, none of his papers can be published for a full twelve months after the death of the last Hale. At that point, however, they are eligible to be entered into the public domain. Nobody's secrets stay buried forever, Carolyne."

Callie expected to see the other woman's face color with rage. Instead, the Widow went completely blank. Callie couldn't imagine having the control to compel her features to refuse all expression. The fact that Carolyne Hale did, was frightening.

"I'm well aware of the provisions in E.W. Hale's will. I'm also in a position to change those provisions if I see fit."

Brad arched a doubtful brow.

"I am the only remaining Hale," Carolyne pointed out. "Which means that now I have the power to do whatever I want. And what I want, is for this so-called project to be scrapped and Callie Jamieson fired."

Callie felt as if her head were caught in a vise, her pain was that intense. She waited for Brad to spring to her defense, to refuse the Widow's instructions to scrap the series and sack her.

Instead, Brad Herring walked across the room and stood before Callie, placing himself between her and the Widow.

"I think you should go now," he said, quietly.

His eyes said they would talk later, but Callie didn't hold out much hope.

With as much dignity as she could muster, she rose and walked out of the office. She didn't look at either of them as she left, nor did she bid them good-bye. She was too devastated to speak.

After she left, Brad confronted Carolyne Hale. His hands were clasped behind his back, his fingers tightly gripped together. He was struggling to contain his anger, both at her and at himself for not being able to protect one of his reporters.

"Why would you do such a thing?" he said, his words squeezed through gritted teeth.

She looked up at him with complete dispassion. "Because I can."

14

She was in a box, her knees butted up against her chin, her arms pressed against her sides. There wasn't much air. There was no light. Her eyes searched for a way out, but there was nothing to see other than a thick, unremitting blackness.

A small door opened, then closed.

Suddenly rats were everywhere, crawling over her, sniffing at her eyes and mouth, gnawing at her flesh. The nails on their claws scratched against the metal walls creating a screeching noise that ran through her like an electric prod. She cringed from the sensation of their coarse fur and scaly tails against her skin. Her nose pinched from the garbage smell that clung to them. She kicked and screamed and flailed about wildly trying to fend them off, to no avail.

She felt a sharp prick in her arm. Then her leg. Then her other arm. Her other leg. Her chest. Her stomach. Her thighs. Her neck. Her body had become a pin cushion.

The poison burned as it passed through her skin and entered her bloodstream. Her body went numb.

Callie awoke with a start. She blinked her eyes and gazed into the darkness, terrified about what additional horror might be lurking in the shadows. Her racing heartbeat slowed, but only for a second. Still straddling the states of sleep and wakefulness, she delicately probed her body, searching for needles. Or animals.

She snapped on the light. Her breath skittered through her lungs, not quite filling them. She was gasping. The skin on her arms felt hot. She glanced down. They were pink and spotty, as if freshly bitten.

Weeping, she slid her arms under the covers, trying to salve her flesh by pressing it against whatever cool spots she could find on her sheets. Slowly, the heat receded.

But not her fear.

After a shower, two cups of strong coffee, and a strenuous yoga session, Callie found herself fully dressed and totally reinvigorated, with nowhere to go.

Brad Herring had left a long message on her answering machine congratulating her on her Dr. Drug story, apologizing for what went on his office, and trying to explain that he needed time to sort things out. Since he didn't tell her to be at her desk at the usual time, she assumed that, at best, she was on a forced sabbatical. At worst, she'd been canned.

Angry all over again, Callie stomped around her apartment, bemoaning her circumstances and loathing Carolyne Hale. Eventually, she wound up in the middle of her living room, frustrated and fuming, full of sound and fury and, to paraphrase Shakespeare, accomplishing nothing.

Callie hated what had been done to her, but she didn't have the influence or the power to be able to demand reinstatement. She wanted to fight back, but her weapons were limited. She had the truth on her side, but Carolyne Hale hadn't been moved by that. She had a successful history with the *Courier,* as well as a blockbuster story that was receiving national attention, but Brad Herring hadn't been moved by that. He needed Carolyne Hale's support on the board more than he needed Callie Jamieson's name on a byline or her expertise in the field.

Then again, Callie had three of E.W. Hale's diaries and a note from Wilty saying something about delving into the past. The more she thought about it, the more certain she was that like a dog in the backyard, he wasn't digging up dirt just because. Somewhere, there was a bone.

Filled with renewed purpose, Callie went into her home office and opened her laptop just as her electricity shut off. She was about to panic when she remembered the notice about some renovations.

She went into the other room and got her cell phone. The night before, she'd spent an hour bending Paula's ear with the details of her hellish encounter with the Widow and Brad Herring, so there was no need for further explanation when she asked to work out of her apartment.

"I'm headed out of town for a couple of days. If you want, you can move in."

"Thanks, but I'll just need to plug into your juice during the day. I'll come home to sleep."

"Do you have your key?"

"I do."

"Great. Work well. See you soon."

Callie hoofed it down the stairs to the lobby only to be greeted by a gaggle of electricians noisily coordinating their assignments with the crew chief.

As Tommy opened the door for her, he complained, "This is going to be a nightmare."

Callie smiled sympathetically. Tommy didn't know what a real nightmare was.

Before she headed downtown, Callie had a few errands to run. She walked over to her bank on Madison, her cleaner on Lex, and a computer store on Third to pick up some extra discs. As she ambled across to Second to catch a taxi going downtown, she thought she heard footsteps keeping rhythm with hers.

Someone else might not have noticed. This was New York, after all. No street was ever really vacant. But Callie had been the recipient of several ominous threats as well as a dead rat in her mailbox. Under the circumstances, caution didn't necessarily equal paranoia.

She slowed her pace. The other person did as well.

Down at the end of the block there was a small lingerie

shop. Callie darted inside guessing that her stalker wouldn't follow. She watched the street through the window, hoping to get a glimpse of him as he passed, but no one went by. He either gave up and turned back, or ducked into a doorway to wait her out.

After ten minutes of trying on bras and workout clothes, Callie, believing she'd shaken her tail, bought a pair of drawstring pants and left. She hailed a taxi and gave the driver Paula's address. The light changed and they headed downtown.

So did an innocuous blue car-for-hire.

Callie let herself into the loft, checked the refrigerator for goodies and settled at the big table in Paula's kitchen. She spread out her notes on the Dr. Drug series so she could finish polishing the next installment and checked her e-mails. Ezra Chapin would be pleased to know she was still receiving hate mail. Today the bulk of it was from addicts. They didn't call themselves that, of course. They referred to themselves as patients suffering from intolerable pain. Naturally, they wished that pain on Callie.

It occurred to Callie that perhaps in his zeal to dance to Carolyne Hale's tune, Brad Herring had canceled the rest of this series. A quick call to Amy reassured her that no such edict had come down from on high. That was a relief.

When she'd put Dr. Drug to bed, she turned to the diaries. Since Wilty mentioned that he'd been at Long House, Callie felt it was safe to assume that the fourth journal wasn't there. From what Brad Herring said about E.W. Hale's private papers being firmly regulated by the Hale Trust, Callie also assumed that whatever wasn't in Wilty's apartment or up at Long House had to be in the possession of someone with a strong claim on the name Hale.

Using her password, she logged onto the *Courier*'s main data base and downloaded the official biography of E.W. Hale. She scrolled through a great deal of it; most people who worked at the *Courier* were familiar with the basics. Her interest peaked when she read the notice of E.W. Hale marrying Constance Shipley in 1904, two years after the death of his first wife, Winifred. He was sixty-four, the new Mrs. Hale was forty-five. They remained married until his death in 1938. She died in 1948.

Callie ran a check on Constance Shipley. With her first husband, she had two children: a son, Walter, and a daughter, Anne. Walter died without issue. Anne had one child, a daughter named Victoria. Thankfully, all of the women in the Shipley line took the family name as their middle names, making it easier for Callie to track. After an exhaustive search of cities Callie thought might be relevant, Callie located a Victoria Shipley Moore in a suburb outside of Cleveland, the city where E.W. Hale laid the foundation for the empire that became Hale Holdings.

When Callie got Mrs. Moore on the phone, she introduced herself as a friend of Wilty's. After a polite, but persistent grilling by the octogenarian, she admitted that she and Wilty had been more than friends. When asked for the reason for her call, Callie fudged the truth slightly, telling Mrs. Moore that Wilty had asked her to collaborate on a project concerning the history of the Hales.

After mourning Wilty's passing and expressing frustration at not being able to attend his funeral due to ill health, Mrs. Moore said, "I spoke to Wilty a couple of days before he died."

"You did? If you don't mind, may I ask if the call was strictly social or was there something specific?"

"I'd like to think it was a bit of both." Callie heard a smile in her voice. "But yes, there was something specific. Several months ago, he called to find out if I had certain diaries."

"What kind of diaries?"

"E.W. Hale kept personal journals. Most were archived up at Long House, the Hale country estate at Lake George. Apparently, Wilty had embarked on some sort of inventory and noticed that certain journals were missing, four in particular. He assumed they were among the ones Mr. Hale had removed toward the end of his life, when he was married to my grandmother. I had three of them, which I sent on to him. I couldn't find the fourth."

"Did he say what had prompted this inventory?"

"He found a letter that upset him. He wouldn't go into it, but it sounded as if he needed the diaries to tell him whether whatever was in the letter was the truth."

Wilty hadn't mentioned a letter, but that must have been what drew him into this "project of personal discovery."

Callie asked how those diaries had come into Victoria's possession. She explained they were part of the personal effects that had been shipped to Victoria's mother, Anne, after her grandmother, Constance, passed on. When Anne passed on, everything came to Victoria, who split both the furnishings and the boxes between her two children.

She assumed that the maids who did the original packing didn't see anything particularly special about these ragged old journals and didn't take care to keep them together. The fourth journal could have found its way into another box. Or the trash.

"Did your grandmother ever talk to you about what was in those diaries?" Callie asked.

"She worried that much of what Mr. Hale wrote could be taken out of context and misinterpreted. E.W. Hale wasn't a likable man, but he was historic. And he did have some very dark secrets. Since he'd made it clear he didn't want those secrets revealed, she kept his confidence."

"Why did he separate these from the others?"

Again there was a pause. "My guess is that if Emmet Hale was preparing to meet his Maker, the diaries he selected to reread contained either the mistakes he wanted to correct. Or the sins he wanted to repent."

It has to do with who E.W. Hale was and what that makes me.

"When Wilty called you the last time, what did he say?"

"Frankly, he was talking so fast, I could hardly understand him." She sounded apologetic.

"That's okay," Callie soothed, her mind racing. "It sounds as if he was agitated. Was he?"

"Yes."

"Did he say what was upsetting him?"

"I asked, but he said it was nothing. He wanted to know if I'd found the fourth diary. He was still curious about what it contained." There was a pause. Callie guessed Victoria was trying to recall the entire conversation. "He didn't sound curious, though."

"Did he sound angry? Worried?"

She deliberated before answering. "Nervous, I'd say." She sighed, her breath quivering. "Perhaps if I had questioned him more thoroughly, I might have been able to help."

Callie heard sniffling on the other end of the line.

"Don't put that burden on yourself, Mrs. Moore. I doubt if there was anything anyone could have done." She didn't know Wilty had been murdered. Callie thought it best not to tell her.

"Well, I've done something about finding that journal."

"You have?"

Victoria explained that her granddaughter, Elizabeth, had contacted her cousins about rummaging through some of what they'd inherited from E.W. Hale.

"She's a professor of English Literature at Case Western. She told them she wanted to see if any first editions were mixed up with the soup bowls and cachepots."

Callie breathed a sigh of relief. "If she finds it, will you call me?"

"Certainly, but I'm afraid I can't give it to you."

"Why not?"

"Because this morning, a Detective Chapin from the New York Police Department called. He told me anything we found had to be turned over to him."

Callie thanked Victoria Moore for her help, commiserated on what a loss Wilty's death was and promised to keep in touch.

Then, she called Ezra Chapin.

"We need to talk," she said when he came on the line.

"What about?"

"Victoria Moore."

"Nice lady."

"Why'd you call her?"

"Wilty called her. I wanted to know what they talked about."

The phone logs. Callie wanted to kick herself. But she wanted to kick him more.

"I came to see you without being asked. I shared those diaries, Wilty's note and other information with you in good faith and now you screw me over by co-opting that fourth diary? That's low, Chapin."

"Where are you?"

"What?" He was zigging again.

"I called you at your office. Your assistant said you weren't in and wouldn't be in for a while. She suggested I try you at home. You weren't there either."

Whatever happened to don't ask, don't tell? Callie wondered, filled with an intense desire to strangle Amy.

"They shut off the electricity in my building."

"So why not work where you're supposed to work?"

The man was insufferably nosy. "Because I'm on hiatus," she snapped.

"Hiatus. My father had one of those."

"Look, I'm not in the mood for your twisted sense of humor."

"How about dinner, then?"

Another zig. She was getting dizzy. And mad.

"I wouldn't have dinner with you if the only way I could get anything to eat was to sit at the same table as you!"

With that, she slammed down the phone.

"Everything back to normal?" Callie asked as she walked through the lobby toward the elevators.

"Depends on what you consider normal," Tommy jibed.

Callie wished him a good night and waited patiently for the elevator doors to close. She wondered if they worked faster when the building was younger.

Callie's apartment was in a rent-controlled building.

Originally, it belonged to Auntie Pennie. Eight years before, she found a convenient loophole in her lease and turned the apartment over to Callie as a college graduation gift. Since Auntie Pennie spent most of her time in California or on the road, it didn't make sense for her to continue paying rent, low as it was, on a residence she didn't use. Callie objected, but, as she'd done for most of Callie's life, Pennie silenced her by saying, "This is what your mother would want for you."

Since Callie and Auntie Pennie shared a preference for contemporary decor, over the years the only real change Callie had made was coloration. The sleek, L-shaped banquette that wrapped around the perimeter of the living room went from charcoal gray flannel to a rich, beige wool. The carpet went from black to taupe. Two cushy club chairs upholstered in creamy linen replaced half-moon chairs in black leather. Lipstick red throw pillows were replaced by a pink cashmere throw. Black vases and silver candlesticks were replaced by crystal. And stark white vertical blinds were replaced by soft, ecru curtains.

Her bedroom bore the same serene, blond aesthetic. The headboard of her queen-size sleigh bed was upholstered in beige linen that matched the carpet and a tufted wing chair. Here, as in the living room, bouquets of pink and peachy toned flowers and the occasional orchid plant attested to the femininity of the chatelaine of this *maison*.

Over time, this apartment had become very much her own space. She never got off the elevator that she didn't anticipate the rush of calm that greeted her when she unlocked her door and walked inside, especially after a day like the one she'd just had. As she turned the key and the scent of her potpourri reached out to greet her, a smile began to form.

The entry light was on. Since the reappearance of the gray people, she'd put it on a timer so she didn't have to walk into a dark apartment. She'd just closed the door when her smile disappeared. Creeping around the corner from the direction of her bedroom was an unexpected splash of light.

She froze, unsure as to whether she should leave, go back downstairs and have Tommy call the police, or tiptoe inside and check it out for herself.

Callie's heart thundered inside her chest. Any minute, she expected to see that burly man from the night before running toward her.

She shut off the entry light and pressed up against the wall, barely breathing. She listened for footsteps. Or the sound of furniture being moved. Or papers being rustled.

The silence was complete. And terrifying.

She listened harder, trying to block out the city noises that drifted up from the street.

The light went off. The apartment became a pool of gray.

She squinted, trying to narrow the field of her vision, yet at the same time, sharpen the focus. Slowly, she panned the dusky living room, looking for shadows. Her eyes moved toward the space where just seconds ago there had been light. Fear intensified the black quiet until it was screaming in her ears.

She inched back toward the door. Her hand clasped the doorknob, but she couldn't move. While her brain began to plot her escape, her body remained frozen with indecision. The door was heavy. If she opened it, it might creak and alert whomever, or whatever, was lurking. Then, there was the elevator. If someone else had used it, it would take forever to rescue her. She could use the stairs, but the doors to the individual floors only opened into the stairwell. Once she started down, the sole exit was the lobby. If her intruder was quick enough to follow her into the stairwell, she'd be trapped.

She was already trapped.

The light went on again.

She gasped and slid deeper into the corner, her hand still tightly gripped around the door handle.

A shadow flitted by. Her eyes darted from one side to another, trying to decide whether the owner of the shadow was outside. Or inside her apartment.

The light went out.

She heard a click that sounded like a trigger.

She reacted as if a starter pistol had been fired. Quickly, but quietly, she turned the doorknob, slipped into the hall, and raced for the stairwell, pulling the door shut behind her. She flew down the fifteen flights, her heart pounding like a jackhammer, her breath heaving, a stream of tears keeping pace with her feet.

When she reached the lobby, her eyes were wide. Her entire body was drenched with sweat. She was trembling.

"Callie!" Tommy ran toward her, clamping his strong paws on her arms to steady her. "What's wrong? What happened?"

"There's someone in my apartment!"

Her breathing was labored from the exertion of her descent. And the height of her fear.

"I heard a click. I think he has a gun."

Fresh tears tumbled down her cheeks. Her hands refused to stop shaking.

Tommy ran to the phone and dialed 911. Then, he settled Callie on the chair behind his station and called the superintendent. Together, they tried to keep her calm until help arrived.

When the police came, Tommy told them what Callie had told him. She filled in whatever details she could, handed them her keys and remained behind while they flagged the elevator. As the brass needle marked off floors along the elevator's climb, a surge of panic took hold of her.

What if her intruder wasn't human? What if the gray stranger had gotten even bolder and had taken up residence in her apartment? She almost choked on the thought. What would the police say? What would they think?

She dropped her face in her hands. Behind her eyelids scenes of other policemen being called in to check out reported intruders began to play like a rented video. She saw them rushing through the doors, bringing dogs in to sniff around closets and in the basement. She could hear them moving furniture, opening and closing doors. And then, the terrible, horrible, humiliating pause as they tried to find a way to tell Mara Jamieson she was mistaken. Again. There was no one in the house who didn't belong there. It must have been her imagination.

"Ms. Jamieson?"

She looked up into the face of a young man with shiny brown skin, a hairless pate and a concerned smile. His name tag identified him as Officer Plover. Before he spoke again, she knew.

"There wasn't anyone there, was there?"

"No. Thankfully, not."

He thought she'd be relieved. Instead, the veins in her neck bulged.

"My partner and I searched the entire apartment. There was no sign of a break-in."

Her eyes looked blank. He wondered if she understood what he was saying. He kneeled down so that they were on the same level.

"The lamp on one of your night tables appears to have a short. It kept clicking on and off. That must have been what frightened you."

"That must have been it," Callie said, her body slumped, her spirit completely flattened. "I'm sorry to have caused so much trouble."

The young officer moved closer to her, speaking softly so only she could hear him.

"I was the one who took the call about your mailbox."

Good, Callie thought. Then he believes me. He doesn't think I'm making this up.

"Mr. Krakowski also tells me that you've reported being disturbed in the middle of the night several times before."

"I wasn't *reporting* anything, Officer Plover!" she said, her face pink with embarrassment. "A couple of times, Tommy asked why I looked so tired. I told him something woke me in the middle of the night." She flushed redder, loath to make this admission for fear of the consequences. "I occasionally suffer from nightmares. That's all. I didn't mean to imply that Hannibal Lecter was standing on a ledge outside my window, for goodness sakes!"

"The last thing I wanted to do was to upset you," Plover said, "but with this coming on top of the other incident, it's my job to ask a lot of questions and follow up on everything. I'd rather be on the safe side and check it all out than have you become the victim of a stalker."

What if you're being stalked by phantoms? she wanted to ask. They don't leave evidence. But they do leave victims.

"Thank you," she said, dragging herself to her feet. "You've been very nice and very understanding. Again, please accept my apology for wasting your time."

"By the way, we think we have a lead on the person who violated your mailbox."

"Really?"

Officer Plover looked confused. "I guess Detective Chapin couldn't reach you."

Now it was Callie's turn to be confused.

"He said he's working with you on a homicide and that when he spoke to you, he'd tell you about it."

Working with me on a homicide? "He must have forgotten. Are you close to an arrest?"

"Don't worry, we'll get him." He smiled at her reassuringly.

Callie made her way to the elevator. Just before the doors closed, she noticed something that scratched at her heart like a fingernail on a blackboard. Tommy, Officer Plover's partner, and the super were staring at her in a way that felt eerily familiar.

That was the way people used to look at her mother.

Callie closed the door behind her. With shaking hands she locked the locks and turned on all the lights, racing from room to room. When the entire apartment was ablaze, she went into the kitchen and boiled some water for tea.

A horn honked. Her head jerked toward the window. The tea kettle whistled. Her heart pounded in her chest.

Quickly, she turned off the gas and poured water into a *Courier, Have we got news for you* mug.

She found a chamomile tea bag and dropped it into the boiling water to steep.

Her legs felt wobbly. She gripped the counter and watched the water turn into a pale, almost celadon green.

The phone rang. Callie jumped. She didn't answer it. She let the machine pick up.

Hi. It's Callie. Well, actually, it's only Callie's voice. I'm either not home or I can't come to the phone for any one of a dozen really good reasons. If you have a good reason for me to call you back, leave your name and number. Thanks.

"Callie, it's Ezra Chapin. You hung up too quickly for me to tell you our guys have a lead on ratman. You were a little cranky this afternoon. Hope this news makes you feel better. If you want to call and express your gratitude, my number is 555-1243."

In spite of herself, she smiled. His call did make her feel better, but she had no intention of calling him and telling him so. Instead, she took her tea into her bedroom.

She turned on the lamp that Officer Plover said had the short and waited to see if it flickered. When it didn't, she breathed a sigh of relief, turned on the television and went into the bathroom to get ready for bed.

She switched on the light. That's when she saw it hanging from the shower: a noose, with a note attached. With shaking hands she turned it over.

LIKE MOTHER, LIKE DAUGHTER.

15

Carolyne was the center of attention. Everyone from the maître d' to the coat check, to the captains, the waiters, even some of the longtime busboys, came over to offer their sympathies. Daniel Boulud, the owner of Daniel, sent an exquisite bottle of Château Latour to their table along with his condolences.

Peter Merrick sat through it all with practiced patience. He'd offered to take her to a lesser known restaurant or to bring dinner in, but she insisted. They'd planned this evening several weeks before and she didn't see any reason to cancel. Nor did she see any reason to sit at a less conspicuous table. Her idea of mourning was to wear black and a dour expression. Anything else was beside the point.

"This must be painful," he said, after the last of her devotees retreated.

"Terribly, but at the same time, it's comforting to know that people care." She lowered her eyes and sipped her wine.

Peter swallowed a smile. No one could sling the bullshit better than Carolyne. It was probably one of the things he found most attractive about her. That, and her ability to slip in and out of her various personas. One minute she was the elegant doyenne—pampered, privileged and proud of it. The next minute she was a street tough who could give as good as she got—and then some. Her proficiency at the art of self-preservation was legendary and admirable.

As for how a river rat from Memphis rose to become one of the pillars of New York society, it wasn't unusual for someone from a disadvantaged background to better herself. All it took was hard work, a steely determination and a clearly visualized goal. Once there, initiates could blend easily into the upper tier via imitation and a compulsive attention to detail. What few in the higher reaches of the social order liked to admit was that while style and class were often innate, sophistication was a product of experience and exposure. Manners and grace could be learned.

Carolyne Hale was one of the few social émigrés who hadn't completely obliterated her original essence. It didn't happen often, but every now and then she allowed her sharper edge to surface. Once, when Wilty insinuated that she'd led a cushy life, she launched into a diatribe about the indignities she'd suffered at the hands of Huntington and Eppie Hale. She painted them with the broadest brush and in the darkest tones imaginable, branding them as her excuse for her indulgences and the cause of her unhappiness.

What interested Peter was that the Hales were the epicenter of her anger. From things she'd confided over the years, there were plenty of others to share the blame. Yet she never went on about the miseries of growing up the daughter of a prostitute and a riverboat gambler, about being shuttled off to her grandmother's house whenever one or both of her parents were jailed, about being teased by her schoolmates whenever stories about them made the papers, particularly when her mother had been beaten by a john and left for dead by the side of a road.

It couldn't have been easy to work her way through college, even with the scholarships she'd earned, but she did. Nor could it have been easy to bring the Crown Prince of Memphis to the altar, but she did. And instead of fading into the background after his death like so many others of her ilk might have, Carolyne moved to New York and flourished.

On some level, she found a way to come to terms with who she'd been, figure out who she wanted to be and move on.

More power to her, Peter thought. He had patients who spent years in therapy for similar problems, yet never conquered their complexes or their rage. He was a professional with dozens of coping mechanisms at his disposal, yet if the truth be known, he would probably have one foot stuck in the emotional mire created by his upbringing until the day he died.

Carolyne was droning on about the effort it was going to take to close down Wilty's apartment and his house in the Hamptons, when a group at the table in the far corner got up to leave. Having watched the waiters parade by carrying an elaborate dessert tray punctuated by sparklers, Peter assumed it was a family that had gathered to honor an occasion.

Inwardly, Peter winced. Just that morning he'd received an invitation to his father's eighty-fifth birthday. He wondered if any of those people had dreaded attending this evening's dinner as much as he dreaded attending the one to which he was invited.

Two of the celebrants stopped by their table to pay obeisance to Carolyne. Fortunately, they did it quickly. The youngest member of the group, a striking young woman in her early thirties, tarried a bit, deliberately letting her family get ahead of her. She, too, wanted to speak to Carolyne, but she wanted to do it privately.

"Vanna, my dear." Carolyne tilted her head so that she could receive a kiss. "Peter, this is Vanna Larkin, a close friend of Wilty's."

"I'm devastated."

"I know."

"I was with him the night before."

Peter noticed that surprised Carolyne, and not pleasantly.

"I wasn't well. Wilty took me home and tucked me in." An embarrassed smile wobbled onto her lips, then collapsed. "I just couldn't believe it when the police told me he'd been murdered."

Peter looked from Vanna to Carolyne, stunned by the news.

"When did you speak to the police?" Carolyne said, deliberately lowering her voice, cueing Vanna to do the same.

"This morning." Vanna's body stiffened, but her eyes became globes of excitement as she regaled them with her harrowing, movie-of-the-week experience with The Law. "These two detectives took me into this really hideous room and went at me," she said, her voice slurring slightly. "They asked me all kinds of things. About me, Wilty, what he was into, who his friends were, how well we knew each other."

Her brow furrowed and she bit her lower lip. Peter could see she was grading herself. She was worried she didn't answer the questions correctly. He guessed total recall wasn't her strong suit.

"They even wanted to know about his relationship with you."

"And what did you tell them?"

"I said you got along."

Carolyne's lips formed an irritated moue. Given the opportunity, Peter believed she gladly would have axed the harebrained Ms. Larkin.

"What else did you tell them about Wilty?"

Vanna shrugged as if it should have been obvious. "Everything." She flushed. "That I could remember, that is. As I said, I wasn't well."

Carolyne patted her hand, the way one might to a doddering old aunt. "I'm sure you did your best." She tried to offer a forgiving smile, but her mouth refused. "I didn't realize you and Wilty had taken up with each other again."

Vanna threw her head back and issued a throaty, tipsy laugh. "I wish!" One look at Carolyne sobered her right up. "Oh! I'm so sorry. What I meant was . . ."

"Why don't you join your family, dear? We'll continue this conversation another time."

As soon as Vanna was gone, Carolyne compelled her jaw to unclench. She took a gulp of wine and looked at Peter.

"I didn't tell you about Wilty because as difficult as it is to comprehend the notion that one's son jumped out a window, it's even more difficult to accept the fact that someone pushed him."

Carolyne was so expert at camouflaging her emotions, there was no way for Peter to gauge her sincerity. He gave her the benefit of the doubt.

She told him about her interview with the aforementioned detectives.

"I can understand how Vanna would have been rattled. They're boorish and cold," she declared. "What's more, they're dogged. They're insisting on accompanying me during my visit to Wilty's apartment tomorrow. Can you imagine?"

It was police procedure, but that wouldn't salve Carolyne so Peter kept it to himself.

The delivery of their first course provided a needed distraction. When the service staff left the table, Carolyne vented about Vanna Larkin.

"My son's regrettable taste in women never ceased to amaze me. If and when he dated women of his status, they were either drunks or morons. Or, in the case of Vanna, both. When he dated women outside of his circle, they were money-grubbers and glory-seekers." She shook her head, as if Atlas carrying the world on his shoulders had it easy compared to her. "Just yesterday, I had to have someone removed from the *Courier*."

"Why was that?"

"Some nobody whom Wilty took up with a couple of years ago came up with the brilliant idea of writing a series of articles centering around that ridiculous old saw, the Hale Curse. She claimed it was a way of giving historical context to Wilty's premature death. I saw it for what it was, a clear attempt to cash in on her limited acquaintance with my son."

Carolyne's tone had turned snide.

"I don't know what possessed him, but Brad Herring okayed the project. Naturally, I demanded that he rescind his approval and assign someone more competent to the task of memorializing Wilty."

"Naturally." Peter wondered whether Brad Herring had recovered yet from his lashing. "What about the reporter?"

Carolyne's expression was one of immense satisfaction. "Ms. Jamieson is in the process of sending out resumes."

"Callie Jamieson?"

"Yes. Do you know her?"

He couldn't, and wouldn't, reveal the fact that Callie was a patient. "Through her work, mostly. This week, in fact, an exposé she authored on doctors and pharmacists colluding to issue illegal prescriptions for painkillers is running in the City section of the *Courier*. It's outstanding."

Carolyne didn't like her judgments questioned. "Then surely another newspaper will rush to hire her and you won't have to be deprived of her talent."

Her pettiness annoyed Peter. He was willing to cater to Carolyne—he did enjoy her patronage—but he had his limits.

"I noticed her at the viewing," he said, slinging an arrow of his own. "She was sincerely bereft. At Wilty's funeral, also, she was moved to tears. Is it possible you misjudged her?"

He took great delight in watching Carolyne swallow her rage at his praise of someone she had designated an enemy of the state.

"The woman has an agenda," Carolyne insisted. "At the funeral, she was on the arm of one of the detectives investigating Wilty's murder. I find that odd. Don't you?"

Actually, aside from finding it curious that Carolyne would even notice something that minor on the day of her son's burial, Peter was heartened to learn that the man who caught Callie during her swoon wasn't a boyfriend, after all.

"She wrote the original story about Wilty's fall," he said. "In a sense, they're both on the same case."

Carolyne offered him a frosty smile. "I don't see it that way, but rather than argue, why don't we simply agree to disagree?"

He raised his wineglass and tipped it toward her. He'd allow her the last word. After all, she might have done him a huge favor. With Callie out of a job, her stress level would elevate. Her dreams would intensify, as would her fears.

Also, without an office to go to, she had the time for longer sessions and more of them. Whatever time she wanted, he'd make available. If she didn't have the funds, he would forgo his fees. Anything, just to get her into his office and on his couch.

The clock was ticking.

It was late. Guy Hoffman was alone in his lab, reviewing his notes. It was an enormous room centered around a large square table which housed several computers, microscopes, as well as other assorted lab paraphernalia. Lining the walls were stacks of cages housing GenTec's community of rodents. Each wall represented a quadrant which was defined by a different experiment, each stack along that wall a different stage in that experiment. A twenty-four-hour ventilation system did its best to keep the animal smell and dust at a minimum. Low wattage ceiling lights kept the main part of the room dim, so as not to overly excite the rodents. A lamp outfitted with a brighter bulb hung just above his head to illuminate his papers.

His colleagues had gone home hours ago. As was his habit, Guy lingered, claiming the need to go over what had been accomplished during that day, and to set goals for the next. In truth, he was never happier than when he was alone in a laboratory. There was something about being surrounded by scientific apparatus that excited him in a way few things did. Whether it was the most advanced microscope or the most basic test tube, it was a miraculous object that provided the opportunity to explore the enormity of the universe, the intricacy of life-forms, the mystery of creation.

It was hard, frustrating, painstaking work, but Guy couldn't get enough of it. He loved the adventure inherent in the task of trying to move the hypothetical into the realm of the practical. He reveled in the singular joy that came from a theory proved or a trial completed.

He didn't know which came first, his fascination with science or his unsociability, but he wasn't a man who was comfortable with people. He didn't do well in communal settings. He had no tolerance for small talk or chitchat or political debates that accomplished nothing other than arousing tempers and creating bruised feelings. He preferred significance, performing tasks that had an end-of-the-day result that moved the world forward in some way. He admired completion, yet respected process and understood failure.

What he couldn't abide was dilettantish behavior and those who simply treaded water in their careers. In his mind, jumping from one thing to another was just as offensive as staying put. The essence of life was asking questions and seeking answers. Everything else was fluff.

He was working out another way of implementing a colleague's theory about the possibility of introducing the protein into the system via inhalation, when he heard strange sounds emanating from the north quadrant. Since it wasn't the usual scratching and sniffling, and whirring of the occasional treadmill, it caught his attention.

Wearily, he got up and went to see what was going on. When he realized which cage housed the noisome rat, he was concerned, yet excited. Earlier, he'd injected this particular row of rodents with a newly formulated solution of p-316. He had increased the concentration slightly to see if that might enhance the effect and motivate the protein to unlock the genetic material inside the cell he'd isolated, the one he believed contained the power of memory. Each cage was marked to show the dosage given to its resident.

While the rats in the lower cages, the ones receiving the smaller doses of p-316 remained relatively undisturbed— one was having difficulty breathing—this one was in the midst of what looked like a grand mal seizure. It was twitching and writhing about, thrashing up against the sides of the cage, banging its head against the floor. Bubbles of white foam had collected at the side of its mouth.

In the cage directly above, a dead rat lay crumpled in a corner, the sawdust beneath its head matted red with blood.

Hoffman bent down and stared into the cage housing the afflicted rodent. It was in the final stages of a fatal seizure. It was a terrible sight to witness.

Guy observed the end with undisguised impatience. He was eager to dissect the animal and put its bodily fluids and tissue samples on slides and into tubes filled with various diagnostic liquids. The seizure indicated that the injected solution had indeed produced an effect. The rat's death told Hoffman that he needed to either correct his proportions or alter the method of induction. But that was tomorrow's task. Right now, he had an autopsy to perform.

16

Ezra Chapin lived in a second floor walk-up on Riverside Drive. It was a large, one bedroom apartment in a narrow building sandwiched between two behemoth co-ops that occupied the corners of Eighty-sixth and Eighty-seventh streets. It wasn't a particularly light apartment, the view of Riverside Park and the river was obscured by trees, and he was subjected to traffic noises most of the day, but its location suited him. When asked, he proudly declared himself to be a citizen of the Great Republic of the Upper West Side, a statement which he believed gave you his politics, his dress code, his religious affiliation and his food preferences all in one quick pronouncement.

With wide, thick moldings, high ceilings, real wood kitchen cabinets, a working fireplace, old glass doorknobs, and floor to ceiling bookshelves on every wall, Ezra's apartment boasted good architectural bones, which was helpful to a man without a scintilla of decorating sense. It wasn't that Ezra didn't have taste or opinions about what he liked and didn't like. Ezra was a utilitarian: if a piece of furniture fulfilled his needs, it could fill a space. It didn't necessarily bother him that the scale of his reading chair was out of synch with the scale of his couch or that neither of them looked comfortable with the oversized refectory table he used as a desk.

He wasn't sloppy, but neither did he suffer any compulsion to maintain a military sense of order and neatness.

Ezra found nothing wrong with disarray, as long as he knew where everything was. Most of the time, he did. It was when he was involved in one of his cold case projects, like now, that remembering where he put what became a chore. To aid his mental organization, he set up a large, old-fashioned bulletin board, the type that used to be seen in elementary school classrooms, with cork on one side, a blackboard on the back, and a tray for pushpins or erasers and chalk running along the bottom.

He'd separated the large board into two rectangles, each with three vertical rows of index cards. On the left were the early Hales, each one described by a different color card.

E.W. Hale was the only one to die of natural causes. His card was white.

Charles Hale committed suicide. His card was blue.

His brother, the first Huntington Hale, was killed in northern Wisconsin when a stack of logs crushed him to death. His card was green.

Hunt's son, Thomas Horton Hale—yellow—fell off a cliff at Martha's Vineyard. His was the only death Ezra thought could qualify as a genuine accident.

He put the second Huntington Hale and his brother, Cole, into the second rectangle along with Wilty. On their cards—blue for Wilty, green for Hunt, yellow for Cole— were all the facts currently available about each case. All three columns were short.

As he surveyed his handiwork, Ezra admitted that just as Callie Jamieson had bought into his crime theory, he was beginning to believe that E.W. Hale had led a secret life, and that the fallout from something catastrophic that had occurred in the course of that secret life might have spilled over into succeeding generations. History was replete with tales of long-standing feuds and continued family vengeance.

His eyes returned to the truncated case histories of Hunt and Cole Hale. Ezra still hadn't heard from Jack Carlson, the Warren Country Sheriff. Either the guy was taking the longest vacation ever recorded or he was lying dead in a pit somewhere waiting for his body to be discovered. Gideon Bryson had forwarded the list Ezra had requested of everyone on staff at Hale Farms at the time of Cole Hale's death, but it contained no surprises and no new leads. Bryson said he'd keep nosing around. Ezra intended to run the list through BCI.

As for Wilty, he and Jorge had interviewed a score of people who'd had contact with the deceased in the days and nights before he died. Nothing unexpected materialized. Wilty rescued some drunken socialite from being mauled at a downtown bar, but she wasn't able to give them much. CSU continued to run tests, including trying to track down the dozens of sets of fingerprints they lifted at Wilty's apartment. The man had a lot of friends. Ezra was looking for his enemies.

The buzzer from downstairs startled him. It was after nine. Ezra pressed the button on the intercom to find out who was paying him a visit at this late hour.

"It's Callie Jamieson. I need to see you."

Ezra buzzed her in. He opened the door and waited for her to ascend. Judging by the edge in her voice, she wasn't dropping by to apologize for rejecting his dinner proposal.

She arrived at his doorstep carrying a stern expression and a shopping bag. He stepped aside to let her in.

Without preamble, she slipped on a pair of latex gloves and lifted a noose out of the bag and laid it on a table. "This was on my shower." She showed him the note as well. "My mother hanged herself," she said, explaining.

He was dumbstruck, not so much by the noose, but by her calm revelation of her mother's suicide. Although looking at her, noting the veins in her neck and the tightness of her jaw, he realized this calm had been reached only through a great deal of effort.

"You left a message saying you had a lead on . . ."

"Ratman," he said, finishing the sentence. Her pallor was chalky.

"Is he in custody?"

"Yes. Plover called me a little while ago to tell me they brought him in."

"Then he couldn't have been the one who left this."

"Probably not." It was the first time he'd seen anything approaching fear in her eyes.

"Who is he? The one they picked up."

"Prodyot Raju."

Callie guessed he was not big and burly. "Do you happen to know if he's related to Hakim Raju?"

"The pill-pushing pharmacist made famous by the Dr. Drug series currently running in the *Courier*?" She gave him a smile. It was faint and fleeting, but he felt rewarded anyway. "He's a cousin. They picked him up in Jersey a couple of hours ago." He paused, weighing the consequences of his next statement. "Right around the time Nelson Plover was checking out your digs."

Callie could tell he wanted to ask why she didn't call Plover after discovering the noose in her bathroom.

"I didn't call Officer Plover because I was beginning to feel like a pest. First, I have a rat in my mailbox. Then I have a short in a lamp. I was afraid if I told him I found a noose in my shower, he'd think I had bats in my belfry."

It was Ezra's turn to smile. "I don't think he would've thought anything of the kind, but I'm glad you believed he would and decided to come to me instead. How about a glass of wine to settle the nerves?"

"That would be nice."

He invited her to make herself comfortable while he went into the kitchen. When he was gone, she looked around, trying to get a fuller sense of the man through his home. She doubted his living room would ever grace the pages of *Architectural Digest,* but she had to admit, it was much nicer than she'd expected. It was comfortably arranged with large pieces of furniture that created an aura of masculinity. Also, it had a lived-in look that said he didn't mind being home alone. Callie was always suspicious of people who couldn't stay in, who had to be out every night for fear of having to spend time with themselves. In her mind, if you didn't want to be with you, why would she want to be with you?

She was surprised by the number of bookshelves in the room and the variety of the titles. Rising, she took a quick tour, eager to learn what, other than bloody murder, interested Ezra Chapin. Aside from the spy and police novels she might have expected, there were nonfiction books ranging from relationship how-to's, to psychiatric journals on psychopaths, sexual predators, serial killers, and violent children. Also, there were dozens of law books.

On one of those shelves stood a nicely laminated degree from Columbia Law School. On the shelf below it was Ezra's college diploma from Brown University.

"My mamma didn't raise no dumb child," he said as he handed her a glass of red wine.

"I see that."

He chuckled at how obviously stunned she was to find out he had a brain capable of something other than conjuring up ways to vex her.

"Since I'm sure the next question is why aren't I practicing law, I'll tell you. I worked in the DA's office for a couple of years, but the justice system, on the legal side, didn't work fast enough for me. And it wasn't in-your-face enough for me. I want to slap handcuffs on the bad guys and toss them in jail. I don't want to be the suit who pleads them out."

Not for the first time, Callie sensed that everything Detective Chapin did and all that he was, came from something personal, something that put a pocket of anger in his gut that simply wouldn't go away.

"How did your mamma feel about you chucking your law career?"

He grinned. "She loves me no matter what."

"I'm sure your second-grade teacher loved you, too." Callie pointed to Ezra's bulletin board. "Colorful and neat and well organized. Definitely worthy of a happy face."

Ezra tilted his wineglass. "I'm glad you approve."

"So much so that I brought you something." She reached

into the shopping bag and extracted the diaries. "In exchange for looking into who left me that . . . thing, I brought you these. To read, not to keep."

He took them gratefully and put them on his desk. As he sat back down, he noticed her eyes gravitating toward the noose. The frightened glint he'd seen in her eyes before had returned.

"I promise to get them back to you as quickly as I can, but before we talk about that, we have to talk about this." He indicated the offensive rope. "Who'd want to scare the shit out of you? And how would they know about your mother?"

Callie sipped her wine. This was hard. She didn't discuss her mother with friends, let alone strangers.

"As you pointed out the other day, Martin Orlando can't be too thrilled with me, but besides him or someone related to the Dr. Drug story, I have no idea. As for my mother, with the advent of the Internet, not much is private anymore."

Ezra had already figured out that whoever left the noose was the same one who'd rigged her lamp. He probably gained access to her apartment by posing as one of the electricians rewiring her building.

"Okay, let's talk curse," he said, pointing to his bulletin board. "I tried to follow your lead, but without those diaries, I had nowhere to go. Wanna help me out?"

"Today, when I was rereading E.W. Hale's bio, I did come upon something interesting," she said, grateful to him for moving on.

Ezra watched her carefully. She appeared to be in control, but she was working at it. Hard.

"One of the reasons E.W. Hale amassed such an incredible fortune, is that at the same time he was buying up local newspapers like the *Cleveland City Courier,* he was also gobbling up small paper mills. That one hand washing the other system worked well for a while, but eventually, Hale Paper wasn't large enough to supply all of E.W.'s newspapers. He began to look around for another paper empire with which to merge.

"He found it in Wisconsin. Tobias Schirmerhorn, the owner of Racine Paper, was up to his neck in financial trouble. He was in debt to the banks and since he had a reputation for defaulting on loan payments, no one was rushing to bail him out. Hale offered to loan Schirmerhorn two hundred thousand dollars in exchange for twenty-five percent of the company. He also insisted on a clause that said if Schirmerhorn defaulted, he'd get twenty-six percent of Schirmerhorn's stock. That would give him fifty-one percent and the controlling vote."

Ezra whistled at Hale's nerve.

"Shortly after the contract was signed and the money had been turned over, Schirmerhorn put all his stock in his daughter's name so if he defaulted—which he ultimately did—he wouldn't have any stock to turn over to Hale."

"Gotcha."

"Not quite. In 1898, Charles Hale married Irene Schirmerhorn. Since the family had no cash to speak of, Irene defied her father and used her shares of Racine Paper as a dowry, giving E.W. control of Racine Paper. Then, for reasons no one can fathom, Charles kills himself. Irene couldn't go home to Wisconsin because Tobias disowned her. Huntington Hale, in a noble attempt to uphold the biblical tradition of the brother taking care of the brother's widow, married the grief stricken Irene in 1901."

Ezra groaned, knowing exactly where she was headed.

Callie nodded, her face a mask of mock despair. "Poor Hunt's up in northern Wisconsin inspecting one of the lumberyards that supplies Racine Paper with its raw timber, when a two-story–high stack of freshly cut logs falls on him and kills him. Instantly!"

"It's the revenge of the Schirmerhorns."

"So it would appear. Anyway, the point to this drawn-out history lesson is that Wilty knew a guy named Schirmerhorn. Ben, I think. I don't know whether he's part of the Wisconsin Schirmerhorns, but . . ."

"It's certainly worth a conversation."

"I hope it helps." Callie stood. "I have to go."

Ezra was disappointed. He stood also. "I'll take you home."

"You don't have to."

"Yes, I do. My mother raised me to be a gentleman. And my badge obligates me to personally examine a crime scene. If you don't mind, I'd like to look around your apartment. It'll only take a few minutes and then, unless you beg me to stay, I'll leave."

He could tell she was relieved. So was he.

This was the part he liked best, watching people who didn't know they were being watched. It used to be he couldn't put more than one camera in a room without being found out, but with these tiny, new fiberoptic snoopers, he was able to catch the action from lots of different angles.

With a bourbon in one hand and a cigarette in the other, he propped his feet up on the side of the table he was using as a desk, positioned the computer monitor so he could see it clearly, punched a couple of keys so that all the rigged rooms were visible at the same time, sat back and enjoyed the show.

He liked being a voyeur, especially when his subjects stripped down and went at it. They thought they were so sexy, grinding their hips into each other, humping and pumping until they jerked about in some final spasm of passion and then flopped down on the bed like fish on a boat. If only they could see how awkward they looked. Dogs rutting in an alley were just as graceful.

It would have been enough to make him give up sex, except a man had needs.

He watched the screen and laughed. The detective, being the zealous type, had checked the phones for bugs, run his hands along some of the moldings and stuck his nose into everything, making certain there was no boogey man hiding behind the curtains or under the bed. He'd come up with nothing, of course, but that didn't stop him. He started on a second go-round. That wasn't good.

If the dick discovered one of his plants, he wouldn't be able to trace it—he never left prints—but he'd send in a crew that would search until every last camera was found. Then, they'd track down who manufactured those particular cameras, where they were sold and by whom. Then they'd grill that putz of a salesclerk. Two seconds after someone flashed a badge in his face, he'd pee in his pants and tell them anything and everything they wanted to know.

A swig of booze quelled his anxiety.

Chapin reentered the bedroom.

He noted the detective's mounting frustration with pride. The guy had conducted a pretty thorough search, but he was up against a master.

The Jamieson broad was nervous. He liked that. He liked knowing that he had the power to make someone feel vulnerable and frightened. It was his way of giving back, of letting the world know what his life had been like.

He gulped his bourbon again and lit another cigarette. He was getting excited. Any minute now, Chapin would find the one little bit of evidence that would push the bitch over the edge.

There. He was hunkered down in a corner of her bedroom. He'd spotted it. Good boy. He reached into his pocket, pulled out a scraper and one of those small plastic bags that the forensic freaks used to collect evidence. Carefully, he lifted the dark pellets onto the scraper and dropped them into the bag.

She asked what it was. The dick didn't want to say. She insisted.

"Rat droppings."

Thank goodness this was in color. If it hadn't been, he'd never have been able to see her turn that deathly shade of white. Or to see the turquoise of her eyes as they widened and darted about the room, frantically looking for other signs of rodent infestation.

If she got an hour's sleep after this, it would be a miracle.

Man, he loved this job!

17

Ben Schirmerhorn wasn't having a good day. At six o'clock in the morning, an hour that normally had no meaning in his life, he was rudely awakened by a heavy hand pounding on the door to his apartment. He tried to ignore it, but the thumping was loud enough and persistent enough to override his soporific slumber. He stumbled out of bed and shuffled to the door.

"Who are you and what the fuck do you want?" he shouted to whatever body was attached to the thumping.

"It's the police. We'd like to speak to you."

Ben scratched his head and raised an eyelid. He could have sworn that man announced himself as the police. He opened the peephole and peered through. Sure enough, standing in the hall, far enough away from the door to allow him full view of the blue uniform, was a member of the NYPD.

"Open the door, Mr. Schirmerhorn." The uniform held his badge up to the peephole for Ben's inspection.

Ben undid the three locks that protected him from the wanton cruelty of city life and opened the door, as he'd been instructed. There were two of them, both a lot bigger and a lot more awake than Ben. He stepped aside to let them in, then closed the door. Out of habit, he redid his locks. When he turned back into the room, one of the policemen was patrolling the living room, eyeing the disarray.

While the other one had adopted an at-ease stance, he looked anything but.

"Yeah," Schirmerhorn grunted.

"Would you mind getting dressed, sir?" the taller of the two asked. His name tag identified him as Officer Viteritto.

"Actually, I would."

Viteritto's partner continued his walkabout, his eyes roaming like a panther hunting prey.

"It'll go much easier for you if you cooperate, Mr. Schirmerhorn," Viteritto said, sneering at Ben's rumpled boxer shorts as if they carried the ebola virus. "We just want to talk to you."

"I have nothing to say to you guys."

"Oh, but I think you do." O'Shea, a bulky, no-nonsense redhead, licked his index finger and nodded to his partner.

Ben's heart felt as if someone had shot him full of adrenaline.

"I think our pal's been doing some cocaine, Ritto."

Viteritto tsked and shook his head. "Sounds like probable cause to me."

"Sorry, Schirmerhorn," O'Shea said, clearly anything but sorry. "We've got to search the place."

O'Shea snapped on latex gloves and began lifting dirty laundry off the floor and the furniture, checking underneath half-read magazines, opening drawers.

"What the fuck is he doing?"

Viteritto's calm stood in stark contrast to Ben's rising panic. "He's conducting a legal search of your property, Mr. Schirmerhorn."

O'Shea moved into the bedroom. Ben could hear him shifting things around. His head began to itch.

"I thought you came here to talk. Okay. Let's talk!"

"Actually, I couldn't care less what you have to say. But we got some pals in the nineteenth precinct who're real eager to have a sit-down with you. They sent me and O'Shea to escort you uptown. So, get your ass dressed, Mr. Schirmerhorn. Now!"

Viteritto had finished with polite and moved on to insistent. Ben had no doubt forceful was next.

"Fine. Then get *him* out of there." Ben tilted his head in the direction of the other policeman. "I gotta pee."

"Go right ahead. The bathroom's clear." O'Shea walked back into the main room. He was carrying a plastic bag filled with orange prescription bottles, loose pills, plastic bags of marijuana and a vial of cocaine. "I left your soap, your toothbrush and some toothpaste. We'll be right here when you're through cleaning up."

"Anything?" Viteritto asked.

"A bottle of Seconal dated March twenty-eighth." O'Shea looked at Ben, mock confusion etched on his face. "Only three left from a prescription for twenty. Having trouble sleeping, Schirmerhorn?" Before Ben could answer, O'Shea shook his head and glanced over at his partner. "No. With all this other shit, his problem would be waking up. Isn't that right, Bennie-boy? You know, Ritto, maybe that's why we had to beat so hard on his door."

"You think?"

The two of them were having a wonderful time. Ben wasn't having any fun at all. The cocaine was enough to get him a court appearance for possession. But then there was the marijuana. And the Ecstasy. He was in deep trouble.

"I'm getting dressed." He glared at O'Shea as if it was the cop's fault that he got caught with all that shit. "And unless you have a search warrant, you'd better keep your fucking paws off my stuff."

O'Shea held up his hands. "Whatever you say, Bennie."

Ben Schirmerhorn stormed out and headed into his bathroom where he dropped to the floor, embraced the bowl of his toilet, leaned over and puked his brains out.

He was slouched in a chair at the end of a metal table. His hair, dark brown and matted, was in desperate need of a barber. He was wearing jeans, a royal blue shirt that had been worn at least once before, beat-up loafers and no

socks. His hands shook as he lifted a paper cup to his lips
and sipped the steaming black coffee. The bagel the police
had provided remained untouched.

When Alvarez and Ezra sauntered into the room, Ben
Schirmerhorn recoiled. He'd been expecting Viteritto and
O'Shea. The sight of two strange men in suits unnerved
him.

Alvarez took a seat across from Ben. "How's the coffee?
Hot enough?" Ben nodded. "Bagel doesn't do it for you?
We can always get you a donut."

"The bagel's fine."

"I'm Jorge Alvarez. This is my partner, Ezra Chapin.
We need to ask you a few questions, my man. I'm hoping
you're gonna be up front with us."

"Ask away," he said. He draped an arm nonchalantly
over the back of the chair, one leg across the other.

"Where were you on April tenth?" Alvarez asked.

"April tenth?" Ben's head pounded. Thanks to O'Shea,
there hadn't been so much as an aspirin left in his medicine
cabinet. "I have no idea."

"I think you ought to fire up the gray matter, Schirmerhorn, and try to remember where you were and what you
were doing." Ezra was leaning against a wall, his arms
folded across his chest.

Ben looked from Ezra to Alvarez. Their faces were
blank.

"What's this all about? Why'd your goons rifle my pad
and drag me down here?"

"Uh-oh," Alvarez said to Ezra. "It's your turn to tell
Viteritto someone called him a goon. I did it the last time."

"Funny," Ben said, but he wasn't amused. He was scared
to death. Whatever this was, it felt far more serious than a
drug bust over a nickel bag of coke, a quarter pound of
grass and a few pills.

"April tenth."

Ezra's voice was quiet and calm, but Ben couldn't count
on him staying that way. The guy was a dick. His job
wasn't about being nice. It was about making his collar.

"Detective, I wish I could help you, but I don't remember where I was on April tenth."

"What was your relationship with Wilty Hale?"

Thanks to his morning upchuck, Ben's color had been white when he'd been brought into the station. His pallor just turned to chalk.

"Wilty Hale." He scratched his head. Then, his eyes boggled. "April tenth. Holy shit! Wasn't that the day he took a header out his window?"

Ezra smiled. "See what happens when you turn your brain on? All kinds of things come back to you. Yup! That's when your pal Hale supposedly took a flying leap."

Ben heard the word "supposedly" and felt his body temperature drop. He began to shiver. Quickly, he broke off a piece of the bagel and shoved it in his mouth.

"Were you guys buds?" Ezra registered Ben's tremors, the change in skin tone, the sweat that was beginning to bead along his brow line.

"Not exactly." Ben gulped down some coffee. "We did some business together."

"What kind of business?"

"I'm a playwright." He saw Alvarez's upper lip curl into a smirk. "Struggling," he said, addressing their obvious critique of his appearance and his lack of name recognition, "but a playwright nonetheless."

"Okay, Shakespeare," Alvarez said, "what kind of business did you and Hale do together?"

"He backed one of my plays in an off-Broadway production."

Alvarez pursed his lips and nodded. "Was the venture successful?"

"He shut it down after only three weeks."

"Did you agree with his decision?"

"Word of mouth on the show was building. He closed too soon."

"That piss you off?"

"It didn't make me happy."

"When was this?" The questioning went back to Chapin.

"A couple of years ago. Two. Three, maybe."

"Was that the end of your relationship?"

"I brought him some other plays."

"When?"

"About six months ago."

"Did he offer to back you?"

"No."

"How'd you feel about that?"

Ben sighed. "Wilty and I shook hands on a deal for him to produce at least two of my plays. When he shut down the first one, I figured he'd honor his commitment to me with the next one. And hey, I gave him a choice of several plays. I didn't shove anything down his throat."

"Not even a few Seconal?" Alvarez loved it when a perp gave him a set-up line.

Ben bounded out of his chair, banged his hands on the table and growled across the table at Alvarez. "What the fuck did you just say?"

"I simply asked if you might have shoved a few Seconal down Wilty's throat on the night of April the tenth."

"You know what," Ben said, too agitated to sit. "I'm entitled to a phone call. I demand to call my lawyer!"

Neither of them so much as flinched. How many struggling playwrights had a criminal lawyer on retainer?

"If you feel you should, go right ahead," Chapin said generously, as if he were helping Ben weigh his options. "After all, we haven't even gotten to the matter of the stash we found in your apartment."

Ben blanched. In his horror over them implying that he might have had a role in Wilty's demise, he'd forgotten all about the drugs. His left eye developed a tic.

"You know what, Ezra? I've heard creative types use drugs for inspiration. Isn't that right, Shakespeare?"

"Fuck you!" Ben snarled.

"See? Look how beautifully he uses the language." And how quickly he forgot about lawyering up.

"You can rag on me all you want, but you've got the wrong guy. I didn't have anything to do with Wilty's death!" Ben's voice was pitched high and loud.

"I wanna believe you, man." Alvarez's tone was frank, not harsh. He looked sincere. But then, he stretched his body across the table, wiped any hint of sympathy off his face and growled, "Just tell me where you were on April tenth!"

"I don't remember." Ben's eyes filled with tears, but he refused to cry.

Chapin exhaled and shook his head. "That's a problem."

"Do you have family in Wisconsin?" Alvarez asked, again throwing Ben a curve.

"What?"

"Wisconsin. I knew some Schirmerhorns, but they came from Wisconsin. They were in the paper business. You related to them?"

Ben was so flummoxed by the question that he answered without thinking.

"Yeah, I am. What of it?"

The minute the words were out of his mouth, he regretted them.

"Are you aware that the Hales have a history with the Schirmerhorns?" Ezra said.

Ben shrugged.

"In fact, they hate each other's guts."

Ben shrugged again and feigned an affect he hoped conveyed that messy family feuds were beneath him. His discomfort was beginning to evidence itself in dark sweat stains on the armpits of his shirt.

"Whatever shit had gone down between his clan and mine was old news."

"Really?" Alvarez asked. "The Hales fucked your family out of a major-league fortune. Are you really going to tell me you and yours don't harbor any hostility about that?"

"You don't inherit hatred, detective," Ben sneered.

"Sure you do. Especially when it involves *billions* of dollars!"

Ben's body deflated the moment the truth pricked a hole in his indignation. His family still bore a tremendous grudge against the Hales and for good reason. Would he have been dragged down here for this little tête-à-tête with the police if his name wasn't Schirmerhorn? And the dead body they were obsessing about wasn't a Hale?

"Hey, man, I get it. You needed help getting your shows produced and you played this feud for all it was worth," Alvarez taunted. "You figured he might feel sympathetic enough to cough up some bucks."

Ben stiffened. "Wilty Hale wasn't a sympathetic kind of guy."

"Not an easy sell, huh?"

"No. But I didn't do anything to make him dead!"

Alvarez fixed his jet black eyes on Ben's. They were as cold and hard as marbles. "Where were you the night of April ninth?"

Ben stared back at Alvarez. His eyes registered complete confusion. "April ninth?"

"I'll give you a hint," Alvarez said. "You and some musclebound sidekick were at a bar downtown."

Ben licked his lips as if he'd been in the desert for days.

"You got in Wilty's face. Am I ringing any bells here?"

"Yeah, okay. I was an asshole! But I walked away, man. I tossed a few insults at him. He came back at me. I saw I was gettin' nowhere fast. And I left."

"Only to worm your way into his apartment the next night, drug his drinks and toss his ass out the window."

"Uh-uh. No way! No fuckin' way!" He started to get out of his chair, but a glower from Alvarez sat him down again. "It wasn't me," he said again, practically weeping.

"Are you dense or something?" Alvarez's voice was rising. Soon, he was screaming. "You're sitting in a police station being asked a simple question that requires a simple answer. Now why can't you remember where the fuck you were when Wilty Hale was drugged and tossed out a nineteenth-story window!"

Ben flopped his arms onto the table and dropped his head into them. He didn't know how he got here, but he wasn't leaving anytime soon.

"Because," he said in a tremulous voice, "sometimes, I have blackouts."

"What kind of blackouts?" Ezra asked.

"I drink too much. I do drugs. I don't lead the healthiest of lifestyles, okay?"

Neither detective spoke.

"Occasionally, I'll go on a toot and have a blackout. I don't remember where I was or what I did."

"For how long? Fifteen minutes? An hour? What?"

Ben looked down at his lap and said a silent prayer.

"Sometimes," he said, "they last for a day. Or two."

Ezra Chapin nodded his head compassionately as he said, "Benjamin Schirmerhorn, you have the right to remain silent . . ."

Callie was exhausted. If she wasn't dreaming about rats or the gray people, she was awake keeping her eyes peeled for rats. Or the gray people.

At some point during this endless night, Callie made the decision to leave New York for the weekend. Wilty's death had hit her hard, but what made it worse was that almost at the precise moment that he died, her nightmares were reborn. Since Callie was a woman who viewed life as a continuum, with even random happenings often connected in a cosmic way, it was difficult for her to shake the feeling that those two events were somehow related. Whether his death had drained her reserves, thereby leaving her vulnerable to an attack by these nocturnal intrusions, or whether the gray people were punishing her for abandoning Wilty, haunting her the way his family haunted him, or if his death were simply a signal for her that it was time to deal with her fears about what she might have inherited from her family, she didn't know. But they seemed strongly linked.

For her own sake, as well as Wilty's, it felt imperative that she figure out what Wilty had found and what he was looking for in those diaries. The only way to do that was to head north and find where E.W. Hale was marooned during the Great Blizzard. And whom he had gone to see.

She narrowed the map of possibilities down to the Adirondacks. The Hale estate Long House was there and the White Hurricane, as Hale called the storm, had ripped into upper New York State after roaring through D.C., Philadelphia and New York City.

According to his account in the diary, it was a place with a big hotel on the main street and a nearby spa where he intended to "take the waters." From that, Callie set down a list of possible destinations.

"You have to start somewhere," Callie told herself as she threw some clothes and toiletries in a bag.

As soon as the exterminator showed up and placed rat traps around her apartment and the locksmith came to change the locks, she'd leave.

The phone rang. She hoped the car rental agency wasn't having a problem. She ran back into her bedroom.

The hidden camera clicked on.

"Hello . . . Oh, Dr. Merrick . . . No, of course it's no bother . . . Yes, actually, I have been thinking about what you said. You were right. The dreams are getting more intense and more frequent, but they're a little different . . . Yes, these are frightening as well, but they're not the same . . . Yes, okay. A session or two would probably be a good idea. The thing is I'm going out of town for a couple of days . . . Okay, great. See you then. . . ."

She put the phone down and returned to the bathroom.

The camera clicked off.

Carolyne Hale strenuously objected to the police escort, but Wilty's apartment was still considered a crime scene. As if to reinforce that fact, when the elevator doors opened, she was greeted by a barricade of yellow tape and a uniformed policeman standing guard. Detective Chapin lifted the tape, then stepped aside, allowing her to enter.

As she walked past him into the foyer, an unexpected rush of emotions hit her, leaving her momentarily overwhelmed. Everything looked as it had when Wilty was alive: neat, elegant, confident. But it felt strikingly different, glaringly vacant. She listened, expecting to hear the click of his footsteps or the baritone timbre of his voice. Instead, there was the incongruous squish of gumsole shoes on marble floors as people shuffled around behind her.

She struggled to filter Chapin and Alvarez out and summon the strength to do what she'd come to do, but their presence was like humidity on an August day, thick and inescapable.

When she turned in the direction of the far rooms, she spied a large bowl of flowers atop the Chippendale mahogany console that once graced the foyer of the Hale mansion in Memphis. The flowers were dead, their petals and leaves dried and shriveled. Small white flakes that looked like fireplace ash dusted the tabletop, the last remains of a spray of baby's breath. The irony insulted her.

"Get Mrs. Hale a glass of water," Ezra said to the policeman by the door. He thought she looked a bit woozy.

"This place is a mess!" Carolyne carped as the officer walked past her toward the kitchen, her tone ringing with patrician umbrage. "Why hasn't anyone been in here to clean up?"

"Our crew is from the police department," Alvarez said. "Not the sanitation department. If you want work done, Mrs. Hale, you'll have to make arrangements through Lieutenant Green."

Ezra shot his partner a look. *Go easy.*

Carolyne Hale also shot Alvarez a look. Her message was more hateful, but equally clear.

Turning on her heel, she proceeded down the hall to Wilty's suite. Ezra and an unrepentant Alvarez followed at a discreet distance.

The Widow's first stop was the master bedroom, a calm, luxurious khaki oasis that belied the violence that had occurred in this apartment only a short while ago. Her visit was brief, probably due to the lack of dressers and drawers; Wilty's wardrobe was housed in a series of built-ins that lined the walls of the adjacent dressing room, which appeared to be where she was headed. En route, her eye caught sight of a small stack of books on the skirted table next to Wilty's bed.

Her back stiffened as she read the titles. One book seemed particularly unsettling. She flipped a few pages, looked around anxiously, then turned back to the book. She flipped a few more pages, glanced over her shoulder again, returned to the book. Ezra didn't know whether she was checking to see if her guardians were present or it was simply a nervous gesture.

When finally, she set the book down and moved on, Alvarez signaled for Ezra to follow. He remained behind to examine the books: two biographies of E.W. Hale and what appeared to be a law school textbook on the subject of inheritance.

Alvarez made a note to send that particular tome to the CSU lab to see if they could tell which chapters had been of particular interest to the deceased.

In the dressing room, Ezra watched as Carolyne Hale slowly and very purposefully rummaged through her son's drawers. Several times, she glowered at Ezra in hopes of intimidating him into leaving. He stayed put.

"Do you have a piece of paper and a pen? I know I'm not supposed to take anything until you gentlemen have completed your work, but there are some items here that are quite personal to me. I'd like to make note of them. Perhaps, Lieutenant Green would allow me to take them out of here before they get misplaced. Or find themselves in an undeserving pocket."

The last she said with deliberate accusation. If she was trying to insult Ezra or goad him into backing off, she failed. He gave her a notepad and a pen, then stood by patiently as she lifted a pair of cuff links, scribbled something on the pad, then returned them to the drawer. As she put each item back, she moved other things around. She thought she was being clever. Ezra found her obvious.

When the dressing room yielded nothing, she proceeded to Wilty's sitting room/travel library. There again, she made a show of jotting notes on the small pad Ezra had given her. She did linger over some of the photographs Wilty had on display. One, taken of the two of them, prompted an honest sigh. Wilty must have been about ten years old. He was posed atop a magnificent horse, dressed in jodhpurs, high black boots, a red hunting jacket and a black riding helmet. Carolyne was at his side, proudly displaying a blue ribbon.

Ezra was glad to know there was a time in Wilty's life when he'd pleased this woman. Judging by his previous interview with her, Ezra guessed those times were few and far between.

Alvarez came in and joined his partner in quiet surveillance.

Carolyne Hale continued her inventory. She opened drawers and peeked inside decorative boxes. She picked up photographs, looked closely at two paintings that hung over a short, squat bureau and riffled through several of the books resting on the island where Wilty kept his travel books and maps.

Alvarez snorted. This was not some bereaved mother on a heartfelt journey. This was a woman on a hunt, groping around for hidden compartments, feeling for false backs or a hiding place where something could be hastily stashed when, perhaps, the doorbell had announced an unscheduled visitor.

She followed the same routine in the main library, picking up small items so she could add them to her list, staring at others in a show of mournful nostalgia, all the while, fingering picture frames and leafing through books in search of something she desperately needed to find.

The only time her frantic pace slowed was when she noticed the picture of Wilty and Callie Jamieson. She didn't touch it, but she stood in front of it for a moment or two and stared. Her expression was one of utter distaste.

After an hour and a half, the Widow Hale announced that she was ready to leave.

"I'm sorry, gentlemen," she sighed. "I'm emotionally drained. This is simply much too difficult. I'll have to come back another day when I'm feeling stronger." She turned to Ezra, knowing there was no chance of sympathy from Alvarez. "Would that be all right, Detective?"

"Certainly, Mrs. Hale. Would you like us to escort you home?"

She shook her head and brushed her hand against her eye. Ezra had seen no tears.

"My driver is downstairs." And she wasn't going home. She had a two o'clock meeting with her aide-de-camp, so to speak.

The uniformed officer pressed the button for the elevator and held the door for her when it arrived.

After she left, Ezra asked Jorge what he thought about the Widow's tour.

"I think your theory about Wilty being killed during a bungled burglary arranged by Mommy Dearest just got legs."

18

First it was "Ball's Town," then "Ballstown Springs," and finally, Ballston Spa, named after the lovely watering place of Spa, Belgium. Like other villages and towns in the area during the late seventeen hundreds, Ballston Spa came into existence because of the magic waters which gurgled beneath the surface. The water tasted salty and smelled of sulfur, but it was said to cure gout, dropsy and asthma. Since there were no medications for those ailments then, the springs were considered miraculous and drew an appreciative crowd.

In its heyday, Ballston Spa was quite grand, boasting a number of elaborate boarding houses for the many visitors who came to partake of the waters. Today, there wasn't a lot of grandeur left in Ballston Spa. Although it remained the county seat, it was no longer the resort destination it once was. In a way, it had reverted back to its beginnings, as a place people passed through on their way to somewhere else. When Callie pulled up to the town hall, she, too, was passing through.

Her intention was to ferret out any record of E.W. Hale having been in the county during those missing years, 1859 to 1864. Callie also thought it might be worthwhile to check out the years following E.W.'s Exile in the Wilderness. The intensity of that excerpt convinced her that wherever Hale was stranded had come to mean a great deal to him.

According to Mrs. Riverton, the clerk in residence, most

of the documents Callie was seeking were so old, either they'd been moved to various historical societies in the area, were in private collections and therefore unavailable to the public, or had been thrown out and no longer existed.

"Before 1880," she explained, "New York State didn't require records of vital statistics like births, marriages and deaths to be kept. Often, only the churches recorded those events."

"Would some of the older churches in the area still have documents like that?" Callie asked, hoping, but pessimistic.

Mrs. Riverton was dubious. "They might but, usually, the documents were given to the families involved."

"What about after 1880?"

"Oh, those are kept in the local city halls."

"Maybe copies were made of some of the older papers before they were donated to the historical societies."

The kindly woman's face crinkled like a piece of paper as she pondered Callie's suggestion.

"We do have an archive section where we store whatever we have from that period. You might look in there."

The records room was a large, musty space jam-packed with row upon row of metal shelving. It took a few minutes, but finally Callie found a section for old deeds, building permits, and tax records. Studying documents that exchanged an acre of land here or a parcel of land there wasn't exactly exciting stuff, but you had to pick through a lot of rock before you mined gold.

In the late nineteenth century, as Mrs. Riverton had alluded, record keeping wasn't very precise. Land that might have been handed down from one generation to the next didn't always have a deed attached. Gentlemen's agreements were sealed with a handshake rather than a contract. Acres of abandoned or barren property got claimed by squatters. Still, Callie slogged on.

Ultimately, she was rewarded. In 1890, Emmet Wilton Hale, of Cleveland, Ohio, obtained a building permit in Saratoga Springs. There were no accompanying documents to tell her whether or not he owned the land, when he bought it or from whom. A further search did yield the name of the person who had paid the taxes on the land before Hale's permit was issued: McAllister. Since she couldn't find the actual deed to the land, she didn't know whether McAllister sold the property to Hale outright, or it was sold to someone else who then deeded it over to Hale. Or if the bill of sale was being preserved in one of the historical societies.

There didn't seem to be any question that Callie's next stop was Saratoga Springs.

Before leaving, she decided to disregard what the well-meaning clerk had said and rummage about for anything relating to births, deaths and weddings from the relevant time period.

Mrs. Riverton was correct, there weren't many files of vital statistics to be found, but at the end of one row of shelves, Callie found a collection of ancient ledgers. She extricated one or two and perused them. A slow smile inched onto her lips. Several contained lists of marriages and births; since they all occurred within a particular year she guessed they'd been compiled for tax purposes. Choosing carefully, she carried a pile of dusty books back to the wooden table in the center of the room, pulled up a chair and began to pore over them. The lighting was poor and some of the printing had begun to fade, but Callie had always been highly energized by curiosity.

At first, the ledgers yielded nothing of any relevance. Callie skipped ahead to the years immediately following the Blizzard. Her eyes were getting tired from the dim light and the strain of reading faded ink and flourishing script. She almost missed it, but on second glance the name called to her.

In Hale's diary, he talked a great deal about looking for the Blessings. He said he would find the Blessings, no matter what it took; that through them he would find Faith and the Truth. She'd thought the Blessings was some religious reference.

"How about a family name?" she whispered as her finger

marked her place and a smile crossed her lips.

In 1894, Miss Sarah Blessing married Dr. Jeremiah Holstein in East Galway, New York, a town a few short miles west of Saratoga.

She wasn't certain how she knew that, but she did.

She also knew that if she could find a Blessing or two, they might be able to tell her about Faith. If they did, she'd be a step closer to the Truth about E.W. Hale. And his great-great-grandson, Wilty.

It was late afternoon by the time she arrived in Saratoga Springs, specifically at the Batcheller Mansion, a Victorian inn built in 1873 that Callie had discovered on the Internet. There were only nine guest rooms. When Callie checked in, she was taken to the Katrina Trask room on the second floor, named for a past Saratoga socialite who, along with her husband, Spencer, founded the famous artists' retreat known as Yaddo. It took Callie all of fifteen minutes to unpack, freshen up and head back out to her car.

She pushed the door out just as another guest was coming in.

"Fancy meeting you here," Ezra said after almost knocking Callie over.

Once she realized with whom she'd collided, it took a minute to respond. His presence was so out of context, it rattled her. "Are you following me?"

"Would you like me to?"

"What are you doing here?"

"Would you believe I'm scouting possible places to stay during fall foliage?"

The man was beyond exasperating. She sighed and cut around him, eager to get on her way.

"Okay, if you won't buy that, how about I'm going up to Lake George to look into Huntington Hale's unfortunate accident?"

That stopped her in her tracks.

"And you?"

After a short debate, and a mental reminder about how

nice he'd been the night before, she explained the purpose of her trip and even divulged the fruits of her labors in Mrs. Riverton's basement. Two heads were usually better than one, she reasoned. And in this case, one head belonged to an NYPD detective. It couldn't hurt.

They wended their way to Union Avenue and headed east in the direction of Saratoga Lake. According to the concierge at the inn, the one hundred acre parcel of land upon which E.W. Hale intended to build was out past the racetrack. Callie noticed that the concierge never mentioned what was on that property.

On the ride over, she and Ezra exchanged information and speculated about what the great man might have built.

Ezra, who'd read all three diaries sometime between getting home from her apartment and interviewing Ben Schirmerhorn, expected a church or some other kind of spiritual sanctuary.

"He went on about an Apocalypse and insisted upon using those religious terms and references. Something happened somewhere around here that affected this man in a major way."

"True, but he also said he wanted to give back to the community that saved him from the blizzard. I think he built a hospital."

After driving past a thickly wooded tract of land surrounded by a high metal fence, they came upon two enormous stone pillars which anchored an elaborate, electrically controlled, wrought-iron gate. A brass plaque hammered onto one of the pillars announced that they had arrived at the entrance to Liberty Park.

Callie got out of the car and pressed a button on a box she assumed was part of an intercom system that connected to a guard house that stood several yards past the gate. Sure enough, a voice asked for her name and the reason for her visit.

"Callie Jamieson from the *City Courier*." She took out her press credentials and held them up, figuring there was a television camera somewhere that was broadcasting her face into the booth. "My colleague and I are working on a piece about E.W. Hale. We'd like to see whoever is in charge of Liberty Park."

"What's the name of your colleague?"

"David Fox."

Neither Callie nor Ezra thought it would be beneficial to announce his affiliation with the NYPD. Since it was obvious they were going to check, Callie gave the name of a fellow reporter she knew was on vacation. The receptionist at the *Courier* would verify their employment— unless Brad Herring had made her termination official— but would tell the caller Fox and Jamieson were out of the office.

"One moment, please."

The box went silent as the sentry called the main house and relayed Callie's request.

Several minutes went by without a response. Ezra got out of the car, walked over to the box and leaned on the button.

"What's the holdup?"

"I'm waiting for clearance, sir. Please be patient."

Patience wasn't exactly Ezra's long suit. Callie tried to interest him in the intricate ironwork of the entry, the way the thick, black metal had been twisted and forged into a forest of sinuous branches and leaves, but he refused to be distracted. He was deep into his monologue on the tediousness of bureaucracy when, suddenly, the gates opened.

Liberty Park was a symphony of green made up of thousands of trees and shrubs that had been harmoniously blended into one verdant oasis of calm. The path from the gate to the main house was serpentine and paved with stone, gently curving away from the highway into the wooded heart of the park. As they wended their way, neither Callie nor Ezra spoke. It was as if each was absorbing the essence of the place in his or her own way.

Callie felt a little like Dorothy in *The Wizard of Oz*, blithely ambling along a brick road in the vague hope of being gifted with a nugget of wisdom at the end of the trail. But, she decided, even if she came away empty-handed, the trip was worth it because the trail was exquisite.

As one who loved the outdoors, Callie couldn't help but respond to the organic tranquillity of her surroundings. She inhaled the soft scent of pine that perfumed the air and watched with childish delight as the sun poked through the foliage and put on a play of color and light. She stopped to read the small signs that had been set out to identify the various evergreens along the way, astounded at the depth and breadth of the variety presented: Norway spruce, Colorado Englemann, hemlock, white fir, balsam, blue spruce, Australian pine. One sign reported that every kind of coniferous tree adaptable to the climate was represented. Another sign boasted of more than one hundred and fifty thousand trees on the property. She was impressed at how natural it all appeared, as if the various trees and shrubs and thickets had arrived there by divine plan rather than horticultural design. They hadn't—the explanatory signs made that clear—which prompted her to wonder whether Liberty Park had been more of a labor of love than a construction project.

Ezra was keyed into a different set of particulars, like why E.W. Hale purchased *this* piece of land. Its sylvan splendor presented the most obvious reason, but Ezra's take on E.W. Hale was that mere displays of beauty weren't sufficient motivation for him to reach into his famously tight pockets. His ascetic background demanded that everything he bought have an essential utility. While it was true that by 1890, Hale was rich enough to indulge himself in a speculative chunk of real estate if he chose to do so, Ezra doubted Hale would buy a large tract of land that promised no financial return, in a town to which he had no ties.

For Ezra, there were only two possible explanations: this was purchased before Hale found the land near Lake George and had been considered as a building site for the family retreat that ultimately became known as Long House. Or, this was where he'd been stranded during the

White Hurricane of 1888. It certainly fit the description in
the diary. At that time, this would have been a desolate
area, off into the hills, far enough away from the main roads
and the center of town for a man to have been lost during
a blizzard. It was pitched high atop a precipice which would
have accounted for the ferocity of the wind. He'd called
his rescue a Liberation, which might have been the root for
the name. He spoke of an Apocalypse and of paying penance. Certainly, a massive replanting of land devastated by
a natural disaster would constitute a significant act of atone-
ment.

But, Ezra thought, why waste valuable brain cells speculating? If E.W. Hale built this park, the answers to all his
questions were here. He could feel it.

The mansion came upon them suddenly and unexpectedly,
rising up from a clearing like Kubla Khan's Xanadu. Constructed completely of stone in the High Victorian style of
the late nineteenth century and built on a rise, it loomed
large over the grand expanse of lawn spread before it. Ivy-
covered walls protected a moat-like terrace that wrapped
around the massive structure, softening the fortress effect,
but only slightly. A three-story center section rose high
above its outstretched, two-story wings, all three heavily
fenestrated with long, narrow windows that reflected the
yellow light of a late afternoon sun.

As they neared the wide, stone stairway that led to the
main entrance, Callie thought she detected motion behind
several of the upper-story windows. Here and there, a curtain parted. A face appeared, lingered for just a moment,
then quickly retreated. Something about the jerky movements of those Peeping Toms unsettled Callie. Her heart
fluttered nervously inside her chest.

"Good afternoon, Mr. Fox. Ms. Jamieson."

Waiting at the top of the stairs was a short, hairless man
with a shiny pate and a foppish air. Garbed in a British
tweed suit, checkered shirt and striped bow tie, he looked

like a page from a Turnbull & Asser catalogue. All that was missing was a bowler and a brolly.

As he extended his hand in greeting, his mouth assumed a smile, but his eyes telegraphed a caution that bordered on distrust.

"Welcome to Liberty Park." He glanced briefly at Callie, then turned his attention to Ezra. "I'm Hiram Wellington. I understand you're here researching E.W. Hale. Unfortunately, I don't believe we can be of any assistance."

"With all due respect, sir," Ezra said, "you can't know that until I tell you what we need."

Hiram Wellington's jaw tightened. "Fair enough. What is it that you'd like to know?"

Callie let Ezra give their pitch. She'd formed an instant dislike for this little man and not because he'd made it obvious that he didn't like having to look up at her; it wasn't the first time in her life a short man resented her height. She didn't like phonies, so his faux-British accent and affected habiliment was an immediate turnoff. Added to that was his Cerberus-like stance atop the stairway as he blatantly guarded against their entering his domain. If he had something to hide, he was being much too obvious about it and, therefore, craved a challenge to his authority. If he had nothing to hide, he was simply being provocative and boorish. Either way, Callie found him completely objectionable.

Ezra told Wellington they were putting together a major piece on E.W. Hale, that in their search for new information about the mogul, they'd discovered a building permit issued to him for this property. They'd come to Liberty Park because they wanted to know more about the genesis of the park and Hale's involvement in its development.

"Construction on Liberty Park was begun in 1893. It opened in 1896."

Callie and Ezra looked at each other. The second diary was written during that year. In it, E.W. Hale spoke of an enormous project having been completed and his pride in that accomplishment, but he'd been short on specifics.

The passage that stood out for Callie was the one in which Hale bemoaned the fact that Faith refused to speak to him.

No matter what I do, she can't forget what I did.

"I wasn't on staff then," Wellington was saying, "so I'm afraid I won't be able to provide you with the kind of first-hand commentary or personal observations you media types covet." He offered Ezra a cold, condescending smile.

"Actually," Ezra said, he too beginning to find Hiram Wellington utterly distasteful, "I couldn't care less about your personal observations. What Ms. Jamieson and I want to know is the history of Liberty Park. If you aren't familiar with the details, you might have a brochure we could take away with us."

Wellington visibly bristled. "We don't hand out brochures, Mr. Fox. This is a highly respected, private sanitarium."

Callie's blood suddenly stopped flowing. She grew lightheaded and shaky, as if her brain had been deprived of oxygen. Quickly, but as unobtrusively as she could, she moved to the side wall and stood against it, taking long, slow breaths in an effort to right herself. No wonder those people at the windows unnerved her. Any one of them could have been her mother.

"I am a psychiatrist," Wellington announced with great hauteur. "My staff consists of medical professionals skilled in the treatment of mental illness. Our patients come to us at the recommendation of their personal physicians, seeking care and, if possible, a cure. I assure you, they're not interested in the history of Liberty Park, E.W. Hale's involvement in its conception or, I might hasten to add, unwanted publicity."

Ezra, who'd deliberately goaded the man into revealing the inherent purpose of the park, was as stunned as Callie was to learn exactly what Liberty Park was. Unlike Callie, who seemed to retreat, he rebounded quickly, determined to capitalize on Wellington's agitated state of pique.

Using a more conciliatory tone, Ezra explained about Wilty's death—leaving out the fact that his apparent suicide was being ruled a homicide—and how it marked the end of a familial line that had been so important to America's history.

"Believe me, Dr. Wellington, we don't want to upset your patients, nor you. All Callie and I are trying to do is fill in some of the blanks."

Wellington, realizing that his visitors had been sincere in their ignorance about Liberty Park's mission, reconsidered his position.

"I'm sure you understand, Mr. Fox. My major concern is my patients' privacy and my ability to maintain an environment conducive to their recovery."

"I'm sure it is." Somehow Ezra suspected Wellington's concern about privacy was right up there with his concern about payment. "I wouldn't want to do anything to jeopardize anyone's recovery, but honestly, sir, I don't see how providing us with historical data would compromise anyone here."

As Ezra and Dr. Wellington continued jousting, Callie surveyed the building, almost desperately looking for the faces behind the curtains. She was about to look away when the light at one of the windows changed. A face appeared. It was a woman whose hair was pulled up in an extravagant topknot. Her face pressed against the glass. Her eyes fixed on Callie. She tilted her head like an inquisitive child. Callie smiled up at her. The woman smiled back, then disappeared.

Callie blinked and stared at the window. The curtain had never been drawn. Whatever she saw, it wasn't in that room. It wasn't of this time.

"Callie." Ezra's voice sounded faint and distant. When she looked at him, he was standing right next to her. "Dr. Wellington has invited us inside."

She nodded dumbly and followed the two men around

the terrace to the front entrance. Her legs trembled as she crossed the threshold.

The foyer was spacious and regal, making it easy to imagine a time when this house hosted elegant dinner receptions and opulent galas. Judging by present conditions, however, that glorious era was long gone. The oak floor was heavily scuffed and partly covered with a richly patterned rug that had seen better days. Dark wood wainscoting shouldered faded wallpaper. A bare, wooden staircase with handsomely turned spindles and newel posts ascended majestically to a second tier; brass carpet rods that once secured a runner stood empty and wanting. Beautifully curved railings formed half circles that outlined the second and third floors, spiraling the eye upward to a painted, triple-vaulted ceiling, which must have been extraordinary in its prime.

Callie looked in the corner behind the stairs for the massive hall mirror with a frame spiked with wooden knobs to hold gentlemen's hats and a narrow trough at the bottom to collect walking sticks. That space was bare, as was the opposite wall where a grandfather's clock would normally reign. There were vacant niches and outlines of places where grand paintings once hung. On the wall facing the staircase, she imagined a cushioned settee and a slim side table, but they, too, were absent.

Feeling wobbly and slightly disoriented, she followed Ezra and Dr. Wellington into what appeared to be the doctor's office; it had originally been one of two parlors on the main floor. In contrast to the impoverished state of the hall, this room was a jewel. It was as if when they came through the door, they had stepped back into those early days in the beginning of the twentieth century when decorative splendor was the norm. The dark Victorian furnishings, the fringed cardinal red draperies and cornices, the globe lights, oriental rug and golden accoutrements, even the wooden plant stands that held pots of mossy fern, felt completely authentic.

Dr. Wellington ensconced himself in the middle of a

tripartite black leather settee, crossed his legs and folded
his hands in his lap. His face was bathed in imperial calm.
It was obvious that this was his throne and no one else was
invited to join him on it.

Ezra selected a straight-backed, wooden dowel chair.
Callie opted for something armed and tufted.

On the marble table in the center of their grouping,
someone had placed a silver coffee service and a plate of
small cakes. Dr. Wellington encouraged them to sample his
chef's baked goods. They were, as he had predicted, delicious.

After the refreshments had been enjoyed, Ezra returned
to the purpose of their visit. He was eloquent and persua-
sive in his arguments, convincing the good doctor that they
were not prying into his medical practices and that the E.W.
Hale story was not a cover for a Creedmore-like exposé on
how poorly the mentally ill are treated. Rather, it was a
tribute to philanthropy.

"When you put it that way," Wellington said, suddenly
extremely forthcoming.

Callie could practically see visions of TV appearances
and newspaper quotes dancing in his head.

"As far as I know, there was never anything actually
printed on why E.W. Hale built this haven," Wellington
said. "My knowledge about its origins is based on local
legends and rumors."

Ezra shrugged. "So far our entire project has been based
on rumor. Legends would be a step up."

According to Wellington, Liberty Park was what Callie
had suspected: this was E.W. Hale's way of thanking the
people of Saratoga Springs for rescuing him when he was
stranded during the great Blizzard.

"Was this built to be a sanitarium?" she asked.

"Yes," Wellington informed her. "It was."

"Did Hale require a sanitarium after being trapped in the
snow? Was that why he created Liberty Park?"

Ezra noticed an edge to Callie's voice. If Wellington did
as well, it didn't show.

"He may have," the doctor said, "but according to the story, it was not *his* need of a retreat that prompted the foundation of Liberty Park. Rather, it was a young woman who'd been the victim of a horrific tragedy and, as a consequence, had suffered a severe mental breakdown. Obviously something about this woman's plight touched a chord in Hale because her recovery became his personal crusade. There's a memorial right here on the grounds commemorating what happened."

"Did he know her before the tragedy?" Ezra asked. "Were they an item? Was she one of the nurses who took care of him after the blizzard?"

Wellington raised his hands, as if to shield himself from the barrage of Ezra's questions. "I don't know how E.W. Hale knew her, but clearly, she was important enough to . . ."

"What precipitated her breakdown?"

Ezra was surprised that Callie butted in. It was unprofessional, but Wellington didn't seem to mind the interruption.

"She lost her husband in a fire. Then, probably as a result of that shock, she lost the child she was carrying. Her grief over both losses was so complete that for several years after, she was catatonic, unable to speak or hear or respond to anyone or anything."

Callie was visibly shaken. Her eyes seemed to glaze.

Ezra was also moved by Wellington's recitation, but he was captivated by the story. He leaned forward, eager to hear more.

"Psychiatry was in its infancy at that time, so Hale brought in doctors from all over the world. He didn't care what their specialties were. He was willing to try anything. Only one seemed to be able to make contact with the poor woman. Hale moved that gentleman to Saratoga, set him up, paid all his expenses, and promised him an institute in return for her recovery. Liberty Park is that institute."

"Did she recover?" Callie sounded hoarse, as if the words had battled their way from her gut to her mouth.

Perhaps for the first time, Wellington looked closely at the tall, pale blonde.

"Would you like some more tea, Ms. Jamieson?" He was concerned about the pallor of her skin.

"Did she recover?" Callie asked, ignoring his offer.

"Yes," the doctor said, his voice low, his eyes clinical. "Eventually, she did."

"Good," she whispered.

Ezra, seeking to cover what he perceived as an awkward moment, questioned Wellington about how Liberty Park was financed. Was it through endowments or fund-raising or patient fees? Was there a limit on how long a patient could stay? Did they accept state cases? Wellington answered all of Ezra's inquiries, but both men remained conscious of the woman seated in the chair between them.

Suddenly, Callie was on her feet.

"I don't feel very well," she said as she started for the door. "If you'll excuse me."

She swooned. Ezra bolted to her side and slid his arm around her waist, catching her before she fell. Wellington was on his feet as well. He suggested that Ezra lay Callie down on the couch. Ezra was about to comply when Callie's eyelids fluttered.

"How about resting on the couch?" Ezra brought his mouth close to her ear and spoke in a near whisper.

"No." She struggled to right herself and regain her composure. Her eyes pleaded with him to get her out of there.

"We've had a long day," Ezra explained to Wellington as he held Callie close, giving her a chance to rally. "I'll just bring her back to the inn where we're staying. All she needs is a good meal and a good night's sleep."

Hiram Wellington escorted them to the main gate and watched as they drove away from Liberty Park.

"She needs a lot more than a good meal and a nap," he muttered to himself. "She needs help."

19

After returning to the inn, Ezra brought Callie up to her room and despite her objections, convinced her to get into bed.

"Either you climb into your jammies by yourself, or I'll be forced to do it for you." His upper lip curled into a lazy, sensuous smile. "Not that I wouldn't enjoy the task, mind you."

It surprised Callie to realize she would enjoy it as well.

"I think I can handle it myself, but thanks for the offer."

"Any time."

As she closed the door behind him, she admitted to a certain amount of regret. She could still feel the strength of his arms around her body as he'd carried her out of the Liberty Park mansion. She could also feel the gentleness of his touch as he eased her into the car, settled her in and brushed her hair off her face.

Her own hand mimicked his caress. The warm shiver she'd felt then, she felt again.

"No," she said aloud, shaking off the incipient twinges of desire she felt creeping throughout her. "Not now. And not with him."

There were too many negatives for anything positive to come from this relationship, she thought, making a mental list. He was too arrogant, too gritty, and much too self-absorbed. She was having nightmares about gray people, seeing people who didn't exist, becoming obsessed with people who lived a hundred years before her, and mourning two people she'd loved and lost, her mother and Wilty.

Her thumbs-down on any romance with Ezra Chapin was well reasoned and solidly based. And at that moment, she meant it.

Half an hour later, Ezra marched back into her room bearing beef stew, freshly baked bread and a bottle of wine, courtesy of the Mansion's kitchen.

Callie lodged an immediate protest.

"Thank you, but really, I'm fine. You don't have to wait on me." She started to climb out of bed, but he blocked her path.

"Believe me. This is not about me waiting on you," he explained as he set a large wicker tray down on the bed in front of her. "It's about making certain that tomorrow, you have enough energy to make it through the day. We are on assignment, you know."

"Look," she began, "I don't know what happened back there, but . . ."

"You probably didn't eat anything all day."

"True." Callie offered him a wan smile. She had to admit, she was hungry. And the stew did smell delicious.

Ezra went to the door where a second tray of food had been deposited. He opted to bivouac in the corner opposite the bed where there was a large red velvet settee. He set out his food on an oval cocktail table, poured himself a glass of wine and dug in. He encouraged Callie to do the same.

For a while, they ate in silence, both content to let the delicate ambiance of Katrina Trask's suite and the hearty taste of the meal work its magic.

Every now and then, Ezra allowed himself to indulge in the tableau displayed before him: a brass four-poster bed bonneted with a lushly draped, lacy white canopy; a ray of lambent moonlight flickering across a white coverlet; an exquisite blonde nestled against a bouquet of white pillows. Despite the fact that she was wearing a cotton tee shirt rather than a silky peignoir and her hair hung loose about her face rather than being confined in a modest chignon, Callie looked as if she belonged in that bed, in this house, from that time.

Ezra decided that was because she appeared so feminine and so delicate, qualities that were highly prized in the era of England's Queen Victoria. Callie's pallor had been whitened by exhaustion rather than cosmetics, and her movements had been slowed by a lack of nourishment rather than an attempt at gracefulness, but still, there was a dainty, refined aura about her that seemed incongruous in this era of Gloria Steinem and Hillary Rodham Clinton.

He looked away and smiled, wondering how Callie—a card-carrying believer in male-female equality if ever he met one—would react if he told her he thought she looked like an old-fashioned girl.

After she'd had enough food to line her stomach, he insisted she have a small glass of wine.

"It'll help you sleep," he said, as he removed the tray and filled her glass.

His sandalwood cologne filled Callie's nose. Just then, it wasn't sleep she was craving, but while the spirit was willing, her body was weak. She accepted the wine and sipped it slowly.

Ezra kept up a steady stream of nonsensical conversation hoping that for once, he would put his audience to sleep. When, in fact, Callie did nod off, he crept quietly from the room, reluctantly shutting the lights and the door behind him.

By the time Callie arose it was past nine. She should have felt rested—she'd slept nearly ten hours—yet it was difficult to rouse herself. She didn't remember waking during the night, yet judging by the way she felt, she knew her sleep had not gone uninterrupted.

Nervous, she looked around the room expecting to see the gray stranger seated on the tufted settee, staring at her, mocking her. The red velvet couch was empty, as was the chaise longue that resided in front of the fireplace. She searched each of the four corners as well as a niche where a specter might have lodged, but they, too, were empty. She was relieved, but knew their current absence didn't negate the possibility of their presence during the night.

Slowly, she climbed out of bed and thanked the golden rush of sunlight that streamed through the tall windows of the suite. It was bathing the room with a yellow strong enough to overwhelm the gray that contained the shadows that insisted on haunting her.

If only she could bottle the power of that warmth and carry it with her, she thought.

After she'd showered and dressed, she stopped by Ezra's room and rapped on the door. When there was no answer, she assumed he was already at breakfast. He wasn't there either. After a quick cup of tea, a glass of juice, and some toast, she asked Beverly, the young woman at the front desk, if she knew where Mr. Chapin had gone.

"He was out early, Miss Jamieson," she said. "But he did leave you a note."

*Went to visit the City Historian. Be back later.
Hope you had a good night. Ezra.*

She wanted to be annoyed that he'd left without her, but she couldn't be. He'd been so kind last night and so disciplined. Never once did he ask what had precipitated her fainting spell. Not that she would have had an answer, but it was nice of him not to press the issue.

"Did Mr. Chapin happen to mention when he expected to be back?"

"No." Beverly thought she spotted a splash of irritation on Callie's face. "I'm sorry. Is there anything I can do to help?"

Callie considered going out on her own, but where? To do what? She wasn't about to go to Lake George without him. She'd picked over everything the Ballston Spa archives had to offer. According to his note, Ezra was already plowing through whatever Saratoga's old records had to offer. And she had no desire to return to Liberty Park.

"My aunt went to Skidmore," she told Beverly, opting for curtain number four. "She talked about how much she loved it here. I thought maybe I'd stroll around the campus. Is it nearby?"

"The current campus is north on Broadway, but your aunt was probably on the old campus."

"Okay. Where's the old campus?"

"Actually, you're right in the heart of it." Beverly handed Callie a map and urged her to walk around the old buildings and then, meander through Congress Park into town. "Saratoga Springs has a really colorful history. I think you'll enjoy exploring it."

Callie set out intending to do just that, but as her morning progressed, a peculiar sensation crept over her. As she had the afternoon before, she experienced moments of disorientation, times when she was at a loss to remember where she was or where she was going. Infinitesimal specks floated before her eyes. She felt woozy and slightly dazed. Frightened that she might faint right there on the street, she slowed her pace, stopping now and then to take a deep breath and steady herself.

Also unsettling were her reactions as she strolled past some of the houses that had been used as dormitories. Many had been built during Saratoga's golden era of gaming and horse racing. Without understanding why, she found herself eyeing them with a certain acquaintance. Like a comic book superwoman, she felt as if she could see past the exteriors of these aging mansions, directly into their drawing rooms and parlors—not the way they were now, but the way they once were: dripping with braided draperies and beaded portieres, heavily wallpapered and darkly paneled. She could envision their hallways lit with gaslight globes, their bedroom bureaus dressed in lace runners and silver-topped containers filled with creams and pomades. She could hear the swoosh of long, bustled dresses dusting the wooden floors as women moved from room to room, their leather buttoned boots creating a tip-tap sound as they passed.

What spooked her was that she was not seeing these rooms in a generic way. Her visions were specific. She knew the color of the walls in that home's kitchen on Church Street, the swag of the parlor drapes in the house on Hathorn. She could describe the chandelier that illuminated the spacious dining room of the large house on the corner of Spring Street. She had a feeling that she had played in the kiosk that stood in the yard behind the one next door.

When she came to the entrance to Congress Park she stopped and shook her head, desperately trying to chase these wild imaginings from her brain.

"It's nothing," she told herself, her breath coming in short, shallow puffs. "You've simply read too many books, seen too many pictures."

She spoke aloud because she was eager to verbalize her thoughts, to get them out in the open where she could hear them and analyze them and defuse them.

"Auntie Pennie probably described these houses in excruciating detail. Maybe she lived in them when she was a student."

It was true that Pennie had waxed poetic about her years in Saratoga. She had often talked about what it was like attending a women's college and living in these quirky residences. And she was a glutton for detail.

It was also true that when she first started looking into E.W. Hale's history, Callie had leafed through books at the library which catalogued the region at the turn of the century. Many were largely pictorial accounts.

"Well, of course," she declared with exaggerated relief. "Like everything else in my life these days, this déjà dizziness is all about Wilty's death! And that damned curse!"

It's not a sign of madness.

"Hey, lady. You want to get run over?"

Callie's head turned sharply in the direction of the voice and the honking horn. A car pulled up alongside her. The window was down and Ezra Chapin was grinning at her.

"Where've you been?" Her tone was fraught, much snippier than she'd intended.

Ezra's brow wrinkled in confusion. "I left you a note. I didn't want to wake you, so I went to visit . . ."

"The City Historian. Right." Callie used the time it took to walk around to the other side of the car to compose herself. "I'm sorry," she said as she slid in alongside him. "I knew that. I guess I was just lost in the moment."

"Well, snap out of it!" Ezra teased as he pulled away from the curb. "We have work to do!"

"I take it you and the City Historian had a nice chat."

She kept her eyes peeled on the road ahead. It made it easier to rein in her emotions. Whatever strangeness had occurred during her stroll, it was her problem.

"Guess what she told me." he said.

"Something good, I hope."

"Something very good! It appears as if your instincts were right on. E.W. Hale did apprentice at newspapers during those missing years. One, *The Morning Times,* which ultimately became *The Times Union,* was headquartered in Albany, but had small bureaus throughout the region. Since E.W. was low man on the totem pole, he traveled around, working a month here, a month there. At some point, he must've settled down, because in the latter part of 1864, his name actually appeared on the masthead of *The Saratogian.*"

Ezra was so upbeat it was hard not to join him in his reverie. Callie rewarded his efforts with a congratulatory smile.

"What that means," he continued, "is that he might've known that woman Wellington told us about. She might've been a girlfriend he dumped before going back to Stroudsburg. Maybe she was who he was coming to see when he was caught in the Blizzard. Maybe he'd heard about what happened to her and had come up here to help her out."

"That's a lot of maybes," Callie said, feeling infinitely better. The gloomy blues that had cloaked her before had waned. And the thought of a possible breakthrough in their investigation into E.W. Hale was genuinely uplifting.

Ezra stopped the car. "You know what? We never asked Wellington the name of the woman who inspired Hale to build Liberty Park. Maybe she was the Faith of the diary!"

"You think?" Her voice was hopeful, yet tentative.

"Yes," Ezra said, pulling away from the curb and making a quick U-turn. "I do."

"Where are you going?"

"Where else? Liberty Park."

"No!" Her voice was one notch below a fright night scream.

Again, Ezra pulled to the side of the road. This time, he shut off the ignition.

"Why not?"

"The place freaks me out." That was the truth. Not all of it, but, she hoped, enough.

It wasn't. "I figured that out already," Ezra said. "Remember me? I'm the guy who picked you up off the floor."

Callie didn't respond.

Ezra refused to back off. "What exactly is it about Liberty Park that freaks you out? Wellington? The color of his curtains? The cut of his jib? The fact that it's a sanitarium? What?"

She faced him, her turquoise eyes begging him to let the subject rest. "All of the above."

Ezra wanted to push this discussion further, but the finality in her voice said let it go.

"Okay. Forget Liberty Park." He'd call Wellington when he got back to New York. "How about Lake George?" The slightly sarcastic color to his tone wondered if Lake George might also freak her out.

Callie glared at him defiantly. "Can't wait."

"Glad to hear it." Ezra smothered a smirk as he turned the key and started the car.

The trip wasn't a complete bust, but it was close. Sheriff Jack Carlson wasn't on vacation and he wasn't dead. He was recovering from a heart attack. Ezra, muzzling his frustration and impatience, corralled one of Carlson's deputies and produced a letter from Assistant District Attorney Matt Felder requesting the full cooperation of the Sheriff's office.

"That list is vital to the investigation of a homicide," he explained.

At first, Officer Billy Gayle appeared unmoved. He didn't quite understand how information from a police report on a crime that occurred nearly thirty years ago could possibly be helpful in solving a present-day murder. But he was obviously impressed by titles and initials. Upon hearing "New York City Assistant District Attorney," followed by the presentation of a gold badge from NYPD Detective First Grade Ezra Chapin, he snapped to attention and assured Ezra and Callie that he would take care of the matter. He would get the list ADA Felder had requested and forward it to the DA's office in NYC, ASAP. If Detective Chapin wanted, before forwarding the list, he would run the names through BCI and ViCAP as a precaution. Of course, he would do this on the QT so as not to arouse any unwanted attention.

After Ezra thanked Gayle, Callie asked if it might be possible for her and Ezra to visit Long House. After seeing those photographs in Wilty's apartment, she wanted to revisit the family retreat to see if it could yield a clue.

Gayle's answer was quick and definite. "N.G."

Permission for such a visit had to be obtained from either a member of the Hale family or someone on the board of the foundation that managed Long House.

"Had I known, I could've asked my buddy, Carolyne, for a pass when last we had tea," Callie said as they headed back to the car. She crossed two fingers together. "We're like this, you know."

"Yeah," Ezra laughed as he pulled away from police headquarters. "I heard."

The ride back to Saratoga was pleasant. Despite being limited to highway vistas, it was still enjoyable to see buds popping and grasses turning that fresh, clear green that

comes in early spring. Ezra was also happy to note that
Callie was evidencing a renaissance as well. Their conversation was light, the drive companionable. She was calm,
responsive. He was beginning to conclude that her previous
bad humor had been nothing more than the result of a dys-
peptic stomach. He'd never experienced such a thing, of
course, but he had heard it was possible for indigestion to
influence mood.

They chatted about a great number of things, but they
always returned to E.W. Hale and what might have drawn
him to Saratoga Springs. Callie was especially curious.

"Do you remember the antique golf clubs in the closet
off Wilty's driving range?" Experience had taught her that
no detail was too small to ignore or too far-fetched to dismiss. "Each one of the antique clubs was carefully labeled.
The putter was labeled 'Liberty.' Maybe before Liberty
Park was a sanitarium, it was a golf course."

"Nope." Ezra shook his head as he took the exit for
Saratoga Springs.

"How can you be so sure?"

"Because the city historian told me it was a horse farm."

Callie's brain began to fizz. The vista before her became
obliterated by a blaze of orange. Familiar ghostly images
crowded her vision with large, gray shapes that rose and
fell in a rhythmic dance. Deep inside, she heard the crackle
and sizzle of flesh caught in the blistering embrace of fire.
She cringed and turned away, but the sound grew louder
and more distinct. It was the shrill, panicked whinny of
horses.

She opened the window, turned her face to the fresh air,
closed her eyes and breathed deeply, imploring the neighing
shadows to retreat.

When Ezra didn't comment, she was relieved. He must
have been lost in his own tale.

Actually, Ezra was focused on the car behind them. He
was certain it was the same silver Saturn that had been on
his tail much of the way up to Lake George. When he and
Callie had pulled into the parking lot adjacent to the police

station, the Saturn had driven on by. Ezra figured it was simply the paranoia that comes with being a cop. It wasn't.

"McAllister, the guy who owned the property before Hale, was a breeder of thoroughbreds," he said, opting to keep his observation to himself. "In a town like this where everything revolves around the track, it must have taken some hell of an offer for him to sell that land."

"Does the why really matter?" Callie said impatiently. "He sold the land to Hale. That's all we care about, right?"

To Ezra, whys did matter. Like, why would Callie find all mentions of Liberty Park agitating? And why should she care whether it was a horse farm or a cornfield?

And why was someone following them?

"I suppose." Ezra pulled into the space provided for guest parking. "I'm just anal-compulsive when it comes to my facts. I like all the strings connected and all the knots tied."

"Sometimes that's not possible," she said. "Sometimes there are strings that dangle no matter how hard you try to connect them to something else."

And dreams that refuse to make sense. And memories that refuse to link up with actual experiences. And fears that never go away.

Ezra locked the car and fell into step beside her as they strolled around to the front of the inn. He was dying to ask her what emotional strings she was having trouble connecting.

Before she went to her room, Callie said, "Thanks for today. I actually had a very nice time."

Ezra responded with a gallant bow of his head.

"I know you said you'd rather starve than have dinner with me. And I realize that the only reason you made an exception last night was because you actually were starving, but the concierge told me about a really great place out at Saratoga Lake. What do you think? Can you be ready by seven?"

"I should be close to starving by then," she said with mock seriousness. "So yes, seven would be fine."

20

The restaurant was out at Saratoga Lake, part of a countryside inn that harked back to another time. It was a
large white house with stout columns, a wraparound porch
and tall, green shuttered windows. According to the maître
d', New Moon was a reproduction of Moon's Lake House,
a place made famous during the late 1800s by its high-
toned clientele and by the fact that this was where the potato chip—known originally as the "Saratoga Chip"—was
invented.

Inside, it was like being in a cozy, Victorian parlor. An
enormous floral needlepoint rug anchored the space. Three
chandeliers, each with eight milky globes, provided lighting
so soft it tricked one into thinking they were illuminated
by gas, rather than electricity. Large paintings added to the
homey atmosphere, as did the spinet piano that seemed to
sit at the ready in the far corner.

Instead of standard restaurant furniture, each setting was
an elegant dining vignette: round tables that seated six or
eight, square tables for four or two, oval tables that allowed
even greater flexibility. Each grouping was unified by the
chairs that surrounded the table. Some were wooden
straight-backs. Others were upholstered and cushioned.
Some had arms. Most did not. There were tablecloths and
candlesticks, tinted wineglasses and patterned china, sprigs
of flowers and lacy place mats. In another room, this hodge-
podge of Victoriana might have looked like a viewing for

a roadside auction. Here, it was as warm and inviting as a pleasant memory.

The maître d' led Callie and Ezra to a corner table distinguished by two armchairs, both of which looked as if they had been needlepointed by hand. When Callie asked, she was told they had been, by the present owner's grandmother.

The menus were handwritten in a flourishing script that made it wonderful to view, but difficult to read. Thankfully, the wine list was printed in a more legible typeface. Ezra ordered for the two of them, starting with a glass of champagne.

"To celebrate our findings," he said after the waiter had come and gone.

They clinked glasses. Callie sipped her champagne, allowing the bubbly liquid to slide down her throat with a soft tickle. A flicker of light outside caught her eye, causing her to glance to the side and catch a glimpse of her reflection in the window.

After they'd returned to the inn, she'd taken a twenty-minute power nap and was grateful that she did. Not only did she look better, but she felt better, more like herself than she had in two days. She was glad, because her escort had planned a delightful evening. It would have been a shame if the gray cloud that seemed to have affixed itself to her had ruined their good time.

After finishing her champagne, her mood was even lighter. She felt as if she'd not simply gone out of town, but had ventured to a place that was out of time. The setting, the ambiance, the company—it was all quite sublime. Especially the company. She didn't know when it happened, but sometime that day a button had been pressed. The sarcasm that had distinguished their other encounters had taken a holiday and they were suddenly easy with each other.

"What got you so interested in solving cold cases?" Callie asked as the waiter cleared the dishes from their first course and poured the Saint-Emilion Ezra had ordered. "It can't be that you don't have enough to do at your day job."

"It was because of my grandfather." He said it simply, but there was a lot of emotion packed into that short sentence. "He had Alzheimer's. My grandmother tried to take care of him by herself, but eventually it got to be too much for her. My mother convinced her to put him into an assisted living facility, which she did. About a month later, they called and told us he'd wandered out of the facility and off the grounds. They had no idea where he'd gone."

Callie was horrified at the thought of a man with no memory and limited skills wandering about with no idea where he was going, where he was or where he'd come from. Ezra's family must have been frantic. She knew how she'd felt whenever Mara became erratic.

"Weren't there guards or an alarm system?"

"They said they heard an alarm but by the time they responded, he was gone."

According to testimony gained later, more than an hour had elapsed between the time the alarm sounded and a staff response.

"The police instituted a massive search effort. The home was near a woods which backed up to railroad tracks. One scenario had him walking through the woods and getting on a train bound for who knows where." His amber eyes turned dark. "Other scenarios were far more gruesome.

"Since Alzheimer patients often experienced blips of long-term memory, we notified police precincts in the Bronx where my grandfather grew up as well as in New Jersey where he and my grandmother lived for much of their lives. The hope was that if he realized he was lost, he'd return to a familiar place."

"Did he have any identification on him?"

"He wore an ankle bracelet that couldn't be removed without special tools."

Which, Callie assumed, meant that if he showed up dead anywhere in the country, the facility would have been notified.

"For months, we held on to the slim hope that perhaps

someone took him in. We couldn't imagine someone that charitable not letting us know he was alive, but my parents and my grandmother convinced themselves that as long as he was being taken care of, they were grateful."

"You didn't buy that theory at all, did you?"

He shook his head. "No. What confused me was the facility's reputation. It came highly recommended by doctors and hospital social workers and people my family respected, yet I knew in my gut something was wrong.

"I was a lawyer then, so I decided to dig a little deeper. What I discovered were three complaints filed against them for shoddy medical practices by people who believed their loved ones had died unnecessarily or suspiciously. Since the patients in question were elderly and quite infirm, it was hard to convince a jury that there was any malice involved or any serious negligence. All three cases were dismissed.

"Since I am dogged by nature, I looked into whether or not there had been any missing person reports originating from this home. There were several, all of whom were afflicted with Alzheimer's. None of those patients was ever found. More to the point, like my grandfather, there were no sightings, no evidence of foul play and no bodies.

"For years, I kept my eye on that place. I was lucky in that I had a couple of friends on the force who volunteered to help me. It took months of questioning people and sniffing around and prowling the property, but ultimately we discovered the truth. My grandfather died from a fall, probably due to negligence on the part of the staff. Instead of telling us, they got rid of his body and told us he'd wandered off."

"What made them think they'd get away with something like that?" Callie was outraged.

"Alzheimer patients wander. It's a well-known symptom of the disease and therefore provides an almost airtight excuse."

"How did you find out what really happened?"

"It took me a while, but I began to believe he never left

the grounds. No one saw him and the canvass was wide and thorough. In the first few hours after he'd disappeared, it might have been possible for him to go unnoticed, but after that, he would have soiled himself or been hungry and disoriented.

"We notified the media. They ran his picture on television and asked anyone who might have seen him to call. There were flyers and radio announcements and notices in dozens of local newspapers. But nothing was reported.

"Also, he had that ankle bracelet. Even if the worst had happened, if someone had killed him and hacked him to pieces, someone would have found that bracelet. When, after three years, there were still no clues, I began to suspect that he hadn't gone anywhere. Ultimately, I got the local police to send in dogs. There were four bodies buried in the woods at the far end of their property. My grandfather was one of them."

"And that's when you left the law."

He nodded. "My legal skills didn't give my grandmother or my mother any peace. My police friends did. Finding his body was terrible, but not nearly as horrific as the things my family had imagined. At least they knew what had happened. They had a body to bury and a ritual to help them find closure."

"And you found a cause," she said quietly.

"Not knowing is the worst. If I can spare some other family what we went through, I'm damn sure going to try."

Callie was very glad she'd brought him that noose. And the diaries. He was relentless and just then, that made her feel safe.

Callie flushed at the other feelings that were roiling within her and swept some bread crumbs away, grateful that the waiter had returned with their entrees.

They chatted amiably as they ate, sliding back into the easy familiarity that had characterized the first part of their meal. When Ezra wondered whether or not to order another bottle of wine, Callie laughed.

"Do you enjoy picking me up off the floor?"

The color drained from Ezra's face. "You're not dizzy, are you?"

"I was kidding. I'm fine. Really."

Ezra debated with himself for a second before saying, "That's good, because in my humble opinion, you haven't been fine."

"I'm sorry. I don't mean to be such a drag."

Impulsively, he reached across the table, took her hand in his and folded his fingers around hers. "Something's bothering you and I'm a really good listener."

Callie slid her hand out of his and retreated. Deep down, she'd known that Detective Chapin could never witness the kind of erratic behavior she'd displayed without asking her to explain it. Also, deep down, she'd known that when he asked, she would answer.

"Occasionally I have really bad nightmares." She looked at him, went through a brief internal debate and in the end, decided to do something she'd never even done with Wilty: tell him the whole truth. "Actually, it's more than occasionally. I've had the same nightmares off and on my entire life.

"I used to think if I was strong and hung in there, they'd go away and stay away, but they've proven to be stronger than I am. Not only have they come back in full force, but I'm beginning to experience them during the day as well as at night."

She said it so matter-of-factly that Ezra might have believed that they weren't as awful as she was making them sound, if not for her eyes. The clouds he had noticed gathering the other day were there. And they were dark.

"What brings them on?"

"I wish I knew. This time, they started the night Wilty died. They've gotten progressively worse." An odd thought crept under her skin, making her very uncomfortable. "It's as if the more I dig into his family's history, the more I try and solve his problem, the more intense my dreams get."

"Are you doing anything about this?" He said it gently,

smothering the flush of jealousy he felt about her loyalty to a former lover.

"I'm working with a psychiatrist known for treating patients with night terrors."

"And?"

"I don't think I'd call the experience positive."

"Was it unpleasant?"

"Recently, he hypnotized me." Her jaw tightened. "That's when I began to have daymares. I stopped going."

"But now you're thinking about going back."

"Have you ever thought about seeing a shrink?" It was her turn to zig.

"Not only did I think about it, but I went." Callie's eyes conveyed surprise. "It was back when I was in college and decided to search for my birth parents. During the process and after, when I realized I wasn't going to find them, I had a tough time corralling my feelings. I was disappointed and angry and guilty and just generally screwed up."

"Did it help?"

Ezra tilted his chair back and stroked his chin as he pondered his response.

"Psychiatry isn't supposed to give you answers. It's supposed to help you gain insight and give you tools so you can take charge of your own life."

Callie moved her fingers up and down like a babbling mouth.

"Did it help?" she asked again.

"Yes." Ezra chuckled at her impatience. "It helped."

"How?"

"Let's see. I acknowledged that my disappointment in not being able to find them wasn't because I couldn't meet them or get a medical history or see whose nose I had. What I really wanted was a confrontation. I wanted them to tell me to my face why they didn't want me."

He swirled the wine around in his glass again, its circling motion as incessant as his desire to know the answer to that question.

"I learned that while I had a right to my anger, it was a

negative emotion that got me nowhere and brought me nothing except more anger and more guilt." The crackle in his voice echoed his struggle. "It's what you said this afternoon. Sometimes there are strings that just can't be connected to something else.

"The bottom line is, I was adopted. My birth parents chose to give me up for reasons known only to them. More important, I came to accept that their giving me up was totally about them and not about me." The shadow that passed across his eyes told Callie his acceptance wasn't absolute. "But the most important thing my couch time gave me was the ability to stop feeling so damned guilty. I left that doctor's office finally believing that wanting to know about my birth parents wasn't a betrayal. It didn't mean I was an ingrate and that I didn't love Laura and Ira."

"Something tells me that's what your parents told you," Callie said quietly.

"Over and over again. But since when do you believe anything your parents tell you?"

"You're asking the wrong one. After my father remarried, he turned my care over to a woman who couldn't have cared less about me."

Ezra knew he was about to trespass again, but he did it anyway. "And your mother? Did you believe whatever she told you?"

Callie turned away from him. Her body language spoke of an inner struggle. She was debating what to tell him. And, if she could empower him with the information. Ezra waited with fingers crossed.

When, finally, she faced him, she was pale. She looked frightened yet determined, like a child on a diving board for the first time.

"My mother was diagnosed as a paranoid schizophrenic. My father had her committed. She died in a mental institution. He blamed himself and never really recovered."

Her words crashed into his skull with the force of an eighteen-wheeler. No wonder she freaked out at Liberty Park.

"I'm so sorry, Callie." He wanted to hold her hand, to touch her, to comfort her, but her posture was rigid, her face blank. "That must have been awful for you."

"The worst part is, I don't believe my mother was insane."

"Then why'd your father commit her?"

"Because he didn't know how to deal with her. The doctors told him she was too sick to live at home. Sometimes, she was violent." She knitted her fingers together nervously. "And, she had these dreams."

Another truck smashed into Ezra's brain.

"You have the same dreams, don't you?"

"Yes."

"Did you have them as a little girl?"

Ezra's insides were a mess. He prayed for the wisdom to do and say the right things.

"Yes." Her expression was a taut mix of anger and confusion and puzzlement. "So, either we're both insane. Or neither one of us is insane."

Ezra leaned across the table and looked deep into her eyes. "I haven't known you very long, but I know one thing for certain: You are not insane," he said, knowing he couldn't vouch for her mother.

"What makes you so certain?"

"I just am."

Small tears gathered in the corners of her eyes. "That's how I felt about my mother. I just knew she wasn't insane, but no one would listen to me."

Ezra's heart felt as if it weighed a ton.

"How about other members of your family?"

"My Aunt Pennie didn't think my mother was crazy, but she couldn't explain away the dreams."

"Did you tell her about your dreams?"

Callie shook her head. "I was afraid if I told anyone I had the same dreams, they would've carted me off to the loony bin as well."

Ezra guessed there was a part of her that still believed that.

"May I ask you something?"

"Sure."

"Is it possible that you only have these dreams because your mom told you about them? You were awfully young. Maybe they're simply the product of the power of suggestion."

Callie considered that, and not for the first time.

"It's true, I used to hear my mother and father arguing about those dreams. And I was terribly young, but she didn't speak to me about them in any detail until the end, until right before my father had her committed."

She pursed her lips as if the bitterness of that memory passed over her tongue, and then continued.

"I already knew most of the details anyway. That's what scared me. I knew what she was going to say before she said it."

"Didn't anyone from the hospital ever speak to you?"

"Nope."

He would've asked if her father ever spoke to her about what she and her mother discussed, but clearly, he hadn't. Nor, Ezra surmised, had Bill Jamieson truly understood the depth of his little girl's desperation. He put the mother away and then allowed the stepmother to push his daughter away. No wonder Callie didn't trust easily.

"Last night I dreamt about visiting my mother in the hospital," Callie said. "But it was all mixed up. Instead of sitting in her doctor's office, the room was Wellington's office. At least I think it was. The round table was there. So was the leather settee. And, I think the windows were the same."

She looked at Ezra as if she needed him to confirm or deny something.

"Callie, Liberty Park is a sanitarium. There's nothing strange about confusing it with the institution where you visited your mother. Or about our visit there dredging up some pretty painful memories."

Her head bobbed up and down, slowly, as if she were reliving yet another awful remembrance.

"The woman in my dream didn't look like my mother, though."

"How was she different?"

"She was a brunette. My mother was a blonde. And she was short. My mom was tall."

Ezra thought about that. "If you transposed Wellington's office over your mother's doctor's office, maybe you substituted Wellington's nurse for your mother."

The woman Wellington summoned when Callie fainted was a short brunette.

Callie quietly digested Ezra's analysis. He could almost see her turning the various faces and settings over in her mind.

"Thank you," she said, finally.

"For what?"

"For trying to help. And for caring."

"I would like to help. And I do care."

Tears pooled in her eyes, yet a smile licked at her lips. "Beneath it all, you're a nice man, Ezra Chapin. I like being with you."

"Believe me, Callie. The feeling's mutual."

While Ezra went to get the car, Callie strolled to the end of the long porch that outlined the New Moon and gazed out onto the lake. It reminded her of a painting she once admired, a moonscape hued in inky tones of navy and black. Like the body of water that dominated that painting, the lake loomed before her like a large, uneven circle of black glass. In the distance, sporadic clusters of twinkling lights defined its shoreline. To her right, a silver finger of moonlight tickled the surface, causing the water to ripple and shimmer like an incandescent veil.

Suddenly, like a chimera emerging from a fog, a small boat appeared.

Callie blinked, uncertain about whether it was real or imagined. She squinted, straining to reel the image in. Slowly, the lines sharpened and the vision became clear. There were two people in the boat. One was the woman from her dream. She was wearing a high-necked dress with a bib front and a bustle. She was holding a parasol and smiling adoringly at a man seated opposite her.

Callie couldn't see his face, but from the back he appeared tall and well built. She watched as he dipped the long oars into the water and pulled back on them, stroking cleanly, precisely, and with authority. He seemed strong. He rowed with an even, unhurried rhythm, yet the boat remained frozen in the center of the moonbeam. It was as if a tape had gotten stuck: The woman flirted. The man rowed. And the boat stayed put.

Ultimately, as if responding to the tug of her curiosity, the boat began to turn, slowly shifting the woman to the rear, her companion to the fore. When he was facing the shore, Callie gasped. It was the man with the pulpy head wound. The man who burned to death in the orange blaze.

21

The ring of the telephone jolted her awake.

"Callie, it's Luke Crocker."

When she heard the voice of her former boss, she roused herself as best she could, considering she'd only had about two hours sleep.

"An OD was called in that looks like it's related to your Dr. Drug story. I'd like you to cover it." He gave her an address on Madison and Eighty-ninth.

"I don't work for the *Courier* anymore, Luke." She hoped she'd strained the bitterness from her voice. It wasn't Luke's fault she'd been tossed.

"Yes, you do," he insisted. "You're just . . . on leave."

That was one way of describing it, she supposed.

"Mrs. Hale was quite specific about wanting me fired. Brad didn't say anything to the contrary."

"He told me what happened."

Callie wondered if he'd been given the complete story.

"No one on the editorial board likes being told what to do, Callie, least of all Brad Herring. Trust me, it'll get worked out."

"Still . . ."

"Come on, where's that famous Jamieson spirit we all know and admire?"

"Same place my creds are: locked away in some drawer at the *Courier*."

"Teddy's already at the scene with your press credentials."

"I can't . . ."

"He's waiting for you, Callie."

Her body was sprawled on the floor of her third-floor bedroom, a pool of vomit near her head. Blood and white foam haloed her nostrils. Rings of tear-smudged mascara raccooned her eyes. Her black slacks were stained and open at the waist, her hair matted with unsavory fluids. A collection of orange pharmaceutical containers lay atop a dresser alongside a small mound of pulverized pills. The elegantly decorated room was thick with the stench of regurgitation and a loosened bowel.

Ezra and Alvarez went through their preliminary walkabout, careful not to interfere with the CSU team photographing the scene. The victim had been identified as Savanna Larkin.

"Looks like she mixed herself some of that Orlando magic," Alvarez said, reading the labels on the various bottles; each prescription had been issued to someone named Sherman and ordered by the pseudonymous Dr. Martin Orlando. He pointed to a metal spatula on the floor beside the dresser. "This must've been what she used to mix her fix."

Jorge's voice resonated with a mix of sadness and confusion. He didn't understand why someone would turn to dangerous drugs as a form of amusement, especially someone who could have afforded other diversions and should have known better.

Ezra too was angry about another senseless drug death, but this one had more significance to him because it appeared to be linked to the man Callie had fingered in her exposé. And, possibly, was the one behind her harassment.

"Any signs of forced entry?" he asked the uniform on the scene.

"No, sir. The front door was unlocked, but all the windows were secure."

That told Ezra someone came in with Vanna and left

after she was either dead or too incapacitated to lock the door behind him or her. Noting the pristine neatness of the townhouse—not a single objet d'art or bibelot was out of place—he also concluded that Vanna's companion hadn't come to pilfer. Either this was a simple instance of two druggies looking to get high and one bolting when the other began to convulse, or this was part of a more specific, more murderous agenda.

"Who discovered the body?"

"The housekeeper, Rosa Fuentes. She came at about seven. When she found the front door unlocked, she was immediately suspicious. Evidently, the vic was very security-conscious."

That was borne out by the three dead-bolt locks guarding the entry from the street, as well as the fancy, but implacable, metal grills on the windows and the motion detectors monitoring both the upper and lower hallways.

"She took a whiff of the stink coming from upstairs and called us."

Ezra studied the room as the ME boys bagged and removed the body. She couldn't have been there long before this happened. It had been a warm night. The likelihood was she would've opened a window. Also, there was no light on in the bathroom and the medicine cabinet was closed. When Ezra opened the cabinet, he found the same drugs that were on the dresser. Obviously, this party was BYO.

As the CSU photographer began to reshoot the scene without the body, Ezra followed Jorge downstairs.

"Have the narcs come up with any leads on Orlando?"

Alvarez shook his head. "The man is in the wind. They've rousted most of his cohorts, but no one's willing to dime this dirtbag."

"What about that Raju guy they picked up for stuffing the rat in Callie's mailbox?"

"The boys had a heart to heart with him. They assured me he gave them all he had to give."

Ezra nodded. In other words, they tuned him up and scared the shit out of him.

"By the way, did you run those plates?" Ezra had called Jorge with the numbers on the silver Saturn that had followed him and Callie to and from Lake George.

"Rented to a guy named Fred Northrup with a Kentucky license. His face matched the photo, but both the name and the address were bogus. The car was taken out Friday at about eleven and returned Sunday morning at ten."

"Any description on the guy?"

"Light brown skin. Six feet. On the stocky side. Shaved head. Blue eyes. The rental agent said she thought he had some kind of thunderbolt tattoo on his left hand."

Callie said she'd met Orlando. While Ezra didn't think Orlando would be out in the open with this much heat on him, he was curious about whether or not this description matched that of the infamous Dr. Drug. And, it was a good excuse to call her.

Yesterday, she left Saratoga at the crack of dawn. Ezra had tried to call her several times, but either she went somewhere other than home, she'd programmed her answering machine to automatically erase *his* calls, or she plain out didn't want to speak to him. He thought they'd had a pretty good time Saturday night, but she was non-communicative on the ride back to the Mansion and couldn't get to her room fast enough. He wasn't planning on putting any big moves on her, but he didn't think a kiss goodnight was out of the question. Obviously, she did.

"We had to kick Schirmerhorn, by the way," Jorge said. "Felder didn't have anything solid to hold him on. I said we'd watch him anyway. Shuttering a play doesn't strike me as a motive for murder, but the families do have a history."

Which reminded Ezra he was expecting a call about a different chapter in one of those families' histories.

After he realized Callie had left Saratoga, he put in a call to Hiram Wellington. He'd just finished explaining who he was and why he'd used a fake name when the good doctor was called away from the phone. His assistant apologized profusely and assured Ezra that Wellington would return the call as soon as the emergency was over. Ezra was still waiting.

"Any link between Schirmerhorn and Vanna Larkin?" Ezra wondered.

"Same drug source: Orlando and Sunshine Pharmacy. Same hangout. Both of them were Onyx regulars."

"As was Wilty," Ezra said, recalling the note on his desk from CSU.

"Are you thinking Orlando had something to do with Hale's jump?"

"I don't know. I had Amanda Maxwell at CSU run another tox screen, specifically for OxyContin. Present and accounted for."

"So Orlando's on the table."

"I think we have to consider him a possibility."

Alvarez grunted.

"I know you hate moving the Widow down to the number two position on your Most Wanted list, but right now we have more on Orlando than we do on her. And, I'm not completely soured on Schirmerhorn."

"We don't have a solid motive on any of them," Jorge reminded his partner.

"Maybe we'll get something from our interview this afternoon."

"With?"

"Someone the bartender said was hanging with Wilty at Onyx the night before he died. Dan Kalikow."

Callie saw him leave the brownstone, so she hung back until he and Alvarez were several doors down beginning their canvass and the Medical Examiner's van had departed with the body. Then, she hooked up with Teddy.

She couldn't speak to Ezra because she didn't know what to say. How could she explain her hallucinations to him when she didn't understand them herself? What should she say, "Thanks for dinner and by the way, I'm going insane so don't bother to call"?

Sunday, she'd risen before dawn so she could drive back to the city without running into him. Then, she'd barricaded herself inside her apartment, let her machine pick up all her calls, and tried to make sense out of the weekend: what she'd discovered about E.W. Hale, what she'd discovered about Ezra Chapin, and all the ghostly confrontations she'd experienced in Saratoga Springs. She was intrigued by the first, infatuated with the second, and frightened by the last.

Thank goodness for Luke Crocker.

While Teddy photographed the brownstone and the crowd gathering on the sidewalk, Callie walked up the steps to Vanna's home. She'd be barred from going in, but the door was open, allowing her to sneak a peek before being hustled away. Inside, CSU was dusting the banister for prints.

She showed the patrolman on guard her credentials and asked a few questions. She was given the name of the victim, the probable cause of death and the names of the detectives to contact. She was coming down the steps when she spotted something on the ground outside the basement entrance. She walked around to the gate for the lower level and crouched down to get a better look. It was a cigarette butt and a matchbook from Onyx. The cigarette butt looked relatively fresh, the matchbook also.

She went back up the stairs, asked to speak to the lead on the CSU team to whom she showed the butt and matchbox.

Then, she and Teddy left. She intended to write her first draft at home. She'd get to the precinct house later. After she'd figured out what to say.

Carolyne Hale was bored. Aside from her dinner with Peter Merrick, she'd been confined to quarters by the rules of appropriate behavior. It wouldn't look good for her to shop, or go to lunch or dinner, or any of the spring galas that she

normally attended, and so she'd stayed home to protect her
image. But not happily.

To make matters worse, that morning she'd been visited
by Harlan Whiteside.

"I found the lawyer who's handling Wilty's will. His
name is Dan Kalikow."

"Who?" Carolyne could feel her stomach knot. It
sounded as if her assumption had been correct: Wilty had
given his last will and testament to someone whose credentials probably included swallowing live goldfish.

"Dan Kalikow. I looked him up in Martindale-Hubbell.
He went to Yale with Wilty. Graduated summa cum laude.
Law Review at Yale Law. Was a top associate at one of the
city's largest, most prestigious firms and then decided to
open a boutique with a bunch of equally brainy friends.
They're in midtown."

"Have you spoken to him?"

"He's not returning my calls."

"Why not?"

"My guess is that a judge issued a gag order on any and
all discussions concerning Wilty's last will and testament
until the police have finished their investigation." There
was a pause while Harlan selected his next words. "This
means that no checks are going to be issued from any of
Wilty's accounts until further notice."

He watched Carolyne's cheeks rouge with pique. She
was a woman who considered control a given. She wasn't
used to chaos. And she didn't like defiance, so she was
going to hate what he told her next.

"I also heard that the police have given permission for
the newspapers to release the fact that Wilty was murdered."

"I told them not to do that."

Coverage would be national and sensational. By alluding
to that infernal Hale Curse, it could invite people to revisit
the deaths of Wilty's father and uncle. By talking about
Wilty's immense wealth, it could inspire some hick in the
hinterland to come forward and claim kinship. Both had the

potential to be personally devastating to Carolyne.

Furious, she headed for the telephone. Harlan cut her off.

"Carolyne, don't make that call."

"Why the hell not?"

"The police are hoping to get some feedback from the story. They feel that when people know Wilty was murdered, someone might come forward with information they didn't consider relevant before. If you demand that they continue to keep this under wraps, it's going to look as if you're deliberately impeding their investigation and they're going to want to know why."

He wanted to know why as well, but he knew better than to ask.

Dan Kalikow's stomach fluttered as he was led into the interrogation room at the 19th precinct. Nervously, he eyed the battered table, the utilitarian chairs, the wall of glass he knew to be a see-through mirror.

Detectives Chapin and Alvarez, the gentlemen who requested this meeting, offered him a seat on the long side of the table. Chapin took one of the short ends, Alvarez a seat down toward the other end. Dan could only look at one at a time. They could both watch him.

"You want a cup of coffee?" Chapin asked. His tone made it clear you drank the stationhouse brew at your own risk.

"Thanks. I've had my fill of caffeine for the day. Bottled water would be good, if you have it."

Alvarez went to the small refrigerator and got what he derisively called, "fancy water," for the attorney.

"So, gentlemen, why am I here?" Dan appeared calm.

"Wilty Hale." Chapin watched for a reaction. There was none. Dan's round face remained placid, his hooded brown eyes noncommittal. "We understand you had lunch with Mr. Hale the day before he died."

Dan nodded. "I did."

"Was that a regular thing? I mean, did the two of you chow down at the Yale Club every week?"

"No."

Alvarez hated interviewing attorneys. They knew to answer only what was asked. They rarely elaborated or freelanced information. Your questions had to be specific.

"Was it more usual for you two to meet at night at a place called Onyx?"

Dan replied evenly, "Yes."

"Were you a regular there?"

"I suppose you could say that."

"Did you drink as much as Wilty did?"

"Some nights, yes. Most nights, no."

"When was the last time you saw Wilty at Onyx?" Chapin took back the lead.

"The night of our lunch."

"Twice in one day," Alvarez observed.

Dan put the plastic bottle to his lips and slugged back a few gulps of water. "Yup. It was a twofer."

"What did you and Wilty discuss over lunch?"

"It was a catch-up kind of thing."

"What exactly were you catching up on?" His tone insinuated triviality.

Dan parried. "Detective Chapin, there is such a thing as attorney-client privilege."

"Your client is dead, Mr. Kalikow. The privilege is erased."

Alvarez watched as Dan wrestled with his conscience. Wilty probably paid him an enormous retainer; he believed he owed it to Wilty to remain silent.

"I don't know if this makes a difference," Alvarez said, "but Wilty Hale's death was not a suicide, Mr. Kalikow. He was murdered."

Dan looked as if a linebacker had just head-butted him in the chest. He choked trying to catch his breath.

"Are you all right?" Alvarez asked, taken aback by how stunned Dan was.

"Give me a minute, will you?" Dan said, struggling to retain his composure.

"Sure thing."

The two detectives sat back and watched quietly as their guest tried to absorb the news.

"I had trouble believing Wilty committed suicide," he said, more to himself than to them. "But *murder*?

"Was it accidental?" he asked, his voice hoarse from trying to stem the rush of grief. "Did it occur during the conduct of a crime? Did he walk in on a burglary in progress or something?"

"No, Mr. Kalikow." Ezra found it interesting that the notion of a burglary instantly popped into the mind of Hale's attorney. "He was drugged and pushed out his kitchen window."

Dan's skin waxed green. He rested his elbows on the table, propped his head against his hands and groaned.

"I realize what a shock this is, but we're on the clock," Alvarez said. "I hate to put it to you this way, but you can grieve on your own time."

Dan raised his head and focused on the two men. "What can I do to help?"

"Answer a few questions."

"Fire away."

"Did you discuss anything unusual at your lunch?"

Dan's jaw tightened as a mix of sadness and outrage flooded his soul. "You bet we did," he said.

22

When Callie called to change the time of her appointment, Peter feared the worst. Then she explained that she'd been called in on a job. He asked if she'd been reinstated at the *Courier,* and wondered whether it was with or without Carolyne's approval. When she said she was doing it freelance, he smiled. Herring was doing an end run around Carolyne. Good for him.

He thought it was good for Callie as well, until she walked in and he saw the grim line of her mouth and the ashen cast of her skin.

"It's nice to see you again, Callie." No matter how horrific the story she'd been covering, Merrick doubted that her glum aspect was born of just that. He'd seen too many patients with her problem not to recognize the wear and tear of constant night terrors.

He escorted her into the consultation room and offered her a chair, or if she preferred, the couch. She opted for the chair. He seated himself opposite her.

Callie didn't know where to put her hands or what to do with her feet. She didn't know whether to smile, or speak, or wait until she was spoken to.

"You look a bit nervous." She also appeared thinner than the last time they met.

"I am," she confessed.

His mouth curved into a comforting smile. "I understand but truly, you don't have to be. As I told you over the phone, we won't do anything you don't want to do."

Callie bobbed her head agreeably, but had difficulty accepting the notion that she was in charge. She hadn't willed any of the events that had transpired over the past several weeks, yet unnerving things had occurred. She didn't want to be here, yet she was. She didn't wish to discuss any of this, but knew she would. Because just as strange, unbidden images had begun to appear before her at various times of the day or night, some irresistible force had brought her back to Dr. Peter Merrick's office.

"Has anything happened since we last met?"

He knew it had. Symptoms suffered by patients like Callie tended to escalate in both frequency and intensity over time.

Callie lowered her eyes. Her fingers worried together, then came apart in a futile attempt at dissemblance. She barely knew where to begin.

"You were right."

Her voice was barely above a whisper. Merrick had to strain to hear her.

"The dreams didn't go away." Nerves prompted a feathery exhale of breath. "I had some . . . visions. Hallucinations. Daymares." She looked at him, her eyes wide and moist with confusion. "I don't know what to call them."

Merrick smiled sympathetically. "We don't have to name them, Callie. We simply have to try and understand them so that ultimately, we can eliminate them."

She nodded again. He seemed so certain they could accomplish that. She was jealous of his confidence. She used to believe in her ability to accomplish whatever she set out to do, but lately . . .

"Tell me what you saw."

Callie decided to skip over the gray stranger at the Royalton, the woman in the window at Liberty Park, the horses, and the bizarre insights she'd had into several Saratoga homes. Instead, she tendered a condensed version of her lakeside mirage: rowboat, two passengers, one of whom sported what appeared to be a fatal head injury.

Merrick noticed the hesitation and knew immediately she was giving him a highly cropped rendition of her recent sightings. He'd seen it before. It was an exercise in self-protection born of the belief that if she told the truth, he would confirm her fear that she was becoming unbalanced.

"What kind of head wound?"

"I think he was the man from my nightmares." Callie noted the glint of recognition in Merrick's eyes and was instantly grateful that she didn't have to describe the wound. Seeing it, talking about it, remembering it, was always so upsetting, so painful.

"And the woman?"

"She's from a different dream," Callie said with an ironic, embarrassed chuckle.

A tilt of Merrick's head assured her he understood how difficult it was to keep track of so many apparitions; his nonchalance implied he'd seen this kind of spectral confusion before.

"Let's deal with one dream at a time, shall we?"

Slowly, Callie painted a portrait of a lady garbed in a bustled peach dress with leg o' mutton sleeves and a ruffled parasol to match. She was quite precise about the details, down to the beehive pattern of the woman's short lacy white gloves and the rakish slant of her straw hat.

"Was she blond?" Merrick was hoping for physical characteristics that might mark the dream lady as one of Callie's forebears. When she shook her head, he masked his disappointment.

"Her hair is a pretty shade of brown. It's glossy and has some red in it, I think. Like the color of a thoroughbred."

She leaned her head to the side, as if listening to what she'd said, considering it. "Of course, it's hard to tell beneath her hat. It was much easier to see in other dreams."

Her eyes narrowed as she appeared to view images visible only to her.

Merrick was rapt. Callie seemed to be summoning dreams at will, retrieving them the way one would call up a document on a computer.

"It's parted in the middle, combed back into a plump roll that rests at the nape of her neck." Again, Callie studied the invisible photograph before her. "Her forehead is broad. Her cheekbones are high, but not sharply planed. Her skin is creamy. White, yet not sickly. Her lips are void of lip rouge, yet don't appear dry. Whoever she is, she's young and lovely looking."

"Are her eyes blue, like yours?"

"They're hazel. More green than brown."

Again, Merrick was denied any obvious physical connection between patient and phantasm.

"Did she wear the same ensemble in both dreams?" He needed confirmation that this woman was indeed someone from another era and not simply someone Callie knew today costumed to fit the continuous drama playing inside her mind.

Callie closed her eyes. Her head drooped as if it was suddenly too heavy for her neck. Merrick feared she was about to faint. Worse, that when she awoke she'd be frightened and would abandon her therapy, permanently.

"This one is white silk," she said, her voice low, almost haunted. "The bodice is pleated, as is the cummerbund that encircles her waist."

Callie's head remained bowed. Her fingers massaged her temples.

Merrick had witnessed that many times before. It was as if the patient was unconsciously tuning a television screen, attempting to make the picture clearer, the images more distinct.

"She's petite. Her hips look quite small."

Several moments elapsed. Callie was silent, but Merrick suspected it wasn't because she couldn't think of what else to say. Something new had materialized on her screen.

"Oh, God! No!" she screamed, lost in whatever terrifying moment was being played out before her. "She needs help! Hurry!"

Callie's eyes popped open and she started up off her chair, but Merrick could tell she was not seeing anything that existed in the present. She was lost in the past.

"What's happening?" Gently, he touched her arm and guided her back into her chair. "Tell me what you see."

"Her waistline. It's gone." She was shaking, obviously quite vexed. Her eyebrows were furrowed. Her breathing became shallow, coming in quick, agitated puffs. "She has a belly. It's round and high." Callie stared at Merrick, her complexion pallid. "I think she's pregnant."

"Why is that frightening?" Merrick worried about the abrupt, dramatic change in her aspect.

"Because she's bleeding." Callie's eyes filled with tears, her voice trilled with barely controlled hysteria. "Because the whole bottom of her dress is red and wet with fresh blood."

She dropped her head into her hands again and sobbed.

"Does she have a name?" Merrick asked.

He could practically see Callie embark on a frantic search, burrowing about in the darkest recess of her mind, venturing into places where, normally, she would never trespass.

"I have no idea who she is." Callie's entire mien was awash with a familiar sense of failure.

Merrick leaned forward and addressed her with honest commiseration. He'd seen the face of rabid frustration many times before, but had rarely felt as moved as he did now.

"Yes, you do," he said.

Callie stared at him, her expression wavering between faint hope and total disbelief.

"You know the names of everyone who appears in your dreams, Callie. Their relationship to you may be locked away right now, but if you give therapy a chance and give yourself time, you'll remember all of it. I promise."

During the ride out to GenTec Sciences in Great Neck, Peter tried to curb his excitement. Callie Jamieson had agreed to another regression. They made an appointment for Wednesday, giving her a full day to recover from this

afternoon's revelations. Peter would have preferred hyp-
notizing her on the spot, but instead of bullying her psyche—as he'd done with previous patients—he reined
himself in and opted for caution. She was too close to remembering the crux of the incident that haunted her, as well
as the names of her ancestors, for him to take unnecessary
risks.

He found it propitious that just after Callie left, Guy
Hoffman called. He'd also experienced a breakthrough and
was eager for Peter to come to his lab so he could demonstrate why he was so certain his p-316 could facilitate
Peter's project. Peter remained convinced that hypnosis
would effect the same result, but after this weekend, he was
open to suggestions.

He'd gone home to Connecticut for his father's birthday
dinner. It was a typical Merrick event, populated with
guests of extraordinary accomplishment who filled the air
with a constantly crackling buzz of intellectual energy. For
Peter, it was two days of fending off the inevitable sense
of humiliation that always came over him in his father's
house.

Since the eminent Kevin Merrick had been one of the
men who developed the techniques for transplanting human
organs, artificial hearts and therapeutic cloning became primary subjects for discussion. Peter's youngest brother, a
neurosurgeon who specialized in spines, enthralled those
gathered in the living room with data concerning experiments using stem cells to regenerate injured spinal cords.
His sister, the future governor, was focused more on the
politics of such research. She conducted her own unscien-
tific poll on the pros and cons of such controversial experimentation, as well as the religious implications inherent in
the practice of cloning. His other brother, the nuclear phys-
icist, did as he always did. He sat in the corner eating and
observing. When you've been nominated for a Nobel prize,
you didn't have to contribute. Your greatness was established. You were a Genius for Life.

As for Peter—his parents, their friends, and his siblings

all asked about his work, but listened to his response with half an ear. They'd heard his views on genetic memory before. True, the Human Genome Project had dusted him with a newly minted sparkle of legitimacy, but until a disease or a cure or a method or a something was named after him, he'd still be The Other Merrick.

Peter didn't know what he'd find in Hoffman's lab, but he was drawn to the quiet, intense microbiologist. Guy Hoffman had also spent years of painful anonymity trying to validate theories he believed to be true so that he could validate himself. He, too, felt as if his life's work had reached a point of no return. Yet, thanks to fate and serendipitous timing, their passions seemed to have coalesced and produced the very real possibility of not only raking in millions and millions of dollars, but also—and this resonated with Peter more than the money—of contributing something so valuable to the world community that it couldn't help but be considered for a Nobel prize.

When Peter was escorted into the conference room, he was surprised to discover he wasn't the only one invited. Carolyne Hale and several other members of the GenTec board were already gathered.

"This is an unexpected pleasure," Carolyne said, eyeing him curiously. "I didn't realize you and Guy had taken your relationship beyond the talking stage."

She sounded annoyed, as if he were somehow obligated to keep her up to date on the state of his various alliances. It made him feel like a kindergarten child who had to tell mommy every single detail of his day. He didn't like the feeling.

"Since we're both dedicated to unlocking the mysteries of human memory," he said, as if she should have deduced this on her own, "collaboration was always a possibility."

Carolyne didn't like his prickly tone. "Guy believes he's ready to conduct human trials. I suppose that's where you come in. Do you have a viable candidate?"

Peter wasn't thrilled with her tone either. "I do have a patient who's exhibiting symptoms of genetic recall."

"Anyone I know?"

"I couldn't tell you even if you did."

"Do you intend to use Guy's protein on him? Or her?"

Merrick shrugged. "I'm not certain. Using his protein on human beings is still a very high risk."

"I thought you liked taking risks."

She had turned coquettish, probably in an attempt to smooth the obvious ripples in their relationship. He wasn't in the mood to play.

"Not when someone's life might be at stake."

As if on cue, Dr. Hoffman invited his guests into his lab. For the next thirty minutes, he attempted to bring his supporters up to date on his Mnemonic Project. To Peter's chagrin, Hoffman made a point of trumpeting Peter's work with patients suffering from night terrors, tantalizing his board members with promises of incredible, historic revelations. Guy was throwing Peter out there as money bait. While Peter understood why, he wasn't certain he wanted his name so closely linked to the Mnemonic Project before he was absolutely certain of its efficacy.

Nonetheless, Peter found Hoffman's demonstrations exciting. They did demonstrate behavior that could only have resulted from inherited memory, but in the process, several rats experienced seizures. One died. Peter found their agony highly disturbing, as did the other board members. Two walked out. Carolyne was rapt.

Guy explained that seizures were the result of an individual subject being given more p-316 than its constitution could handle.

"It's like a doctor trying to find the precise amount of Coumadin to thin the blood without causing hemorrhaging. Even when all the variables like height and weight are taken into consideration, no response is certain."

He assured them that he and his associates were toiling relentlessly to establish a way of controlling the dosage/response ratio.

One board member, a doctor at a renowned research institute, wondered whether the method of induction was the issue, whether inhalation was better or worse than in-jection or ingestion.

Hoffman felt ingestion was too slow and opened the pos-sibility of compromise due to a natural chemical exchange with whatever was in the food; injection offered the greatest control, but had proven to be the trickiest to calculate. In-halation was certainly the easiest method of administration, but its effectiveness was dependent upon the depth of the intake.

Another director felt that perhaps Hoffman should con-duct additional pre-clinical trials on a larger animal before moving on to humans.

Hoffman's response was diplomatic, but he made it abundantly clear that he believed conducting experiments up and down the evolutionary ladder was a waste of time.

Peter was torn. He could see the progress Guy was mak-ing and more than agreed with his assessment of the po-tential for p-316, but low survival rates raised a number of red flags. Clinical trials were still a crap shoot, but Hoff-man's rats had proved the possibility of genetic memory in three out of four attempts. Peter would have to work very hard to convince Callie Jamieson to participate in these ex-periments, but he had to work just as hard to deny that the end—the prospect of all that money and all that fame—wasn't worth the means.

He'd be gambling with his career—and her life—but, as Peter's father always said, "The only way you reap big rewards is to take big risks."

Shortly after Ezra and Alvarez returned to the stationhouse, Callie walked in. Ezra noticed how puffy her eyes were, how sallow her complexion had become. She wasn't sleep-ing well.

"I was assigned the Vanna Larkin story," she said bluntly. "What can you tell me?"

Jorge flashed Ezra a "What's up?" look.

Ezra shrugged. He thought the weekend had gone well.

Judging by the chill emanating from the lovely Ms. Jamieson, she felt otherwise.

"I'm going to see if the labs have come back," Jorge said to Callie as he pushed away from his desk. "Chapin can fill you in."

"Fine," she said crisply as she took a seat. "Thank you."

Ezra told Callie about the pills, the name on the prescriptions, the fact that the door had been left unlocked, that the house was undisturbed, and that the neighborhood canvass turned up little except that Vanna Larkin was a night owl. She took diligent notes.

"We had to kick Schirmerhorn," Ezra said, hoping to keep her there a while longer. "We can't find anything that places him at the scene. Whatever we have is circumstantial: an argument he had with Hale the night before the murder and a half empty bottle of Seconal."

A look of guilt passed over Callie's face. "If not for the coincidence of his name and his distant relationship to the deceased, he never would have been brought in."

Ezra knew she was regretting her role in Schirmerhorn's detention.

"I don't believe in coincidence," he said flatly. "Schirmerhorn may not be a killer, but our uniforms found enough drugs in his apartment to supply the entire borough of Brooklyn for a week, including a packet of OxyContin. I've got two people dead from those drugs. Two people he knew. As far as I'm concerned, the guy's involved."

His voice was low, his words were clipped and his eyes bore into her with the heat of a torch. He was angry and hurt and confused. Mostly angry, Callie thought.

"The DA's office may want to consider him a witness for the prosecution when the results of narco's investigation goes to trial," she suggested, bravely meeting his gaze. "I bet he'd be happy to flip on Orlando, et alia, if it would erase his name from the police blotter."

Ezra tilted his head to the side and studied her. "How'd you get so smart?"

"Bergdorf's was having a special on brains. I bought a large."

Ezra, sensing a thaw, wanted to ask her why she left Saratoga without so much as a wave, but she was still sending out No Trespassing signals. She obviously had more pressing matters on her mind than his bruised ego.

"How'd you like to go to a photography exhibit tomorrow night?" he said.

Zig. "Come again?"

"I read about it in this weekend's *Courier*: 'Titanic,' an exhibition of photographs taken in the late 1800s. Interested?"

He knew she would be.

"Sure," she said, knowing that accepting his invitation was emotionally risky. "Why not?"

Not long after Callie left, Ezra's telephone rang. He prayed she hadn't changed her mind.

"Detective Chapin? It's Hiram Wellington returning your call. I'm sorry it took so long. We had a major crisis here and it took a while to get things under control."

"That's okay. Thanks for getting back to me."

"What can I do for you?"

"When I was going over my notes, I realized I never asked you the name of the woman for whom E.W. Hale built Liberty Park. Do you happen to know what it was?"

"I do, indeed," Wellington said. "Her name was Sarah Blessing."

23

Ezra leaned back in his chair, plunked his feet up on an ottoman and clicked on his TV. He played with the remote, but his brain was too buzzed with thoughts of Callie to commit to a movie or a weekly drama with characters he didn't know wrapped in story lines he didn't understand. It was like walking in on people in the middle of a conversation, which had never been his favorite thing to do.

All the way home from Saratoga, he tried to figure her out, but the woman was an enigma, soft and seductive one minute, snippy and off-putting the next. Still, he was attracted to her. Whether it was because he'd come to see that beneath her steely armor was a pool of vulnerability, or because she consistently challenged him, or simply because he thought she was hot—and she didn't seem to return the compliment—he had a major crush on Callie Jamieson.

His finger was on automatic pilot, his eyes half glazed over when the word Alzheimer's poked him awake.

". . . decoding the mnemonic gene is one of the final steps along the way to finding a cure for Alzheimer's."

The zipper running along the bottom of his television screen informed him C-SPAN was rerunning an interview conducted earlier by prominent CalTech scientist Ansel Moreland of Dr. Guy Hoffman, head of GenTec Sciences. From what Ezra could pick up, Hoffman was a microbiologist conducting experiments designed to unlock the key to human memory. Ansel Moreland, a straw-thin man with gray eyes and a thatch of silver hair that didn't speak well of his barber, was heading a forum on where medicine was going in the new millennium.

"You can't pick up a newspaper these days without finding at least one article concerning the sequencing of the genome. In a nutshell, Dr. Hoffman, what's it all about?"

"Figuring out what makes us tick."

Pleased with the sound bite, Moreland encouraged Hoffman to provide a bare bones primer to the Human Genome Project.

"The genome is a vast chemical database. What we're trying to do is identify each gene within that genome, figure out what it does, what makes it work, and how to make it work better, if need be."

"Most of us know that database as DNA, correct?"

Hoffman nodded, his facial expression emitting a whiff of intellectual patronization. "Yes, but the importance of DNA goes way beyond the forensics of TV detective shows. It's the substance of heredity. It gives us our hair color, our personality, our medical destiny . . ."

"And," Moreland interrupted, "according to you, the memories of our grandparents. In your opening address, you spoke of an experiment you're conducting concerning genetic memory. Tell us what you're doing and where you're going."

Hoffman briefly explained what genetic memory was so that the uninformed—like Ezra—wouldn't be at a loss. He wasn't quite as forthcoming about his experiment.

"The Mnemonic Project is still very early stage. If, and when, we have any concrete evidence that generational memory is encoded in genetic material, you can be certain we'll release our findings to the public immediately."

Moreland wanted to know why this was important.

So did Ezra.

"Just as much of our genetic material derives from our parents, we've received genetic gifts from past generations as well. We believe those gifts include pieces of the past that are stored somewhere in our brains. If we could find a way to release this information, we'd be able to view history as it happened, through the eyes of those who were there."

Ezra's reaction was disbelief mingled with utter fascination. The thought of having an eyewitness account to the start of World War II, or the pillaging of Rome, or the settling of the American West, or the crucifixion of Christ buried somewhere in his brain was so unfathomable, yet so profound, it made him dizzy with the wonder of it all.

"This isn't to imply that each of us is hoarding a vital piece of history, mind you. Most of our predecessors probably weren't witnesses to anything more dramatic than their family's personal history, but because those memories are set in another time, often in a different place, even simple scenes of domestic life become vital to our understanding of the human continuum."

"Why can't we simply bring these memories forward by ourselves?"

"Why do we use only ten percent of our brains? There's a great deal about the workings of the human brain that remains unknown. Releasing stored data is only one aspect."

"How do you propose to unlock these memories?"

Ezra leaned forward, his breathing momentarily suspended.

"One method entails working in concert with psychologists and psychiatrists trained in regression therapy. Hypnosis often helps identify whether the patient is suffering a neurotic episode, or reliving something from a long ago past."

Memories passed on from one generation to the next. Regression therapy. Hypnosis. Was this what Callie was going through? Were her dreams, the ones that were exactly like her mother's, an example of genetic memory? Ezra felt small, cold bumps on his skin.

"And if therapy's not successful?"

"We've been working to isolate a protein that will compel the mnemonic gene to fully unburden itself."

Ezra didn't like the sound of that.

"Is there any danger to that aspect of the treatment?"

Hoffman's left eye twitched and he licked his lips before responding. Ezra had interviewed too many perps not to know that either he was about to tell a whopping lie or reveal some uncomfortable truth.

"There's always a danger when we move from laboratory experimentation to human trials."

Moreland steepled his fingers and eyed the man opposite him. "Proteins are volatile. Do you know how a human brain cell will react if tampered with?"

Hoffman shifted in his chair, uncrossing his right leg, crossing his left.

Ezra read that as a nervous stall.

"At this point, we're not absolutely certain."

The silence following that admission loomed large.

"Could the patient's memory be destroyed?"

Hoffman's chin jutted forward; beads of sweat dotted his brow. "I can't say for certain."

"Is it possible?"

"Anything's *possible,* Dr. Moreland."

"Could the patient die?"

Hoffman backtracked, hoping to provide greater context. "The public thinks they know what Alzheimer's is, but if they haven't experienced the ravages of the disease firsthand, they have no idea how devastating it is. More to the point, they don't want to know."

Ezra admitted that was true.

"Aside from trying to effect a way to eliminate Alzheimer's, another of the more serious goals of the Mnemonic Project is to help those suffering from night terrors. These people are tormented by dreams they don't understand because their visions relate to another time and another cast of characters. Some of these patients are on the brink of insanity."

Ezra's blood descended into his feet, leaving his face stark white, his hands ice cold.

"The public doesn't really want to know about them either, yet they are the ones I'm trying to help," Hoffman insisted.

"How do your experiments help if patients completely lose their memories? Or wind up mentally deformed, or dead?"

Hoffman paused, as if needing to reconsider the consequences of his words.

"It won't help them," he said with appropriate reverence. "But as you well know, Ansel, science often succeeds on the back of its failures. It always has. It always will."

The taxi stopped on Tenth and Avenue B, right on the edge of Tompkins Square. Alphabet City was not Callie's usual stomping ground. If she partied downtown, it was in the West Village or Soho. The East Village, of which Alphabet City was a part, was still a little rough for her tastes. While it wasn't the drug and crime infested slum it used to be, it was still a neighborhood in flux: one block might be lined with trendy new boutiques, upscale co-ops and bistros; the block behind it might boast buildings that housed rats and squatters.

Like many of the storefronts-converted-into-bars down here, Onyx had high ceilings and wooden floors. It also had a cloud of cigarette smoke that hovered over the room like a giant parachute. Black curtains suspended from a brass rod covered the bottom half of the front window, providing the one and only soft touch in an otherwise gritty decor. The remaining glass framed the globe of an outside street lamp and, in the background, an abandoned building, a visual as stark and lonely as an Edward Hopper painting.

The place was busy, but not packed; ten o'clock was early for the bar scene. There were about a dozen tables, none large, all filled. A thick cluster of patrons were bunched into a tight knot at the end of the bar nearest the door. Several smaller groups were scattered about, as were individuals who looked momentarily unattached.

As Callie made her way inside, several sets of eyes, both

male and female, followed her with incipient lust. She took a seat at the rear of the granite bar and ordered a Cosmopolitan. Following Paula's advice, Callie had eaten before setting out on her adventure. She even had a piece of bread tucked into her purse, just in case.

The last few days had been harrowing. In between grieving for Wilty, being battered by hallucinations, and trying to stave off the deepening of her feelings for Ezra, Callie was working overtime convincing herself that the only way she was going to survive was to focus on *what* was happening to her instead of *why,* and what would make it *better* instead of what might make it *worse*.

Callie shivered. If she didn't, if she surrendered to the spirits the way her mother had, she could wind up like her mother, committed to an institution.

But, she told herself, she wasn't her mother and she didn't have to repeat her mother's tragedy. She had the power to change course. Therapy was one way of shifting momentum and pulling order out of chaos. Work was another—which was why she was here at Onyx.

From her perch, she surveyed the crowd, which was thickening. The ones that jammed the space in front of the door were the twenty- and thirty-somethings who'd anointed Alphabet City the latest happening place. For them, this was the fraternity/sorority scene with better clothes and better booze. The assembly near the bar appeared to be slightly older, less codependent, more sophisticated.

Callie's eyes moved to her left, to the velvet-curtained booths. They were a definite curiosity. Onyx wasn't a sex club, yet the most obvious presumption was that the games being played inside those booths involved neither cards nor checkers. There was something ominous about them, something that raised the specter of *Les Liaisons Dangereuses,* and things reminiscent of de Sade.

Callie wondered if that was their sole purpose—to simply emit the scent of menace, to capitalize on the reality-

TV lure of watching others put themselves at risk from a safe distance.

Those in the younger crowd glanced over at the booths frequently, almost hopefully, as if they couldn't wait to witness something salacious or decadent. Yet they never moved any closer. The older group was flush up against them, as if their kicks came from testing the depths of personal vulnerability: Learning what tempted them. What frightened them. What turned them on.

Is that what happened to Wilty? The small veins at her temples pulsed wildly. Had he put himself into the mouth of the lion once too often?

She bowed her head and massaged the stinging pain of grief away.

"Can I get you something else?"

Callie looked up into the piercing eyes of Gus the Gigantic.

"Thanks, but I'm good." Her drink was still half full. "I could use some information, however."

Gus didn't strike her as the type who responded to fakery or manipulation.

"About?"

"Vanna Larkin." Quickly, before he could shut her down, she reminded Gus that she'd been at Onyx several times with Wilty. She also told him she was a reporter on assignment for the *Courier*.

Gus's thick, black eyebrows pressed toward the bridge of his nose, looking like a vulture in flight.

"What about Vanna?"

"She OD'd last night. I'm trying to figure out what happened." She paused, knowing she had to tread lightly. "I'm also trying to find out if there's a link between her death and Wilty's."

"Why come to me?"

"Because they came to you. They were regulars here. I want to know who they hung with. And who supplied their drugs."

Gus planted a beefy arm on the bar, rested his considerable weight on it and leaned in close to her. His breath smelled stale.

"What exactly are you getting at?"

Callie met his angry stare head on. "Two people you and I knew are dead thanks to something called Orlando Magic."

Gus's eyes told her he'd heard the phrase before.

"The guy responsible for that deadly cocktail, Martin Orlando, is being sought by the police. He's gone underground, but someone's pushing his pill mix for him. I'm on the hunt for that someone."

Down the bar, a man in need of a refill grew impatient. Gus went to assuage the beast. Callie sipped her Cosmopolitan, keeping her eyes open, in case their conversation had provoked interest in any other corners.

"Vanna Larkin was doing some heavy shit," Gus said upon his return. "But I never saw a buy go down. She either brought her own or the guys she partied with supplied her. As for Wilty, he was a drunk, but I didn't think he did drugs."

Neither did Callie, which meant the OxyContin in his bloodstream probably had been introduced to his system without his knowledge.

"Did Vanna leave here last night with anyone?"

"Tell you the truth, she was spreading her favors around." Gus's face registered disgust. "At some point, I tuned out. Know what I mean?" Callie nodded. "So if she left with one of them, I missed it."

"Did Vanna ever party with Ben Schirmerhorn?"

Gus laughed. It was an explosive, booming sound. "No way. Vanna liked her men beefy and tough." His smile faded as he remembered something. "Come to think of it, Schirmerhorn was here last night and yeah, they did a couple of minutes in a booth."

"Did he do a lot of booth time with your customers?"

"More than he should have," Gus admitted. It was the first time he'd ever thought of himself as an accessory to the drug trade, or worse. Judging by his expression, he wasn't proud of his negligence.

Both Gus and Callie agreed that Schirmerhorn was probably pushing to support his own habit. The question was who was supplying him.

Callie took a police sketch out of her backpack. "Ever see him around here?"

Gus studied the sketch. "Maybe. I can't say for sure. Who is he?"

"Orlando. If he comes by, do us all a favor and call the police."

"I will." Gus took her card, pocketed it and went on about his business.

Callie nibbled on some bar nuts and gazed into the mirror over the bar. As she panned the crowd, her eye caught someone who looked vaguely familiar. It took a minute for her to place him as the burly guy who'd been standing across the street from her apartment the night she found the rat in her mailbox. He was smoking a cigarette and staring at her, his upper lip curled in a way that made her feel as if she'd just swallowed a glass of sour milk.

She spun around, got off her bar stool and made her way to his table. "Who are you?"

"An admirer." He sucked on a non-filter cigarette. His blue eyes were rheumy from vodka and half closed in response to the freshly exhaled smoke.

Callie noticed a zigzag tattoo on his left hand.

"Why were you standing outside my apartment the other night? And what are you doing here? Are you tailing me?"

He leered at her and licked his lips, slowly and deliberately.

"I don't know what you're talking about, babe. I'm just a guy enjoying a night out. If you want to enjoy the night with me, come and get it." He pushed back from the table and slapped his hands against his thighs, encouraging her to sit on his lap.

Callie's face registered utter disgust at the thought. He made a hitching sound, as if giving a giddyup to a horse, and pointed to his crotch with an oh-yeah grin.

Callie leaned toward him, getting up close and personal. He reeked from tobacco and liquor. "Stay away from me," she hissed.

She turned, left money on the bar for Gus and made her way to the exit. As she pushed open the door, he blew her a kiss.

She went to the corner to find a cab, but there were none. Figuring she'd pick one up on the other side of Tompkins Square Park, she headed west toward First Avenue. It was dark and she was uncomfortable walking by herself, but it would take a car service twenty minutes to get to her. She could be on her way home by then.

She was approaching Avenue A when an arm closed around her neck. She jerked to the side, trying to pull away, but he had her in a chokehold. With his free hand, he covered her mouth as he dragged her across the street into an alley.

When they reached the anonymous safety of darkness, he shoved her face against a wall and brought his mouth up against her ear. "You're gonna pay for what you did to me, you fucking little bitch."

Too afraid to think, Callie allowed her karate training to take over. She spiked an elbow into his ribs, hoping to loosen his grip on her neck. When his body recoiled, she spun around and snap-kicked her foot into his groin. He buckled, giving her a chance to hunker down and launch a roundhouse kick to his chest. He fell backward, but enraged and fueled by adrenaline, he recovered quickly.

He lunged at her, slamming her into the wall. Her head and back went numb from the pain of the impact. He thrust his body against hers and stuck one of his legs in between hers, trying to immobilize her. Before he did, she scratched at his face.

A fist came at her, hard. The first punch landed just under her left eye. The second and third were aimed at her gut. The hits were punishing, doubling her over until she crumpled like a rag doll. Blood dribbled from her nose. Her head throbbed.

"Now you know how it feels to get the shit kicked out of you," he hissed.

Despite the pain, she pulled herself up to a sitting position and confronted her attacker.

"Nobody did anything to you, Orlando. You did it to yourself. You knew what those pills could do and you prescribed them anyway." She glared at him with fiery defiance, secretly trying to gather her strength in case he came at her again. "Another one of your *patients* died last night. Vanna Larkin. Remember her?"

"Shut up!" he shouted, his agitation as raw as a salted wound.

"There were a bunch of pill bottles lying right there next to her body. Guess whose name was on the scrips? The same name that's going to be in all the headlines. And on the murder indictment."

He pulled a gun out of his belt and pointed it at her. His hatred for her was as hot as desert sand and just as gritty.

"One more word about me in your fucking newspaper, and I'll kill you," he said.

She stared back at him, refusing to feed his power trip with a response.

"Don't test me," he warned as he backed out of the alley. "As you've already pointed out, I have nothing to lose."

When she was sure he was gone, she crawled to where her backpack had fallen, found her cell phone and called 911.

24

It took a while for Callie to get to the door. She'd been sleeping, compliments of some painkillers administered by the ER doc who treated her at St. Vincent's. She was more than a little surprised to find Ezra Chapin standing in the hall. He was agape, to put it mildly. Then she remembered her black eye and swollen cheek.

"You should see the other guy," she said, in a feeble attempt at humor.

"I heard about your encounter with the infamous Dr. Orlando." His eyes trolled her body, assessing the physical damage. Her slightly bent posture told him the blows to her stomach had left purple bruises. Her face spoke for itself. "The guys downtown knew Alvarez and I were working the Larkin case," he said, explaining his presence.

"Come on in." She stepped aside so he could enter.

"I thought these might cheer you up." Like a kid on a Hallmark card, he stuck out his hand and shyly handed her a bouquet of pink peonies.

She tried to smile. "That's sweet. Thanks."

He followed her into the kitchen and watched as she found a vase, filled it with water and arranged the flowers. He carried them into the living room.

When they were settled, she told him what happened. He told her what the detectives from the 9th were doing about it.

"They've got sector guys out looking to grab up Orlando, but he's in the wind. They said scratching his face was a good thing. It makes him stand out."

"It wasn't exactly a conscious thing," Callie admitted.

Inwardly, Ezra seethed as images of Callie being attacked and beaten flashed before his eyes.

"The boys wanted to have a chat with our pal, Schirmerhorn, but he's also disappeared."

"I seem to have that effect on men," Callie said, dryly.

"Pardon me, Ms. Jamieson, but I wasn't the one who cut out of Saratoga without so much as a see-ya."

Callie flushed. "That's true."

"I'm going to forgive you, but only because you got the crap knocked out of you last night. Otherwise? Not an ounce of pity."

"You know, I had you pegged as a heart-of-stone kind of guy."

"And you were right." He swallowed a smile, delighted that her spirits weren't as bruised as her body. After what his colleagues at the 9th had told him, he didn't know what to expect.

"Good. I like being right," she said.

"Yeah, I got that."

Ezra didn't want to frighten her any more than she already was, but the guy in the silver Saturn might have been Orlando. He needed to check.

"By the way, what does this Orlando look like?"

"White, about five-eleven, brown eyes, thinning brown hair. He must be working out somewhere, because his body is a lot bulkier than the first time I saw him."

Ezra's eyebrows knitted together with concern.

"Why? What's up?"

"When we were driving up to Lake George, I spotted a tail. Alvarez ran a check on the plates. It was a rental to a guy with a fake license. The photo matched, but nothing else. I thought it might have been Dr. Drug. Guess not."

"What does that guy look like?"

"Mixed race skinhead. Blue-eyed. Lightning bolt tattoo . . ."

"On his left hand."

Ezra watched Callie's eyes go dark and her jaw tighten. "How do you know that?"

She explained about seeing the burly guy outside her building the night a rat was deposited in her mailbox, and running into him at Onyx.

"Could he be working for Orlando? Or could this be related to what happened to Wilty?"

Ezra's only response was a shrug. There was no way to know until either he or Orlando was picked up.

"Look, I don't know who this guy is or what he wants with you, but tomorrow, Jorge and I will put the word out on him."

Callie smiled. His tone was tough, but his eyes were soft.

"Have you heard from Victoria Moore?" he asked, changing the subject.

"No, have you?" she said, reminding him that he had co-opted her attempt to secure the fourth diary for herself.

He chuckled at the jibe. "No."

Callie, noting the onset of dusk, suddenly became aware of the time. "When is that gallery opening?"

"What? Who cares? You're not going anywhere," Ezra said, dumbfounded that she had even remembered their date.

"I've been in bed all day. I feel fine and I need to get out of here. I'm getting cabin fever." She stood and headed for her bedroom. "Do you know how to make coffee?"

Ezra harrumphed. "I am a fully self-sufficient male. Of course I can make coffee!"

"Then get to it. I have to shower and change."

The Reinish Gallery, like most in Chelsea, had been a ware-house in a former life. Now, where trucks once loaded and unloaded cargo, men and women swathed in city-chic black mingled on a steel dock that served as a porch. Inside, the high-ceilinged space was crowded and dimly lit. The walls, which usually boasted several coats of white paint, had been softened to a dun gray that complemented the black-and-white photographs on display.

As they walked in, Ezra picked up a sheet of paper containing critical comments on the show. He shared one with Callie that interested him.

" 'When I read the invitation and saw whom they had cast as Titans, I took issue with the title. Tyrants would have been far more accurate.' "

"Do you agree with his assessment of these men as tyrants?" Callie asked.

"Were they singularly focused on success? Yes. Were they ruthless with their adversaries? Yes. Were they cold and calculating and, more often than not, emotionally vacant? You bet. But they were the ones who saw opportunity, seized it by the throat and rode it to glory." Ezra smiled at his own idol worship.

"Maybe one has to be tyrannical to achieve the level of Titan," Callie mused.

Ezra threw up his hands and grunted with the pain of self-discovery. "I knew there was a reason I wasn't rich and famous. I'm too nice a guy!"

Callie laughed. "Yeah. That must be it."

They headed into the main room and meandered from one bay to the next, studying each of the photographs, allowing themselves plenty of time to become immersed in the mode of the day. The least interesting items on display were the ubiquitous power portraits of stern-faced men, snarling and glowering at the camera as if hoping to intimidate anyone and everyone who sat in the boardrooms where they once hung. Callie half expected to hear J.P. Morgan growl when she came in close to fully examine his likeness. Andrew Carnegie and Jay Gould weren't much more appealing.

Neither was John D. Rockefeller, if all one viewed were the images preserved from his later years. Hairless due to alopecia and leathery from age, Rockefeller's narrow face appeared pinched, his smooth white skin and light eyes making him look almost albino. When he was younger, when his wide forehead was outlined by hair and his upper lip sported a thick, brushlike mustache, his face looked fuller, less sour. In one or two shots, he actually looked as if he were smiling.

Studying the differences in expression, Callie wondered if people who changed the world as dramatically as he had, looked back at what they had wrought and were disappointed. Or, having done so much, found it painful being too old to do more.

The last of the Titans was E.W. Hale. They hadn't planned it, but somehow, Callie and Ezra wound up viewing this section of the exhibition in reverse, traveling from the latter stages of Hale's life backward to his youth. They could have circled around to the other end of the bay and started at the beginning, but this route felt more appropriate.

There was a power portrait, of course. In it, Hale appeared as baronial and frightening as his peers, his starched shirt collar tight under his chin, his black bow tie plump, but neat, his dark eyebrows canting toward each other in a vulturine scowl. He, too, had a mustache, but his was thinner, better clipped and more carefully waxed than Morgan's or the young Rockefeller's.

Callie, recalling Wilty's penchant for neatness and order, wondered if anal retentiveness was an inherited trait.

Naturally, there were photographs that chronicled E.W. Hale's rise to power and prominence: The young newspaper magnate proudly standing outside the *Courier*'s original building in Cleveland, a squat, single-story brick structure that wouldn't adequately house a clothing boutique today. The three Hale brothers dwarfed by trees in a forest that fed Hale Paper its pulp. E.W. in his Hale Holdings office after he'd moved his headquarters to New York, as well as several other portraits, each as draconian as the last.

His passion for golf was evidenced in several photographs of him with his cronies standing arm in arm on a tee at Hale's private golf course, and one of him in slacks, a woolen jacket, and a cloth cap having just smacked a ball down the fairway.

Callie thought of those clubs she'd found in Wilty's closet. Maybe one of them was the one in this photograph.

A small alcove within the larger bay was devoted to Hale's beginnings, starting with a stilted, but interesting group portrait of the Hales in Stroudsburg before E.W.'s father, Addison, died and the rest of the family dispersed. The children were poorly dressed, particularly when contrasted to Addison in his fancy brocade vest and gold fob watch. Charlotte, E.W.'s mother, centered the picture, much as she had centered their lives, her round face and softly dimpled chin somewhat incongruous with the pioneer toughness she projected.

Alongside that picture was one of E.W.'s parents standing atop a mountain, looking dour-faced, dusty and exhausted.

"That must have been when they first arrived in Pennsylvania," Ezra said, offering Callie some of what he'd found about E.W. Hale's personal history.

Charlotte Wilton had come from Salem, Massachusetts, the eldest daughter of a gentrified family with strong religious convictions and an accomplished ancestry. Addison Hale's resumé had more holes in it than Belgian lace, but he was a man of considerable charm, able to smooth over his shortcomings with a genial manner and a raconteur's ability to spin a yarn.

After Charlotte and Addison were married, and a generous dowry had been paid, the newlyweds packed up their belongings and headed west.

"Suddenly, this well-bred, well-educated schoolteacher who was accustomed to being transported from place to place in an elegant carriage, found herself trundling along in a canvas-topped prairie schooner," Ezra said. "Needless to say, she wasn't a happy camper.

"By the time they reached the Pocono Mountains, Charlotte had had it. She refused to go any further, literally. She climbed down off the wagon and started unloading her luggage. It may not have been where Addison had planned to stake his claim, but he acceded to her wishes and built their home on the very spot where Charlotte's forbearance ran out. They named their parcel, Patience's End."

Callie laughed. "Good for Charlotte!"

And good for Ezra, she thought, impressed at both his breadth of knowledge on the subject, as well as his obvious joy in the process of acquiring it. His mama not only raised a smart child, but a curious one. She liked that.

As in the other rooms, there were numerous photos of people who had some association with the Titan on display, particularly their wives. There were several portraits of Winifred Colfax Hale, all of them formal. One was a glamorous study of her with her hair done up and her body swathed in a floor-length, velvet opera cape trimmed at the neck with a ruff of feathers. Another, a moody profile in which she wore a low-cut dress meant to display an envious collection of jeweled ropes. The lighting was soft, yet the planes of her face remained sharp and sculpted.

There were several family tableaux, with Charles Hale, Huntington Hale, and Charity Hale gathered around their parents, everyone unsmiling and stiff as statues.

"If I remember correctly, Charity Hale married Thomas Brighton, one of the editors of the *City Courier*," Callie said. "I don't think they had any children."

Once again, Ezra was johnny-on-the-spot with the facts. "She had two babies who died within their first two years, and several stillbirths."

"I wonder why she didn't adopt."

Ezra's upper lip curled in a sardonic half smile. "Winifred was adamantly opposed to the Hale name being given to a child that didn't flow from their bloodline."

"And how did that particular factoid hit you?"

"I called my parents and told them how much I loved them."

Callie smiled. She liked that, too. "How about E.W.? Did he object?"

"Apparently not. According to this particular biography, E.W. encouraged Charity and Thomas to adopt, but Winifred made such a stink about it that even after Winifred died, they remained childless."

Callie recalled that in the third diary, the one written in 1902, E.W. Hale had rued Winifred's influence on his children, claiming *"she'd done them more harm than good."* Later, however, he confessed that, *"my extended absences didn't help. They were an indulgence and, I'm sad to say, an abdication of my paternal responsibilities. If Winifred failed our brood, so too have I."*

E.W. Hale's aspect softened as the years retreated and he was returned to his youth. His scowl disappeared, his eyes looked warmer, his hair became less lacquered, his mien less starched. Ezra, who thought the older pictures conveyed an ambiance of sadness, noted that the earlier snapshots—all lighter in tone and mood—were dated before 1888, before Hale's life-transforming Exile in the White Wilderness.

Near the end of the bay, they came upon a bewitching portrait of a woman in a pleated white dress. The woman's hair was dark, parted in the middle and turned under in a soft roll that rested gently on her neck. She was young, with big, doe eyes and a plush mouth that looked as if it had been lightly tinted.

Callie stopped and stared at the picture. As she did, her face flushed. Her breathing grew shallow.

"What's the matter?" Ezra was afraid this outing would be too much for her. He slipped his arm around her waist to steady her.

"That's the woman from my dreams. She was the one at the sanitarium. She was the one in the boat with the dead man."

He had no idea what she was talking about.

Her body felt rigid and still, but her eyes darted about the portrait, studying it from every angle, examining it like a radar beam searching the skies for enemy aircraft. She was rattled. In truth, so was he. Something odd was going on here. How could Callie have two different dreams about a stranger who somehow or another had ties to E.W. Hale?

It was much too much of a coincidence. Especially for a man who didn't believe in coincidence.

While Callie continued to gawk at the woman in white, Ezra read the card on the side of the photograph.

"Callie," he said quietly, not wanting to jar her, "this is Sarah Blessing, the woman for whom Liberty Park was built." He relayed his conversation with Hiram Wellington.

"She's the one who went catatonic?"

"That's what Wellington said."

Callie's brow crinkled in concentration. "What was Hale's connection?"

"Wellington didn't say."

"I think I'm spooked."

"Let's not go off half-cocked," Ezra said, hiding his own apprehension. "You saw a brunette. The world is filled with dark-haired beauties. This young Miss Blessing is charming, but not unusual looking. She's ubiquitous, if you know what I mean."

Callie shook her head. "Everything you say is true, but Ezra, *this* is the woman in my dreams. I may not be certain about much else, but I'm sure of that."

Ezra couldn't argue the point, so he didn't. It was possible that Callie saw this picture at another exhibit at another time or in a book when she was preparing to go up to Saratoga. There might have been a photograph of Sarah Blessing at Liberty Park that Callie saw and he missed. He'd give Wellington another call.

"This looks like it could be a wedding dress," Callie said, glancing at the card to the right of the picture. "But this isn't the year she married that doctor in East Galway. This was taken in 1887. She married Jeremiah Holstein in 1894."

"True, but remember, her breakdown was caused by the death of a husband and a child. Holstein was the doctor Hale brought in to take care of her. This could be from her wedding to hubby number one."

Though Callie wanted to linger, Ezra encouraged her to

move on. There was nothing more to learn standing here, he told her. She agreed, but halfheartedly.

They browsed through pictures of E.W. and his daughter, Charity, pedaling down Euclid Avenue on a tandem bicycle; E.W. peering out from the back of his touring car; E.W. lounging against a bale of hay eating sardines on a camping trip out West; the entire Hale family picnicking on the lawn of Long House.

It was the final photograph in this segment of the exhibition, however, that struck Callie and Ezra as the most curious: E.W. Hale with his arm around a very beautiful woman. They both looked to be in their early twenties. His hair was free of oil, windblown, a dark lock falling loosely onto his forehead. He was wearing a high-necked, black jacket that was more typical of country men than city men. His eyes were bright, glistening almost, and his mouth was caught in a soft smile.

The woman nestled into the crook of his arm had lighter hair, which was drawn back and plaited into a long single braid that scrolled around her neck and rested against the bodice of a white, shirred cotton blouse. Her eyes were pale and her cheeks were round. Her mouth, like that of her companion, also curved into a gentle, satisfied smile.

The man was E.W. Hale. The woman was Liberty McAllister. The date was 1863.

25

Most of their dinnertime conversation centered around M.E.W. Hale and his women: Liberty McAllister, Winifred Colfax Hale, someone named Faith, and Sarah Blessing. Callie remained certain she was the woman she'd seen on the lake.

By the second glass of wine, Ezra felt emboldened enough to ask, "Would it disturb you to tell me about your nightmares?"

Callie shored up her courage with a deep breath. She reminded Ezra about her dream of a woman in the doctor's office, the one she'd had after visiting Liberty Park.

"The woman in that dream was Sarah Blessing."

Ezra couldn't help but wonder about the implications of something as bizarre as being haunted by a stranger who lived in another century.

"The second time I saw her I wasn't asleep," Callie continued. "I was standing alongside Saratoga Lake waiting for you to bring the car around."

Callie recounted her vision of the woman and the man in the rowboat that went nowhere.

"Back at the gallery, you said she was in the boat with the dead man. What dead man?"

"He's one of the gray people." Unexpectedly, she smiled. "I guess now you'll want to know who the gray people are."

"That would be helpful." Ezra smiled back at her. He

wished he could tell her how amazing he thought she was. And how brave.

"I'll spare you the really gruesome details and just give you the highlights."

After she finished reciting the short version of the gray people saga, Ezra sat silently as he tried to absorb it all.

"The woman in that dream isn't Sarah. Right?" he said.

"Right."

"Do you recognize her?"

"No. Somehow, I never can make out her face." Her brow furrowed. "Maybe I don't want to."

"Have you ever had any other dreams about that gray lady?"

"No. The dreams about her are always the same. But I did have another vision of Sarah." She told him about the episode in Peter Merrick's office when she saw Sarah in a white dress, pregnant and covered with blood. "Obviously, that was when she lost her baby. But why would *I* see that?"

"You got me," Ezra said.

Callie offered him a rueful smile. "Not to worry. Dr. Peter Merrick, shrink extraordinaire, is on the case. He assured me that I know the names of everyone in my dreams and that one day, they'll come to me." The smile became a laugh. "I only hope it's not when I'm so old I forget it all two minutes after I remember it."

Ezra laughed with her, but the mention of Merrick's name raised a flag. When he and Callie discussed this over dinner in Saratoga, he asked if it was possible that her dreams were the result of the power of suggestion. Callie said no, that the suggestions weren't coming from her mother. But what about from her therapist?

Ezra wondered whether Peter Merrick was one of the psychiatrists to whom that Hoffman guy had referred, regressing patients in an attempt to coax ancient memories from the recesses of their brains.

The thought that someone might be using Callie as anecdotal evidence in an experiment turned Ezra's stomach. It also unnerved him.

"This has been a long night. How 'bout I get the check and we get out of here?"

"That's fine with me, but I saw at least ten yummy desserts on this menu."

"Not interested." He motioned to the waiter.

Callie, having witnessed Ezra's love of things sweet, reached over and pressed the back of her hand against his forehead. "Are you okay?"

He took her hand and brought it to his mouth for a soft kiss.

"I just want to be sure you're okay," he said.

"I will be," she said, stunned at the gesture, but happy.

As they rode up in the elevator, Callie wondered if he'd ask to stay and what she'd say if he did. He must have been wondering the same thing, because the elevator was working at its usual snail's pace and there was no conversation between them.

When Callie opened the door and they walked into her apartment, any romantic thoughts they might have been entertaining disappeared. Someone had been there. Lights were on. Furniture was disturbed. Cushions had been tossed onto the floor, tables overturned. In Callie's office, papers had been moved, drawers opened, files taken from their cabinets and strewn about. Callie's computer was on, as was her PalmPilot.

Callie's eyes teared at the violation, but her jaw was set.

With Ezra right behind her, she headed for her bedroom. When she opened the door, she gasped. Staining the center of her beautiful peach bedspread was a blotch of color that looked a lot like pooled blood. Brownish red spatters tattooed her pillow shams and headboard. And at the end of the bed was a bloody blanket that was wrapped around something with a shape that was difficult to define.

Ezra moved quickly to the bed and prevented Callie from unwrapping the blanket.

"Leave it. Don't compromise the scene."

She nodded, but every nerve ending in her body wanted to scream and to cleanse her home of this hideous desecration.

Ezra grabbed his cell phone and called the stationhouse. He described what they'd found, gave the address and assured the desk sergeant they would leave everything as it was. Then, he took Callie's arm and led her back to the living room. He sat her down on one of the couches and went to get her a glass of water. While in the kitchen, he looked for any additional signs of disruption, but there didn't seem to be any. Either the intruder wasn't looking for anything in the kitchen, or had run out of time.

When Officer Plover and his partner arrived, they had members of the Crime Scene Unit in tow. Ezra filled them in on what had happened to Callie the previous evening.

"Miss Jamieson," Officer Plover said, extending his hand. "How're you doing?"

"I'm all right." Callie recognized the two uniforms as the ones who'd followed up on her false alarm. "I don't think we can blame this on a faulty light switch."

"Nope. I'd say we have a real, live B and E on our hands." Plover smiled. He understood she was still embarrassed about the last time he and his partner had been called in.

As the two of them talked, Crime Scene technicians hunted for fingerprints in the entry foyer. One of them interrupted to explain to Callie he'd have to fingerprint both her and Ezra to facilitate the identification process. He also asked if anyone else had regular access to her apartment. She mentioned Skip, the daytime doorman—he occasionally dropped packages off or let in repairmen—and Tommy, the nighttime guardian of the gate. Other than those two, she couldn't think of anyone else.

The tech went on to dust the entry and living room area—walls, door frame, pictures, light switch plates, table tops, plant leaves. His partner was doing the same in the dining room/office. When they'd finished there, they would both move into the bedroom. Plover apologized about the black powder and the time, but he explained that collecting trace evidence was painstaking, heavily detailed work. They would probably be working in the apartment for several hours.

"I'm afraid you won't be able to use your bedroom tonight," Plover said. "Do you have somewhere else you could stay?"

"Paula's out of town," Callie muttered, thinking out loud. "I could go there. My father's place is in New Jersey. I'd need to rent a car. No. That's a pain. Besides, it's too late. I suppose I could go to a hotel." Her voice sounded shaky and unsure.

"You could stay with me," Ezra volunteered. "I'll bunk on the couch."

"I don't want to . . ."

"It's not an inconvenience," Ezra said.

Plover looked from one to the other and decided that since this was not a police matter, he'd check on his partner.

"And frankly, if you'll forgive this chauvinistic, knight-in-shining-armor display of protective fervor, I'd feel a lot better if I knew where you were and that where you were was safe and secure."

Despite her desire to steer clear of all romantic entanglements, Callie was falling in love with this man.

"I don't want to put you out," she said.

"It won't be the first time I've sacked out on that couch. Although this time, it'll be a conscious and deliberate choice, as opposed to an alcohol induced happenstance."

"I think I should let my father know. We're supposed to have lunch this week."

Callie got her cell phone and joined Ezra on the couch.

"I'm sorry if I woke you, Serena. It's Callie. May I speak to my dad?"

As she waited for her father to come to the phone, Callie tapped her foot *Allegrissimo,* as if she believed Serena was stalling deliberately to annoy her.

"I didn't know if you'd call here or at my office, so I thought I'd better let you know I'm not working in the office, and I'm not going to be home in the morning. Something happened . . . no, I'm all right, but someone broke into my apartment. . . . Calm down, Daddy. I'm fine. Really. . . . Yes, the police are here. . . . No. It doesn't appear that they took anything. . . . Thanks, but I'm going to spend the night at . . . a friend's."

Ezra swallowed a chuckle when a noticeable blush rouged her cheeks.

"Yes. I'll call you first thing. . . . I love you, too." She returned the phone to the kitchen, then came back inside.

As she did, Officer Plover asked if Callie and Ezra would join him in the bedroom. Ezra took Callie's hand and they followed Plover down the hall. Once inside her bedroom, Callie's heart sank. Her beautiful, pale aerie looked as if it had been attacked by a plague of polka dots. Everywhere she looked, there were dusky patches of powder or rusty spatters of blood. She couldn't even begin to imagine what it would take to get this room back to the way it was, if that was even possible.

One of the CSU technicians lifted the bloody bunting off the bed; it had already been photographed, tagged, dusted and searched. Slowly, he unwrapped it.

Inside the blanket was a blood-soaked baby doll.

"What the hell is this supposed to be?" Officer Plover said with obvious disgust. "Is this some anti-abortion thing?"

Callie's voice was low and whisper-soft. "It's a miscarriage." She turned to Ezra. There was raw fear in her eyes. "This is Sarah Blessing's dead baby."

26

When Ezra first issued his invitation to spend the night, Callie thought she might feel awkward—there seemed to be a lot of emotional dust in the air whenever they were together—but in fact, the opposite was true. When the door closed behind her, she felt welcome and safe.

Ezra took her overnight bag and headed for his bedroom. Callie plopped down in a comfortable chair. She was thoroughly exhausted, yet her brain continued to work at full throttle, conjuring a host of unsettling images: a bloody doll; a stained bed cover; a photograph of a woman she thought lived only in dreams; her apartment defiled and besmeared; the disquieting introduction of someone called Liberty McAllister; the continuous, haunting presence of the unknown, unseen, Faith.

She studied each of them, moving them about like puzzle pieces to see where and if they fit, trying to meld them into an understandable whole. After a few minutes of this mental juggling, thoughts and emotions from everything that had happened, everything that could have happened, and everything that still might happen collided like rain clouds, hitting Callie with the sudden intensity of a summer storm. Consumed by the enormity of it all, Callie's head fell into her hands, her palms pressed against her eyes in an effort to repel whatever tears threatened. She refused to give whoever had befouled her home the satisfaction of crying. Instead, she sucked in a gulp of air and lifted her head in a defiant thrust.

White specks of light danced before her eyes. Her brain felt tight and tingly. Realizing she must have raised her head too quickly, she took a long breath, opening herself to the healing powers of oxygen. Slowly, the specks faded, but in their place were other disturbing images: Mara being led from the house, the solarium at Stonehaven, the lobby of Liberty Park.

Antsy, unable to stem the anxiety welling within, she pushed herself up from the chair. As she came to her feet, her eyes caught sight of Ezra's bulletin boards. Drawn like a tropism she stood before them, folded her arms across her chest, and confronted the Hale historical tree.

Her gaze journeyed across the neatly arrayed index cards, stopping at various highlighted signposts: E.W. Hale's birth, those five missing years, his marriage to Winifred, the births of his children, the death of the infant Josiah, his Exile in the Wilderness. Ezra had added a card noting the establishment of Liberty Park and the name of Sarah Blessing. He'd also amended Wilty's card to read: "cause of death—murder."

"What am I supposed to do with this, Wilty?" she whispered to the spirit of her former lover. "What was this journey you were on and what were you looking for?"

A nascent thought nibbled at her consciousness. Callie tried to bring it forward, to prod it into a full realization, but it remained stubbornly resistant, like when she worked a crossword puzzle and the right word lurked at the edge of her mental fingertips but refused to be grasped.

More and more, she was coming around to the belief that Wilty's inference that E.W. Hale's past was informing the present was not a supposition, but the truth. Initially, she may have embraced the concept of a curse for its promotional value, but if one juxtaposed what she and Ezra learned in Saratoga and Hale's diaries, along with the photographs they saw tonight, it was beginning to seem possible that there was some kind of carryover from then to now; that grievances or feuds or rifts from a hundred years ago were literally coming back to haunt the Hales.

But what could have happened then that would have affected Wilty today?

The thought of Wilty having ghosts struck Callie hard, knotting the veins in her head until they pounded against her skull. She closed her eyes and massaged the lids to disperse the pain.

Ezra, who had been watching Callie from the doorway, said, "You can either hit the sack or pig out on cookies and milk."

"Curtain number two," Callie said, returning to her chair.

Ezra seated himself on the couch, set down two glasses of milk and a plate of goodies and indulged immediately.

"Any thoughts about who and why?"

"If you're asking if I know of anyone who'd want to trash my apartment other than the psycho who attacked me last night, or the one who stuffed a dead rat in my mailbox, no. I haven't a clue."

Ezra heard the anger in her voice. It was an emotion he preferred over fear.

"What I can't figure out is how either of those two loonies knew about my dream."

"The most obvious source is your therapist." He said it gently, knowing how deep her sense of betrayal would be if this proved true.

She didn't respond right away. When she did, her words were measured and hesitant, as if she were thinking out loud, still working it through.

"The man is a renowned doctor, for goodness sake. His family is famous. His brother was nominated for a Nobel prize."

"So?" Ezra was unimpressed with Merrick's family history as a defense.

"So, there's no way he would jeopardize his reputation, not to mention his medical license, with a stunt like this." She sighed, her breath trembling. "But it is true that other than you, he's the only one who knows about that particular dream, the one about Sarah in the bloody white dress."

Her distress was obvious. She would've preferred almost any conclusion other than this. She'd invested a great deal of trust in this man.

But, was he worthy of that trust? Storming to the front of Ezra's brain was the interview he'd watched on C-SPAN and the unsettling realization that some of the facts presented there coincided with what was happening to Callie. Dr. Hoffman said he was working with psychiatrists who had patients suffering from night terrors, people who dreamt about people they never met and places they never visited. He said it was possible that these dreams were the experiences of others passed on through the generations. He said many of the patients taunted by these memories were on the brink of insanity.

"Who else could have known about that dream and what would they gain from harassing you?" Ezra's interest in Peter Merrick was growing more intense by the minute.

Callie started to express ignorance, but then, her face paled with the shock of enlightenment. "I made a tape of my session with Dr. Merrick."

Ezra's nerve endings twitched with anticipation.

"Remember, I told you the hypnosis frightened me?"

Ezra hadn't forgotten. "You decided not to go back."

"Then, we went to Saratoga. What happened to me there convinced me I had to find a way to exercise greater control over these . . . visions."

"So, you resumed therapy."

"Yes, but my reporter's instinct wasn't comfortable with the possibility of not having full access to the facts. If I'm in a trance when the information is brought forward, I'm at the mercy of the therapist. Rather than risk him suppressing something either for my own good or his, I wired myself up to a voice-activated device. Maybe whoever trashed my apartment listened to that tape and then went out to get that doll."

Ezra knew that scenario wasn't likely, and said so. It

was too time-consuming and created too much unnecessary exposure. But the notion of someone listening, or watching, gnawed at him like a burr. He'd checked for bugs the night she found the noose in her bathroom and come up empty, but he wasn't as savvy about the latest listening devices or cameras as the department techs. He could've missed something.

"Since I can't think of any way Martin Orlando could have known about that dream," Callie was saying, "I think we have to eliminate him."

Ezra agreed, but he hadn't eliminated Merrick. He wouldn't have needed a tape. He could have hired someone and told them exactly how to set the scene.

Callie shifted position in her chair. As she did, Ezra's bulletin boards once again came into view. That thought, the one that had nibbled at her, suddenly gained heft.

"The diaries! Whoever it was, was looking for the diaries. Or the letter Wilty said jump-started all this." She sat up, newly energized. "Ezra, I can't be the only person Wilty spoke to about this so-called journey. If Wilty's killer knew about the diaries and the letter, it's not a stretch to think he knew Wilty sent them to me."

She looked at Ezra, a frisson of fear prompting a shudder. "What the hell is in that diary?"

"Corroboration for what's in the letter," Ezra said quietly.

"And you know what that is?" Callie was incredulous and annoyed at the thought that Ezra was keeping information from her. "Since when?"

Quickly, Ezra told her about Dan Kalikow's interview.

"Evidently, a document exists that questions the legitimacy of the line of descent leading from E.W. Hale to Wilty. Wilty had the original. He showed Kalikow a copy. When Kalikow offered to help Wilty verify some of the facts, Wilty declined. He said he was already working on it."

Callie tried to digest the hunk of meat Ezra just fed her, but it was difficult to swallow.

"Whew!" she sighed, her eyes wide with wonder. "This is huge!"

And, it explained that line in Wilty's letter: *It has to do with who E.W. Hale was and what that makes me.*

"If this . . . stuff is true and Wilty isn't a Hale, what does that do to the *Courier* and to Hale Holdings?" A spiteful giggle bubbled up inside of her. "What does this do to Carolyne Hale?"

Ezra caught the smile and joined her in a guilty pleasure. Then, he leaned forward, moving closer to Callie. He wanted to be certain that, momentary amusement aside, she truly grasped the enormity of this, because it might have consequences that would affect her.

"It upsets the power structure at one of the most important media empires in the world. It challenges the fortunes of people who've become accustomed to being rich. And it opens the door to the possibility that there are other Hales out there who, for more than a hundred years, have been denied the wealth, the power and the prestige that should have been theirs. This is more than huge," he said. "This is cataclysmic."

"It's also a motive for murder," Callie said, quietly stating the obvious.

Ezra's face remained calm, but his body was drawn tight, as if he were already girding himself for battle.

"What makes it so powerful is that it almost doesn't matter whether it's true."

Callie looked surprised.

"Anyone who's at risk of losing their precious status quo can't afford to take the chance of something like this finding daylight. Whispers can be as devastating as howitzers if they pose the right questions."

"And legitimacy is a question that demands to be answered," Callie said, her skin prickling with a growing sense of menace. "Especially when it involves control over a billion-dollar fortune."

"Exactly. Wilty's killer won't stop until he finds the original of that document *and* the diary. Which is why we have to find both of those missing items . . ."

"Before I wind up the way Wilty did," Callie said, finishing his sentence.

Edgy, she rose from the chair and began to pace. Ezra stood and waited for her to circle around to him. When she did, he put his hands on her arms and held her in front of him. Tears of fear and frustration dotted her cheeks.

"Nothing's going to happen to you," he promised, tenderly brushing away her tears. "I won't let it."

Callie recalled her father saying that to her mother.

"If you want to protect me," she said, trying to hide all that she was feeling, "why don't you and Alvarez start by finding that lunatic Martin Orlando?"

Ezra's eyes widened, as if he never would've thought of that on his own. His face was inches from hers. "You know, that's a really good idea. We'll get right on it. But in the meantime . . ."

Callie took his face in her hands, brought his mouth to hers and kissed him. It was so impulsive, it stunned them both, but when Callie went to back away, Ezra wouldn't let her go. He held her tight against him while his lips explored her mouth, tracing its contours, tasting the sweetness of her flesh. When his tongue met hers, Callie melted, praying that the sensations coursing through her were real and not imagined.

Ezra's hands traveled slowly down her back, ranging over the firmness of her rump and the softness of her thighs. His lips followed, grazing the side of her neck on its journey southward. When his hands slid between their bodies and his fingers traced the vee from her stomach to her groin, Callie felt her legs go weak. Instinctively, she pressed her hips against him, needing to know if his excitement matched hers.

Their lips locked again and for a while, they fed on each other, allowing their feelings to evolve and take shape. When she felt him begin to unbutton her blouse, her skin actually tingled. She hadn't been with anyone since Wilty, so for her, this was a revival, a reawakening of passions that had been dormant for way too long. What a delicious revelation to discover that all the sensations and feelings and responses she feared had been buried by the weight of current fears and former failures were very much alive.

Invigorated by a sense of liberation she, too, began to explore, eagerly running her hands beneath his shirt, sliding her palms over Ezra's chest. His body was taut and muscular, much tighter and more powerfully built than it appeared in his clothes. As her fingers traversed his strapping physique, she was confounded by a mix of emotions. She was turned on by his brawn, but what thrilled her even more was knowing that his body was as strong as his will and that his physicality was more than able to back up his promises to protect her.

As if he'd intuited her thoughts, he lifted her in his arms and carried her down the hall into his bedroom. When he set her down in the darkened room, she saw a question in his eyes. Her answer was to remove her blouse. Without looking away, she undid her slacks and slipped out of them as well. Then, clad in nothing but a bra and panties, she went to his bed.

Ezra approached her, his amber eyes hot with yearning. He sat next to her and ran his hands down her arms. The only light in the room came from the hallway, a yellow wash that bathed Callie in a golden veil. As his eyes took in the wonder of her, he noticed a livid bruise on her stomach and a black and blue mark on her face which he hadn't seen before. Both were remnants of her encounter with Orlando. Passion was momentarily replaced with anger.

Callie moved toward him, her blue eyes as intense as jewels. As much as he longed to protect her, his longing to possess her long, lean body took precedence. He drew her to him and kissed her with a feverish wanting.

As they sank onto the bed, she pushed his shirt off and again, caressed his sinewy frame. Her hands undid his belt and his trousers. She slid her hand down and felt his power building. He unhooked her bra. She waited for his lips to find her breast. When they did, she gasped and closed her eyes, luxuriating in the exquisite pleasure Ezra's mouth was providing.

Just then, she wanted him desperately, yet despite his need, he had slowed the pace. Instead of racing toward consummation, he lay next to her, his fingers langorously drawing lines on the insides of her thighs, arrows pointing the way to the place they both wanted to be. Her hips responded with the undulating dance of heightened sensuality but, still, he played with her, his tongue and his fingers working in concert to raise her desire to an excruciating pitch.

With trembling hands, she relieved him of his trousers and his shorts, marveling at his naked virility. She touched him and he shivered. She stroked him and he sucked in his breath, holding it as his body went into that odd calm that only came during sex, that moment of suspended animation when one was aroused almost beyond control, yet managed to brake the action and prolong the flood of sensation.

Envious of his obvious pleasure, Callie, too, longed to be naked, to be with him flesh on flesh, yet instead of encouraging her, he stopped her from slithering out of her panties. It was as if he were keeping them on to prevent both of them from rushing the moment, particularly him.

Again, he looked at her with a question in his eyes. Again, she granted him permission to lead.

Slowly, he moved down her body, his lips searing her skin as he kissed her thighs and traced the line of her panties with his lips. Her hips writhed as voluptuous waves of desire swept over her. Sensing her need—well aware of his own—he removed the last of her clothing, sheathed himself and moved onto her, slowly covering her body with his. It felt like an eternity before his lips came down on hers and the void between her legs was filled.

She moaned as they went about satisfying their craving for each other, touching and probing, using their lips and their hands and the physical manifestations of their gender to give expression to emotions that had been building since the moment they met. As their mutual passion erupted, Callie experienced an incredible explosion of joy, followed by an equally wonderful flood of tranquillity. For the first time in a long time, Callie was truly content.

Later, after they'd made love again, Ezra fell asleep. Callie lay next to him, reliving the evening and thanking fate for bringing this man into her life. As she listened to the even rise and fall of his breathing, she marveled at the power of the heart. After all she'd been through over the past twenty-four hours, her thoughts should have been about protecting herself. Instead, she was focused on Ezra and the fact that she was falling in love with him. And he with her.

They hadn't said so. There had been no verbal declarations. But even before their lovemaking, the emotion between them had been so taut it bounced off the walls and ceiling as if the words had been shot from a cannon.

Was the heart stronger than the mind because love was more important to the survival of the species than thought? she wondered. Or was it because the mind was designed to search and catalogue, conclude and debate? The heart was made to feel.

Callie snuggled up against him, her lips curled into a tired, but happy smile.

Slowly, the tide of slumber rose. Callie could feel herself drifting off into that middle distance where she wasn't awake, yet wasn't totally asleep.

And then, she heard it. *'Til death do us part.*

In her foggy state, she received it as a message of promise.

'Til death do us part.

The voice was louder, more insistent. She climbed back into wakefulness. Once more, the voice said: *'Til death do us part.* But this time the tone was dark and foreboding.

Her eyes filled with tears. Her heart, so puffed with pleasure a moment before, deflated. This wasn't a harbinger of happy times ahead. It was a warning.

'Til death do us part were the last words her father spoke to her mother before the madness took over. And killed her.

27

Ezra was as happy to see Carolyne Hale as she was to see him, which was to say, not at all.

It was eight-thirty in the morning and once again, Ezra and Alvarez had dared to interrupt her morning ritual. This time, however, she made them wait in the entry until she was good and ready to receive them.

"This is becoming a very unpleasant habit, gentlemen," Carolyne said as she wafted into the foyer and reluctantly led them into her living room.

"It's no pleasure trip for us either, Mrs. Hale," Ezra groused. "But you know what? If you were honest with us, we wouldn't have to keep coming back."

Jorge glanced over at his partner, slightly astounded by his tone. Normally, snide was his shtick. Ezra was the educated one, the lawyer, the diplomat. He was the street guy. Judging by the look on Carolyne Hale's face she'd been taken aback as well.

"I don't know what you're talking about," she sniffed.

"According to our notes, you claimed you hadn't seen your son after your lunch at the Four Seasons."

Carolyne didn't respond. She simply continued to stare at Ezra, outraged at his lack of respect.

"We have witnesses who say he came to visit you at around seven P.M. the night he was murdered."

In his initial interview, the doorman at Wilty's building said Wilty went out about seven and returned just after ten.

He hadn't called a taxi; Wilty said he preferred to walk. The doorman across the street remembered seeing Wilty turn west, toward Fifth. Ezra and Jorge had been waiting for Carolyne's doorman to return from vacation to find out whether or not Wilty had ended up at her place. This morning, he said Wilty had.

"Somebody's fibbing," Ezra said, his eyes glued to Carolyne's face. "Who could it be?"

Jorge's jaw nearly dropped open.

"I refuse to be insulted in my home," Carolyne huffed. "I'm afraid I must ask you to leave, Detective Chapin." Her arm jutted out, her finger pointing to the foyer in a dramatic gesture of Begone!

Unfazed, Ezra shrugged her off. "Fine, but if we leave, you're coming with us."

Carolyne Hale looked as if she were about to bare her teeth and growl like a Doberman.

"Look, Mrs. Hale, I don't give a damn whether we conduct this interview here or back at the stationhouse, but one way or the other, you're going to answer our questions." The tenor of his voice dropped. It resonated with annoyance. "Now, I'll try it again. Was Wilty here the night he was murdered?"

Still, Carolyne hesitated.

"Maybe that last visit slipped her mind," Jorge said, in a stage aside to Ezra. "Mrs. Hale's a busy woman. It must be hard to keep track of all her appointments."

"Call me obsessive," Ezra sarcastically confided, "but I think I'd remember seeing my son the same night he died."

"Me too," Alvarez said. "But hey, we're just working stiffs. What do we know?"

Carolyne seethed at their mockery.

"Yes," she said, finally, practically spitting the words in Ezra's face. "Wilty was here."

"And you didn't tell us that because . . . ?"

"I don't know." She screwed her face into a mask of grief, raising her hand to her chin and biting her lip. "The pain of hearing about my son's death was so enormous, I must have blocked it out."

Yeah, that must be it, Alvarez thought.

"Was his visit social," he said, "or did you have some kind of business to discuss?"

Carolyne was juggling a selection of responses with their possible consequences, struggling to keep all the balls in the air at the same time.

"Business?" She sounded almost amused at the notion that she and Wilty would discuss business. Both detectives recognized it as footdragging.

The telephone rang. It was picked up in another room on the second ring.

"You know, a fortune that's here today and gone tomorrow. That kind of business."

She looked as if a car had just run over her foot. "I'm sorry, Detective Alvarez, but really, I'm at a loss."

Ezra'd had enough. He was finished pussyfooting around with this woman.

"Wilty came to see you that night to tell you he'd found a document which challenged his birthright. Isn't that true, Mrs. Hale?" His tone signaled a growing impatience with her prevarication.

"It was such an upsetting evening . . ."

Ezra walked close to her chair and stood over her in a manner designed to invade her space and make her feel claustrophobic.

"I don't know what drama you think you're starring in, but I'm giving it a big, fat, thumbs-down. Now cut the crap and answer the question!"

For the first time, Alvarez sensed a touch of fear coming from the Widow. Ezra had hit a nerve.

Carolyne worried her fingers and studied her lap. Finally, she sucked in her breath and confronted her interrogators.

"Yes, Wilty came here that night to tell me he'd discovered something that contradicted his descent. As was his habit, he used it to taunt me with the notion that if it proved true, the Hale fortune would be taken away and we would be left with nothing." A sour thought crinkled her mouth. "More to the point, I would be left with nothing. As he delighted in telling me, he might be able to salvage his properties and the profits from certain investments. Since I was dependent upon his largesse, had no property in my name, and only limited high yield investments, I could wind up practically penniless."

Again, she grimaced, unable to completely cloak her hostility.

"He found it amusing to quote Tennessee Williams and tell me I would have to rely on the kindness of strangers."

"That's cold," Jorge said, taking his turn at playing the good cop by buddying up to the Widow.

She turned to him, seeking sympathy. "It was more than cold. It was cruel. No matter what your preconceptions are, Detective, I did have to rely on the kindness of my son. That's not always easy."

She was acting so pathetic it made Ezra's stomach lurch. Did she really expect them to feel sorry for her? To believe that she was the victim and Wilty was the villain? On a good day, he wouldn't buy into that pap. And this was not a good day.

Lourdes tiptoed into the room and softly cleared her throat.

"Mrs. Hale," she said tremulously. "Dr. Merrick's on the phone."

Ezra's eyes widened. Carolyne Hale and Peter Merrick. His brain couldn't even begin to organize his thoughts about that association.

The Widow stood and started to leave the room. Ezra held up his hand like a school crossing guard.

"Tell Dr. Merrick, Mrs. Hale will call him back," Ezra said to Lourdes.

Carolyne opened her mouth to protest, but thought better of it. She nodded to Lourdes, giving her permission to do as the detective had instructed. Then, she returned to her seat.

"Is Dr. Merrick a friend or are you a patient of his?" Ezra caught Jorge's look of disapproval, but he couldn't resist. Hearing Merrick's name in Carolyne Hale's home seemed too much of a fluke to ignore.

Carolyne's instant defensiveness validated his curiosity.

"I don't think that's any of your business," she said.

Ezra's jaw tightened. "I'm investigating your son's murder. You haven't exactly been forthcoming. That puts everything you say and do in the questionable column. It also means that until Detective Alvarez and I solve this case, everything about you is our business. Including your phone calls."

Carolyne recoiled at Ezra's intensity, but she was too experienced a warrior not to know when a tactical retreat was in order.

"He's a friend," she declared. "He's probably calling to see how I'm doing. Most people have respect for the emotional burden of the bereaved. They either leave them alone with their grief, or offer their company as comfort."

Ezra's upper lip curled at her attempt to reprimand him.

"Most people weren't in the alley behind your son's building when his remains were loaded into the Medical Examiner's van. I was."

Her face blanched at his words.

Ezra, sensing her discomfort, took command of the conversation and insisted that they return to the night Wilty was murdered.

"What went on here? Did Wilty threaten you with the incriminating document? Did you have a knock-down-drag-out? Or a tiff, after which, you kissed and made up?"

"We did argue," she admitted. "But mainly because I felt he needed to have the document authenticated. People of . . . well, of extraordinary wealth often find themselves deluged with crank documents disclaiming heredity or never-before-heard-of relatives who appear from out of nowhere and demand a seat at the table. Since he only showed me a copy, it was difficult to tell how old it was."

She yammered on about Wilty agreeing that her thoughts

had merit and leaving with no hard feelings between them. She made the point—several times—that she never left her apartment, a fact she knew her doorman would confirm.

The other point she tried to hammer home was that she had nothing to gain from Wilty's death. In truth, the opposite was true: Wilty was her meal ticket. Without him, she'd have no access to the Hale fortune.

She went on, but Ezra didn't bother listening to her tale of woe. Once she said, "he only showed me a copy," he tuned out.

When he and Jorge had entered her apartment, they had means and opportunity. She just handed them a motive. Now, all they needed was proof.

"If I didn't know better," Jorge said on the way back to the house, "I'd say you were suffering from PMS. Man, you were pissy!"

"I got the job done, didn't I?"

Alvarez conceded that he had. He was dying to ask Ezra what was bugging him but, instead, he took an educated guess, stamped Callie Jamieson's name on the bug up his partner's butt and left it alone.

Back at their desks, Jorge concentrated on writing up their interviews. Ezra made the calls necessary to requisition both Carolyne Hale's phone logs and Peter Merrick's. His request for the Widow's calls were easily explained, they were part of the investigation into Wilty's murder. Explaining why he wanted Merrick's phone records took a little tapdancing, but he managed to link it to the same crime. What he was really after was finding out how close the relationship was between Carolyne Hale and Dr. Peter Merrick. And if Merrick knew Dr. Guy Hoffman.

The administrative assistant for the squad walked over and dropped off several papers. "These came in while you were gone."

It was BCI's response to Ezra's inquiries. Two of the names on Noah Bryson's list came back listing prior arrests: one, Elton Biggs, was a groomer at Hale Farms. He

had a string of small robberies, but after Cole was dead—
and his steady meal ticket was gone—he hooked up with
a gang and pulled an armed robbery. He died in prison, not
of natural causes.

The other guy, Delwin Campbell, was a handyman. He
had a string of minor burglaries to his credit, as well as a
couple of drunk and disorderlies. He'd also done time for
aggravated assault. He was sixteen. His father and younger
sister had been killed by a drunk driver. When Campbell
arrived at the scene, he went berserk and viciously attacked
both the driver and the passenger. It took three men to pull
them apart.

Ezra studied Campbell's mug shots, but it was the list
of distinguishing marks beneath it that caught his attention:
a lightning bolt tattoo on the left hand.

Ezra felt a familiar fizz inside his head. He was having
a *brain itch*. It occurred whenever something completely
unexpected popped up and, when examined, appeared to be
linked to something else that was completely unexpected,
a juxtaposition of unrelated facts that tickled his curiosity
and wouldn't go away no matter how vigorously he
scratched. Like hearing Merrick's name in the Widow's
apartment. Like discovering that his upstate tail was the
same man who'd been stalking Callie, the same man who'd
been at Hale Farms when Cole Hale died. That man was
in New York now and might have been here when Wilty
Hale died.

Quickly, Ezra riffled through his file to see if Campbell
was at Long House when Hunt Hale died. According to
Officer Billy Gayle's list, he wasn't.

That didn't mean he couldn't have been somewhere else
in the Lake George area. Ezra placed a call to his pal in
upstate NY to give him an FYI on the report from BCI
concerning Delwin Campbell. Next, he had to figure out
Campbell's connection to these three murders. If he was
involved, Ezra needed to know how and why.

He jotted down a few ideas, then tore them up. He went
on-line thinking he'd research Campbell's background that

way, then couldn't decide where to go. His head was
jammed with thoughts of Carolyne Hale and Peter Merrick
and Delwin Campbell. And Callie.

He sat and stared at the phone as if he could will Callie
to call him and tell him she'd left because she wanted to
return to her apartment and straighten things out, that she
meant to leave him a note but didn't know what to say,
and that, yes, last night meant as much to her as it did to
him.

When the phone did ring, he almost leapt out of his
chair.

"Callie?" he said.

"No. I'm sorry," a woman said. "If you're expecting
another call, I'll call back. It's Elizabeth Winters. Victoria
Moore's granddaughter."

Ezra had spoken to Elizabeth several times, at Victoria's
request. Elizabeth was a scholar. She'd read the other diaries, as well as dozens of biographies of E.W. Hale. Victoria felt Elizabeth would be a better contact.

"Of course," he said, his curiosity heightened about the
purpose of her call. "How are you?"

"Fine, and you?"

"Frantic, but that seems to be my normal state these
days, so I guess I'm fine."

"I found the fourth diary," she said, in her typical, no-
nonsense way. "One of my cousins found it stuffed in a
box of table linens."

Ezra detected a certain lilt in her voice. Obviously, this
wasn't one of those diaries in which Hale delineated his
daily business triumphs down to the last excruciating detail.

"What year?"

"Nineteen hundred," she said with a tad of bravura.
"And a chock-a-block year it was. I sent it off to you this
morning. You should receive it sometime tomorrow."

Ezra wanted it NOW. "How about giving me a little
preview?"

"No," she said, turning serious. "It's a very poignant

journal, one which I believe has to be read in its entirety and in sequence. But, Ezra . . ."

"Yes."

"It's the one you're looking for. It's the one with the answers."

28

A t first, Callie didn't hear the phone. She was vacuuming, still trying to get her apartment cleaned up from the break-in. When she did hear it and shut off the vacuum, she thought twice about answering. The ominous voice in her dream, on top of this twisted violation of her home, had truly unnerved her. Then she remembered she'd had Caller ID installed. When she recognized the number as Paula's, she eagerly picked up.

The camera clicked on.

"Where have you been?" she was practically shouting.

Paula reminded her she'd been out of town on an assignment. When she opined that Callie sounded borderline hysterical, Callie laughed.

"I passed over that border a couple of days ago. I am now officially, completely and totally hysterical."

She hadn't realized how badly she'd needed to speak to her best friend, until now. She filled Paula in on the anonymous gift that had been deposited in her mailbox and the follow-up which had been left in her bed. She recounted Vanna Larkin's overdose, Luke Crocker's invitation to freelance, as well as her painful encounter with Martin Orlando's fists. She neglected to mention spending the night making love to Ezra.

"You're right, as always," she said when Paula observed that Callie sounded strung out. "What I need is some serious R and R."

Paula suggested going out to the Hamptons.

Callie brightened. "I forgot we have the house to ourselves. What a wonderful idea! I'll tell you what: I have a session with Dr. Merrick. Then, lunch with my Dad and Auntie Pennie . . . Yes, I am excited. It's been a while since the three of us have broken bread together . . . It was his idea. He said he has something important to tell me."

Callie had a few things she wanted to talk to her father about as well.

"Anyway, when I finish with them, how about if I go out to the house and fix us . . . okay, okay. I lost my head for a minute. I'll *buy* us some hors d'oeuvres. You can do your dinner thing when you get there."

They were just about to hang up when Paula said, "Don't get crazy. I know I've been there dozens of times, but once I turn off Montauk Highway, where the hell do I go?"

Callie laughed. Paula's inability to remember directions and find her way was a standing joke between them. For one of Paula's birthdays, Callie gave her a can of bread crumbs, to make sure she'd never get lost.

"Write it down. Make the left off Montauk Highway. Go three blocks, take a right, then a quick left. It's the third house on the left. Got it? Good. See you there," she said. "Can't wait."

"Neither can I," said the man watching her.

Before Callie opened the door, she took a moment to reconsider what she was about to do. All morning, she'd debated the wisdom of going through with this session. In the end, two things brought her here: One, the fact that her night with Ezra—so unbearably special—had been followed by a spectral warning about death. This made her more determined than ever to rid herself of these invasive voices and visions. She wanted to be in love and live her life without always looking over her shoulder for ghosts.

And two, if Merrick was gaslighting her or using her as a guinea pig to further his career, or simply doing something twisted, she was going to find out what it was and stop it. She was taking a risk, but life was a risk. If she wanted one, she had to accept the other.

"Take three deep breaths," Peter Merrick said softly. "Breathe in deeply, with your mouth open. Now slowly, breathe out."

Callie lay quietly on the couch, her eyes closed, inhaling, exhaling, beckoning the bliss that accompanies a state of complete relaxation.

"Crystals are protection. Search for a crystal, Callie. Watch for it and accept the first clear glass crystal that comes toward you."

Her eyebrows slanted toward each other. Merrick was pleased. She was searching.

"Have you found one?"

She nodded.

"Good. Get inside it and make yourself comfortable. It's a safe place, Callie, one in which you'll receive love and light."

He watched the movement of her chest slow as she began to slip into a trance.

"Tell me the shape of the crystal you're in."

Her head tilted ever so slightly to the side, as if she needed to take a closer look.

"It's a teardrop."

Merrick considered her response. Square, rectangular, and jagged shapes indicated the presence of an anger that had come from the past and was prompting mental defenses against it now. While the teardrop indicated enormous sadness, the fact that Callie had chosen a rounded shape assured him she was in touch with her present-day feelings and was working to detach herself from past karmic linkages.

"A circle of white light is forming in front of you. Bring the light down through the top of your head. Let it flow throughout your body, head to toe like a stream of clear water. Take your time. Let the white light saturate any place in your body where you feel darkness or heaviness. When you're ready to move on, say so."

For several minutes, Callie lay in an almost stony stillness. Her breathing was slow and deep. Her face appeared to be peaceful. Merrick observed her carefully. This was an important session. He wanted everything to proceed perfectly.

"I'm ready," she said.

Merrick smiled. She was quite beautiful when she was asleep, even with her facial bruises.

"We're going back in time, Callie, back to that familiar place that lives in your mind and in your dreams."

Her head bobbed slightly, hesitatingly. She was nervous.

"There's nothing to worry about. There's nothing for you to do. Just relax and let the past come to you."

Again, she breathed deeply. Her body slackened as the tensions of the present left her and the calmness of the journey backward took hold.

"The white light is your guide to your long ago, Callie. It's taking you back to that day from the past that's been demanding your attention."

Her breathing accelerated. Her fingers splayed, then rested.

"You're not alone, Callie. I'm there to help you. You're safe with me."

He watched as her eyelids fluttered. He waited until her breathing steadied.

"Let's start our visit later in the day, after the gray erupted into orange and then returned to gray. After you found the man and woman on the ground." His voice was quiet, deliberately monotonous, soothing. "It's quiet now. There's no movement. No noise. Just you. And me."

Slowly, she allowed herself to retreat into the mysterious world of memory.

"Slip into the moment as if you were putting on an overcoat. Feel who you were in that time, where you were." Again, he waited. "Are you there?" he asked, watching her closely. Under hypnosis, a nod was little more than a barely perceptible movement of the head.

"Yes."

"Good. Now, look down at your feet. What are you wearing?"

"Shoes." Her tone implied she thought his question was silly. But it wasn't the present-day Callie who was speaking.

"What do they look like? Describe them."

"They're sort of brown. And the laces go up my legs. And they're very, very dusty."

"Are you wearing a skirt?"

She nodded. And tsked. Another silly question.

"Is it long?"

"Uh-huh."

"What color is it?"

"Blue. That's my favorite color."

"Mine, too," he said, speaking to the child that had taken Callie's place. "Now, take me with you. Take me to where you are."

"I'm in the gray, but I'm standing away, behind something. There's dust. And ash." She crinkled her nose.

"Come out from behind whatever it is," he instructed. "Move around in your surroundings." He waited. Her toes flinched as her brain commanded that she take a few halting steps. "Where are you?"

"In a clearing." She paused, surveying. "There's something tall over there. It looks like it used to be a wall, but it's shaped funny."

Merrick assumed she was describing whatever remained standing after the fire.

"Have you been there before? Is it a familiar place?"

"Yes."

"Is this place your home?"

She nods.

"Is the wall part of a house?"

"No. The house is over there. A ways away." Her eyelids tighten. She's looking around. "I'm in a place with a fence around it."

"Is it a barn?" he asked, guessing.

She sniffed. "Yes. There's hay. And horses." She grimaced. "And burned wood. And charred flesh."

From beneath her lashes, several tears dribbled onto her cheeks.

"It's awful," she said, her voice low and mournful.

Her body stiffened.

"What's happening?"

"I hear a loud bell clanging. And lots of hoofbeats. And people shouting."

Her head slapped from side to side. She pressed her hands against her ears to block out the noise. The tears continued to fall.

Suddenly, her words came in a rush, catching on sobs as they flowed out of her.

"There was this man. He was awful. He yelled at them. He hurt them. Then he burned the place down. He wanted to hide the bad things he did."

The cadence of her speech had changed completely, becoming rapid and even more childlike.

"Tell me what's happening."

She snuffled and wiped her nose with her sleeve.

"I yelled at him. I tried to get him to stop." The tears were coming in torrents, now. "But she told me to go, to run away."

"Who told you?"

Callie pointed to the ground, where the bodies lay. "Mommy." She choked on the word.

Merrick needed to shift the focus. If she lingered on the fact that this woman, whom she purported to be her mother, was dead, she'd become grief stricken and he wouldn't be able to get her to move on.

"Who are you talking to?"

"Sarah."

"Who's Sarah?"

A smile escaped her lips. The child within Callie's mind loved Sarah, whoever she was.

"She's married to Mac." Suddenly, Callie's smile faded and the tears reappeared. "Oh, God! Mac."

Callie's body began to tighten. Her eyelids fluttered as if she were about to waken. Obviously, the scene was so unpleasant, her subconscious, seeking to protect her, was luring her back to the present. Merrick couldn't let that happen. Not yet.

"Is Mac one of the people the bad man hurt?" he asked, keeping his own voice even and soporific.

Callie bit her lower lip, which trembled fiercely. She nodded. "Uh-huh."

Merrick assumed Mac was the one who'd been battered by the two-by-four, the one whose head was now a bloody pulp.

"Who is Mac to you?"

Callie's chest heaved. "He's my brother."

"And who are you?" Merrick asked.

"I'm Faith."

Carolyne debated taking a Valium. Those awful detectives had frayed her nerves to the point where her hands were shaking. Instead, she told Lourdes to make her some chamomile tea and bring it into her study. She'd center herself by returning phone calls and finalizing arrangements for her weekend in the Hamptons. She'd been invited to several dinner parties. It was time to decide whom she'd favor with her presence, whom she'd disappoint.

As she pondered her choices, she wondered if it would be inappropriate to bring an escort. Peter Merrick had called. His name and his good looks made him more than welcome in the homes of the *beau monde*. The fact that he'd treated many of them and was privy to their deepest, darkest secrets only added to his cachet. Perhaps she'd invite him to come out to the house and be her partner for various evenings. He was always such a delightful companion.

And, she thought greedily, a deliciously wonderful lover.

She smiled as she slithered into the chair behind her desk, conjuring memories of bedtimes spent with the elegant doctor. Beneath his bespoke suits and silk ties, the man was quite savage, which was the way Carolyne liked it.

Physical affection was visceral. It was quick and satisfying and without any requirements beyond the duration of the afterglow. Emotional affection came with strings and obligations and a script for role-playing she couldn't abide, especially if the role assigned to her was that of a supplicant.

Her eye caught Lourdes's list of other messages. One was from Guy Hoffman. He was another possibility. He wasn't as social as Peter, nor was he as agile and creative in the bedroom, but he had a certain gravitas that might project a more flattering image at this particular moment. She was in mourning, after all. And, if she had interpreted the inferences of those two policemen correctly, under investigation for possible complicity in the death of her son.

There was a third message, this one from a man who was neither social nor sensual. Truth be told, he was barely palatable, but just then, he was more important to her well-being than the others. She put her sexual fantasies and her social plans on hold, picked up the phone and dialed the number. It was answered on the first ring.

"What do you want?"

"The good news is my surveillance project paid off. The bad news is I don't know what it means."

He told her what he'd overheard.

After a leaden silence, she said, "I don't like this."

"I didn't think you would."

She viewed the situation from several angles, seeking an upside, weighing the consequences of the downsides. In the end, she decided she didn't have many options.

"Do you have a plan?" She knew what his response would be, but in matters of this sort, she preferred that someone else took the initiative.

He laid out his thinking and his demands.

"Fine," she said. "Take care of it."

• • •

Penelope James clucked over her niece until her brother, Bill, had to push her aside so he could hug his own daughter. After embracing Callie, he held her at arm's length, studying her face. His hand brushed lightly against her cheek.

"You look exhausted."

"Actually," Callie said, trying to force a smile, "I am."

"Let's sit." Auntie Pennie hustled them into the corner booth at "21." She'd turned down her usual front and center table near the bar, requesting instead to be seated near the back. She also told the maître d' she didn't want to be disturbed—by anyone.

At her father's request, Callie described the scene at her apartment the night she'd called him. Naturally, that required an explanation about her being rescued, so to speak, by a detective assigned to Wilty Hale's murder. Since she didn't want to linger on the subject of Ezra Chapin, knight in shining armor, she rushed to fill them in on her dismissal from the *Courier,* thanks to the Evil Queen, and the apparent underground movement to bring her back on staff.

Their main concern, of course, was who had caused the purple bruise on her cheek and what was being done about finding and punishing the perpetrator of that assault. One look at Bill's face told Callie he wouldn't be satisfied until there was an arrest, a confession, and a beheading.

"It was revenge for my Dr. Drug series," she said, condensing all the Orlando-linked incidents to a simple explanation.

"Are the police looking into it?"

"Yes, Daddy, they are." She smiled at his paternal angst. It had been a long time since she'd been warmed by that level of protective intensity.

"Speaking of police, tell me about Ezra Chapin."

Callie chuckled. Auntie Pennie sure knew how to change a subject. She was even better at it than . . .

"What about him?" she said quickly, clearly uncomfortable.

"That's what I'd like to know. What about him? And you."

Callie fidgeted with her napkin.

Bill, divining a great deal from her unease, said, "I suppose what Pennie's asking, in her uniquely indelicate way: Is this man something more than a port in a storm?"

"We're working together on a case."

Pennie was about to dig in, but Bill shot her a look that silenced her. Instead, he shifted the conversational focus onto himself.

"I don't know whether the two of you will consider this good news or bad news," he said, "but the reason I scheduled this lunch was to tell you that I've left Serena. I am temporarily, yet happily, ensconced in the Lowell Hotel."

Pennie was stunned, but her smile of satisfaction was immediate. Callie was speechless.

"I want more than what I have."

Bill paused, his expression one of enlightenment. It was as if by making this momentous decision, he'd thrown off whatever emotional shackles had imprisoned him and allowed his heart to embrace feelings that had been moribund for way too long.

"More to the point, I want what I had," he said quietly. "To be with someone who loves me passionately and whom I love passionately in return. Serena isn't that someone. She never was. She was a fill-in-the-blank."

Callie was visibly staggered by her father's announcement. "What happened?"

Bill spread his hands and shrugged. "Nothing *happened*. I've simply spent far too many years in an unfulfilling relationship."

"What are you going to do?"

He smiled at his daughter and caressed her cheek. "I'm going to do what I'm always telling you to do: Take the best that life has to offer and not settle for whatever comes along."

"Words to live by," Pennie intoned.

"It's good advice," Callie agreed. "Unfortunately, I have

some things I have to clear up before I invite anyone to share this chaos that is my life."

Callie was grateful to the waiter for interrupting with their lunch. One of Bill's favorite dishes was the "21" hamburger. Callie hoped it would provide at least a momentary distraction.

It did, but only for a moment.

"So where are you in your life?" Pennie probed.

"Mired in the past." Callie winced at her own double entendre. "Speaking of which, did Mom ever mention the name Sarah Blessing during her . . . ramblings?"

Pennie shook her head. Bill put down his fork, swallowed the last of his meat, and studied Callie. "Not that I recall. Why? Who's Sarah Blessing?"

"I've been seeing a therapist," she said. "About my dreams."

The last time Callie had been besieged by night terrors was the summer before her senior year in college. She'd been staying with Pennie, and since she had no other way to explain away her midnight bouts of hysteria, she confessed her familiarity with the gray people to her aunt and, subsequently, to her father. Despite their best efforts to drag her to a psychiatrist, Callie refused. Her reasoning was difficult to argue with: her mother had sought help and she wound up in an institution. Callie, on the other hand, had experienced these nightmares for most of her life, and while they were disturbing and frightening, to be sure, she'd managed to deal with them. Until now.

"Once they began to affect the conduct of my life, I decided to do something about them."

"How did they affect your life? What did you do?" Bill had visions of Callie freaking out, talking to herself in public places, screaming at strangers. All the things Mara had done.

"It's what I couldn't do," Callie said, softly. "I couldn't sleep. I was having trouble concentrating on my work. I wasn't eating. I couldn't allow anyone new into my life. And I couldn't convince myself that I wasn't going mad."

Bill started to say, "You're not going mad," but stopped himself. He'd said that to Mara, yet her behavior continued. After a time, he assumed she had indeed gone insane and ultimately had her committed.

"Are you pushing this detective away because you're afraid you're going to turn into your mother and, if you do, he'll turn into me?"

Callie couldn't believe he said that.

"Underneath it all, yes, I think that is what I'm afraid of," she admitted, recalling how she'd felt when she was with Wilty, what she feared with Ezra. "That's why I went into therapy."

"Who's the therapist?" Pennie asked.

"Peter Merrick."

Sensing her father and her aunt needed further assurance of Merrick's qualifications, Callie told them he'd written several books, and that *Before and Again,* concerning past lives and genetic memory, was a best-seller.

"So you think that since your mother had similar dreams, they were genetically passed on?" Pennie hadn't dismissed the notion, but she wasn't convinced.

Callie struggled with how best to respond. It was all so complicated. "I don't know how to explain certain things any other way."

Callie described the core dream; from the looks on their faces, they'd heard that dream described before. Then, she told them about the hallucination she'd experienced at Saratoga Lake and the way she felt at Liberty Park. She expected her aunt and her father to become agitated or to back away as she detailed her episodes. Instead, they were riveted in a way that let her know they believed her. They had no idea what that kind of support meant to her.

Then, she told them about the photography exhibition at the Reinish Gallery, about how one young woman was so familiar.

"Her name was Sarah Blessing. She's the woman I saw in the rowboat at the lake. She's also the one I saw with the blood on her dress."

Bill was searching the deepest vaults in his mind, trying to recall whether or not he'd ever heard the name, Sarah Blessing, before. He hadn't.

"It could be that Mom didn't experience that particular vision because she never went to that lake." Bill's sense of logic demanded that he follow up on that thought, bringing him to the conclusion that, "Perhaps Saratoga Lake and Liberty Park provided the stimulus because those places have something to do with the origin of the dream."

Callie had begun to believe the same thing. She'd even toyed with the notion of revisiting Hiram Wellington's psychiatric fiefdom, but before she did, she had another name she needed to check out.

"Did Mom ever mention anyone named Faith?"

Bill blanched. "She used to say she *was* Faith."

29

The shade was down, but there was enough space between it and the window for him to survey the street. His eyes swept the limited landscape, studying even the most minute change in the status quo as if inspecting a still life for artistic authenticity: a trash bin moved, a door ajar, a strange glint coming off a window, a car circling the block one too many times. Other than the usual flow of traffic and a couple of parked cars, the street appeared quiet and empty. Now and then, someone strolled down the block; if the gait appeared honestly purposeful, he allowed himself to relax.

But only for a moment. Instinct said they were watching. Either from a rooftop or from a window across the street or from someplace he'd never even suspect. And if they weren't now, they would be. The NYPD wasn't known for its patience. Sooner, rather than later, they were going to come for him. Maybe even with guns blazing.

His heart pounded at the thought. He didn't want to do time, but dying wasn't high on his list of things to do either.

He wanted to blame his current situation on Callie Jamieson, but plain out, he fucked up. If he'd kept his mouth shut and hadn't messed with her the other night, he'd still be happily anonymous, able to come and go whenever and wherever he damned pleased. Instead, the cops were out gunning for him.

How could he have been so stupid? He knew she had a

detective for a boyfriend. He knew she worked for a major newspaper with snoops and snitches everywhere. He also knew she had a surprising amount of street smarts for an uptown girl.

What he hadn't realized was how resilient she was.

Oh well, he thought, as he packed his weapons in a bag. That only made the hunt more exciting. And the kill more satisfying.

Peter canceled the rest of his morning appointments. Again and again, he listened to the tape of Callie's session. He was as drained as she'd been when she left. This was a major breakthrough and both of them knew it. Callie Jamieson was a reliquary of ancestral history. Now, it was up to him to determine whether her revelations were truth, or merely imagination; a continuance of her mother's memories, or symptoms of her mother's illness.

He should have been elated to have come this far but, instead, desperation rose slowly but surely inside him, like a malted through a straw. The sweet satisfaction of success was so close he could taste it. But because he was so near to achieving his life's goals, he became frightened—for Callie.

He'd come to care about her, probably more than he should. Not in a sexual way, although she certainly appealed to him, but in a protective, avuncular way. This unbelievably beautiful young woman was struggling to free herself of the hideous burden of repetitive night terrors. He'd watched her tremble with fear and collapse with exhaustion. He'd heard her cries and her screams and, most pathetic of all, her whimpering pleas for peace.

Just this morning, after he'd brought her out from the hypnotic state, they'd talked about her life and what it would mean for her to be free of those specters she called, "the gray people."

"I'd feel free to let myself be loved," she'd said.

He asked her if she had someone in mind. He knew about Ezra Chapin, so he wasn't surprised to hear her say, "yes." When he asked about her romance, she said she'd ended it that morning. He asked why. Her answer broke his heart.

"It's not safe to love me," she said.

His forehead pleated with concern. And guilt. If, as Callie explained, she used the past as a guide, it might not be safe for her to trust him. His history was also writ with tragedy.

As he did whenever he felt himself sinking into a quagmire, Peter picked up the telephone and called his mentor. The minute Peter heard his voice, he relaxed; Hiram Wellington had always had that effect.

"Peter," Hiram said, clearly equally pleased. "It's been a while. What are you up to?"

Peter told him about his patient and her dreams. He described their talk sessions, as well as the results of her hypnosis.

"Congratulations! It sounds as if you've finally found your definitive subject," Hiram said.

"I agree, but I'm nervous. I need to present the scientific community with valid, qualitative evidence of my findings. To do that, I have to verify exactly *when* these events took place, as well as precisely who the individuals involved in these events were. For obvious reasons, I'm afraid to push too hard."

"I think that's wise, Peter. Besides, if you proceed slowly, you might be able to coax all that information out of her."

"I don't know if I have the time," Peter lamented.

He told Wellington about Guy Hoffman's p-316 and Guy's suggestion that its use would fast-track the regression.

"He's a brilliant man," Peter said, "and I don't doubt the efficacy of his lab experiments, but there are extenuating circumstances that lead me to believe he might be advancing to clinical trials too quickly."

"The funding's dried up, correct?" Hiram was quite familiar with the pressures placed on those who were compelled to rely upon largesse. He had a stack of projects that had been halted midstream because of a grant that wasn't renewed or a philanthropist whose attention span had reached its limit. It was a miracle science ever moved forward.

"Let's review the case. First, who is your patient?"

"A young woman named Callie Jamieson."

"An investigative reporter for *The Courier*?"

"Yes. How did you know that?"

Hiram explained about Callie and Ezra's visit to Liberty Park.

"In fact, their questions and their interest in Liberty Park inspired me to delve into the history of this place."

"Were they interested in anything specific?" Merrick's heart was pounding.

"Ms. Jamieson was fixed on the woman for whom this institution was founded. If you recall, it was a young woman who'd been a victim of a tragedy and had fallen into a deeply catatonic state. Her benefactor researched the field until he found Dr. Jeremiah Holstein. He brought him to Saratoga, set him up, and told him to help this woman. Ultimately, he did."

Peter's throat was so dry he could hardly speak. "What was the woman's name?"

"Funny, Detective Chapin wanted to know the same thing."

"What was it?" Peter would think about Ezra Chapin, what he wanted to know and why, later.

"Sarah Blessing."

"Sarah," Peter said in a hush. "Was she married to a man named Mac?"

"This must be your lucky day," Hiram chortled. "I've been digging around in various archives and yesterday, I hit pay dirt."

"Tell me," Peter said, his nerves frayed.

"Sarah Blessing was indeed married to a man named Mac. They hadn't been married very long when he and his mother were killed. The mother was strangled. Mac was bludgeoned."

"And the murderer set the barn on fire to incinerate the evidence."

"Exactly." It was Hiram's turn to be breathless. "Is that part of this woman's dream?"

"It's the crux of it. It's what's been torturing her for most of her life." Peter felt Callie's pain. His eyes welled with sympathy. "She believes it's what put her mother in an institution."

Hiram was silent for a long moment. "This is quite extraordinary, Peter. Beyond anything you've imagined."

"Why?" Merrick heard the awe in Wellington's voice. "Who are these people?"

Hiram took a deep breath and exhaled.

"The woman who was murdered was Liberty McAllister. Her son, Mac, was married to the former Sarah Blessing. There was another child as well."

"Faith," Peter said, in a tone that could only be described as reverential.

On the other end of the phone, there was also the hallowed quiescence that usually follows the discovery of something miraculous.

"Yes," Hiram said. "Faith." Again, he paused, knowing that what he was about to say was going to cause a seismic shift in many people's lives. "What's extraordinary about this, Peter, is who Liberty's husband was. Who Faith's father was: E.W. Hale."

Peter's chest felt tight. He was certain he was having a heart attack.

"How is that possible?" he said. "Hale lived in Cleveland, then New York."

"I don't know anything more than what I've told you. Liberty McAllister Hale and Mac Allister Hale were murdered. Sarah Blessing Hale, who was pregnant at the time, lost her baby and suffered such an extreme mental breakdown that she was catatonic for years. It was because of her, his daughter-in-law, that Hale sought the services of

Jeremiah Holstein and funded the construction of Liberty Park."

"When did all this take place?"

"Liberty Park opened in 1893. That's all I know. I read the story in an undocumented record."

"Do you think it's a made-up story?"

"No. Especially after listening to you describe your patient's dream. She's retelling the tale pretty much as I read it."

Peter was a wreck. "Who murdered the mother and the son?"

"No one knows. The case remains unsolved."

"Faith knows," Peter said, his head swirling.

"Yes, I assume she does."

"And Callie is Faith."

Again, there was a heavy silence on the other end of the phone as Hiram Wellington went over his own memories: Callie Jamieson in his office, the way she reacted walking through the lobby, her intense interest in the woman who was at the heart of Liberty Park. None of that was unusual when placed within the context of Sarah's sister-in-law coming to visit during her hospitalization.

"You do know what this means, don't you, Peter?"

"I think so."

Hiram heard the tremor is his protégé's voice and assumed it was the shock of such a stunning revelation; he was struggling with the task of putting all this into perspective as well. Hiram always said, Success wasn't without its burdens. Peter's burden was twofold: presenting the world with proof that there was such a thing as genetic memory, and presenting his patient with her past.

"We still need to prove it," Hiram warned, "but if Callie is the keeper of Faith's memories, then Callie Jamieson is a Hale."

30

Callie looked at her watch. If she didn't leave soon, the Long Island Expressway was going to resemble a parking lot. She'd returned to her apartment because she had a few things she needed to do before heading off.

When her doorbell rang, she felt her stomach tighten. No one had buzzed up to announce a visitor. She walked to the door, opened the peephole and found herself staring into a familiar set of amber-colored eyes. Their owner held up a Dunkin' Donuts bag and a box of Munchkins.

"I thought you might be hungry," he said. "You left without having breakfast."

She opened the door. Ezra walked past her toward the kitchen.

"I . . . ," she started, phumphering.

Without waiting for an invitation, he set down the bags and proceeded to set out their coffee.

"Breakfast is the most important meal of the day," he tsked, sounding like a Norman Rockwell sampler. "Miss it and the rest of the day is nothing but nutritional catch-up."

He opened the Munchkin box and handed her a napkin. She selected a cinnamon donut hole; he opted for powdered sugar. Callie was tempted to ask him about the nutritional value in Munchkins, but thought better of it.

They ate their donuts and sipped their coffee quietly, companionably, as if Ezra bringing a snack for her was the most normal thing in the world.

"I had to go," she said plainly, hoping he'd leave it at that, knowing he wouldn't.

"Because?"

"Because there are things I need to do . . . for me. Things that have nothing to do with either Wilty Hale or Vanna Larkin. Things that don't concern you."

Ezra took his time picking through the Munchkin box. When he found a butternut, he popped it into his mouth, chewed slowly and stared at her. His face divulged nothing of what he was thinking or feeling.

"I respectfully disagree. Everything about you concerns me."

Callie started to say something, Ezra held up his hand.

"I don't do love easily." When he saw the look of confusion in her eyes, he continued. "A couple of years ago, I tried love. I liked it, but that woman walked out on me and broke my heart. I swore I wouldn't let that happen again.

"Then, you came into my life." His eyes perused her. "A stunning package, filled with everything I always said I wanted in a woman, and then some. You, however, don't make relationships easy, and since I didn't think I wanted to deal with something difficult, I told myself to back off. Then, last night happened."

For a moment, he didn't say anything more. His eyes simply embraced the entirety of her, engulfing her in a cloud of emotion so thick she could feel it on her skin.

"Despite my best efforts at emotional fortification," he said, his gaze still holding her in his thrall, "the barricade was breached. I love you. And because I do, I feel free to claim entitlement to all your travails, whether they occurred in this century, the last century or, even, the century before that!"

Callie wanted to leap across her desk and fall into his arms and tell him she loved him, too, but she restrained herself. Despite her father's exhortations about grabbing on to the now, she couldn't even think about it until she'd exorcised the then. Bill had appeared strong and resolute this afternoon, but this was twenty years after the fact.

Twenty years ago, his wife took leave of her sanity and he became a shell. Callie could still see his lifeless eyes, hear the listless tone in his voice, sense the ponderous void that was where his heart had been. No matter how much Bill assured her she wasn't Mara and Ezra wasn't him, Callie wasn't about to take that chance.

"I appreciate your concern for my well-being," she said in a tone more appropriate to a business discussion than a romantic declaration, "but I don't share your feelings. Last night was purely recreational. We got a little carried away. We had sex, but we're not a couple. We're not really even colleagues. We're simply involved in an investigation and, if you don't mind, I'd like to confine our conversations solely to that."

Ezra's face displayed no angst, no devastation, no sign of having suffered an emotional angina attack. Rather, he stroked his chin and tilted his head from side to side as if he were considering which garbage disposal to buy. He didn't care how much she protested, she loved him. He saw it in her eyes. He heard it in her voice. He'd felt it in her touch. And he knew it deep down in his soul.

"Okay, then." The man in love disappeared behind the implacable face of the detective. "What have you decided to do about Merrick?"

Inside, Callie rued her request. More than that, she hated how quickly he acquiesced to her demands.

"I don't think that's any of your business," she snapped.

"Maybe not, but I flat out don't trust him."

"You don't know anything about him."

"I know that he's in cahoots with some mad scientist known as Guy Hoffman."

"What?"

"Guy Hoffman is a biogeneticist who runs a lab called GenTec Sciences. The other day, I watched an interview he did with Ansel Moreland, on the possibility of each of us containing generational memories. When Moreland asked how these memories might be accessed, Hoffman said there were psychiatrists using hypnosis as part of their therapy protocol. When asked what would happen if that didn't produce the desired result, he hemmed and hawed about some protein he'd isolated. If injected or inhaled, it apparently blows open the door to the memory gene. There is one little negative, however. It hasn't been proven safe or effective."

Callie's heart thumped inside her chest. She knew none of this.

"When Hoffman was asked whether this protein was dangerous, he fluffed it off by saying science moves forward on the backs of its failures. Do you find that comforting? I didn't."

"What does any of this have to do with Peter Merrick?" Callie's lips were dry.

"I looked GenTec up on the net and guess whose name was listed as a consultant." He saw her blanch. "Then, I ran a check on Merrick. His reputation's solid, except for three patients who committed suicide while in his care." He hated scaring her like this, but she needed to know the truth. "Each had been diagnosed as a schizophrenic."

Callie tensed.

"Each of them was someone Merrick *claimed* exhibited signs of genetic memory." Ezra leaned across the table. His eyes locked on hers. "Please, Callie, find someone else. Anyone else! I don't care how many books he's written or how exalted his family tree is, or how many seminars he's given, his resumé is worrisome. His relationship to Hoffman is even more worrisome."

"That's a lot to absorb," she said, her face pinched and pale. "Thank you, I guess, for being so incredibly thorough."

"I don't always like what I find, but I always try to find the truth."

Callie's head was churning from a swirling confluence of disparate pictures and words, each of which was challenging her notion of what was real and what was imagined. Was she a guinea pig in a risky experiment or a patient undergoing legitimate treatment? Was she on the path to madness or the road to wellness? Were the compelling revelations of this morning the natural outgrowth of honest, hypnotic therapy or the result of carefully insinuated suggestions? She felt weary from the weight of it.

"By the way," Ezra said, noticing how rattled Callie was. "Elizabeth Winters called. She found the fourth diary, the one from nineteen hundred."

At first, Ezra's news didn't register. He repeated it.

"Oh! Wow! How fabulous!" she said, grateful for the distraction. "Have you read it?"

Ezra shook his head. "I just got it. I thought I'd read it tonight. Actually, I was going to make it your bedtime story, but since you don't want to do bedtime, I'll have to go through it on my own and report my findings to you in the morning."

"Sounds like a plan," she said, swallowing a smile. "Now, if you don't mind, I have places to go and people to see."

He eyed her curiously. She didn't know why, but she felt compelled to tell him her plans.

"I'm meeting my friend, Paula, in Bridgehampton for a weekend of R and R."

"Sounds great." Ezra stood and started for the door. "Listen, Callie, I know you believe your therapy with Merrick is on the up-and-up, and despite my devout skepticism, it probably is." He paused, studying her face, evaluating the impact his words had already had on her. "When it comes to hypnosis and new age therapies and crystals and stuff like that, I'm a registered Neanderthal, so I apologize for visiting my rampant incredulity on you. But please think about what I said. Please be careful. And . . . well . . . if you need me, please call."

"I will. And, Ezra?"

"Yes."

"Thanks."

When he was gone, she returned to her computer, logged onto the net and ran her own search on Peter Merrick. There were dozens of hits, so she quick-scanned them, looking specifically for something that would either confirm or deny Ezra's findings. She needed to be sure his dislike of Merrick hadn't colored or exaggerated the facts.

After wading through endless articles about the more celebrated members of the Merrick clan, she found the article Ezra had referenced. He hadn't embellished a thing. Merrick had treated three patients for symptoms he claimed presented evidence of genetic memory. All three were institutionalized schizophrenics. All three took their own lives. No one blamed Merrick; suicides were not inconsistent with schizophrenia.

Callie hadn't found that comforting when the doctors at Stonehaven told that to Bill and her. She wondered how the families of those three people felt about Merrick being found blameless.

Apprehension shimmied up her spine. Again, she wondered if she was part of some experiment.

She continued scrolling down the seemingly endless list of Merrick mentions until one caught her attention: a speech he'd given to the American Institute of Psychology. In it, he defended his crusade for acceptance of the genetic memory theory and credited an early mentor with introducing him to the intriguing, unexplored world of mnemonics during a specialized psychiatric residency at a private sanitarium. The institution was Liberty Park. The mentor was Dr. Hiram Wellington.

Callie stared at the screen, captivated by the cursor that blinked incessantly over Wellington's name. *Liberty Park. Hiram Wellington. Peter Merrick.*

Ezra couldn't have known about this. He would have said something.

Callie tried another search, this time for information on Guy Hoffman. He, too, produced numerous mentions, most of which had to do with the work GenTec was doing. She scanned a number of headlines, impressed with the awards he'd won over the years and the many accolades he'd been accorded. There were several articles about his Mnemonic

Project, but no mention of Peter Merrick, a miraculous protein, or clinical trials.

She was about to shut down when, for some unknown reason, Callie ran a search on Carolyne Hale.

31

La Belle Haven, Carolyne Hale's Southampton manse was an architectural jewel set on five acres of prime beachfront property. A cedar-clad home of blond shingles, thick Doric columns, turrets and gables, it was set back far enough from the road to insure privacy, close enough to the shore to afford a commanding view of the water. Outlined by a grand porch that stretched across the back of the house, a curving south side verandah and a portico entrance, it was a typical Hamptons' house, writ large.

Carolyne loved this place, even more than her Fifth Avenue apartment or her Palm Beach spread. There was something about the spaciousness of the rooms, the grand sweep of the architecture, and the importance of its location that signified station. It declared that she, Carolyne Faessler Hale, was not an *arriviste,* but a full-time, full-fledged resident of the upper tier.

From April through November, Carolyne spent most weekends here, either entertaining guests, attending charity galas, or simply kicking back. This weekend, she craved seclusion, something La Belle Haven offered in abundance.

As her car moved east along Dune Road, she passed Wilty's house. It was an elegant, white stucco structure reminiscent of a French château. Eppie Hale had been its original occupant and when she was in residence, one could almost see the imperial flag flying. When Eppie died and Wilty inherited the house, he stripped it clean of all its

fancy French trappings, took it down to its bones and refitted it to suit his very American tastes. There was the
occasional antique, an impressive collection of folk art, and
rural American paintings throughout but, basically, the interior was dedicated to the relaxed lifestyle implicit in the
term country home.

Outside, he had created an elegant playground that provided opportunity for both physical and visual pleasure.
He'd enlarged Eppie's prize rose gardens and expanded her
meticulously cultivated rows of rainbow perennials. For
added color, he constructed a pergola near his pool that was
swathed in screaming pink bougainvillea and bounded his
terrace with large stone planters that burst with lividly purple blooms. For recreation, he had a tennis court, a horseshoe
pit, a handball court, a croquet course, and a regulation golf
hole.

As she passed by, Carolyne spotted the red flag dancing
happily in the wind. Replete with a wide tee, two sand
traps, a grass bunker and a tiered green, Wilty's golf hole
occupied the far corner of the property, situated so an errant
shot couldn't hit a passing car or find its way into a neighbor's yard. A flyer would find itself either on the beach or
in the ocean. Since he'd emblazoned the golf balls with the
Hale crest, passersby often picked up the balls and kept
them as souvenirs.

Carolyne wondered how many she'd find when she un-
packed the various golf bags that were stacked in the trunk
of the limo. These were the only items the police permitted
her to remove from his apartment; everything else had been
declared "part of the ongoing investigation." Her plan was
to store the newer clubs for use by future houseguests. The
antique ones, she'd display at her beach house.

La Belle Haven was built around a completely different
concept than her son's retreat, one which had derived from
Carolyne's Southern roots. Her grounds were more expan-
sive, less cluttered; she preferred that the visual emphasis
remain focused on the house, rather than its gardens. Like
many of the gracious plantations that had filled her favorite

childhood picture books, as well as the real-life mansions she had known during her years in Memphis, La Belle Haven was set high on a gentle knoll, reigning over the land, rather than simply sitting on it. The drive from the road to the entrance was straight and tree-lined. Instead of incorporating staff quarters into the main house as so many of her neighbors had, Carolyne's staff was kept separate: in a fully equipped, beautifully decorated, two-bedroom house, with a golf cart for transportation.

Her pool area was replete with glorious flowers and shrubs, but the mistress of this domain had no interest in, nor derived any pleasure from, mulching, seeding, or otherwise groping about in the soil; she liked her vegetables thoroughly cleaned and her flowers precisely cut. Since she had no desire to provide a camp for overgrown children, Belle Haven offered nothing in the way of amusement other than the pool. Carolyne's attitude was: If her friends wanted to play tennis, golf, or croquet, they should join a club.

She and Wilty often debated what constituted a welcome atmosphere. He believed it was a host's obligation to treat guests the way one would treat oneself; in his case, that meant bacchanals of constant overindulgence. Naturally, Wilty's guests raved about weekends spent at his house and begged to come back. Carolyne provided elegant surroundings, entertainment when appropriate, interesting companions, and scrumptious victuals, but she never went overboard. She wasn't looking for return business, she used to tell him. Nor did she want her invitations to be so frequent or easy to come by that they could be rejected on the theory that there were plenty more where that came from.

Wilty always scoffed at that as a boorish, social superiority complex, born of a stubborn, self-imposed social inferiority complex.

"Don't try so hard," he used to say.

He never understood that, to him, it appeared easy to do, because he never had to do it. He was a Hale, born and bred. He could walk into a room falling down drunk and still, he would get respect. She could perform a Vaticancertified miracle and someone would whisper something demeaning behind her back.

Wilty claimed part of that was her own doing; she wasn't the world's most likable woman.

Carolyne's lips twitched in a quick smile of admission. That was true. And, if she were to continue down the path of complete honesty, she didn't really give a damn who liked her or didn't. It was who did what for her that mattered because that implied power, which to her was more meaningful than winning a personality contest.

Before Nigel, as well as Lourdes, departed, Carolyne had him bring Wilty's antique golf clubs into the den. This was the venue she'd selected for his homage: Wilty always said it was the most inviting room in the house. Oak-paneled and furnished with large couches upholstered in a soft, black-and-white plaid, spare Stickley tables and Native American pottery, everything was centered around the huge stone hearth that dominated the far wall. She brought the bag in and stood it in a corner created by the jut of the fireplace.

She stepped back and marveled at how the quiver-like bag seemed to nestle into its new home. Aside from nicely filling the space, the provenance of the collection actually added a certain gravitas to the room. Curious, she took out two or three of the clubs. She read the labels and examined the wooden heads and shafts of the longer clubs. The names were amusing and quaint, especially the short one, Liberty. Recognizing it as a precursor to the putter and, feeling oddly playful, she went back out of the foyer for the Hale-crested golf balls she'd found in one of the other golf bags, and returned to the den.

She placed four balls on one of the kilim area rugs, set down a flat, hammered brass plate to serve as the cup, picked up the Liberty and tried to putt. Tentative and awkward, she either topped the ball, moved it two inches, or missed it completely. Intrigued by the fact that putting wasn't as easy as she'd presumed, she practiced her stroke before setting up the ball again. More determined this time, and therefore more forceful, she hit one ball against the far wall, lost another one under a chair, and nearly toppled a table with a third.

"Okay," she said, feeling a bit like Goldilocks. "That was obviously too hard. Those first ones were too soft. We're going to try this again and this time, we're going to get it just right."

Bringing the club back slowly, she stroked it through the ball. When it stayed on line, climbed up over the lip of the brass plate and slid triumphantly into the center, Carolyne rejoiced, her mouth erupting into a huge grin. She was so delighted, she hoisted the putter into the air and smacked it on the head, giving it a high-five, of sorts.

She was stunned when the head broke off and fell to the floor with a hideous thud. She was even more surprised when she noticed a tightly scrolled piece of paper peeking out from the hollow shaft. Extracting whatever it was, she sat down on the nearest couch, laid the damaged putter alongside her, and gently unwound the papers. They were yellowed with age and slightly fragile. Carolyne's heart pounded. This was it, the document she'd been looking for, the one Wilty believed contained the power to erase their future.

The handwriting was lavish, but small, with elaborate serifs and flourishes that made it difficult for her to read. Thankfully, her eyeglasses were strung around her neck. She slipped them on and, again, tried to decipher what was written.

> *I, who am about to end the torturous malignancy that is my life, hereby offer my last confession. Forgive me Father, for I have sinned.*

It was long and rambling and full of regret, but, just as Wilty had said, it didn't give any explicit details. There was no definitive explanation of why Charles didn't deserve to bear the Hale name, but the inference was clear: thanks to something E.W. Hale had done, Charles, in trying to rectify his father's mistake, had done something worse.

After reading the note for the third time, Carolyne seriously considered tossing it into the fireplace and burning it. Then she remembered Harlan Whiteside's call. He'd reached her on her ride out to Southampton. Dan Kalikow had finally gotten back to him.

"Wilty did give him a copy of that document you felt was so incriminating. He, in turn, handed it over to the probate court. As I suspected, a nationwide search for possible descendants of E.W. Hale has been launched. The probate process won't go forward until the court is satisfied that every attempt has been made to find the legitimate heirs. He thought you were entitled to know."

Carolyne paced as she considered her options. There appeared to be only one: to burn this suicide note along with the broken golf club and pray that no one else knew where Wilty had stashed it. She had no way of knowing how many other copies were floating, but if the original never saw the light of day, there could be no scientific verification of the date on which the note was written. No court was going to award the Hale fortune to a Wilty-come-lately with only a Xerox copy to support his claim. Without another unassailable form of corroboration—and to date, she knew of no such possibility—the wannabe would be turned away and she would be able to make a case for herself.

Carolyne rolled the papers up again and tossed them into the fireplace along with the shaft of the broken putter and a starter log she took from a brass holder. She struck a match and held it to the log until it burst into flames, taking Charles Hale's last words and E.W. Hale's damnable golf club with it.

Then, she went to the bar and fixed herself a really stiff drink.

She unlocked the door to the Bridgehampton cottage and nudged it open with her hip. Her arms were burdened with bundles of fresh vegetables and flowers from one of her favorite farm stands. She deposited them in the kitchen, opened a few windows, and turned on some lights. When everything was put away, she selected a bottle of white wine from a large brass and wrought-iron wine rack and put it in the refrigerator to chill.

She brought her suitcase upstairs to the front bedroom. Since she was the first to arrive, she had first dibs. She staked her claim by putting the novel she was reading on the nightstand and unpacking her toiletries in the adjoining bathroom. Then, she went back downstairs.

A satisfied smile decorated her face as she filled a few vases with flowers and put them out. A quiet, girlfriend weekend was just what she needed.

She looked at the time and thought about starting the salad. Before she did, she turned on the outside lights, letting them bathe the grounds with an ambient glow.

The property was small, but sylvan, lush with trees and shrubs that bolstered the illusion that the amoeba-shaped, black-bottomed pool was really a pond in a secluded glen. In summer, wildflowers danced freely amidst the tree trunks. A waterfall that looked as if it originated in a far-off brook, gently cascaded over a cluster of rocks into the pool, causing soft, languorous ripples. A verdant patch of lawn led to stone steps and a spacious patio. At the far end, elevated slightly so that its inhabitants could enjoy the view, was an enclosed gazebo housing a built-in Jacuzzi that could be used year-round.

She opened the French doors and walked out onto the terrace. It was a beautiful night. Tiny song birds entertained her with their vespers while a couple of crickets competed for attention.

She checked her watch again. By now, the traffic was probably brutally snarled. She'd left the city early, but it was beginning to build even then.

Just then, her eye caught a twinkle of reflected glass at the other end of the Jacuzzi. She walked into the gazebo and found a tray with wine goblets, an open bottle of Chianti and a hastily scribbled note.

*Went to the store to get a few things for our Spring
Fling banquet. Chill out with a glass of wine and
a soak. Be back soon. xoxox*

She smiled. The wine was one of her favorites. She
poured some into a glass and indulged.

So good.

She took the glass, went into the house, turned on some
music, and returned to the terrace.

It was nearly seven o'clock. She wondered if she should
worry. She looked at the note and decided shopping for a
banquet took time. She poured herself more wine and
looked at the Jacuzzi. The heater was already on. Steam
rose from the hot water in a vaporous finger that seemed
to beckon to her.

"She told me to chill out with wine and a soak," she
reminded the birds. "And so I shall."

Slowly, she stripped off her clothes and sashayed over
to the Jacuzzi. She giggled as she dipped her toe into the
steamy pool, recalling the wild days of their youth when
they used to skinny dip in the pool behind her house whenever the parental units were out for the evening.

She laughed out loud, recalling the time the adults decided to come back to the house for coffee and cake and
found about six girls splashing around naked in the pool.

She leaned down and placed her wineglass on a ledge,
gripped the stone wall that surrounded the simmering tub
and stepped in. Sliding down to the bottom, she sighed as
the water embraced her. The heat felt deliciously erotic
against her skin. She lay her head back, closed her eyes,
and lost herself in a world of wine and water.

When she opened her eyes, it took a minute to reorient
herself. Her head was fuzzy and her insides were beginning
to feel weird. She'd consumed a lot of wine on an empty
stomach and was beginning to regret it.

She checked her watch. It was almost eight o'clock.

*Where the hell is she? Could she have changed her
mind?*

No. She was here. She left a note.
The handwriting looked funny.
Maybe there was an accident.

Her hands were trembling. She was beginning to sweat.

She climbed out of the Jacuzzi. Unmindful of her na-
kedness or the water dripping off her body, she stumbled
into the kitchen and found her cell phone. Instead of a human voice, she got one of those annoying messages that
said the person she was calling was either unavailable or
out of range.

Damn! She has her phone shut off.

She dialed the apartment. An answering machine picked
up. Again, she looked at the clock. Something was wrong.
She knew it, but she was too tipsy to think rationally. Instead, she opted to switch to automatic pilot. She'd do
whatever felt right and hope for the best.

At the moment, what she felt most was cold, so she
ambled back out onto the terrace. Her clothes lay in a heap.
The thought of bending down to pick them up made her
stomach lurch. The Jacuzzi loomed as an easier alternative.
Slowly, bracing herself against the stone wall, she made
her way back into the hot tub.

The steam made her nausea worse, but she knew she
was too woozy to climb back out. She tried taking deep
breaths, but her body was out of synch with her brain so
all she did was hiccup. She was beginning to feel ill. And
frantic. She didn't know why she felt the way she did, but
she did know that she *needed* help.

Her eyes closed without her wanting them to. She
slipped down into the tub. Water filled her nose. Her eyes
snapped open. Again, she gasped for air.

The swish of the whirlpool would wake her up, she
thought. The thrust and sting of the water would restore
energy to her legs and arms. She'd be able to get out and
get dressed.

She took another deep breath and reached behind her,
groping about until she found the various switches, one that

would turn on the jets, another that would turn on the lights. She flipped them both.

The water slapped at her. She was so out of it, her body was weightless. The waves buffeted her from side to side. Her nausea was increasing, as was her sense that she was losing control. Desperate, she reached behind her, searching for ballast. Through bleary eyes she saw the metal stair rails that flanked the steps into the Jacuzzi. She stretched out her arm and willed herself close enough to grab on to one of the bars. Her hand was shaking as it closed around the railing. Then it stopped.

Three minutes later, Paula was dead.

32

The first red flag went up when Gus, the bartender from Onyx, called to say that Ben Schirmerhorn had been in demanding to know who'd ratted him out to the cops.

Then CSU notified Ezra that prints taken off the prescription bottles at Vanna Larkin's home matched those taken from a glass used by the ubiquitious Mr. Schirmerhorn during his visit to the station house. That gave Matt Felder, the ADA assigned to Vanna Larkin's and Wilty's cases, probable cause. A warrant was issued for Schirmerhorn's arrest.

When the phone rang for the third time, Ezra expected it to be the guys from the 9th precinct saying they'd found the pill-popping, drug-selling, possibly murderous Schirmerhorn and grabbed him up. It was the sheriff's office in the Hamptons.

Callie sat on the couch in the living room. All around her, police and forensic technicians tended to the tedious and gruesome tasks necessitated by the discovery of a felonious crime. They tiptoed around her and tried to keep their voices at a respectful timbre, but it didn't matter. There could have been a hundred people in that room; Callie saw nothing except Paula floating face up in the small Jacuzzi, heard nothing except the sound of her own voice screaming for help.

When the police arrived, she'd been sitting in the gazebo

alongside the Jacuzzi, maintaining a heartbroken vigil at the water's edge. They tried to get her to go inside, but she wouldn't leave Paula. Only after she was assured that Paula was safe from any further harm did she agree to go into the house.

Callie was numb, her body a heap of desolation, her face stained with disbelief, grief and, most of all, guilt. A doctor called to the scene offered a tranquilizer, but Callie refused. She needed to feel every sting, every stab of pain created by this loss. Paula Stein had been her best friend since she was ten years old. She deserved to be mourned, which Callie did in abundance.

She thought she'd cried herself out, but when Ezra and Alvarez walked in, a fresh wave of tears flooded her cheeks.

Jorge expressed his sympathy, then found a discreet place to stand, near enough to hear what was said, far enough away not to intrude.

Ezra sat down next to her. Phrases like "how are you" and "are you okay" felt empty and stupid, so he said nothing. He simply held her and let her cry into his shoulder.

"It was supposed to be me," she said, finally, her voice barely above a whisper and breaking with emotion. "You know that, don't you?"

Ezra nodded. "That's probably true."

"I got here late." Her eyes were vacant, her voice wooden. "All the lights were on. There was music playing. I called out, but she didn't answer. The doors were open, so I went out onto the terrace." She gasped, revisiting the horrific scene that had greeted her. "She was naked, floating in the Jacuzzi.

"I ran inside and called 911. I thought maybe she was still alive. Or could be saved. Or . . ." She broke into a spate of wrenching sobs. "I didn't know what else to do."

"There was nothing else to do, Callie."

She looked at him, confusion hooding her eyes. "The police said there was a note and a bottle of wine. They said it was made to sound like it was from me."

Ezra glanced over at Alvarez, who exited to confer with the team working the scene.

Just as another wave of grief washed over Callie, a man burst through the front door trailed by a Hamptons police officer. Tall and blond, his face deeply scored by stress, his body wired with worry, he rushed toward Callie and wrapped her in his arms.

Ezra assumed this was Callie's father. He stood and stepped aside.

As Bill tried desperately to soothe his bereaved daughter, Ezra slipped out back and joined his partner who was being brought up to speed by the Sheriff.

Lester Hancock had picked Ezra and Jorge up at the airport and driven them to the house. In that time, he told them a neighbor had reported a car parked down the block and across the street from the cottage. It had been sitting there for about two hours.

"The minute Jamieson shows up, he beats it out of there. I don't get it. Did he suddenly realize he'd whacked the wrong woman?"

"Yes," Ezra said, stunning the older officer. "That's exactly what happened."

As Ezra approached Hancock now, he studied the man. A sexagenarian, he was a crusty sort who reminded Ezra of an old chair: battered by age, soft in the middle, fraying at the edges, yet still sturdy enough to be useful.

"Has the coroner determined the cause of death?" he asked.

"She was electrocuted."

Ezra looked at Jorge. That wasn't what he'd expected either.

Hancock called over one of his uniformed cops and introduced him as Ed Fertig. He was the first patrolman on the scene.

"Tell 'em what you told me," Hancock directed.

Fertig paused to collect his thoughts. He didn't want to misspeak or overlook an important detail or otherwise embarrass his boss in front of NYPD detectives.

"I went to check for a pulse. When I grabbed her wrist, it felt like I was touching a live wire." He expelled a nervous breath and looked at his hand, reassuring himself his fingers were still attached. "That water was highly charged, Detectives."

"Any idea how the current got into the water?" Alvarez asked.

Again, Fertig thought his answer through. "No, sir. The heater was off, but the jets and the lights were on."

A thought gnawed at Ezra's brain, making it itch.

"Was there a short? A circuit breaker flipped?" he asked.

"I don't think so," Fertig said, but admitted he hadn't checked that out.

Jorge took him off the hook. "If there was a short, nothing would've been on."

Ezra's itch wouldn't go away, so he continued to scratch. "Were all the jets on?"

"Yes, sir."

"And the lights?"

"Actually, no. One of the bulbs was out."

Ezra knitted his fingers together as his brain attempted to put the disparate thoughts that were nagging at him into a coherent whole.

"Somehow, the perp knew Paula and Callie were coming out here. And that one was expected earlier than the other." Ezra sighed with frustration and looked again at the open bottle of wine. That invitation was just too blatant. "Have your lab test for OxyContin," he said.

Hancock assured Ezra they would, nodding to Fertig, who took the bottle and left. "We'll also check for it in the blood."

"Are you thinking Orlando's behind this?" Jorge asked.

"I'm thinking a lot of things," Ezra admitted. He held up the note and studied it. "Wine and a soak. What could be more soothing than that?"

"I don't know that I'd exactly call it soothing. Mixing water and electricity is even more toxic than mixing drugs and alcohol."

So is working on high-voltage lights with the power on, Ezra thought, recalling another death by electrocution.

Ezra called Mike over, the electrical tech Jorge had spoken to earlier, and asked how the current could have gotten into the pool.

"One of the officers on the scene said there was a light out," Ezra said.

"Yeah, I know. When I got all the wires disconnected so I could examine the pool without getting fried, that was the first thing I checked, because a burned-out bulb shouldn't have been a problem. Turns out, the problem was there was no bulb at all. And the glass casing that's supposed to cover it was broken."

Ezra absorbed that information slowly. This was not exactly his field of expertise.

"Were there any burns on the victim's hands?"

"One hand was practically charred."

"From grabbing the hand rail on the steps."

"Exactly."

Alvarez wanted to know how Ezra knew so much about electricity.

"Something came up on one of those cold cases I've been working that got me interested in all things electrical."

"What kind of things?"

"Like how there could be power when the switch controlling the power was off. And . . ."

"That's easy," Mike said, interrupting. "You just reverse the wires so that off becomes on and vice versa."

That went a long way toward scratching Ezra's itch, but it wasn't gone yet. "Did you check the GFI?" he asked Mike.

Alvarez and the sheriff both looked confused.

Mike explained. "The GFI is the mechanism that grounds the electricity for the Jacuzzi. If it's installed properly, there could be a short, or a bulb out, or some other kind of electrical glitch and you'd still be okay. But this pool was juiced, which means someone jimmied around with the GFI."

"Think about what this bastard did," Ezra said, his anger growing. "He takes out a bulb and breaks the casing so that when the switches are thrown electricity gets into the pool. The victim's groggy from the wine, which was probably laced with drugs. She tries to get out, but she's wobbly so she grabs on to the railing. The minute she touches the metal outside the pool, she becomes the grounding element and electricity shoots through her like a lightning bolt."

Alvarez was taken with—and disturbed by—the intricacy of the plan.

"There are lots of ways to kill someone, Ez. Electrocution isn't usually the method of choice. It's complicated stuff which means it takes time to set up."

Ezra's jaw hardened. "Only if you don't know what you're doing. If you know how to rig it, it's quick and effective. And most of the time, it doesn't leave a trail."

Unless you create a pattern. Then, it becomes your signature.

33

It was two A.M. when Ezra got home. Too wired to sleep, he spent the rest of the night reading E.W. Hale's journal from the year 1900. Elizabeth Winters was right. It was the diary with the answers.

Unfortunately, Ezra still had a long list of questions.

Dawn had just broken when Carolyne Hale was awakened by the loud jangling of the telephone. Her hand groped around for the receiver. Still half asleep, she placed it next to her ear.

"Something went wrong." The voice was low, but pulsing with agitation.

"How wrong?" She was groggy, but his nervousness seeped through the phone like poisonous fumes, jolting her into wakefulness.

"Very wrong. But that's not why I called you. The shit's about to hit the fan. If you want to be there when it all goes down, you'd better drag your ass out of bed, gas up the Benz and get on the road."

Hyped by what he read in the diary and delighted to have any excuse to check on Callie, Ezra made Callie's apartment his first stop. She wasn't there. Bill Jamieson was. He'd brought Callie home and spent the night on her couch.

"So you're Ezra Chapin," Bill said cordially, as he invited Ezra inside. "I saw you at the cottage last night, but . . ."

"It wasn't exactly a time for pleasantries," Ezra said.

Jamieson sucked in his cheeks in an effort to control his emotions. "I am pleased to meet you, Detective Chapin, even under these dismal circumstances."

"Yes, sir. Likewise." He felt awkward. The other man did as well. It prompted Ezra to wonder what Callie had told her father about *them*. "In case you're wondering, even though Ms. Stein's death occurred outside of our jurisdiction, my partner and I are overseeing the investigation."

"Thank you. Paula was special. This is a terrible loss, for both Callie and me."

"I'm sure it is. Mr. Jamieson, where is Callie?"

Bill Jamieson noted the abrupt change in subject, as well as the worry underlining Ezra's eyes.

"She left early this morning."

"Where'd she go?"

"Saratoga Springs."

At once, the detective's face became starched. His eyes grew dark and contracted. His entire mien projected concern, which only served to amplify Bill's already heightened anxiety.

"Did she say why she was going there?"

"To check out some things for a project she's working on," Bill said, unable to escape the feeling that Callie hadn't told him everything. "Something about Wilty Hale."

Outside, a restless cloud must have vacated its patch of sky because a brilliantly yellow shard of sunlight suddenly sliced through the window into the room. As it did, Ezra thought he saw an incongruous glint in the corner above Bill Jamieson's head. His eyes fixed on the spot, but the cloud reclaimed its space and the sunlight disappeared, as did the mysterious wink of light.

Ezra put his finger to his lips, signalling Bill not to question him. He grabbed a chair, moved it into the corner where he saw the glint and climbed onto it. He reached into the gap between the wooden molding and the wall and extracted what appeared to be a fiberoptic camera. It was the size of a dime and not much thicker. No wonder he'd missed it. These things were so small they could be all over this apartment and still escape detection.

As he climbed down, it hit him. He and Callie were in this room when they discussed going to the gallery and out to dinner. They talked about Orlando, Schirmerhorn, and the tattooed man who'd been stalking her, as well as Victoria Moore and the fourth diary. When she and Paula made their plans for the weekend, Callie was probably here and not on her cell. No wonder the killer knew what she was up to, where she was going to be, and when. Worse, whoever was watching knew she was gone and where she was headed.

Ezra took a breath. "If you'll wait here for a moment, sir. I'll be right back."

He went out into the hall and, using his cell phone, called Jorge.

"I'm glad you called in."

Ezra knew from Alvarez's voice it wasn't good news. "What's up?"

"Schirmerhorn's dead. He'd called into the house wanting to give himself up. Narco worked a deal. He helps them pull a sting, they drop the charges against him. Too bad nobody told Orlando the rules of the game. He stuck Shakespeare with a needle filled with enough of that Orlando Magic to float a barge."

Ezra felt as if he'd been pumped full of drugs.

"I take it Orlando is still out there."

"They've got APB's out on him from Miami to Maine."

Ezra was quiet. Alvarez never liked it when Ezra was quiet. "Where's Callie?" he asked.

"Gone." Ezra quickly told Alvarez about the cameras. "They're expensive, which in my mind, screams Orlando. He has to be sitting on a stack of cash, more than enough to finance fancy surveillance."

"Merrick's not exactly poor," Alvarez said, wanting to

remind Ezra there were other possibilities. "We got his
phone logs. Not only did he speak to The Widow several
times, but he placed a couple of calls to Guy Hoffman, the
one you dubbed the mad scientist. The Widow also spoke
to this Hoffman character, by the way. More than once."

"Interesting."

"If you think that's interesting, this is gonna make your
socks roll up and down. Yesterday, Merrick called someone
at a Saratoga Springs exchange. Hiram Wellington."

"I don't like that one bit," Ezra said.

He told Alvarez about Callie heading up there, reiterat-
ing what he'd revealed on the ride back into town the night
before about Merrick and Hoffman's brain-bending experiments.

"Speaking of Hoffman," Alvarez said. "Yesterday, while
we were on our way out to the Island, there was a B and
E at his lab. Some kind of serum was taken."

The hair on the back of Ezra's neck was standing at
attention. "I need one more favor, Jorge. Call Felder and
ask if we can get a warrant to search Merrick's office."

"What're you looking for?"

"I'm not sure, but the guy creeps me out." Ezra looked
at his watch. "Gotta go."

"Yeah, me too. After I call Felder, I've got to arrange
for a plane to take us to Saratoga." Ezra started to protest.
"You may be running up there to play white knight for
your lady love, but I'm working a case. Besides, I've never
been to Saratoga. I hear it's lovely this time of year."

Ezra smiled. "I'll meet you at La Guardia."

"Hiram, it's Carolyne Hale. I'm driving up to Long House
and I thought I'd stop by so we could go over the Hale
Foundation's annual endowment to Liberty Park. Will you
be around? . . . Wonderful. See you soon."

Ezra struggled with how much to tell Bill Jamieson. In the
end, he felt the man had a right to know that someone was
trying to kill his daughter. He encapsulated some of what

had occurred, making certain that each time he laid out a grim possibility, he softened it with details about what he and Alvarez were doing to protect Callie. When it came to Peter Merrick, Ezra opted for unvarnished bluntness.

"I'm not discounting the therapeutic process, but to be honest, I'm not sure she should be putting all her faith in this particular doctor."

"When Callie and I had lunch yesterday, we talked a great deal about Dr. Merrick. She mentioned that you have reservations about him."

Ezra found that interesting. First, because Callie and Bill had talked about him. And second, because if she laid his reservations about her shrink on the table, she wasn't as secure about Merrick as Ezra had believed.

"She does as well, but she's conflicted. She's afraid of what further therapy will reveal. Yet at the same time, she believes her life can't move forward until she finishes with the past."

Ezra remained skeptical. "She can't change what happened a hundred years ago. And really, what difference does any of it make now?"

"It makes a big difference." Bill's voice resonated with experience. "Something is haunting her. She needs to put it to rest. If she doesn't, she'll never have any peace."

Ezra steepled his fingers and studied them as if they were runes.

Bill watched him with mixed emotions. This young man was so in love with Callie it oozed out of him.

"Why did you come to see Callie this morning, Ezra? I have the feeling it was something unrelated to the tragedy with Paula."

"Actually, it was. I read something last night that took my breath away. It's historical dynamite."

"From one of those diaries Wilty sent Callie? Or the one that was missing?"

"It's the one E.W. Hale wrote during the year nineteen hundred."

"Would you mind telling me about it?"

Bill Jamieson needed a distraction. Ezra was delighted to provide it.

"It seems that E.W. Hale had a second family. He had a wife named Liberty and a son named Mac. Mac was married to Sarah Blessing. She was the woman in the photograph that Callie said was in two of her dreams."

Bill Jamieson stared at Ezra in an odd, unsettling way.

"Hale also had a daughter named Faith."

Bill's face turned dough white.

"Excuse me, sir, but is what I'm saying upsetting you for some reason?"

"Yesterday, Callie had another session with Merrick. She went through the dream again, the gray people dream. Merrick asked her to describe the people in the dream. She did. He asked her who she was talking to. She said, 'Sarah.' He asked who Sarah was. She said she was Mac's wife. When he asked who Mac was, Callie said he was her brother. Merrick asked who she was. She said she was Faith."

Ezra felt as if he'd been body slammed. His chest seemed to cave in as his breath shot out of his mouth. "Are you sure?"

"I heard the tape."

Ezra's fingers drummed on his knee as his head digested what Bill had told him.

"That's why she recognized Sarah Blessing at the gallery. That's how she knew the music that was played at E.W. Hale's funeral. That's why she flipped out at Liberty Park." He stared at Callie's father, wide-eyed with revelation. "That's where this all took place."

He gasped as other thoughts and worries rained down on him, particularly the realization that if any of this was true, Callie was a Hale.

Bill, who'd heard the tape, but hadn't put the pieces together until now, appeared astonished.

"I'm having trouble wrapping myself around the thought that my daughter is a descendant of E.W. Hale. It's quite unbelievable, don't you think?"

Ezra smiled in agreement. A second later, his smile faded and angst took its place. "Does Merrick realize she's a Hale?"

Bill considered Ezra's question. "I don't see how. All he'd get from Callie's dream was that a hundred years or so ago, something terrible happened to a relative of hers."

"How about Callie? Does she suspect a genetic connection to the Hales?"

Bill shook his head. "To her, this is about the gray people, the ghosts her mother left her, not about E.W. Hale's line of descent."

Ezra debated whether in this situation, ignorance was indeed bliss.

Bill must have intuited Ezra's thoughts. "How dangerous is this for Callie?"

"We're talking about billions of dollars, Mr. Jamieson. People in control of that kind of money don't like to be told it could be taken away from them and handed over to someone they never heard of before."

Bill's lips stretched into a tight, angry line. "We have to find her."

"We will," Ezra assured him.

But would *they* find her first?

34

Callie spent much of the ride up the New York State Thruway trying to clear her head. It hadn't been easy. She was exhausted, drained of energy and spirit from too many tears and too little sleep, thanks to a barrage of vivid nightmares that vacillated between heart-wrenching visions of Paula and the familiar hauntings of the gray people.

She didn't know what one had to do with the other, but at some point during this endless night, the brutal knowledge that whoever had killed Paula meant to kill her became entangled with thoughts about Wilty's savage death. Callie couldn't explain why, but she felt certain the two incidents were related.

Ezra believed Wilty's quest to verify his place in the Hale universe was the reason he was killed. According to Dan Kalikow, he'd discovered something about E.W. Hale that had the power to alter the course of his life. For answers, he'd resorted to Hale's diaries.

Callie couldn't imagine whose universe she'd invaded and why her presence in that world would impel someone to kill her. Her only enemies were the gray people and, if Dr. Merrick was to be believed, they were dreams and as such, had no power over her.

But should she believe Dr. Merrick?

She was making progress with him, but was she being programmed or deprogrammed? She knew from listening to her tape that she was the one producing the details. He wasn't inventing or embellishing anything. But she hadn't taped their first session. He could have put things into her head then to extract at a future date. He might even have shown her a photograph of Sarah Blessing while she was under hypnosis. Maybe that's why she looked so familiar at the gallery. And why it was that particular face which insinuated itself on the woman in the rowboat. And the woman having the miscarriage. Those visions all occurred after that initial regression.

Then, there were the things Ezra had told her about Merrick's association with Guy Hoffman, plus what she'd downloaded off the net. Certainly, that had raised some very legitimate questions about whether she could trust Peter Merrick with her mental health.

If she polled her inner circle, the answer would be a resounding no. Ezra thought Merrick was playing with Callie's mind to suit his own ends. Paula had been supportive only because Callie seemed so troubled. Her father had warned against placing unconditional faith in a doctor out of desperation. He was also less than impressed with Merrick's claim that he was a specialist; to Bill, specialist was a synonym for narrow, a perspective he deemed unwise when dealing with matters related to the mind. Auntie Pennie echoed one of Ezra's main concerns, that Merrick's objectivity as a therapist was compromised by his ambitions as a writer. Even Callie's research portrayed him as unorthodox and far too aggressive in his therapy.

Still, the gray people had been with her all her life. The people she saw during her regression yesterday were the very same people. Merrick couldn't program that.

Then again, she and Ezra had spent a great deal of time talking about someone named Faith. That name could have lodged in the back of her brain, surfacing when Merrick specifically asked her for a name. Her saying, "I am Faith," could have been a subconscious attempt to solve a nagging mystery, two unrelated synapses bonding together to form a coherent answer that had no basis in fact. Anything was possible.

Except that her father said Mara used to claim she was Faith.

Then, too, was the basic question of Faith's identity. Declaring that she was Faith didn't tell her who Faith was.

"Arghhhhh!" Callie groaned, loudly voicing her frustration.

The only thing she knew for certain was that she needed to return to Saratoga Springs. There, she'd experienced such strong visions and such powerful sensations of déjà vu, she had to believe that if she allowed herself to suspend the cynicism of the present, she could access the truth of the past. If she went down to the lake or back to Liberty Park or wandered around the streets of old Saratoga, the astral static charging the atmosphere in those places would infuse her with telepathic omniscience. She would know whether the Faith of E.W. Hale's diary had anything to do with her gray people. She would know whether the Sarah of her dreams was the Sarah who had inspired Liberty Park. And, perhaps, she would learn why she and her mother had been singled out for a lifetime of spectral obsession.

Ten miles west of Saratoga Springs was the village of East Galway. Callie followed the directions she'd gotten off the web to the chapel where Sarah Blessing married Jeremiah Holstein in 1894. On the drive up, Callie had called the woman in charge of the historic chapel and arranged to meet her there. She wasn't sure what she was looking for, but she hadn't forgotten the feeling she had when she discovered Sarah's marriage certificate. She'd known that East Galway was only a short way away from Saratoga, which was strange because she'd never heard of the town before.

It was a charming site, small and intimate, the kind of white clapboard church from those early times that made one think of Sunday suppers and family hymnals and community sings. As Callie walked inside, a blip of memory flashed before her eyes: men in waistcoats and top hats; women in puffed sleeves, corseted waists and bonnets; small boys with their hair slicked back, their sisters sporting pigtails or corkscrew curls. It was there and a second later it was gone, yet if she closed her eyes, she could almost hear the varied timbres of that congregation raised in songful prayer.

When she opened her eyes, she felt displaced, shaky, as if she'd traveled a long distance. She had, but she knew it was more miles and many more hours than the trip up from New York City.

Slowly, she moved through the wooden pews, down the aisle toward the altar. Two large books sat on the pulpit. On top of them was a note from the woman she was supposed to meet. Something had come up, she couldn't stay, these were the ledgers Callie had asked about. She apologized, wished Callie good luck, and told her where to put the ledgers when she was done.

Callie ran her fingers across the ancient velvet cover of the first book. This was the ledger brides and grooms signed before their nuptials. It was large and thick, encompassing several years. Callie was curious about 1863, the year the picture of E.W. Hale and a woman named Liberty was taken. She turned the pages slowly, studying the signatures, admiring the decorous handwriting that distinguished a time when typewriters were only used for business and computers weren't even part of a visionary's subconscious, let alone the popular vocabulary.

When she came upon it, it startled her, even though she'd been expecting it:

> *Liberty McAllister and Emmet Wilton Hale, married this day, the sixteenth of March in the year of Our Lord, 1863, in the village of East Galway, in the county of Saratoga, in the state of New York.*

So that's what he was doing during those lost years. He was courting a woman named Liberty, a woman he married in 1863.

According to bios, Hale returned to Cleveland in 1864 and married Winifred Huntington Colfax in 1869. Callie stared at the signatures, begging them to explain. Did Liberty die? Was E.W. Hale widowed before he married Winifred? Or was he divorced? Was that the big secret? That he'd been married before and never told anyone?

He wouldn't be the first man to keep such a secret. Even today it wasn't unheard of for someone to fudge their marital history. In the late eighteen-hundreds it would have been a snap to do. Saratoga Springs was a long way from Cleveland. Communities, particularly small suburban ones like Saratoga, were still somewhat isolated. Hale could have married Liberty, gone back to Cleveland after it ended, and married someone else without ever having to say word one about it.

But according to his journals and some of the biographies she'd read, Hale returned to Saratoga many times after his marriage to Winifred. He built an institute there out of respect for a woman who seemingly had no relationship to him. If his marriage was over, why would he continue to come back? Had she and Ezra guessed right? Was Sarah Blessing his mistress?

Callie set the first book aside and turned to the second, the one that included the year 1894, when Sarah Blessing married Jeremiah Holstein. She found their signatures and stared at them, sliding her fingertip across the dried ink, willing the ghosts to speak. She closed her eyes and waited. What followed was that same fraught soundlessness with which she was so familiar. It was a quiet that wasn't quite still, a susurrant hush that told her the ghosts were there with her, but remained unwilling to reveal themselves.

Annoyed with their refusal to make themselves manifest, she opened her eyes and scowled at the silence, cursing the stubbornness of the specters.

"Damn you!" she said. "I don't know who you are or what you want from me, but I am going to find the answers to all of this."

Shaking, she turned her attention back to the page. Her

breath caught in her throat when she noticed something she hadn't read the first time: after the date of the marriage, November 6, 1894, were the signatures of the two witnesses—E.W. Hale and Faith Blessing.

35

Callie gave her name to the gatekeeper and waited. Within minutes, the large wrought-iron gates swung open. Slowly, she made her way to the main house, using the time to review all that she'd learned and to shore up her courage. Suddenly, she wasn't sure coming here alone was such a good idea.

Hiram Wellington was waiting for her at the steps leading into the mansion.

"Ms. Jamieson. What a delightful surprise," he said, extending his hand in greeting. "To what do I owe this unexpected pleasure?"

His smile was fixed. Callie thought he looked a bit tense.

"I needed to speak to you," she said. "And to visit this place."

"Would you like to come to my office? I could have some tea . . ."

"No." Callie didn't mean to be so abrupt, but she remembered what happened during her last visit. "When I was here before, you mentioned that there was a memorial to the founders of Liberty Park somewhere on the property. I'd like you to take me there."

"Certainly, but may I ask why?"

Callie studied her fingernails, the toes of her shoes, the blades of grass on the patch of lawn beneath her feet. She'd rehearsed this a dozen times on the ride up but, still, she felt awkward.

"You're considered something of an expert in the field of mnemonics," she said, finally looking up.

He tilted his head in acknowledgment of the implied compliment.

"You've written a number of papers and given speeches about genetic memory."

"Yes, I have."

"So, I can assume you believe it's possible for memories to be inherited."

"I do indeed." He eyed her cautiously. "May I assume that you've raised this issue because you've experienced visions from another time?"

"I think so." Her gaze became harder, more direct. "Dr. Peter Merrick, my therapist, was one of your acolytes. Hasn't he spoken to you about me?"

Wellington didn't offer an answer to her question. Instead, he started away from the mansion, heading behind it, in the direction of the woods. As expected, Callie followed.

"What role does this visit to Liberty Park play in your treatment?"

Her body language spoke of a roiled interior, yet her words were concise and considered. "During my last visit to Saratoga, I had a number of hallucinations. I was overcome by sights and scenes from an era way before my time. I had emotional reactions to incidents I hadn't experienced. I knew things I shouldn't have known, about people I don't remember knowing." She glanced around, back at the mansion, forward into the woods. "The emanations from this place were particularly strong."

"And you believe the memorial is somehow related to those hallucinations?"

"I don't know. That's what I want to find out."

"Well then," he said, "onward."

The next minute or so passed in silence. Then, Callie stopped and faced him.

"Is it true that some therapists implant names and images

in a patient's brain while they're in a state of partial unconsciousness?"

"To what end?" Wellington's cheeks were pinched with indignation.

Callie shrugged as if she were pulling answers out of the air, but she had thought a great deal about this. "To speed up the flow of memories from a stubbornly retentive patient. Or to fill in a few blanks so whatever story they're recalling could come to an end. The patient feels satisfied. And the doctor feels like a rousing success."

"Absolutely not." Wellington had inhaled so deeply, the sides of his nose were pressed flat against each other. "Memory is a highly speculative field of study, but one which has attracted dozens of highly qualified scientists, many of whom are conducting barrier breaking experiments as we speak."

"Is Dr. Merrick involved with any of those projects?"

"If you have questions about my work, Callie, you really should ask me directly."

Callie spun around and found herself face to face with Peter Merrick.

"Where did you come from?" Her heart was pounding and her skin prickled from an unaccountable fear.

"The house." His blue eyes fixed on her. "I drove up here to discuss your case with Dr. Wellington. As you've obviously gleaned, he was my mentor. I still regard him as a valuable and reliable colleague."

"Is Guy Hoffman a valuable and reliable colleague?" she asked, her voice steadier than her legs.

"Yes, but he has nothing to do with you, Callie."

"You're on the board of his company. You're both working to prove the theory of genetic memory." The more Callie thought about Hoffman, the more agitated she got. "He's got some protein he wants to inject into human beings to see if it'll prod the past into coming forward." She glared at him. Her hands were shaking. "I'm not a lab rat, Dr. Merrick."

"I would never experiment on you, Callie. I can't believe you don't know that."

Callie didn't know what she knew anymore.

"Besides, we're making such wonderful progress on our own, we don't need outside inducements." His voice was smooth, almost soporific. "Our last session was a breakthrough. You went further into your dream than you'd ever had. Correct?"

She nodded dumbly, like a five-year-old saying yes, she'd understood she wasn't supposed to play in the mud.

"You were able to recount names and faces and relationships, but you want to be able to put it all together, is that right?"

Again, she nodded.

"That's what I want as well." He stood directly in front of her, making it impossible for her to see anyone but him. "My job is to help you go back into the past so you can understand what happened there and reconcile the terrible conflict that's haunted you all these years. Best of all, you'll be able to let the past rest in peace and get on with your life." He patted her shoulder, gently encouraging her on her mission. "And you'll finally feel safe in your own skin."

Callie's eyes welled with tears. It was as if he'd read her mental diary and verbalized her exact thoughts, an intuitiveness that rocked her. She wanted to challenge him, to vent her anger and test him with questions that would either support or alleviate her suspicions about him, his methods, and his motivation. But she couldn't. Not now. She was on a journey. He was her guide.

"Would you like to continue on to the memorial?"

"Yes." Her voice was hoarse.

Merrick signaled to Wellington he should leave. Quietly, he did so.

The forest closed in around them, blocking the sunlight and enveloping them in a brambly cocoon of low-slung limbs and crowded tree trunks. The scent of pine was strong and pervasive. Old branches and dead foliage crunched beneath their shoes as they proceeded deeper into the thicket. Neither one spoke. It was as if they were treading on hallowed ground. Callie believed they were.

She could feel the edge of the woodland even before she came to it. Her senses shifted to high alert, turning her skin into gooseflesh. Her pace quickened. Like a kidnap victim who'd been blindfolded, yet had managed to memorize the route to the hideout, she knew exactly how far away it was, that she had to veer slightly left to avoid a chronic low spot, that if there was a wind, it would be coming directly at her, from the north.. Her eyes contracted from a glaring ribbon of sunlight that laced through the greenery. It disoriented her, but only for a moment.

As they approached the clearing, the first thing she saw was a silhouette, a dark sketch set against a clear and brilliant sky. It was tall and spare, a remnant from a building that had been savaged by fire, yet somehow summoned the tensile strength to survive. With the wooden slats of its bulk burned and gone, all that remained was the skeleton of a single wall, looming like a life-size drawing of what was going to be, representing instead, what had been.

There was only the pitch of the roof, the outline of the loft's window, the struts and sides of the outer wall, yet Callie saw it whole. She saw the huge stable from the outside, with its wide planks, small windows, thick roof and double doorways. She could see inside to the broad avenue that ran from front to back, the narrow horse stalls, the tack room, the place where bales of hay were stored.

She was about to move forward when she was engulfed in an orange fog, the same heated, orange fog that blurred the faces in each of her dreams and muddled her ability to get to the truth. She held her hands up in front of her eyes and stepped back, but not out of fear or confusion. She had come too far and it had taken her too long to get here for fear to paralyze her. Fully resolved to see this through to the end, she closed her eyes, sucked in as much air as her lungs would hold and pushed through the coppery cloud.

• • •

When her eyes opened, the orange was gone. The light was clear and she was standing on familiar ground, in the same place her mother, her grandmother and all those who came before had stood. The gray people were there as well. Callie had seen them her entire life, yet now it was different: they were three-dimensional. They were life-size. And they were close enough for her to touch.

She, too, was different. As she looked around, she realized everything seemed bigger and taller. More to the point, she was smaller and younger. She had entered that other world, the one in which she was Faith, this was her home, and two of those people were her family.

The three figures were inside the barn, near the doorway. She was also inside the barn, hiding behind some bales of hay. She closed her eyes and breathed deeply, trying to get her bearings. Her nose itched from the strong scent of hay and horses. Here and there she picked up the sound of hooves stomping on the dirt floor. A horse or two neighed. One snorted. Another whinnied. But she wasn't listening to them.

The gray stranger had announced the reason for his visit. *Your very existence is an affront to my family.*

The other gray man, the one she knew as Mac, wasn't cowed.

I might say the same about you.

The stranger was offended, more by Mac's refusal to be intimidated than by his words. He parried with an insinuation that Mac and his mother weren't equal to the stranger's family, pointing to their clothing and their surroundings as proof of their inferiority.

The argument became louder, more pointed.

If it's money you want, I'm prepared to give you a sizable cash settlement. There would be conditions, of course.

Faith stretched her head to the side and peered out from behind a bale of hay. The woman standing next to Mac— Faith's mother—spotted her. Her turquoise eyes widened, then narrowed as she dropped her hand behind her skirt and

shooed her child away. Faith retreated behind the hay, but
she didn't leave.

Money isn't the issue.

The stranger threw his head back and laughed as if Mac
had just told the funniest joke ever.

Money is the only issue, the stranger said.

Mac stepped forward, deliberately trespassing on the
gray stranger's space. The stranger stood his ground, his
hands balling into fists as he tried to control his rage. The
two men glowered at each other, inching ever closer.
Faith's mom stepped up, slid her arms between them and
forced them apart.

*I don't know the purpose of your visit, but if you're
going to speak ill of my husband or my children, you're
not welcome here, sir.*

The gray stranger retreated, and bowed his head ever so
slightly in a reluctant display of respect.

Faith smiled. Her mother had subdued him. Unfortunately, his retraction was momentary.

*You may not like what I'm saying, Madam, but I am the
son of Emmet Wilton Hale.*

Faith's eyes grew large and her mouth fell open in disbelief. How could his name be Hale? Hale was her name.

Mac and the man who claimed to be Charles Hale exchanged another fusillade of words. Both of them were
flushed with rage.

Faith tried to read the emotions on her mother's face.
There were many. Anger. Betrayal. Fear. Disappointment.
What disturbed her was that underscoring this medley,
hummed an uncharacteristic uncertainty, as if the stranger's
words had knocked the usually steady and stolid Liberty
off her bearings.

Faith crept around the haystacks, moving close to where
the trio was standing.

The stranger demanded to know when Liberty had married E.W. Hale. Mac vehemently protested. He shoved the
other man, seething at his nerve, yelling that he had no right
to question his mother. Liberty answered anyway.

Emmet and I were married on March 16th, 1863. My son was born in 1864.

The gray stranger's face fell. The swagger that had characterized him to that point collapsed.

When were you divorced?

Mac's eyes widened. Confused, he looked at his mother. Her face was tight, but confident.

My husband and I took vows to love one another until death parted us.

Faith watched as the unwelcome visitor struggled with the impact of hearing verification of something he wanted desperately not to be true, but she felt no sympathy for him.

What was the year of your birth, Mr. Hale?

The man stood statue still, as rigid and gray as marble.

When were you born, Mr. Hale?

Liberty's tone was no longer polite, it was insistent and filled with challenge.

Charles's voice quivered as he intoned, *1870.*

Faith didn't understand exactly what was going on, but she knew by their expressions that her mother had trumped the stranger. Verbal fisticuffs ensued, with invectives and threats and angry words being hurled like mythical thunderbolts. And then it happened.

At almost the same moment that Charles Hale picked up the two-by-four and slammed it into Mac's skull, there was an explosion. The orange fog returned, obliterating everything and everyone.

36

Peter raced to Callie's side, raised her upper torso off the ground, and held her in his arms. Her body was lifeless, her breathing shallow. He pressed his fingers against her neck, seeking a pulse. He found one, but it was weak. Her color was as white as snow, her skin just as cold.

Distressed and nervous about what had caused her collapse, he debated whether or not to carry her back to the mansion where there were trained personnel who could help her. He worried that it would take too long and take too much out of Callie.

Peter checked her pulse again. It was getting weaker. Convinced that anything would be better than doing nothing, he was about to pick her up and head for the house when he heard someone approaching the clearing. He breathed a sigh of relief. Either Wellington's curiosity had gotten the better of him, or he'd anticipated complications.

Within seconds, a golf cart emerged from the thicket, driven by a man in the white uniform of the medical staff. Alongside him, dressed in casual slacks and a sweater, looking as if she were about to tee off on the front nine, sat Carolyne Hale.

Peter quelled his surprise at the incongruity of seeing Carolyne at Liberty Park and eagerly directed his attention to her companion, who'd already grabbed a black bag and bounded out of the cart.

"Dr. Wellington sent me. He thought you might need

assistance," he said as he made his way to Callie.

"I do. Thank you. She fainted."

The medic plunged a needle into her arm without any further explanation from Peter or even a cursory examination of the patient.

"What is that?" Peter demanded to know. "What are you giving her?"

Hiram's staffer drained the fluid in the needle, then extracted it from her arm. "Adrenaline."

Peter's anger abated slightly. The man may have acted less cautiously than Merrick would have liked, but under the circumstances, an injection of adrenaline was not inappropriate. It accelerated the heartbeat and infused the body with energy.

He kept his fingers on Callie's wrist and studied her face, waiting for some indication that she was coming around. There was none.

"Are you sure that was Adrenaline?" Callie had been given a large dose of the hormone. She should have had some response by now.

"I said it was, didn't I?" the attendant snapped, tossing the used needle into the black bag.

Peter didn't like his attitude. He looked for a name tag so he could discuss the matter with Hiram. There was none.

"What are you doing here?" he said, turning to Carolyne.

"I stopped off on my way to Long House to speak to Hiram about this year's endowment to Liberty Park. When he said you were here regressing a patient and he was sending Delwin out to assist, I begged to come along."

Her eyes left his and traveled slowly down to Callie, who remained unconscious.

"We could see something was going on through the trees, so we hung back and watched. It was fascinating, Peter. All that silent gesturing and dancing about. So geisha-like."

Her eyes lingered on Callie, then found his again, but they'd turned flinty.

"I had no idea that pesky reporter was your patient. You should have told me."

The tone of her voice grated on Merrick like a branch scratching on glass, but he ignored her. Just then, Callie's health had precedence over Carolyne's pique.

Gently laying Callie back down on the ground, he rose. "How many CCs did you give her?"

The man folded his arms across his chest, responding to Merrick's challenge with a gladiator-like pose of belligerent silence.

Peter looked from the white-coated man to Callie to Carolyne, his head pulsing with unpleasant speculation.

Carolyne did serve on the boards of both Liberty Park and the Hale Foundation, but she wasn't a serendipitous woman. She didn't just stop off or pop in. She knew he'd be here with Callie.

But how? And why would it matter?

The only way Carolyne could have known he and Callie would be here was if she bugged both Callie's apartment and his office.

If she had listened to his session with Callie and his conversation with Hiram, she knew it was possible that Callie was a Hale.

And last, but hardly least, there was the radio report he'd heard on the drive up about a robbery at the GenTec lab.

"She was reliving the past on her own," he said, trembling with rage and violation as he put the pieces together.

"How do you know that? She wasn't speaking."

"Because I know." Merrick kneeled down and pressed his fingers against Callie's neck. Still, no improvement.

"What *exactly* do you know?" Carolyne's tone grew sharp and urgent.

"She recalled a murder." Though he managed to sound calm, his mind was racing, trying to figure out how to get Callie out of there.

Carolyne glanced down at the young woman on the ground. "Who died?"

"A woman and her son."

"Who did it?"

Just then, Callie's arm shot up. Her body went into a spasm. Her head slapped from side to side. Merrick bent down to soothe her, but she pushed him away. Her eyes opened and she bolted upright, using her hands to gain purchase. She blinked to clear away the residual fog. Slowly, she looked from one to the other, studying their faces as if trying to recall who they were, where they were, and why.

Fearfully, she scrambled to her feet, holding her hands out in front of her in a gesture of self-protection. With small, tentative steps, she backed away from Merrick and the others.

"Don't come near me," she said, her eyes bulging with alarm. Despite the breeze, a line of sweat dotted her brow.

"It's Dr. Merrick," Peter said softly. "Look at me, Callie."

Her breathing was rapid. She looked befuddled. "I'm Faith. Faith Hale."

"What is she talking about?" Callie Jamieson's one-woman show had just turned much too personal for Carolyne's taste.

Peter, who hadn't taken his eyes off Callie, spoke quietly, hoping that Carolyne and her aide-de-camp would stay put and let this play out.

"Faith is the daughter of E.W. and Liberty Hale."

"E.W. Hale's wife was Winifred," Carolyne insisted.

"Winifred was his second wife. E.W. Hale was a bigamist."

Callie's eyes squinted angrily. Her mouth was tight and her fingers were bundled into knots of nervous energy.

"I don't have all the particulars, but it appears he married a woman named Liberty McAllister and had two children with her, Mac and Faith."

He smiled at Callie, acknowledging Faith's existence and her heritage, but the defensive child wasn't appeased. Instead, she growled back at him.

"Some years later, he returned to Cleveland and married

Winifred Colfax. There's no record of a divorce, which
makes him a bigamist."

"And Winifred's children illegitimate." Carolyne felt
faint.

As Peter reiterated the Hale history, he continued to
study Callie, trying to ascertain whether her disorientation
was a result of hitting her head, the introduction of p-316,
or in fact, that she'd slipped back in time.

Callie straightened slightly, clearly poised for flight.

The movement created a stunning pause as everyone assessed each other.

Gingerly, Peter took a step toward her.

Callie reached down, lifted up an imaginary skirt, and
ran into the woods.

Callie ran as fast as she could, deliberately heading deeper
into the forest where she believed Faith had an advantage.
There were a hundred acres of land at Liberty Park. Merrick
had studied here, but Faith had lived here. At some point,
Callie realized that, somehow, the universe had put the past
and the present in a cosmic blender and shaken things up
to where Callie and the spirit of an ancestor had come together in a synthesis of time. She didn't know how it had
happened or why, whether it was good or bad. All Callie
knew was that if she could just keep Faith Hale with her
in the here and now, she'd be able to elude her pursuers
and find her way back to the road and her car.

Her feet flew over the landscape, hurdling over rocks
and branches, landing as softly as possible so as not to give
away her location. Still, she could hear them behind her,
the determined footsteps of men on a hunt.

She ducked under a dead tree trunk that had toppled over
under the weight of the winter, then pushed it to the ground
before veering left around a large boulder, hoping those two
obstacles would confuse or at least slow the progress of her
pursuers. As she ran, her eyes spotted a primitive path
formed by the deer and elk and large brown bears that
claimed original ownership of this place. Snaking her way

onto it, she smiled as she realized her gym membership was actually paying off. Without sapping her strength or her breath, she was able to get into a brisk runner's rhythm as she slalomed through the thick maze of trees.

Suddenly, she stumbled and fell, hitting the ground hard. She hadn't tripped on anything. Her legs had simply turned rubbery and collapsed beneath her. Her head felt dull and cottony, yet the back of her brain fizzed like a shaken bottle of soda. Her pulse was racing, yet her body felt heavy and sluggish. She held her arms out in front of her and shook them, trying to get some feeling back in her muscles. She breathed slowly and deeply, trying to oxygenate her blood and restore her energy. Still, she didn't feel right.

Behind her, the footsteps grew louder. They were getting closer, but something had changed. There was only one runner. And he was gaining on her.

She inhaled sharply, sucking in the stinging scent of pine as if it were ammonia. Revived, she clamored to her feet, looked through the branches to fix the position of the sun and took off again.

The clearing where the memorial stood was behind her, which was east. The mansion was further east. She considered doubling back and heading there, but she didn't think she could trust Wellington any more than she trusted the others. Feeling as if she had no choice, she headed north instead of continuing west, wondering if the second runner had expected her to do just that and was already lying in wait. He might, but she couldn't worry about it. The other man was on her heels.

The duskiness of the thicket diminished as the horizon loomed ahead of her. Beyond the unremitting green of the freshly leafed forest she spied an endless, clear, blue-white light. As she ran toward it, she wondered if Faith might have led her into a trap. Possessed of local knowledge she couldn't explain, she knew the reason there was so much sky was that the property's north end was the mountain's edge, a craggy border guarded by a steep precipice that was almost impossible to descend.

Her pace slowed as she debated whether to change direction or continue on. Logic said she was lost, yet there were other voices in the air. Frightened, she prayed for guidance. Should she trust whisperings from the past? Or rely on tangibles?

A recollection flickered before her. There was a back road. That's where Faith was taking her. It traced the rim of the mountain and wound around the thickest part of the forest, ultimately coming out behind the mansion. All she had to do was get there.

She paused to catch her breath.

He grabbed her from behind, yanked her arm around her back and pinned it against her. Pain shot up her arm, into her shoulder. She tried to wrestle free of his grasp, but he was strong and she was still battling whatever drug she'd been given. He pushed her toward a large tree and pressed her against the trunk, using his entire body as a restraint.

She glared at him with heated defiance.

"I don't want to hurt you," he said. "I just want to know what you saw."

She scrunched her face like a child being told to drink cod liver oil.

"I need to know what happened. So I can help you."

She swung her head from side to side. "Uh-uh. You don't want to help me. You want to hurt me."

"That's not true."

"You killed my brother."

He had no idea what she was talking about. "No, I didn't."

"You did," she insisted. "You killed my brother, Mac. And my mother, Liberty."

He couldn't believe what he was hearing. She thought she was a little girl who'd lived a hundred years before. "It was an accident, Faith. I'm really sorry."

Again, she shook her head. "No. It wasn't. You picked up a big piece of wood and you smashed Mac's head in. Then, you pushed my Mommy to the ground. And then, you started the fire." Her eyes filled with tears and she began to sniffle. "I had to run and get help. When I got back with the policemen and the firemen and the doctor, they were dead. And you were gone."

"I was afraid," he said, hoping he was following her script.

"I knew who you were." Her voice was girlish, the cadence of her words childishly taunting. "They asked me, but I didn't tell because Sarah said not to. She said if I told, you'd come back and hurt her and me."

"I wouldn't have hurt you."

"She changed my name to Blessing so you wouldn't find us."

"That was smart."

She affirmed that with a vigorous nod of her head. "I'm smart, too."

"I'm sure you are."

She stared at him for a long moment. Her gaze was less wide-eyed, more direct. "This time, I'm going to tell the police who you are and what you did."

The gist of the conversation had shifted. "What exactly do you think I did?"

"You killed my really good friend."

His face remained expressionless, yet his body tensed.

"Wilty. Didn't you know he was my friend? Well, he was."

"What are you talking about?"

He looked into her eyes. Faith was gone. His accuser was Callie Jamieson.

"You went to Wilty's apartment to steal Charles's suicide note, but he walked in on you. Somehow you explained what the hell you were doing there and made amends. Maybe by talking about people you had in common and having a couple of drinks.

"Wilty got wise to you, but by then it was too late, wasn't it? You'd already drugged his vodka so he'd pass out." Her eyes burned with anger and grief. "But then it dawned on you: if you dumped him out the window you could get the note, the fame and fortune that came with it, and get rid of Wilty, all at the same time."

"Shut up!" he screamed, his face flushed crimson.

He cocked his arm and clenched his fist, but she was ready. Before he could land his punch, she geed to the side and lurched forward, freeing herself from his clutches. She tried to get past him, but he grabbed her and slammed her back up against the tree, igniting a flame in her shoulder. His forearm pressed against her neck, blocking her windpipe. Summoning what little strength she had left, she kicked his legs out from under him. His grip on her neck loosened. Hungrily, she filled her lungs, then kick-punched him in the gut and watched with great satisfaction as he doubled over. She should have run, but she couldn't.

"I need to know why you wanted to kill him. Was it just because he was a Hale?"

Delwin "Buddy" Campbell, the man with the lightning bolt tattoo, gathered himself up onto his haunches. His face was a storm.

"Shut up!" he screamed again as he rose to his full height.

Reflexively, Callie dropped down to a crouch, her hands high, all of her senses *en garde*.

"You killed Hunt and Cole just because they were Hales."

"That's not why," he blurted, his entire body rigid with resentment.

"Then it must be because they were the drunks who killed your father and sister."

Campbell blanched as she reiterated the truth that had guided his life.

"They ran your father's truck off the road, but they were never charged."

He snorted, his breath exiting his nose in a bullish explosion of air. His eyes bulged with the white heat that can only come from the deepest, most personal rage.

"When you got to the scene and beat them both into

hamburger, you got sent away. They killed your family and got nothing."

His eyes watered as he revisited that horrible night, his little sister's body lying in the middle of the road broken and bloody, his father ripped in half by the steering wheel when his truck slammed into a tree.

"They paid off the cops to say the road was slippery, that it was an accident." He spit onto the ground, as if the Hales' bribery and manipulation had tainted his saliva with venom sucked from a snake. "My father and sister were black and poor. To those rich bastards, their lives weren't even worth the cost of a trial. All I did is get me some justice," he said without remorse.

"No," Callie said. "What you did was murder."

37

Peter Merrick hobbled over dead tree limbs and rocks, his ankle badly sprained from a fall. Pain spiked up his leg, yet propelled by fear, he continued making his way through the woods. When, finally, he caught up to his quarry, they were at the far end of a small clearing, positioned precipitously close to the mountain's edge.

Callie's eyes were closed. Her hair was blowing. Her arms were scraped and bloody. Her right foot dangled over the side. The bogus medic was leaning over her, his hands tucked beneath her arms.

"Stop!" Merrick shouted, gritting his teeth as he jumped on top of the other man and tackled him to the ground. "What the hell are you doing?"

"Trying to keep her from committing suicide."

"Suicide?" Merrick was so startled, he could barely get the word out. He looked at Callie lying only inches away from the chasm. *Could it be?*

"She was about to throw herself off this ridge."

Anxious and disbelieving, Merrick rose to his feet, ignoring the pain in his ankle. The other man backed away. Callie continued to lie motionless.

Slowly, carefully, Merrick slid Callie away from the precipice, settling her behind a large boulder he hoped would provide shelter from the wind, which had begun to gust, kicking up swirls of dust and gravel. Her pulse was almost non-existent. Also, a skinny string of white bubbles clung to her bottom lip; she'd suffered some kind of seizure.

"What happened?"

"She was raging on and on about her mother and brother being murdered by some lunatic wielding a large board." His eyes got big, like a child telling an amazing tale. "Then, all of a sudden, she gets all freaked out about not being able to help them and runs for the edge. I came at her and she fell. Probably hit her head on a rock."

He was lying. When Merrick moved Callie, he'd checked for injuries. Other than the scrapes on her arms, there was no blood, no swelling, no sign of a contusion. She was unconscious because of whatever had been in that needle.

"Carolyne knew Callie was a Hale before coming up here, didn't she?" he said, finally putting it together.

"The bigger question is, when did you know and why didn't you tell me?" Carolyne Hale said, as she emerged from the woods. Her slacks were speckled with burrs and she was out of breath, but her voice pealed with anger and betrayal.

"Yesterday." Peter's stance was defiant. "And I had no reason to tell you."

"If she's a Hale," Carolyne said through clenched teeth, "you had *every* reason."

"I don't *know* that she is," he taunted. "I was hoping Callie could fill in the rest, but you and your hired muscle probably ruined that."

They all looked at the comatose woman on the ground. Callie was barely breathing.

"You better hope she pulls through," Merrick said to Carolyne.

"Why? If she and her memory survive, I'll be ruined. If she survives but her memory doesn't, your career will be ruined. Why would either of us want her to live?"

"What are you suggesting?" Peter feared there was another needle filled and ready to be used.

"I'm not suggesting anything. I'm simply laying out the facts."

"Here's a fact for you. If anything happens to her, I'll make sure you go to prison."

"I don't think so, Peter. You see, you and Dr. Hoffman devised a plan to use his protein to prove your theory. You brought this poor girl here for some kind of therapeutic outing. It goes tragically wrong. She dies. And *you* become the most logical suspect."

A malevolent, yet satisfied, smile slithered across her lips.

"Your colleagues will shake their heads and mutter about the oh-so-ambitious Dr. Merrick, how he pushed too far and tried too hard. Again."

She looked at him through cold eyes. "Four patients. Four regressions. Four deaths. That's not a Nobel Prize–winning resumé, Peter. That's a rap sheet."

Merrick started for her, but stopped. She had turned to Buddy and flicked a finger at him, as if there were a task he'd left unfinished. Peter expected to see Buddy pull another syringe from his pocket. Instead, the burly man folded his arms across his chest and did nothing.

"What do I look like, your own personal pit bull?"

"Who do you think you are, speaking to me that way?" Carolyne snapped, unnerved by his unexpected disobedience.

"He's your brother."

Callie's voice was weak, yet the words tolled with absolute assurance. While the others had been slugging it out, Callie had come to and propped herself up against the boulder. She was weak and struggling hard to regain her physical stability, but her eyes were clear and focused.

"And he killed your son because you ordered him to."

Before either Merrick or Campbell could stop her, Carolyne lunged at Callie, grabbed hold of her arm and started dragging her toward the edge. She was so overwhelmed with murderous intent, she never saw it coming. A large body, with the lethal dedication of a missile, swooped down and ripped her off Callie with painful brutality.

Ezra, Jorge and Bill Jamieson had come from the road that traced the rise of the mountain behind the woods in a large golf cart navigated by a highly agitated Hiram Wellington. Even before Wellington came to a complete stop, Jorge jumped out to back up his partner while Ezra rescued Callie from the ridge. Wellington braked the cart, grabbed his medical bag and followed.

Ezra shoved Carolyne to the side and surprised Campbell with a punch to the jaw that staggered him. Then, he spun around and glared at Peter Merrick, practically inviting him to do battle. His amber eyes blazed and his body quaked with the desire to beat someone to a bloody pulp.

While Bill cradled Callie, Wellington gently pressed his stethoscope against her chest. He didn't like her color or the shallowness of her breathing.

"She's suffered a seizure," Merrick said.

Hiram gave Callie a shot of phenobarbital. "It'll help stabilize her," he said.

Slowly, she came around.

"He killed Wilty," she said, pointing a finger at Campbell. "At her instruction." She shifted her gaze to Carolyne, who stared back with feral eyes.

"Less than an hour ago, she was chasing ghosts in a clearing. She hears voices and sees dead people, for goodness sake. This woman isn't an eyewitness. She's an experiment." Carolyne glanced over at Merrick. "And if he were half the doctor he thinks he is, he would commit her here and now."

Callie, who hadn't taken her eyes off the imperious Mrs. Hale since she'd awakened, struggled to her feet.

"It wasn't hideous enough that you killed your son, a man I cared a great deal about, but then you killed my best friend." Her voice trembled with barely restrained fury. "As God is my witness, I'm going to make sure you pay for that."

Carolyne's back stiffened, but she refused to display any fear or remorse. The truth was, she had none.

"First, I'm going to tell my story to the press. The *Courier*. The *Times*. The *Post*. Then, I'm going to talk to every network, cable and radio announcer that will give me a mike. I'm going to tell them what a reptilian, Medusa-like creature you are. And when I'm done with them, I'm going to tell the same story to a judge."

Carolyne narrowed her eyes and fixed them on Callie. "Wilty didn't do much that I approved of, but he was right to get rid of you."

"He was right about you, too," Callie countered. "He wanted to love you, but couldn't find a single reason to do so."

"And how about your part in all of this, Mr. Campbell?" Ezra said. "What did you stand to gain from tossing Wilty into the alley?"

"I didn't toss nobody. He jumped." Buddy's eyes darted from side to side as he searched for a way out.

Alvarez had positioned himself at the perimeter of the clearing to prevent any escape attempts. "Try again, Buddy-boy," he said. "We've got your prints on his slippers. And on the gate at the Hamptons cottage."

"Let's not forget about Cole Hale."

Buddy's head snapped from Alvarez to Ezra, who said, "In case you forgot, you killed him, too."

"Nope. Uh-uh." Buddy waved his hands and shook his head and any other body part he thought he could use to deny the charges being levied against him.

"A little while ago, I had an interesting chat with Officer Gideon Bryson in Memphis. According to the warden at the pen where you did some time, you apprenticed as an electrician." He looked at the tattoo on Buddy's hand. "You learned your lessons well, Campbell, I'll give you that. Switching the wiring in the stable so that when Cole turned the power off, he was actually turning it on. Planting bugs throughout Callie's apartment and Dr. Merrick's office. Dismantling the GFI at the pool in the Hamptons. You're good, but this time, you're the one who's gonna get burned."

Buddy shook his head insistently. "I was interviewed and released. I had nothing to do with Cole Hale's death."

"That's a lie."

Everyone turned toward Callie.

"You confessed to killing both Hunt and Cole Hale." She reached into her blouse and extracted a small recording device which had been taped to her midriff. "I have it all on tape."

Ezra stared at Callie with naked admiration. Alvarez whistled. Campbell's eyes bulged and grew wild.

Carolyne was beyond wild. Afraid of what Buddy had said when he and Callie were alone, recalling things she had said, she raced toward Callie with arms outstretched and claws bared. Callie saw her coming and turned her back toward Carolyne, creating a human blockade. Carolyne rammed into her and was repelled, but fueled by the juices of self-preservation, came at Callie again, determined to wrest the tape from Callie's hand. As Carolyne reached for it, Callie threw the recorder down, grabbed her arm and twisted it until the other woman screamed in pain. When Callie let her go, Carolyne fell to the ground.

Buddy, seeing an opportunity, broke for the road. Jorge jumped him from behind and brought him down, but not easily. Buddy was a big man with a hot temper and quick fists. He was also desperate. Alvarez took some heavy hits, but he had a few moves of his own. When Buddy reared back, Jorge rammed a fist into Buddy's ribs and then came right back to clock him in the ear. Campbell, his head ringing, went down.

Ezra picked the tape recorder up and put it in his pocket. "What were you afraid of, Carolyne? That your brother might have ratted you out?"

The Widow's eyelids flickered nervously. Things were spiraling out of control. People she thought she could rely on were deserting her. People she thought could be defeated easily, were proving to be quite stubborn. Incensed at the insolence of everyone around her, Carolyne drew herself up and sneered at Campbell.

"Do you really think *that* is related to me?"

"You can deny it all you want," Callie said, "but Delwin 'Buddy' Campbell is the son of your mother, Evangeline, and Homer Campbell, one of her boyfriends. She moved in with Homer when she found out she was pregnant and stayed with him for a while. When she tired of him, she did to Homer just what she did to your father, she moved out, left Delwin behind and went back to the life. After Buddy was orphaned, he moved in with your mother's mother, but for years, you barely acknowledged his existence. It was only when you discovered that life with the Hales wasn't the fairy tale you expected it to be, that you became Buddy's fairy godmother. You gave him money. You got him a job. You did whatever you had to do to insure his loyalty. The rest was easy.

"You knew the Hales had killed his family. You knew how much he hated them and how badly he wanted revenge. You wanted revenge, too, but you wanted yours in cash. The only way to do that was to be the last Hale standing.

"First, you had Buddy get rid of Cole. Then Hunt. When the old lady died, only Wilty stood in your way. As long as he gave you what you wanted, he was safe. The minute he threatened to take it all away, you called Buddy."

"Where in the world did you come up with claptrap like that?" Carolyne huffed.

"On the Internet. I ran a check on you and found your grandmother's obituary. Earlene Campbell lived upriver from Memphis. Her husband and daughter—your mother—had predeceased her. Her only survivors were a grandson, Delwin, and a granddaughter, Carolyne Faessler Hale."

"The next place both names will appear," Alvarez said, "will be on a court docket. You're both under arrest for murder."

Carolyne strolled over to where Campbell lay and looked down at him as if he were a worm she could crush with her shoe. "As you police types are so fond of saying, he did the crimes. He'll do the time."

As she turned to walk away, Campbell rose to his feet with a large, jagged rock in his hand. Just as the rock was about to come down on Carolyne's skull, a shot rang out. Campbell dropped the rock. Carolyne fell to the ground.

For a long moment, the two of them lay in the dust. Merrick started for them, as did Wellington. Ezra held up his hand. "They're fine. Leave them alone."

Campbell's arm was bleeding where the bullet grazed him. Carolyne was unhurt.

"Read them their rights," he said to Alvarez.

While the two detectives went about their business, Hiram Wellington and Peter Merrick hurriedly bundled Callie into the golf cart next to her father.

Ezra, seeing they were about to go, quickly ran to her side. "Are you about to disappear on me again?"

"I think so," she said, her voice weak, her color seesawing between chalk and lime. "But don't take it personally." She offered him a wan smile. "I had a shot of something that didn't agree with me."

Callie was taken to Saratoga Hospital and treated for dehydration and the other aftereffects of a seizure. She had an MRI, a PET scan, as well as a complete battery of other tests, all of which came up clean. She'd suffered no permanent damage from Hoffman's protein induction. She did have some residual memory loss, but the doctors assured her it was temporary. They insisted upon keeping her overnight for observation.

She was exhausted, but she couldn't sleep. Her mind was racing with the events of the day. As she looked out her window onto the dark canvas of night, she shivered, recalling Buddy Campbell's cold confession of murder. And Carolyne Hale's complete dispassion about her role in the deaths of four people, including her own son.

She also couldn't stop thinking about how she'd felt at the site of the burned-out barn and what she'd heard on her tape during her out-of-body time, the things she said when she was, for all intents and purposes, Faith Hale.

Callie wondered whether Dr. Merrick considered his work with her a success. She hoped so. He did help her retrieve memories from someone who lived during another time. He did reveal a part of her heritage she wouldn't have known otherwise. And, if the diary Ezra gave her before he left earlier this evening was accurate, her visions weren't dreams. They were the truth.

Among other fascinating revelations in that diary, were entries that explained why E.W. Hale constructed the Hale Trust the way he did. He admitted that having two families was wrong, but swore he'd done his best to provide for both according to their wants and needs. Liberty was content with very little. The one thing she wanted more of was time—with him and their children, as a family. Winifred couldn't get enough—of anything.

After he'd read Charles's suicide note and learned what he'd done to Liberty and Mac, E.W. decided that, *If Winifred was so venal and so avaricious that she could poison her children to the point that for money, a son would commit murder in her name, none of her offspring should be gifted.* Which was why, in the Trust, he specified that *only those of his blood line born in wedlock or legally adopted could inherit.*

Callie chuckled in amazement at the thought that she was that wily old man's descendant, but her amusement was shortlived. While it was true that the diary Elizabeth gave to Ezra laid out the facts of her ancestry and established her right to claim membership in the Hale dynasty, and that those facts were corroborated by Charles Hale's suicide note—during a police interrogation Carolyne admitted she'd burned the original—there would still be legal challenges and DNA tests and who knew what else.

Certainly, the board of Hale Holdings would have something to say about the extent of her acceptance into the Hale universe. After all, a woman who yesterday had been a staffer—and a suspended one at that—was, technically, their new Chairperson.

Callie laughed out loud as she visualized striding into

the fabled Hale boardroom and taking her seat at the head of the twenty-foot polished teak table. What a Rolaids moment that would be!

Her smile faded when the starker realities of her new situation came into focus. She was the Hale heir. While she didn't know all the details, the essence of that simple statement was that she was entitled to a fortune—one that came with some pretty heavy strings attached.

Wilty had told her the terms of the Trust demanded that he become the head of the board, that he take a more active role in the running of Hale Holdings. Did that apply to her? Would she have to give up her career as a journalist? Was her financial inheritance dependent on her corporate involvement?

It couldn't. She was a reporter, not a capitalist. She'd never even attended a board meeting, let alone run one. Then again, she'd never been a Hale before.

Callie groaned, her head swimming with a thousand questions for which she had no answers.

Though she tried to calm her jitters, she couldn't stop thinking about Wilty. That he was dead, for one, and that his own mother had instigated his murder. Carolyne's homicidal greed made Callie sick.

The other notion that curdled her stomach was the shocking recognition that she and Wilty had been cousins. Granted, they were very far apart on the family tree, but they were cousins who'd been lovers nonetheless. It was way too hillbilly for Callie to deal with, so she didn't.

Instead, she lay back against the pillow and willed herself to concentrate on the future rather than the past. Despite her best efforts to think happy thoughts, she kept seeing Wilty. Not the charming, bon vivant of their early courtship, but the morose, self-deprecating, sodden boor he'd turned into toward the end of their relationship. It hurt to remember him that way, to recall how solemn and drawn his face had become, how self-destructive his actions were, how little fun he had. It hurt even more to acknowledge how many times she'd dismissed his fears about taking on

the mantle of the Hale dynasty as if his hesitancy was born
of laziness. She insisted he had the brains and the resource-
fulness to overcome any and all hurdles if he really wanted
to. He claimed she was naïve and didn't understand the
enormity of the burden that came with being a Hale.

He was right. She hadn't understood. That heritage was
hers now and all she could think about was whether she,
too, would fold beneath its weight.

Fortunately, she didn't have to worry long. Within
minutes of closing her eyes, she succumbed to the lure of
her medication.

After a short nap, she awoke feeling refreshed, and much
steadier emotionally. Buoyed by renewed strength and
spurred by a nagging curiosity, she took a deep breath,
trying to summon the spirits that had plagued her for most
of her life. She waited and took another breath. And then
another. She almost cried with relief when her repeated
invitations got no response.

A wave of sadness swept over her. If only Mara had
found a therapist who believed that some dreams had their
roots in past realities, maybe she wouldn't have felt so
alone and so afraid. Maybe she wouldn't have gotten lost
in that dusky netherworld that bridges the then and the now.
Maybe everyone would have known what Callie knew, that
Mara Jamieson wasn't insane. She was haunted.

Callie's nose twitched. There was a strange smell in her
room. Not strange as in stomach wrenching or disgusting,
but strange as in not belonging. When she turned toward
the door, nervously expecting a gaggle of spectral visitors,
she laughed. It wasn't anything ghostly or strange. It was
Ezra and he was carrying a huge carton of food.

"Since the hospital is practically right around the corner,
I dropped in at the Batcheller Mansion. You know, *our*
place?"

Ezra set his package down on one of the chairs and
began to unpack his bounty.

"When I told them what happened, they gave me two
beef stew dinners, complete with hot rolls, real butter, and

an exquisite bottle of red wine. Of course, you can't have any wine because you're on drugs, but it's the thought that counts, don't you think?"

He took one of the cloth napkins and tucked it into the top of her hospital gown.

Callie grabbed hold of his shirt, pulled him toward her and kissed him.

"Whew! I can hardly wait to see what happens when I put down the tablecloth."

"I love you, Ezra Chapin."

"I love you, too," he said, his mouth wreathed in a smile. "In fact, if you recall, I said it first."

"That you did."

"But you had places to go, ghosts to see, things to do, and a hundred years to relive before you could give me a tumble."

"That's true," she confessed. "But it's done. The ghosts are gone."

She didn't fully understand what had happened, how or why, but sometimes the only way to deal with inexplicable circumstances was to take a leap of faith. This felt like one of those times.

"Great. In case you haven't guessed already, when it comes to romance, I'm not a fan of competition. I play much better on a clear field."

Callie smiled. "I had guessed that."

"Smart woman. So? How relieved are you that all this is over?"

"Very."

"But?"

"But how odd is it that Wilty's death was the catalyst for me taking back my life? I might have arrived at the same place at another time, but really, it was his letter, those diaries, and my desire to do right by him, that compelled me to see this through.

"In a sense, he was on the same journey. We were both searching the past to clear the way to the future." Her eyes widened. "And where did we wind up? As part of the same family. And victims of the same woman."

"You're not a victim," Ezra said, gently stroking her cheek. "You're a survivor."

"I am, aren't I?" She heaved a sigh of honest relief and wiped a tear from her cheek. Wilty hadn't been as lucky.

"Along those lines, I thought you'd like to know they arrested Orlando today." He didn't tell her about Ben Schirmerhorn. There'd be time enough for things like that. "They picked him up outside of Philadelphia."

"Good."

Ezra continued laying out their dinner, breaking off pieces of a roll for her to nibble. For himself, he uncorked the wine, poured some into a plastic cup, and toasted her.

"You were amazing today," he said, his voice choked with emotion.

"I had a lot of help. Particularly from one daredevil cowboy who saved me from being tossed off the side of a mountain." He looked away, but she spotted a blush. "Then, too, there was my father. My new best friend, Jorge Alvarez. Hiram Wellington. And Peter Merrick."

Ezra glanced at her over the rim of his wineglass. "Okay, I read him wrong. You win that one. And Jorge wins for having had the Widow in his sights from the get-go."

Callie winced, thinking back on her murderous confrontation with Carolyne. And conjecturing about what might have been.

"Just so you know, I was scared today," Ezra said.

"Coulda fooled me."

"I was afraid of losing you." His eyebrows scrunched together and he looked at her with such fevered intensity, she thought he'd burst into flames. "I would have killed any, or all of them, if they hurt you."

Again, she brought his lips to hers. "I'm glad you didn't have to. You wouldn't look good in an orange jumpsuit. And you'd never survive on prison food."

He laughed. She sat back against her pillows and looked at him, lovingly.

"Carolyne and Merrick did give me a gift, you know. By forcing me to confront my ghosts, they allowed me to resolve a conflict that had haunted everyone from that terrible day in 1887 until today. They freed me from the past and gave me the gift of a future."

"That's a very big gift."

"Only if it's shared with the right person."

"And that would be me, I hope."

Callie smiled, and not just at Ezra. She smiled at Liberty and Mac and Sarah Blessing and Faith and E.W. Hale. Without them, she wouldn't be who she was. Without them being gone, she couldn't do what she was about to do.

"Yes," she said, as she let the past go and followed the clear, unfettered path into the safe haven of Ezra's arms. "That would be you."

Read on for an excerpt from
Doris Mortman's next book

SHADES OF RED

Coming in hardcover from St. Martin's Press

Prologue

It's hard to remember a time when I didn't hate her. Despising her feels as natural as breathing, as ordinary as putting one foot in front of the other. Not a single day goes by that I don't think of ways to torment her, yet I don't consider this an obsession. It's simply part of my emotional gestalt: Hating her is who I am.

I used to lie awake at night planning things to do to her. I'd invent exquisite tidbits of torture that would infect her with fear, small, excruciating moments of persecution that would gnaw at her like hungry maggots and make her skin crawl with the terror of anticipating what I'd do next.

How thoroughly delicious those crucifying imaginings have been!

But I've had enough imaginings. They don't satisfy me anymore. It's time to move on, to make my punishing fantasies a reality.

I'm certainly well prepared. Over the years I've amassed a stockpile of ways to make her life miserable and I intend to execute each and every one of them.

And then, I plan to execute her.

Vera Hart's mouth went dry. She was a powerful woman who rarely felt helpless, but just then her knees were weak. An avalanche was threatening to bury her in a ferocious storm of accusations. If she couldn't divert it or stem it or stop it, everything she had taken a lifetime to build would be destroyed.

"Hart Line International is guilty of gross accounting irregularities which must be addressed before the next peer review. If they're not corrected, you run the risk of being investigated by the government, which could result in enormous fines and possible imprisonment. At the very least, with today's climate of consumer rage against corporate corruption, it's likely that you could wind up becoming a scapegoat for the sins of others. At worst, your company will go under."

Vera read the memo for the third time, still in a state of disbelief.

When she came in that morning there was an envelope on her desk stamped FOR YOUR EYES ONLY. It was unsigned, but the details described the author as someone who was more than slightly familiar with the inner workings of Vera's corporation. As she read the comparison of the public financial statements for HLI, the parent company, and the internal financial statements, she realized that she was indeed in serious trouble. As the nameless whistleblower put it, "your books have been cooked."

It infuriated her that something this potentially catastrophic had caught her so off guard, but to be fair to herself, she didn't conduct regular line-by-line reviews of the company's financials. That's what staff was for. Years before, when she added clothing and accessories to the Hart Line's cosmetics business, she'd put together an outstanding team of business and accounting specialists and gave them control over the numbers. It was a move that was alien to her basic, control-freak nature, but early on she recognized that she simply couldn't do everything and be everywhere.

She was the centerpiece of an enormous conglomerate that manufactured all manner of lifestyle products, from nail polish to sectional sofas. She was also the public face of Hart Line International, marketing herself and her talents every waking minute of every single day. She did the weekly television show, *Vera Hart at Home,* made public appearances, edited the magazine *Hart to Heart,* promoted the various products at stores and malls throughout the country, supervised the addition of new merchandise, and personally tested each and every new idea that came her way. She didn't have time to be a bookkeeper as well.

Aside from the unthinkable prospect of her stock tanking and taking HLI with it, what disturbed Vera was the notion that she could be targeted for investigation. Enron had collapsed. Tyco was in shambles. WorldCom's stock wasn't worth the paper it was written on. And yet she knew the whistleblower was right: Given the opening, the government would look to make her the poster girl of corporate corruption. The reasons were obvious: She was a woman in a man's world, she had been an actress, not an MBA graduate, before going into business, and she had been extremely successful. It seemed unfair to Vera that once again she was about to be screwed over by a system that judged her on her celebrity rather than her success and by her gender rather than her judgment.

Vera Hart had been a star from the day she made her cinematic debut in *Little Girl Blue* at the age of nine. Until her film career came to an end, her name on a theater marquee had practically guaranteed eight-figure grosses. Her face had graced the cover of every high-circulation magazine in the world. And her image had spawned so many desperate wannabes that at least once a month some well-known psychologist took to the airwaves to urge teenage girls not to disparage themselves if they looked in their mirrors and came up short. Vera Hart, they explained, was simply exceptional.

She was tall and model-slim yet with enough curves to be described as sensuous, her skin was gardenia-white, her nose so perfectly sculpted for her face it was as if the proportions had been mathematically calculated. She had a wide mouth with full, ripe lips that always seemed to be teasing for a kiss and eyes that positively startled. Framed by wing-shaped brows, they were large, clear, aquamarine demilunes that could glisten with emotion one minute, go dead and cold the next. Straight across on the bottom, softly rounded on top, they were neither a true sapphire blue, nor an absolute emerald green, neither the pale, yellowless blue of a Vermont sky in winter, nor the bleached-out green of a backyard pool overdosed with chlorine. They were pure aquamarine gems: rich and precious and mesmerizing.

At fifty-nine she owned a penthouse in New York, an oceanfront mansion in Palm Beach, an estate in East Hampton, and a compound in Westchester that included a television studio that was the envy of the networks. She had been named to the Best Dressed List Hall of Fame fifteen years before and even with the natural effects of aging was still considered one of the most beautiful women in the world. More important, she was one of only two females on the New York Stock Exchange. Her personal wealth was calculated in excess of five hundred million dollars; Hart Line International was a multibillion-dollar-a-year enterprise. She was a force to be reckoned with.

Again, she went over the figures. Then she picked up

the phone and instructed her secretary, Tess, to set up a
six-thirty meeting that evening with the CFO, the COO,
and the heads of the various Hart Line divisions. She didn't
care if anyone had social plans or family obligations. There
were to be no absentees and no excuses.

"If they're not at the meeting tonight," she said, "they
don't have to bother coming to work in the morning."

There were days when Bryan Chalmers hated his job. He
was an assistant district attorney for the city of New York,
sworn to uphold the laws of the state and to ensure that
justice was done. That part of it he loved. What he hated
was that after the police and the Crime Scene Unit and the
DA's office had gathered the evidence and sorted through
the facts and put together a case that would obtain a conviction and take a criminal off the streets, the system kicked
in with loopholes like plea bargains and parole and, most
laughable of all, time off for good behavior.

Take the case he was working on: A woman was gang-
raped under the boardwalk in Coney Island. She was so
badly beaten that three months after the assault she was
still in a coma and therefore unable to assist the police in
making a positive ID on her attackers. DNA had led the
police to two of the assailants. They needed help nabbing
the other three: an eyewitness who could place them at the
scene, a snitch who'd heard one or all of them bragging,
another forensic clue, or, as happened here, for one of them
to roll over on the others.

Once Bryan explained the hard-time consequences of
their night on the town, Ramon Ramirez gladly ratted out
his friends. In exchange for that noble exercise in civic
cooperation he demanded—and received—immunity from
prosecution.

A knock on Bryan's door announced the delivery of a
package. It was from Tony Borzone, a detective from the
Central Park Precinct. A young woman had been accosted
in the park, savagely beaten, and raped.

The victim, a white woman in her mid-thirties, had suf-

fered multiple blows to her face and head. The beating was
so savage she was almost unrecognizable. If not for an alert
patrolman finding her driver's license in nearby brush, they
would have had to rely on dental records.

Her pants were down around her ankles. Her bra had
been ripped off so violently it had sliced into her skin. Her
T-shirt remained on, but her arms had been twisted in such
a way that her right arm coiled around the left side of her
neck, her left arm snaked around the other side. Her wrists
were lashed together with a shoelace from one of her sneak-
ers; a twig served as a garrote. If she struggled too hard to
escape, the shirt would tighten around her neck and make
it difficult for her to breathe. One of her socks was stuffed
in her mouth as a gag.

A wave of nausea washed over Bryan as he studied the
photographs. Whoever did this had stalked this woman,
swooped down on her, beaten her just enough to immobilize her, then raped, sodomized, and bludgeoned her to
death. When he was done, he painted her face and body
with lipstick.

In his note, Borzone promised Bryan a clean collar.

Bryan promised the victim there would be no plea bargains, no loopholes, no deals.

Greta Hart had a headache the size of Ohio. First, Vera's
secretary had informed her there was a mandatory meeting
at six-thirty in the boardroom. A few minutes later, her
date, Bryan Chalmers, called and canceled. He was sweet
about it, and she obviously had to work late as well, but
Greta couldn't bear to give up a single moment with him,
let alone an entire evening. They had only been seeing each
other for a few months, but she hadn't felt this way—ever.

Then her secretary handed her a copy of the program
for the Women of the Year Banquet. The cover was Hart-
red paper with a satin finish and a richly embossed Hart
Line logo. It was simple and elegant, the only flourish a
red rope tipped with a feathery tassel that ran down the
spine of the booklike program. Greta opened it and leafed

through the white pages, each of which featured the bio of a recipient. She was more than a little surprised when she came upon the 2002 Hart Foundation honoree for scientific achievement, Dr. Marta Phelps.

Normally Greta was afforded the opportunity to screen the nominees for the various categories. She wasn't on the Foundation board, so she didn't have a vote per se, but her opinion mattered. If there was someone she felt was completely wrong for the Hart Line's image, or there was a candidate whom she felt was undeserving of recognition by the Foundation, she said so. Since she didn't abuse the privilege and the few times she'd raised objections they'd been borne out, the board heeded her warnings.

There was the time the nominating committee had proposed a young pianist for the award in arts achievement. A Russian émigré, she had made a splash on the classical music scene by winning a major competition. Everyone on the committee was wowed by the woman's musical genius. The fact that she was extremely good-looking didn't hurt; the Hart Line, after all, was a cosmetics company. Greta, who over the years had created a network of informers and had several very private detectives on her payroll, was told that Tatiana Godonov's real talent was in the bedroom. According to Greta's sources, Tatiana had slept with every one of the judges—male and female—and probably would have slept with a Great Dane if it would ensure her victory.

The nomination was hastily withdrawn.

Then there was Bess Whitelaw. She ran a rehab facility for teens. Her track record for turning out recovered addicts who went on to complete high school was beyond remarkable. She seemed like a shoo-in. Until one of Greta's private eyes told her that not only was Bess skimming the money she received through charity events, but also she had a sideline venture with her brother who dealt the very drugs that hooked those kids in the first place.

Her name was also removed from consideration.

Logic dictated that the only reason Greta wouldn't have been given the complete list of this year's candidates was if Vera had specifically told the head of the Foundation not to do so.

Typical, Greta thought.

Much as she liked to believe she was her mother's confidante, Vera kept her own counsel. She told others, Greta included, only what she wanted them to know, when she wanted them to know it. Like when Greta had asked Tess what was on the agenda for that evening's meeting, Tess said she knew nothing other than it was a command performance.

As Greta read Dr. Phelps's bio she tried to swallow the jealousy that quickly soured her throat. Greta was a highly accomplished woman. She was the COO of a major public company, a Harvard graduate with an MBA from Harvard Business School, and a well-respected, much envied doyenne of New York society who, like her mother, had graced the Best Dressed List many times. Yet suddenly she felt like the fourth runner-up in a backwater beauty pageant.

It was the quality of the achievements, she supposed. This Dr. Phelps was like some super Girl Scout who went around winning merit badges for performing beyond the norm; Greta simply made money.

Also, Marta Phelps was perfectly gorgeous.

In an almost Pavlovian response, Greta grabbed a mirror and studied her reflection. Even to her highly critical eye, she was indisputably attractive. Her pale, snow-white complexion, complemented by lustrous auburn hair that fell softly to her shoulders and aquamarine eyes combined in a palette as delicate as a watercolor. In contrast, her aristocratic nose and high cheekbones were sharp and angular. While that sort of sculptural classicism was deemed enviable by most, Greta felt it made her appear hard, underscoring the soberness of her personality.

Her eyes, those fabulous azure orbs, were a genetic gift from her mother and unquestionably her most arresting feature, yet there too she found a negative. Despite their luminous color and the fact that they were enlivened by a keen intelligence and unceasing curiosity, they were often void of humor. Greta studied and perused and considered; she rarely twinkled or sparkled or gleamed.

And then there was that damnable scar beneath her right eyebrow. No one else noticed it. It was barely visible and easily covered by makeup, but to Greta it stood out like a red badge of imperfection. Despite the oohing and ahhing of the fashion press about her stylishness; despite the accolades from the business community about her managerial cunning; despite what she knew to be true about who and what she was, that damnable scar served as a patent reminder that she was flawed.

Greta shoved the mirror back in its drawer and slammed it shut.

The phone rang. Startled, Greta hesitated before picking it up. Her head was throbbing; the last thing she needed was more bad news. Then again, maybe her date was back on. A romantic late-night supper would be lovely. She popped two Tylenol into her mouth, took a quick gulp of water, and picked up the phone.

"Hi," she said, purring even before she heard his voice.

"What the hell do you think you're doing?"

Greta smiled and leaned back in her chair. She'd been expecting this call.

"Whatever do you mean?" she said in her best Melanie Wilkes voice.

"There is no way I'm giving you a divorce!"

"I take it you got the papers."

"Yes, I got the papers."

"Well, I'm sure you're as devastated as I am that our marriage has actually come undone, but really, Tripp, we've always known that ours was not one of those happily-ever-after unions. Eight years wasn't a bad run and it was fun while it lasted."

"Fuck you!"

From the shrill timbre of his voice she knew his face was hideously florid.

"You wish."

She hung up the phone, but that wouldn't be the end of

it. Trevor Runyon III, known as Tripp, was a libertine. Work was not his strong suit, leisure was. As someone lucky enough to have been born into a family with a pedigree, he adhered to the philosophy that lineage translated into entitlement. His idea of a good day was brunch, golf or polo, drinks, a nap, not necessarily alone, drinks, dinner, never alone, drinks, and then to bed, again not necessarily alone. Work was what he did when he wasn't playing.

Greta had married him because he'd been a terrific catch. He was handsome in that fair-haired, blue-eyed, chiseled Wasp way. He looked spectacular in a tuxedo or a navy blue blazer, the two requisite wardrobe pieces for the socially prominent male. He'd graduated from Princeton, thanks to numerous tutors and a generous endowment from the family trust. And while he could never be mistaken for an intellectual, he had a certain savoir faire, was at ease on a dance floor and adept at witty cocktail party repartee. Most important, he was a Runyon.

The Runyons were Mayflower descendants who owned the Seafarer Bank of Boston, a lending institution established in the late 1700s to finance international trade for the Colonies. Skillfully run by Trevor Runyon, Junior, the family continued to maintain its niche position as a venture capital source for the shipping industry with branches in New York, San Francisco, Seattle, and Miami. Lowell Runyon was the executive vice president. Malcolm Basking, husband of Bethany Runyon, was a senior vice president. And Bethany served on the Seafarer board. Tripp was the only Runyon who didn't work for the bank. He worked for HLI.

By divorcing him, Greta was also firing him. She couldn't imagine that he would go quietly, but no matter what he said, did, or thought, he would go. He had been a husband of convenience. He was no longer convenient.

It was a redbrick Tudor-style home on a quiet street in a modest neighborhood in Mercerville, New Jersey. There was an open, square porch off the dining room at the back, two large oak trees in the front whose roots had entered into a territorial battle with the sidewalk, an old-fashioned one-car garage with a door that could only be raised manually, and at the rear of the small yard a willow tree overlooking a pond that in summer became a breeding ground for mosquitoes.

Inside were three bedrooms, one and a half baths, a kitchen with a dinette, a living room, dining room, and small den—each decorated within an inch of its life with Hart Home Line products. Everything from the carpets to the cachepots were inspired by Enid Polatchek's idol, Vera Hart. Several rooms had been reproduced directly from Hart Line catalogues. Others had been cloned from episodes of *Vera Hart at Home*. Enid's greatest regret in life, and she had many, was that her husband, Dolph, wasn't rich enough to allow her to change décor as often as Vera did.

For Enid the joy of cooking was being able to work alongside Vera Hart. Of course, that meant Vera was on television and Enid was in the kitchen, but she didn't quibble about such details.

This afternoon the mission was Arctic Ambrosia, an all-white cake that looked as if it had been constructed of icy glaciers and snow-peaked mountaintops. Enid's eyes darted from the television mounted on a shelf to the mixer on the island countertop. Small beads of sweat dotted her forehead as she concentrated on whipping the egg whites to the proper consistency: not too wet, not too dry.

Vera lifted the whisk out of the bowl. The glob of shiny white meringue stayed on the whisk, sparkling with perfection.

Enid lifted the whisk out of her bowl, examined her egg whites, and smiled. They too seemed perfect.

Step by step she followed Vera's directions, stuffing the meringue into a canvas piping bag fitted with a wide-mouthed tip and squeezing its contents onto the top of a three-layer white cake that had already been frosted with vanilla cream.

"Squeeze a large, lovely dollop of meringue onto the top of your cake. Then swirl the top around, narrowing it as you go. Twist the tip just so," Vera said, flicking her wrist and gazing at her effort with gushing admiration. "It should look like a tiny bell atop a jester's hat."

Squeeze. Swirl. Twist. Make each white cap exactly the same size and height as the one next to it. Watch Vera. Squeeze. Swirl. Twist.

"There!" Vera exclaimed, proudly displaying her finished product. "How gorgeous is that?" she asked her adoring audience. Her face glowed as if she could actually hear millions of viewers clapping their approval.

Enid watched enviously as Vera bent down to perform the final check. With a cathedral hush to accompany her, she eyeballed the high, round cake, carefully verifying that each white cap was precisely the same height as the others. When she was satisfied, she tilted the cake forward so the camera could get the full effect and uttered her signature line: "If it's from Vera Hart's home, it has to be flawless."

She smiled. The credits rolled. The show was over.

Enid examined her Arctic Ambrosia. Two peaks were higher than the others. A third had drooped. A fourth had collapsed altogether. She looked at the cake, looked at the fading image of Vera Hart on her screen, curled her lip down in disgust, and dumped the cake into the garbage.

Tim Polatchek walked into the kitchen just as Enid's Ambrosia met its inglorious end. If he could have sneaked out before she spotted him he would have. He'd forgotten what time it was. Visiting his mother before or after *Vera Hart at Home* was never a good idea. She was either too ecstatic to talk about anything other than how she kept up with the miraculously gifted Goddess of Perfection or too despondent to do anything other than mourn the fact that she wasn't worthy of sharing the same air as the High Hoo-Hah of Hearth and Home.

"Having a bad day, Mother?"

"It wasn't flawless," she said with the same breathless incredulity as someone trying to explain how a gun went off accidentally and killed a philandering husband. "I tried, but as usual, it wasn't perfect."

Tim didn't bother to console her. Words wouldn't soothe her, nor would they alter the script. After the mea culpa came a few tears. Then there would be the diatribe on how if Dolph really cared about what made her happy he would make enough money for her to go to cooking school so she could be in the same kitchen with Vera Hart and not be humiliated by harebrained mistakes such as not being able to get two dozen gooey egg-white balls to stand at attention.

"I brought you some things that might make you feel better," he said, handing her a box of Harty Chestnut hair dye, a red vinyl pouch with makeup from the Hart Line's fall color story, and a peach velour warm-up suit from the Hart Line Leisure Collection, size 12.

Like a daytime game show contestant who'd just won a refrigerator, she jumped up and down, giggled, and clapped her hands with delight. When she grabbed the hair dye box and didn't throw it back at him, Tim breathed a sigh of relief. Enid's latest incarnation, Harty Titian, was an abomination. In her eternal quest for Hart-like beauty Enid tended to go overboard, especially when it came to hair and makeup. She thought if you could put it on and wash it off if it didn't work, it couldn't be a bad thing. She was right, but she was wrong. She wasn't doing anything dangerous or permanently scarring, but more often than not the results were scary.

For the last couple of years she had been on a fruit and vegetable kick when it came to her hair, dying it shades that could only be described as orange, eggplant, carrot, pepper, kumquat, cherry, or cantaloupe. As for her makeup, the palette coordinated a bit too closely with the hair. The concept of subtlety was completely absent from her maquillage.

After she had gone over every item—twice—she kissed her son and patted his cheek lovingly.

"You're such a good boy. Thank you, Timmy."

"It makes me happy to see you happy, Ma." Tim had

repeated that sentiment so often over the course of his life-time he wondered if that was destined to be his epitaph.

For as long as he could remember, pleasing his mother was Tim Polatchek's unattainable goal. As hard as Enid tried to be Vera Hart, Tim tried to be a good son. The task of eliciting a smile or a word of praise from her became more important than any other achievement, a misapplication of effort that resulted in a life steeped in mediocrity. While he did have some successes over his forty-three years, Enid had set the bar so high that unless they were spectacular they felt like failures.

As a boy Tim was smart, but too undisciplined to be an honor student. He had attitude problems with teachers. They thought strictness might be a more effective motivational tool; he had enough of that at home. He was an okay athlete, but not a particularly likable kid, so he was the last one picked for a team, a distinction that didn't inspire a great deal of esprit.

He wasn't cootchy-coo adorable as a child, but as he grew into manhood his aspect enhanced to where he was attractive, though hardly an Adonis. Six feet tall and well built, he had the slender frame of a runner with muscles toned by weights from regular workouts in a gym. His face was wolfish, with a wide forehead, a shock of thick pitch-black hair, and an attenuated jawline rough with stubble. Bushy eyebrows that hooded flat, deep green eyes the color of seaweed added to the sense of a man whose personality was guarded, hidden in a thick emotional swamp at the bottom of which was a bubbling anger rooted in a need for approval.

He'd gone to college, tried his hand at a number of different occupations, but ultimately wound up an accountant, like his father. To Enid that was anathema. She couldn't imagine a more dead-end job. And said so, over and over and over again.

Then Tim landed a position with Hart Line International. Suddenly he was the sun and the moon and the stars. The fact that he was one of many financial managers didn't matter. Her son worked for Vera Hart. If he were President of the United States she couldn't have been more impressed.

"So how's work?" It was her favorite question.

"Fine. Same as usual." It wasn't. He'd heard a few rumors, but he wasn't one of the privileged few. If something was happening he wouldn't know about it until it was a fait accompli or his inside sources filled him in. As of that moment, those sources had been extremely closemouthed.

Enid's nose crinkled with dissatisfaction. She relied on him for the inside scoop on her idol. "Fine" didn't cut it.

"I am going to the Hart Foundation Awards Gala," he said, knowing it would thrill her, annoyed that something so trivial was more important to her than what was really going on in his life. "Someone gave me a ticket."

Enid almost fainted. "Will you take pictures? Can you get me her autograph? Can you get me a ticket?"

"No to all three." He shook his head. He hated when she sounded so sophomoric. But it upset him more when she got that look of tragic disappointment on her face. "I'll bring you whatever souvenirs I can. Okay?"

She patted his cheek again. "That's a good boy."

Tim nodded dumbly. Sometimes he felt more like her pet than her son, but like any good cocker spaniel he continued to jump through hoops for her favor. The only thing he would never do was roll over and play dead.

He did that once. It didn't turn out too well.